WINTERSET HOLLOW

WINTERSET HOLLOW

A Novel

JONATHAN EDWARD DURHAM

credo
house publishers

Winterset Hollow: A Novel
Copyright © 2021 by Jonathan Edward Durham
All rights reserved.

Published in the United States of America by Credo House Publishers,
a division of Credo Communications LLC, Grand Rapids, Michigan
credohousepublishers.com

ISBN (Hardcover): 978-0-578-39587-6
ISBN (Softcover): 978-1-62586-208-2
ASIN (Ebook): B09F9YKSRT
ASIN (Audio): B09TS335GG

Cover and interior design by Believe Book Design
Editing by Eleonor Gardner
Illustrations by Jay Labelle

Printed in the United States of America
First edition

For my family

without whom I would be nothing and nowhere.

Part One

The Rabbit in the Rye

The table was set and all were met with barleywine and beer
There were kin around and smiles abound as Barley Day was here
Glass-blue skies and pumpkin pies and bellies full of bread
Stories of old about glory and gold and the paths the elders tread

The Hollow was never so peaceful amid the buffalos' retreat
The foxes were never so impish, the owls ne'er sang so sweet
The breeze was never so warm as it was on that September day
Every frog in his own little bog and not a worry to weigh

Every leaf a perfect breath of orange, green, and brown
And every blade of grass seemed fit for every patch of ground
Every bowl of chowder warmed the whole of every heart
As did the sweet potato pies and leek-and-onion tarts

But as the sun began to chase the lighthouse and the sea
The party tired of games and song and settled in for tea
And though the light was dwindling, which the children thought unfair
There were still two empty seats, you see, for Runny and the bear

Still two empty oaken chairs, two pastries left untouched
Two empty steaming cups of brew just waiting for their clutch
Two absences unspoken as they held their children tight
For he to whom their feast was owed was missing in the night

'Twas on the hill the barley mill had stood for all this time
The rabbit found a spot to sit and let his fur unwind
His ears pressed back against his head, no taller than the grass
He waited till the rumble of the buffalo had passed

He waited till his mouth was just too tired to curl a frown
Till his nervous leg was spent sounding its thump against the ground
Then arose his furry nose, his ears, his eyes to see
His bear friend's bitter end as he sat slumped against the tree

And even in the dusk he saw the red among the grass
The spot he'd set the duel for which the buffalo had asked
And there next to his kindred bear, old Runny sat and cried
With no one near to shed a tear for the rabbit in the rye

ONE

John Eamon Buckley didn't even know his first name until he was already a young man, but such was the timbre of the wake in which he was raised. There were of course countless landmines that had been buried during his upbringing, but as far as he could remember, that was the first one to jump up and take a sizable bite out of his reality. A decade later, he could still recall hearing it for the first time—the strong, singular syllable dripping from the mouth of some social worker who looked as if she'd been unboxed along with her prefab desk, the building around her cold and gray and still teeming with the ghosts of the police station or madhouse or whatever awful thing it used to be. *John? Can I get you some water? How are you doing with all of this, John?*

Eamon still didn't know how to answer that question, and over the course of his journey to adulthood he had grown comfortable with the understanding that he would just never be able to put it all into words, and moreover, he wasn't sure that he even cared to. *How do you go about telling somebody a story like that? How would you possibly make them understand?* Night in and night out, Eamon still asked those things of himself while wide awake at some obscene hour with his fists clenched around nothing and his eyes glued to his flat's vanilla stucco ceiling. He wanted to turn back the clock and force himself to tell her everything. He wanted to make himself scream it so loudly that a decade later he could still hear its echo. He wanted to wrap his arms around his younger form and promise that everything would be okay or speak one of a hundred other impossible niceties, but the urge to lie to himself was always too bitter for him to indulge, even in the very moment it began to bubble up his throat. So there was no screaming and there was no answer from the newly minted John and there was no story about where he'd been and how he'd lived. Not for some stranger stuffed behind a desk anyway. Not even after all these years.

Things weren't necessarily bad in the days before Eamon's father disappeared, but they were certainly different. Different in a way that only someone raised by a man who was left wholly unchecked to indulge his raging instabilities and violently agoraphobic whims could grasp. Different in a way that only someone who didn't know truth from tale and had heard nothing but the words of his father until he was forced into the great wide open at the age of fourteen could ever relate to. But there was at least some peace in those days before Eamon knew any better and things were still simple—some ease of mind when there were boundaries and he slept well and soundly under the unfiltered light of the stars and amid the chorus of crickets and night owls. Things were easy and uncomplicated back then, and though there was plenty space to roam and too much time to kill, there were unfortunately no french fries . . . and *that* was a landmine over which he was always happy to trip.

"Oh my god, these are amazing," said Caroline, her diction muddled by a mouthful of perfectly fried, golden-brown potato wedges. She was shoehorned into the window side of a red vinyl booth next to her boyfriend, Mark, the pair of them seated across the table from Eamon, who as usual had nobody on his shoulder to play his better half. He was something of a loner by circumstance of comfort rather than anything more pointed, but the three of them had become a familiar clique over the past few years and so Eamon, despite his solitary nature, never really made the jump to unambiguous hermit . . . and he was patently aware that he had the two of them alone to thank for that.

Eamon chose his next victim from the heaping pile of starch in the middle of the table, swiped it through the thick puddle of ketchup on the side of the plate and popped it into his mouth only to surmise that something was missing and immediately reach for the saltshaker.

"I already salted those," objected Mark. "You watched me do it. I watched you watch me do it."

"I watched you salt the top layer, but we've just eaten the top layer, so now somebody needs to salt the fries that are on the lower layer. It's really not that complicated," Eamon said with a well-intentioned smirk as he gave the newly unearthed goodness a dusting of God's chosen crystal.

"See, he gets it," jabbed Caroline, taking a freshly seasoned bite and miming her unbridled pleasure for Mark to see. "Perfect."

"You've really put a lot of thought into this, huh?" said Mark.

"The mechanics of salt as it relates to fries are uncomplicated, but that doesn't mean they don't require some reflection. I think the question you should be asking is . . . why haven't *you* given them that same consideration?" returned Eamon before blessing the pool of ketchup with a few shakes of his wrist. "Tomatoes need love too, you know . . . not to get too technical or anything."

Caroline shoved another fry between her typically demure lips, put a hand on her chest and collapsed against the window, overcome by the sheer deliciousness of it all. "God, he gets me in a way you never could," she razzed, never missing an opportunity to throw a barb the way of her beau. "Tomatoes need love too. *So* much love."

Mark gave her a half-hearted frown and barked, "Yeah, well, if you think there are any actual tomatoes in that bottle . . . I've got news for you."

"I love news!" replied Eamon. "What is it? Something exciting?"

"You know what I mean. Don't make me come over there."

Eamon, of course, knew exactly what Mark meant, but he always relished the opportunity to play obtuse any time his friend gave him an opening, and he was never above partnering with Caroline to snipe at Mark's simpler nature. Mark may have been uncomplicated, but that was more a virtue and less a shortcoming in the eyes of his companions as he was never too wrapped up in himself to share a moment with them. Even if it was nothing more than a shallow back and forth, it was typically wholly welcome, and truthfully, Eamon usually preferred that to anything that might require any unwanted introspection. Mark was far from an artist in any facet of his life, but no matter the painting at his fingertips, its promise was always sweeter than a mirror.

Caroline, too, was a source of support for Eamon in his constant struggle to adjust to the world beyond his upbringing, albeit for entirely different reasons, and though her outlook wasn't nearly as plain and positive as Mark's was, she understood Eamon in a way he didn't. She knew what it was to feel like an outsider, even in familiar situations. She knew what it was to look at the table and not see a seat, even when the table was her own, and most of the time, all it took was a gentle glance in Eamon's direction or a friendly hand on his shoulder to remind him that he wasn't the only one who felt lost and encumbered by his circumstance of birth. To remind him that she also had a history laced with mirrors.

The milkshakes arrived to silent, smile-laden approvals from Mark and Eamon and actual applause from Caroline who clapped her hands together like a schoolgirl as a tall glass of strawberry slurry was set in front of her. As for Mark, he could never say no to chocolate in any situation where it was an option, and Eamon, it seemed, still hadn't evolved beyond the delicious predictability of vanilla.

"Can I get you anything else?" the waitress added, already halfway through her turn back toward the kitchen when Eamon stopped her with a question of his own.

"Actually, I was, uh . . . I was just wondering . . . is this Runny?" he squeaked while pointing to a line sketch of a rather fancy-looking rabbit on the front of the laminated menu just under the diner's name, Millie's Place.

"Is it *what*?" the waitress fired back as if Eamon was speaking some long dead language.

"Is it Runny? The rabbit in the rye? I just figured that what with—"

"You want runny *what* on rye?" she asked through a pair of baggy eyes.

"No, no . . . I was asking if the drawing on the menu was—"

"Turkey," Caroline interjected. "Tomato, lettuce, no onion, and mayo on the side. And can we get that to go if it's not too much trouble?" Their server shrugged and scribbled something on her pad before turning on her tattered flats and plodding back to the kitchen. "Guess she's not much of a reader," added Caroline before playfully kicking Eamon's shin under the table.

"Yeah, but that doesn't mean she's dumb," barked Mark, pointing his finger at both of his comrades as if to ward off an attack he knew to be coming. "Some of us non-readers are totally smart and stuff. And like . . . super handsome."

"Uh huh. It also doesn't necessarily mean she's *not* dumb," Eamon retorted, raising his eyebrows and slurping his shake as Caroline stroked her boyfriend's chubby cheek with her perfect, graceful fingers. "Although, for a woman, I must admit she's *quite* handsome."

"Right, but like . . . not as handsome as me, right?" offered Mark as he craned his neck and smoothed his imaginary lapel, tacitly aware of his forgettable looks but happy to be in on a joke, even at his own expense.

Caroline grabbed one of the menus and took a moment to look at the drawing on the cover—a perfectly fine charcoal sketch of a hare hiding among some tall grass, his fur covered by a plaid overcoat and his head topped with a gray flatcap. "I mean, it *does* look like him," she said. "With no one near to shed a tear for the rabbit in the rye."

Books were omnipresent during Eamon's youth as there wasn't really any manner of entertainment apart from stories, games, and the endless paradise of the outdoors in the Idaho desert of trees where he was brought up. But despite the seemingly endless collection of volumes from Verne, Defoe, London, Dumas, and Twain on the ramshackle shelves that lined his cabin, Eamon had never even heard of *Winterset Hollow* until his brief and bitter stint with his first foster family. It was a remarkable story and an inter-generational marvel, and even after the very first time Eamon sunk his teeth into the charming tale of a clan of animals scrambling to prepare for their yearly Barley Day feast, he immediately understood why the acclaim for E. B. Addington's masterpiece had only grown throughout the decades since it was first published.

Winterset Hollow was one of those timeless, inimitable books that was simple and pure and patently entertaining on the surface, but so much more underneath. It spoke about life and loss and struggle, fear and bravery and sacrifice in a way that was so approachable it was almost easy to miss, and it immediately wormed its way under Eamon's skin and stayed there like good, strong ink from the day he first opened the cover. Its pages were filled with simple poetry and complicated lessons, and even at the age of twenty-six, he still cherished every word of it as if they were his alone. He loved every turn and every character, and though there were lovely, lively pieces to them all, Runny the rabbit always held a special place in his being as Eamon understood all too well the desire to escape to the tall grass and be still until nothing and nobody knew him to be there. With no one near to shed a tear. No one at all.

Sixty-some years after its publication, *Winterset Hollow* remained many things to many people, but it was also the reason that Eamon, Caroline, and Mark found themselves in the sleepy little hamlet of West Rock, Washington—a small town nestled along the coast of the Pacific Ocean that was wholly unremarkable save for its most famous resident, E. B. Addington himself. They were on a pilgrimage of sorts . . . there to pay homage to the man who had given them so much even though he never knew their names. There to pay respects and gaze upon the grounds of the estate that famously inspired his book, if only from afar.

They were there to say thank you and to let him know how much it all meant to them . . . and they were close now. So close.

West Rock was pointedly charming only in the way that it wasn't pretending to be anything other than what it truly was. Surprisingly enough, there were no bookstores stocked with copies of Addington's work, no gift shops selling keychains adorned with tin cutouts of his characters, and no guided tours tracing the streets he once walked. In fact, there was no mention of him at all among the storefronts and street signs that dotted the heart of town as it snaked along the rocky coast for no more than half a mile. To Eamon's eye, it was really no different than Boise except that it was a bit smaller and seemingly less concerned with being a crossroads of nearly identical subcultures and regional freight lines. And as they walked along the shore toward the only pier in town, he couldn't help but feel like West Rock didn't care a whit that they were even there to begin with, and a new and unfamiliar comfort bloomed through his being. Three rabbits in the rye and nothing else at all.

Mark and Caroline found themselves bouncing along Main Street, playfully bumping shoulders and ribbing one another about their respective literate interests, she munching on her turkey sandwich and he with his hands in his pockets as Eamon lagged several steps shy of their pace. A moment or two behind their heels was the position Eamon usually preferred when in their company, and though he was well aware that pacing typically painted him as some charity case of a third wheel, those were colors he was happy to wear if it meant being able to see the two of them together. It made him happy to see *them* happy, and it made him feel a little less existentially tortured to see such incongruity in this world seem so natural and so inarguably correct. Mark and Caroline were like proof to him. They were proof that it could all work out even if it shouldn't. Proof that different didn't necessarily equal broken, even when the math seemed so sure.

Mark was a small mountain of a man, a former high school lineman who stood a head taller than most and carried his weight with a surprisingly effortless comfort. His strides were long and confident as he navigated the coast, and even though his pale cheeks were turning red from the salt-stained sea breeze, his jaunty disposition never skipped a beat. Caroline, on the other hand, was strikingly fit, the habits she'd learned from a lifetime of track and field at the same school where the three of them had met having served her well through college and into adulthood. She was as graceful in motion as she was in empathy—her olive-brown skin holding its own against the early September sun and her jet-black curls swinging with every turn of her legs. As a couple, they seemed antithetical at a glance, but to anyone who knew them even in passing, they were simply incomplete without each other. Two halves of the same lump of clay. Two breaths of the same kick of wind.

Eamon himself was physically reflective of nothing but the patchwork fabric of the country in which he was born. He was shy of six feet tall and cursed with thick locks of red hair that he was careful to keep short enough not to be a bother, and though he was scrawny and sinewy and unassuming, that by no means meant he wasn't capable. A lifetime of hunting, tracking, and foraging had grown his senses to be sharper than most, but whereas such things were once paramount to the survival of him and his father, now they were just fossils he was keen to ignore lest he dwell too sharply on the baggage that made him feel so out of place so often. There were times when he wanted nothing more than to be chubby and uncoordinated and unaware of everyone and everything around him . . . times when he wanted so badly to be something other than what he was. Anything really. Even a pair of blue eyes would do.

As they made their way closer to the pier, which looked more like just a big dock than anything official or city sanctioned, Eamon fiddled with the free ferry passes to Addington Isle that he had stowed away in his hip pocket. He knew they were there, but that didn't stop him from running his fingers over their surfaces and feeling the creases along their midlines to be sure he hadn't made some horrid oversight that would derail their little pilgrimage. They had come to him through a subscription to a *Winterset Hollow* fan magazine called *The Frog's Feast* that had found its way into his hands through a strange bit of coincidence that he was happy to have fallen into.

He and Mark had shared an apartment since the year they graduated high school, but even from the day they christened their new pad with a six pack of something cheap and awful, Eamon knew it was only a matter of time before his best friend would want to share his home with Caroline. There was no jealousy or hard feelings on Eamon's part the day that Mark approached him about moving out, and truthfully, their relationship never even skipped a beat. He was happy for them and knew their future together would be stronger for it, but that didn't make the prospect of being a bit more isolated any less daunting. There was always something about having a roommate that forced Eamon to be more sociable than he otherwise would be. Something about sharing his life that behooved him to sharpen his social graces and be more open to the idea of compromise, even on a superficial level, but there was also a part of him that was terrified that he would slip back into the darkness he had fought so hard to escape the moment he set foot in a space where he needn't answer to anybody.

It was a challenge that Eamon was loathe to face at twenty-three, but he knew it to be a necessary one, and so he found himself a flat in a forgettable corner of Boise that he could afford on his meager retail assistant manager's salary, packed his paltry belongings into his hatchback, and marched once again into the great unknown. *The Frog's Feast*, oddly enough, was waiting for him in his mailbox as if it was part of some strange and serendipitous welcome package. It was addressed to the previous tenant, but it felt like it was meant for him as if somebody somewhere was trying to tell him that maybe he wasn't so different. As if maybe the rye was searching for him too.

That night, Eamon sat on the bare floor of his apartment and read his new rag cover to cover under the watch of four stark white and empty walls. It was filled with fan fiction of the worst kind, reviews of the various *Winterset Hollow* cartoons that had been produced over the years, and page after page of user-submitted artwork, but it was hardly the content that mattered to him in that moment . . . it was the connection. A connection that he still felt every time a new quarterly issue showed up buried among the bills and credit card offers. A connection that made his decision to take a weekend trip to Addington Isle somehow free of the bulk of his normal anxieties when, tucked into the pages of praise and homage, he found a handful of coupons for a free ferry ride that were good for only one day of the year—September 7. Barley Day.

There were seven other people waiting for them at the pier, most of them looking no older than thirty-five and no younger than twenty, but all of them seeming more than a little bookish even at a distance. Eamon couldn't remember the last time he'd been in the presence of this many young strangers without seeing any plaid, but there were myriad corduroys and fashionably questionable sweaters and almost all of them were sporting glasses of one thickness or another.

"Well, these certainly look like your people," said Mark, nodding at Eamon who was now walking abreast of him and Caroline.

"My people!? Did you hear that?" Eamon replied with a snoot. "My people have been through a lot and frankly, we don't need your insensitive stereotyping right now, okay?"

He waited for Caroline to support him with some amount of feigned disdain, which as requested, she expressed with a perfectly judgmental "Mmhmm."

Eamon continued, "And look, just because they're all staring at their shoes and clearly horribly uncomfortable in their own skin doesn't mean they're *my* people."

"What about the one with red hair?" challenged Mark.

"Actually, he *does* kinda look like you," Caroline added, looking the young man closest to the water up and down. "Maybe if you lost three inches and gained thirty pounds?" Eamon couldn't disagree, but before he could conjure something witty to say, the most boisterous and rotund among the strangers took it upon himself to welcome them in shamelessly theatrical fashion.

"Good morrow, fellow Hollowheads!" he barked, stepping away from the rail with a leather-bound copy of Addington's opus under his arm. "Hast thou come to share the feast of Barley with this party of wayward souls?"

Mark stopped dead in his tracks and rolled his eyes so hard that both Caroline and Eamon could hear his corneas etching new wrinkles into his gray matter. "Okay, I'm going home," he said, turning on his heels as Caroline stepped in front of him to lend some perspective.

"You be nice! It's only a ferry ride. It's not like you're spending the weekend with any of them," she said.

Mark took a resigned breath and forced a pitiful smile, returning the gentleman's greeting in the words of *his* people, the largely unaffected. "Sup."

"Ah, a man of letters," said the group's self-appointed spokesperson.

"He's making fun of me, isn't he?"

"Nooo, no, no. He's just—"

"No, he's definitely making fun of you," Eamon interjected, turning his attention back to the others. "Are you guys all waiting for the ferry?" he asked, brandishing his free passes from *The Frog's Feast*.

"Indeed!" crowed the town crier. "We are but weary travelers in search of passage to—"

Mark held his finger aloft in such a singular manner that it stopped him mid-sentence, and he wasted no time in turning his attention to the one who resembled Eamon as if to say, *you . . . you may speak.* "Yeah, man, we're just waiting to get over to the isle," said the redhead as the rest of the motley gathering confirmed as much by nodding and waving their own free passes in the salty September air. "It's been almost an hour now."

Mark spun back around as if his word was final and said, "Well, there you have it, no ferry."

"Actually, now that you mention it, I don't even see any signs or anything," pondered Eamon, looking around for any indication that they were even in the right place to begin with.

"Guess that's that," Mark said, spinning on his heels again only to be forcibly turned around by Caroline.

"Give it a couple minutes, Babe. We're already here. Come on, we drove like seven hours."

"Fine. But if I have to hear any more from Captain Renaissance Fair over there, I'm gonna shove that book so far down his throat he won't be able to joust right for a month." Eamon bobbed his head from side to side as if he was evaluating the merit of Mark's threat. "What?"

"I don't know," he protested. "I mean, that was okay, but I would've gone with like . . . 'so far down his throat that he'll be shitting whist cards for a fortnight,' or something like that."

"Ooo, that's way better!" chimed Caroline.

"I hate you both so much. And for the record, whist cards are just regular playing cards, so who's the smart guy now, smart guy?"

"Certainly not me," Eamon squeaked, but as he looked down at the suddenly useless freebies in his hand, his silent reverie for their weekend trip was interrupted by the sturdy chug of a big diesel engine and they all turned to see an old fishing trawler limping in from the sea. The haggard boat swung a wide turn across the shoreline and idled to a stop before reversing until its stern was close enough for Eamon to see that *The Standard* was painted on the hull in faded lettering. The boat was in rough shape and its captain didn't appear to be faring any better as he stepped out of the wheelhouse sporting canvas pants, a hefty fleece, and a beard befitting a very particular image that he clearly had no intention of avoiding.

"All aboard!" he said as he grabbed a thick rope and tied his craft to the nearest cleat. The entire party gave him a skeptical eye, but it was Mark, having never met a stranger he was too shy to engage, who elected himself consigliere.

"All aboard for what?" he barked.

"You guys wanna go to the isle or not?"

"Wait, this is the ferry?" Eamon asked as the rest of the congregation slowly crowded around them, prompting the captain to point to a large people-carrying craft that was docked a hundred or so yards away and looked as if it had been left there to die.

"Nope. *That* is the ferry. *This* is *The Standard*," the captain said, gesturing broadly with his hands out to his side.

"Well, when does the ferry come?" asked Eamon.

"It doesn't. Been out of commission for five, six years, something like that."

Caroline took the coupons from Eamon's grasp and flipped them up for the captain to see. "But why are they still sending out coupons?" she asked to a chorus of supportive mumbles.

"I look like the goddamn mayor to you?" snapped the captain.

"Watch it," Mark warned.

"Sorry. Didn't mean nothin' by it, Captain Gene," he said, stepping up to the dock and offering Mark his hand as he clocked the empty to-go container Caroline was still clutching. "I imagine Millie didn't wanna lose her tourism bump," he offered with a chuckle and a nod toward the diner. "Pretty sure she's been sendin' those out for a decade or two at this point. Anyway, I've been pickin' up the slack here for a while. Takin' people to the isle in between fishing charters and runnin' hunters out to some of the other islands. Guess everybody likes a little extra jingle in their pocket. So, you guys havin' a good buckwheat day or what?"

"Barley Day!" shouted the big mouth from the back of the pack.

"Whatever. Look, twenty bucks a ride, round trip. Now, I may not be much for books and fake holidays," Gene said as he climbed back aboard his craft and opened up a cooler stocked with cold beer and a few bottles of Jack Daniels. "But that doesn't mean I don't know how to celebrate."

Suddenly, Mark felt much better about the whole excursion. "I like this guy," he said as Gene grinned and kicked open the little half-door that was cut into the stern. "I mean, we *did* drive like seven hours."

"That all it takes?" asked Eamon of his friend. "A cooler full of beer?"

Mark turned to him with the blankest of expressions hanging from his face and said only, "Have we met?" He stepped onto the boat and immediately everyone felt a bit more comfortable with the situation at hand, and one by one, they all followed suit. And as Mark cracked a beer and downed a good portion of it with his first grateful gulp, he raised a silent toast to a book he had never read and gave himself over to a man he barely knew as they set a course for Addington Isle.

TWO

The seas were choppy but both Gene and *The Standard* seemed up to the task. The captain clearly knew the waters like the back of his hand, navigating between the swells with ease and cutting clean, familiar lines around the crowded collection of little islands that dotted the coast before breaking out into open water. It was terrain that Eamon had never encountered before, and he was glad to have a moment to soak it in amid the relative silence of his fellow travelers clutching the rails and trying their best to avoid swallowing their lunches for a second time. Eamon had never actually seen the ocean, and even though his view looked nothing like the pictures of the limitless, perfect blue he was taught to expect, it was nonetheless breathtaking. There was a power he could feel even through *The Standard's* calloused hull, and it moved him right back to the days when the unbridled force of nature was of genuine concern and respect for its fury was a necessity for survival. He had a captain then as well, but while Gene was preoccupied with getting him safely to somewhere else, his father's only wish was to keep them both from going anywhere at all.

Eamon hadn't seen his father, Jack, in fourteen years, but still he heard him bellowing from the corners of his lateral mind from time to time. His voice had become warped with age and indistinct with distance, but it remained undeniably loud, particularly in those moments when Eamon was embarking on an adventure to somewhere new. *There's no town around here worth a visit, not even for a second. There's nobody worth talkin' to but me, and there's no land worth crossing except for ours and God's. You understand me? You are here . . . and you are here forever . . . and that's the only way you're gonna get through this life. I won't have you end up like the rest of them.* The blanket of Eamon's youth was trimmed in a thick fabric of crazed, xenophobic ramblings, and until the day he left the shelter of his childhood cabin, he had no way to parse their truth, as any counter to his father's arguments simply didn't exist in their world. There was only their life . . . and the surefire curse of anything else, and nothing in between. *Anybody comes to the cabin when I'm gone . . . you run. You come across anybody when you're out in the woods . . . you run. You so much as hear anything that isn't the creak of the pines and the rustle of the wind . . . you run.*

Eamon knew no relatives that might've told him any different, as according to his father, they had all died out there in the world beyond theirs. Even his own mother had passed during childbirth, so to a young man who couldn't possibly know any better, the gift of a lonesome life was always to be valued over the death of living otherwise. That sentiment was etched so deeply in his heart that it took Eamon years of painful adjustment to understand that nobody really cared enough about him to wish him any sort of hereditary mortal harm, and though that gave him some solace from his childhood anxieties, it also made him feel somehow more insignificant. There were times when he wished he *was* the center of some grand conspiracy, if only to feel like the focus of something other than a handful of utility bills at the end of the month. Times when he wished that somebody would pay enough attention to hate him. Anything really.

As usual, it was Caroline who snapped Eamon out of another one of his existential daymares with a friendly bump of her shoulder. "You okay?"

"Uh, yeah. Just taking it all in," he replied, gesturing with a glance at the unmistakable wonder that surrounded them.

"I've never been out here before either. It's beautiful," she said.

"Looks like it just goes on forever. You know, I actually like that idea better than knowing there's another shore out there somewhere." Eamon took a moment to let his shoulders sway with the dip of the deck and feel the spray of the whitecaps land salty and unfamiliar against the pink of his lips. "Almost makes you wonder why anybody would bother trying to find the other side at all."

"There's beauty in the unknown, but there's also beauty in truth," she answered. "I guess some of us like to believe . . . and some of us just have to know. Betcha I can guess which one *you* are." Caroline managed to coax something of a smile out of her friend with another jab of her shoulder before her gaze drifted to Mark who was hamming it up with

Gene over a can of something sudsy. "Aww, I think he made a friend."

"Shocking," whispered Eamon with a well-intentioned roll of his eyes. It did indeed look like Mark had made a friend, and although Eamon couldn't hear their conversation over the roar of the diesel engine and the crash of the Washington waters, he rightly assumed Mark was trying his best to sound interested and knowledgeable about some aspect of Gene's world.

"*The Standard*, huh? Solid name," said Mark with an unreasonable confidence. "What's it mean?"

"It's a noun that means something by which other things are measured."

"I . . . I know that. I just meant does it have like a deeper meaning or something?"

"Dunno," replied Gene as he adjusted his line through the waters. "You'd have to ask the guy I won it from playin' poker."

"Whoa. You won a *boat* playing poker?"

"Nah," the captain said with a chuckle. "But that's a way better story than I bought it on the cheap at a repo auction, right?"

"Yes. Yes, it is." Mark took another swig of brew as his gaze wandered to a cubby hole in the dash where he spotted a .45 caliber hand cannon that would've made Billy the Kid blush. "You expecting trouble?"

"If I was expecting trouble, that baby would be on my hip," Gene said as he pointed his bow toward a large island in the distance. "Nothing you have to worry about unless you're actually a well-spoken bear, which . . ." The captain paused mid-sentence, taking a moment to look Mark up and down before continuing, "Ah, never mind."

"There's bears out here?"

"Big ones. Grizzlies. They'll eat a nine-millimeter for lunch, so I don't take any chances."

"Damn. You ever have to shoot one?"

"Not yet, but the day is young," Gene said with a sparkle in his eye as he took a swig of his beer and pulled back on the throttle.

"Oh, I forgot to show you what I brought!" exclaimed Caroline, taking her daypack from her shoulders and opening the zipper to the scent of peaches and lavender—a surefire tell of the hand cream she had come to swear by over the last few years. It was a scent Eamon had grown to love, as anytime it was near, he knew he wasn't more than an arm's reach away from an ally, and as she rifled through her bag and tossed aside an industrial-sized tube of the stuff, she extracted a glossy hardcover volume entitled *Addington's Hollow*. "Found it at the library."

Eamon leaned into her shoulder and together they flipped through page after page plastered with stunning pictures of the author's island—a place teeming with so much precious life and blanketed in so much breathtaking beauty that it had famously moved him to write his beloved masterpiece. It was a purely visual history of the grounds he once called home, but the photos were so vibrant and their subjects so worthy of immortality that truly nothing else needed to be said.

"Wow," was all that Eamon could muster as they churned through the snapshots of scenic vistas and rolling hills, thick forests and rocky cliffs and daunting waterfalls and even a lighthouse, which according to the caption, was the inspiration for the barley mill that played such a pivotal role in *Winterset Hollow*. "It really does look like the Hollow," he said as he took the book from her grasp and set it about his own lap. "I wonder if we'll be invited to the feast?"

"I mean, I brought crackers," she replied as she took some saltines she had swiped from Millie's Place from her pack. "You can totally have some if you want." Eamon chuckled as he perused the rest of the idyllic images that were laid across his knees, and as Caroline slathered her hands with peaches and lavender to save them from the wrath of the salty ocean air, they heard a begrudging chug from *The Standard's* guts as Gene eased back on the old boat's throttle and took up a more pointed angle toward what was now the only island in sight. It was the only land that Eamon could see at all anymore, and after one last glance over his shoulder to be sure that the coast, West Rock, and every last thing beyond it were now nothing more than promises buried by the horizon, a grand and graceless grin beat a path clear across his countenance.

Eamon was certain that Addington Isle would be quiet and quaint and plenty cozy, as every brush he had ever seen including Caroline's photographic history had painted it as such, but even on approach it was clear that it was a massive and mighty piece of earth that stretched for miles in every direction. The coastline was cluttered with heavy, jagged rocks and the island's shoulders were so brawny that it was impossible to tell exactly where the shore began to turn, but the sheer scale of what lay on the other side promised so much wonder that even the rickety dock sent shivers through Eamon's soles from the moment he set foot on the first warped board.

The landing looked as if it hadn't been touched in the better part of half a century and the grounds that flanked it weren't much different, their boundaries hopelessly overgrown with weeds and the old boat-house that stood watch over it all ruined and rotten and leaning to the east as if it badly wanted to sip the morning sun. Eamon let the tips of the hairgrass that studded the grounds tickle his palms as he walked the same path from the sea that he was sure Addington had followed during his days there. It was a wild and woolly place, but there was an inherent beauty to its feral edge, almost as if Edward's passing had returned it to its once-natural state, and now that the isle was no longer his home, it was free to be nothing but wilderness once again. Nothing, that is, except for the fence and what surely lived within its embrace.

It was easily two stories tall and made of heavy bars that were spaced too closely together for a man to pass through, and though there was a drive that looked as if it wound all the way back to where they knew the manor house to be, it was blocked by a stately gate emblazoned with the letter "A" and secured by heavy chains. Eamon strained to see further into the property, but the home itself was set so far back and the trees were so thick that the only thing any of them could parse at all was the great spire that stretched just above the canopy. It was something of a disappointment that the mansion wasn't going to be part of their day trip given the circumstance of its security, but Eamon and Caroline had read so much about the famous manor and were so enraptured by the spirit of their journey that it was treat enough just to lay their eyes on its crown and be near its history.

Edward Bartholomew Addington was a titan long before he'd even conceived of *Winterset Hollow*. His family had been textile industry royalty in their native England for generations, and so already wealthier than any one man should rightly be when he decided to spread their interests overseas sometime in the early 1900s, he only thought it proper to build a castle befitting his stature upon arrival. He commissioned a towering, lavish Victorian mansion replete with sprawling gardens and facilities for all occasions and more rooms than he could count, and as he had always fancied himself something of a social butterfly, Addington Manor quickly became the hub of high society in the still-nascent Pacific Northwest. The regal grounds played host to every party, feast, and ball worth attending for decades after its christening, each celebration drawing politicians, actors, writers, artists, and barons of industry in droves to take full advantage of the devilry that was storied to lay beyond Edward's open doors. And as the roaring twenties swung into being and *Winterset Hollow* began to make waves among the literati, legend had it that the festivities rarely ever stopped until the crush of the Great Depression and Addington's untimely passing emptied the halls of his manor forever. Eamon wrapped his paws around the iron that skirted the island proper and knew that he didn't belong on the other side, but as far as he was concerned, it was an honor just to commune with the ghosts of the place and bear witness to its bones. Everyone who was anyone was a guest on Addington Isle at one time or another, and now . . . now John Eamon Buckley was too.

Once everybody had their fill of puttering about the clearing and throwing gauzy stares through the fence, it wasn't long before they all began to gather by the gate, and though the access they had to the grounds was lackluster, the character of their gathering was far from it. Rowan, the other redhead, and his college roommate, Patrick, each lit a candle and tucked it into the links of the chain that secured the entrance as if they were attending a vigil for a dearly departed friend. Paige and Thomas, a young couple who had come to the island with their friend, Gareth, the crier from the pier, managed to find a few flowers scattered among the brush and tied them into little bouquets which they set at the base of the gate. The two oldest travelers, Talia and Percy, who seemed even on first impression to be a bit self-serious, each slipped a handwritten letter through the bars as if Edward himself had been expecting them, and Caroline, who was something of an artist in her younger days, left a collection of simple sketches she had drawn as a child—one rabbit, one bear, one fox, one frog, and one owl.

Eamon hadn't thought to bring anything in the way of an offering, but he felt compelled to leave something behind, so he collected a few handfuls of rocks that had been polished smooth by the tide and simply spelled out *Thank You* in the middle of a naked patch of ground just to the side of the property's entrance. It wasn't anything fancy or premeditated, but he meant it with his whole heart, and though he knew it was folly to believe that Addington's work somehow meant more to him than it did to everybody else in attendance, he still couldn't help but think it.

Winterset Hollow was the story of a community of animals that never saw a sour day until an ever-curious rabbit named Runnymeade poked his nose outside of their sacred grounds and spooked a pack of war-weary buffalo that were moving west in search of better lands and sweeter food. It was a simple tale about a naive tribe's first brush with the real world and the first Barley Day feast that almost wasn't, but it was so much more than that to so many people including Eamon, who at one point in his life sorely needed an ally to help him parse the mechanics of society at large. He still believed with every fiber of his being that if it hadn't been for Addington's relatable, poignant, beautifully illustrated narrative, he might not be around to preach its graces and savor its lessons. *Winterset Hollow* saved him from himself as much as it saved him from his father's wake . . . and that little pile of rocks, meager as it seemed, was the sincerest thank you he had ever offered to anybody.

After everybody had said their piece at the gates, they all felt a little more connected to one another, and it wasn't long before conversations began about favorite characters and impactful passages and which adaptations everybody loved or hated or felt otherwise indifferent to. To nobody's surprise, Gareth was quick to profess his love for Flackwell Frog, the boisterous, theatrical amphibian who prided himself on his culinary acumen, and Thomas, who was a cook at some ubiquitous chain restaurant in some cookie-cutter strip mall in some nothing corner of the suburbs, couldn't help but agree. Talia and Percy, who wasted no time in announcing their statuses as PhD candidates in English literature, both praised the complexity of Phineas Fox's character and went on and on about his searing flaws and generationally seeded emotional baggage until the candles in the gate had burned themselves down to nubs. They spoke about his mastery of games and love for sport as being nothing more than an excuse to ignore the more important trials of life and how his tragic turn was simply the result of his long-suppressed self-hatred and fragile masculinity finally bubbling to the surface after so many years. It was all patently exhausting, but in the spirit of the day, everybody seemed happy enough to swallow their exasperation let them have their say until their sermon had run its course.

Caroline was the first to speak up for Binghamton, the builder bear with the biggest hammer in all the land, though she wasn't the only one to count herself among his fans. She admired his quiet, constructive nature—always there to fix a neighbor's hut or build a new table when a family welcomed a litter and never one to linger long enough for a reward, as the simple pleasure of his craft was always payment enough. Truthfully, she was always a bit envious of how easy Bing made it seem to be so at peace with what he was . . . how effortlessly he molded himself into something so invaluable that a community not tailored for his size would come to depend on his grace for their very survival. He was something of a talisman for her, and though she knew him to be nothing more than a figment of some author's creativity, Caroline couldn't help but save a special place for the imaginary beast in her flesh-and-blood heart.

And while some of the others spoke of Runnymeade Rabbit and his penchant for politicking and nervous leg, Eamon held his tongue as some things, he often felt, were better left unsaid, particularly those that were made somehow more sacred by his presence on Addington's Isle. Runny was gregarious and outgoing and impulsive, and while Eamon was none of those things, he often felt the guilt of somebody who was. He knew what it was to make a decision from which there was no release, and to loathe himself for it, even if nobody else did. He knew the sting of watching his world crumble from the echo of simply putting one foot in front of the other, and he knew all too well the pull of the rye. But after all the words had been said and the sun began to chase the horizon, an unexpectedly welcome curtain began to rise as Gareth framed himself in front of the iron doors, opened his leather-bound copy of Addington's masterpiece, and began to read aloud. Eamon and Mark shared a scoff at the first few words, but it didn't take more than a stanza for everyone in attendance to realize that Gareth had an undeniable talent for performance, and one by one, they all settled in as his voice boomed to the shore and back with words they all dearly loved . . .

> *I wish to see the world, he said, with all his heart and half his head*
> *I wish to graze the grasses I don't know my way around*
> *I wish to see the water's edge, I wish to race beyond the hedge*
> *I promise I'll be swift and wise and barely make a sound*
>
> *But Runny, said the frog, undone, I know I'm not the only one*
> *Who doesn't want you off on some adventure on your own*
> *Your place is here, it's here with me, it's here among your family*
> *Your place is in the Hollow where the barley's always grown*

It was quite a reading and even Mark had to admit he was enjoying himself, sitting there with Caroline in his arms and a blanket from her pack wrapped around their shoulders to protect them from the breeze that had started to roll in from the coast. Captain Gene, too, was unexpectedly soaking it all in, having moved his lounge chair from the dock to the gravel clearing where everyone was seated. This entire sojourn was something of a show for him—an excuse to sate the morbid curiosity that humans all seem to carry about those from different walks of life—but he was undeniably tickled by Gareth's performance and made sure that anyone who was thirsty had a cold beer and anybody who was shivering had a dram of whiskey to warm their bones.

> *What harm is there that I could do? It's only for a day or two*
> *The barley will still be here in its place when I return*
> *The sun will set, the breeze will blow, the children will still play, you know*
> *And I will be the better for my journey past the burn*

> *What could you want that isn't here, the frog said with a somber sneer*
> *What could you possibly expect to find beyond that hedge?*
> *The air is clear, the water's clean, the grasses are the greenest green*
> *The Hollow is your home and there's no me beyond the edge*

There's no me beyond the edge. A powerful line spoken with a powerful voice . . . a line that made everybody who was coupled hold their loved ones a little tighter and everyone who wasn't long for somebody else's embrace. Eamon was used to being alone, but that didn't make it any less tiresome, and while he understood why his inability to let anyone inside his shell made relationships an impossibility, he had always hoped that one day he would outgrow his issues and learn to be vulnerable enough to be with somebody else. But that time hadn't come and Eamon felt there was little he could do to speed its arrival, so he learned some years ago to be content to let his life unwind at its own pace and his nature evolve as it saw fit. It was a maddening current, but it had carried him this far, and while it hadn't brought him to the place he wished to be yet, it had taken him out into the world and for that, if nothing else, he was thankful.

> *You know I love it here, said Runny, you know I am a happy bunny*
> *But still I wish to spread my wings and fly beyond the trees*
> *I promise you that I'll be back, I promise I'm not lying, Flack*
> *I promise I just need to go see what I need to see*

And with those words, his shoulders dropped, and Runny hopped a mighty hop
And turned to face the hedgerow that he'd known for all this time
And jump, he did, as rabbits do, for this was sad for Runny too
It was no treat to go and leave his bestest frog behind

There's no me beyond the edge. Eamon had barely heard Gareth bellow the last two stanzas, for he was still feeling those words with every breath. All of a sudden, he was twelve years old again. All of a sudden, he was being called John by some stranger stuffed behind a desk again. All of a sudden, he was standing at the side of some road he didn't recognize with everything he owned stowed in a pack, countless miles from the only home he had ever known and sure his father was never coming back. All of a sudden, he was certain he would be terrified for the rest of his life, and all of a sudden, he was all of these things and nothing all at once.

It was Caroline, of course, who noticed Eamon's eyes welling with tears and Caroline, of course, who came to his rescue. As soon as Gareth came to the end of the next phrase, she began to applaud, and though he clearly wanted to continue, his doggedness was no match for hers, and shortly thereafter everybody else joined in. They all rose from their seats and crowded around Gareth to show him their appreciation for his reading, and it was somewhere in the distraction of that bustle that Eamon was able to find a thankful moment to collect himself. Gareth took a bow and seemed genuinely grateful for the show of thanks, and as he popped open a beer that had been thrown to him like a bouquet of flowers, he felt a bit like Addington himself for a heartbeat or two . . . but even in the wash of that feeling, Gareth could do little to allow them past the gate.

Their little party was surely a pittance compared to the decadent affairs that were commonplace on the isle during its heyday, but it was warm and it was honest and every last one of them felt like they were the better for it. All of them, that is, except for Captain Gene, who was fast asleep in his folding lounge chair with a half-empty bottle of whiskey still nestled in his lap.

"It's getting cold. You think we should wake him up?" asked Mark amid a modest shiver.

"Not unless you want him to drive us home plastered," answered Eamon.

"I understand how that *sounds* like a bad idea, but you don't need to be sober to make something float. I mean how hard can it really be to drive a boat . . . on water."

"I don't think I wanna learn the answer to that question today, to be honest."

"Besides," interjected Caroline, "it's not *that* cold out here, you big baby. Let's just enjoy it while we can."

Mark turned his gaze skyward at the clouds that were rolling in from the sea. "Yeah, well, we'll see who the big baby is when it starts raining."

"You," Caroline returned. "It'll be you."

"It will definitely be you," added Eamon, the scowl on Mark's face only making their exchange sweeter. "Let's go for a walk."

"A walk? A walk where?" asked Mark.

"Anywhere, man. Come on, let's go. I wanna try and get a better look at the house."

"You mean the one surrounded by the giant fence? You mean *that* house?" protested Mark with his hands on his hips as Eamon and Caroline started working their way up the spindly dirt road that ran the perimeter of the island.

Eamon looked back over his shoulder and yelled, "Up to you, man! I'm sure Gareth is a ton of fun after a few beers! You guys can talk whist and turkey legs and shit!"

Mark had never made a silent decision so quickly. "For Christ's sake, fine. Wait up," he said, jogging to make up the distance between them. "You guys know I don't actually play whist, right? Guys?"

The foliage was dense and savage on either side of the path, and while the trio had walked several miles or close enough to make no difference, they hadn't caught so much as a glimpse of Addington Manor itself. In fact, they seemed no closer than when they were sitting by the gates listening to Gareth pour his heart out in front of old strangers and new friends.

"Listen, I don't mean to be *that* guy, but I'm pretty sure we're not gonna see anything besides this road on this road no matter how far we walk," barked Mark.

"I hate to say it, but he's probably right," added Caroline.

"What do you mean you *hate* to say it?"

"Did I stutter?"

"You know, if I didn't love you so much, I would really, *really* dislike you."

Eamon, who was walking ahead of the two of them instead of lagging behind, as was his typical nature, turned and began to backpedal. "Just another mile or so, okay? Then we can go back."

"Just another mile of trees and shrubs and dirt? I mean, we can see all that on the way back," offered Mark.

"You never know, maybe there's something worth seeing around the bend."

A knowing smile came over Caroline's face as she wrapped her arm around Mark's waist and leaned into him with her whole being. "Let him go a little longer, he just wants to see a rabbit."

"A rabbit?" said Mark incredulously. "We can go back home and see rabbits. Boise is like drowning in them."

"Yeah, but he wants to see one *here*."

"Why?"

"I just wanna see what he saw, you know?" said Eamon, trotting along with his hands buried in his pockets. "Addington said he wrote *Winterset Hollow* in part because he felt so bad about disturbing the wildlife when he started building his mansion here. He said it was all so beautiful that he couldn't help but write about it. That the guilt would've eaten him alive if he didn't find a way to honor it."

"Come on, Babe," urged Caroline. "I've told you that story a thousand times."

"Well, in my defense, I probably wasn't listening." Mark reached out and flicked the iron fencing that was still running the inside of the path they were treading. "He felt so bad he put a giant metal fence around the entire thing, huh? Sounds like he was *really* broken up about it. What is it about his book that you love so much anyway? I know the poems are good and everything and I've seen the cartoons and stuff, but—"

"I don't know," answered Eamon. "Haven't you ever read something and felt like it was written just for you?"

"No."

"Sorry, let me rephrase that. Haven't you ever read something?"

"Very funny," returned Mark. "Also no."

The three of them shared a chuckle before Eamon reached into his bag of sincerity. "It's hard to explain. It just . . . it taught me a lot of things that I needed to learn at a time when I really needed to learn them. It made me a little less scared of everything. A little more willing to stick my head of out of the hedge, I guess."

"Oh, that's one of them, uh, metaphors, right?"

"God, I love it when you play dumb," said Caroline, standing on her tiptoes to give him a peck on the lips.

"I can be dumber if you want." Mark stopped and wrapped his arms around her, and she tilted her head up toward his. "I can go full Lenny . . . right here, right now . . . with Eamon watching and everything. What do you think?"

"*Now* who's making rabbit metaphors!?" Eamon shouted from a few dozen yards ahead. "See! Feels good!"

When Mark and Caroline finally caught back up, they were surprised to see Eamon standing in front of a once-towering spruce that looked as if it had been felled by the wind. It was lying across the path with its roots to the waterside and its trunk driven clean through the sturdy iron fencing, and Eamon, who was clearly awed by the stature of the thing, was running his fingers over the bark as if he was about to whisper some sage advice about dying with dignity.

"That's a big tree," said Mark, the poet.

"You're not kidding," added Caroline, gazing skyward at the roots of the thing which were easily twice as tall as she was. "Must've been one hell of a storm."

"Had to be pretty recent," offered Eamon. "It's still alive." He explored a series of grooves in the tree's skin with the tip of his finger before looking over to the crater it had left to see that the earth looked freshly uncovered and free of seedlings.

"Are you having a moment . . . with the tree?" Mark asked dubiously. Caroline jabbed him in the kidney with her fist just hard enough for him to get the picture. "Sorry." Eamon was indeed having a moment with the tree—a moment that was only interrupted by a rustle of leaves and a flash of fur from underneath the trunk.

"Did you guys see that?" asked Eamon, his eyes lighting up like oil lamps.

"Don't tell me, you saw a—"

"A rabbit. I saw it too," confirmed Caroline. "Ran right through the fence." All it took was one look from Eamon for Mark to understand what was about to happen, and a glance at Caroline did nothing to persuade him that she felt any different. Mark's only protest was a roll of his eyes and a reluctant shift of his weight, but even he could sense the breath of adventure in the air. Even he could feel the kismet of it all and appreciate the romanticism of having a rabbit play usher to a dream so pure, and before he took his first step toward whatever was on the other side . . . even he looked back over his shoulder and across the great sea to be sure that everything he knew was nowhere to be seen.

THREE

They lost sight of the rabbit the moment they stepped onto the grounds, but it made little difference now that they were treading the same earth Addington had tread and breathing the same crisp air. Truthfully, the land just inside the fencing didn't look much different than the area they had already covered, but that didn't mean it wasn't immediately recognizable as special. There was a feeling—a character to the space that sent the best kind of chills racing up Eamon's spine and set the hairs on his arms reaching toward the heavens. It was all so electric and vital and sublimely necessary, and the knowledge that he would have to leave in a matter of seconds or minutes or even hours was already making him nostalgic for its embrace. It was like the most blessed sense of home and Eamon's biggest, bluest vein was already twitching for more.

The terrain further in from the coast, however, was beautiful and surprisingly varied. The bulk of it was covered with thick pines, mighty firs, kingly redwoods and stately spruces, but there were also rolling hills and peaceful valleys, rocky outcroppings and pockets of meadow and rivers and streams that seemed to almost sing as they bumbled their way toward the coast, which was nothing more than a memory now. It was as if the outside world was of no consequence . . . as if the rigors and nuisance of daily life simply weren't allowed passage through the endless, evergreen canopy, and the stench of modern madness was silenced by the scent of flowering bushes and wild grass. Even half a mile into their journey, Eamon understood why Addington had picked this place to build his castle, and he also understood his reticence to change it, even if just to make sure that it was his forever. Good god, it was ever lovely.

Mark and Caroline followed Eamon's lead as he pushed toward what felt like the middle of the isle, as there was really no way for any of them to tell just how big the piece of land truly was. They knew it to be finite, but it was sprawling enough to feel like it had no end, and every last piece of Eamon wished that were the case. He led them through rashes of thick forest and across lazy pastures, along the banks of a steaming river and over to the other side where they watched it twist its way into the distance, and for once, it was Mark and Caroline's turn to lag behind their friend and smile at the very sight of him being happy. Eamon looked correct in the island's embrace, and whether it was his familiarity with the outdoors coming home to roost or simply the serendipity of finding something real to attach to those feelings that had bloomed within the pages of Addington's book, it mattered little to his comrades as long as they could watch him grin.

When they felt like they needed a breather from their trek, they found a quiet little pond and sat about the rim. Caroline joked that Eamon, who was lost in the ripple of the waters, was waiting for a frog to come and greet him with a snack, but the truth was that he was thinking about home again. He was thinking about the waters he used to fish and how much his reflection had changed since those days. His eyes looked so heavy, and his chin was angular and masculine, and though the stubble on his cheeks was familiar now, it was still new to the glassy surface staring back at him. He could still hear his father calling after him as he played possum at the bottom of the lake near their cabin, and for a moment, he swore he saw his father's boots on the shore right next to the ragged slip-ons that Eamon was so fond of. He could still see them clear as day—perfectly worn and patched a hundred times and emblazoned with a capital "J" that he had carved into the leather on the back of the heel. "J" for Jack. "J" for the now-and-future John that never was.

Soon, early evening began to push its way down from the rafters, and while Eamon and company had started to angle their way back toward the coast, knowing full well that they still had a boat to catch, they couldn't help but stop when they came across a clearing filled with tall, hearty grass. Eamon's heart almost burst when he saw the rye stretching for acres in every direction, and though time was running short, nobody seemed to begrudge him the instinct to sit himself down in the middle of it all, wrap his arms around his knees, and simply be. It was a pervasive and timeless peace with his eyes tucked below the tide of seed heads and the crickets weaving their song into the fabric of the day's end, and as Eamon began to breathe with his whole chest instead of just his lungs, he felt for the first time in his life that he was part of the axis instead of just a piece of the wheel. It was reassembly like he had never experienced, but it was truly getting late, and it didn't take more than one frigid gust of sun-starved air to remind them all that their time in the wild was running short . . . so with his heart in the rye field and his head once again swimming with mainland anxieties, Eamon led his friends back toward the dock.

They pushed past the rolling grasses and back through the thicket of woods which offered them some quarter from the billowing breeze, and while the urgency of their gait spoke to their worry over missing their ride, even Mark couldn't ignore what they found once they came to the next rash of hills. It was a plinth meant for a statue—set with care on top of a gentle rise in the earth and affixed with a blank copper dedication plate about the center. There were no other details at all to tailor their interest in the thing, but the choice to place it in the middle of an otherwise unremarkable field gave it a strange and alluring gravity that Mark couldn't help but immediately soil. He jumped on top of the stony canvas and tucked his hand inside his jacket like some oversized Napoleon, but just as he was about to spew some lighthearted nonsense, he caught something out of the corner of his vision and marched over to the crest of the next hill.

"Is that a hedge maze?" he asked as the others arrived to share his view.

"I don't know what else it could be," answered Eamon. It looked to be a hundred yards square and built of thick, towering bushes that had once been meticulously cared for but were now wild and overgrown and infected with legions of snakish vines that had managed to worm their way through every opening and over every pathway before they died.

"This is some serious white people shit, huh?" Caroline chimed, a little spurious but equally intrigued as the three of them made their way toward the labyrinth.

"You mean you didn't have one of these growing up?" jabbed her beau.

"What's that in the middle?" Eamon nodded toward a domed wooden structure set plum in the center of it all, its summit peeking through the cloud cover of the brush like some great mountain.

"I don't know," said Caroline. "Only one way to find out."

"We *really* need to get back though," reasoned Mark as he stopped.

"Then head back!" Caroline called over her shoulder. "I'm going to see how the other half lives!"

"Alright, fine, but if we die here . . . I'm gonna be really upset with both of you," Mark lamented with his hands on his hips. "I may even write you a strongly worded letter. You guys even listening to me?" he asked as the two of them bounded away. "I said I might even—"

"Oh, this is some teetotaling flapper nonsense for sure," sniped Caroline as she stopped by the outer edge and waited for the straggler to catch up.

Mark toed the line next to her, and noticing something at his feet, bent down and snatched up a bullet casing, cradling it in his palm and adding, "Yup, that Addington was *some* animal lover. Guess it must've been a big bunny, huh?"

"More like a small bear," returned Eamon, taking the casing and inspecting it. "Looks like a .257 or a .303 or something. Like a deer rifle round." Eamon looked for any markings on the bottom of the casing, but the weather had not been kind through the years, so he simply slipped the fossil into his pocket.

"You just gonna take it?"

"I'm not gonna keep it, just . . . I don't know, it doesn't feel like it belongs here." Somehow, that made sense to Mark. After all, this was a place of staggering beauty and the presence of a tool of war felt incongruous, and as Eamon and Caroline disappeared into the hedges, Mark found two more casings lying about the grass and likewise slipped them into his jacket.

"Darling, would you care to join me in the hedgerow for a martini or two!?" Caroline bellowed from inside the walls in her best continental accent.

The interior of the maze was narrow and dark but almost perfectly overgrown, the spidering vines forming something of a canopy through which the last dwindling rays of the sun sparkled down. The place was littered with twists and turns, dead ends and false exits, but the three of them soon found themselves at the center only to discover a puzzle of a completely different timbre.

"What . . . what is this?" Caroline asked as they approached the domed structure they had seen from the hill—a curious thing that eventually revealed itself to be a tightly latticed cage about twenty feet in diameter and made of thick, lacquered bamboo. Mark grabbed ahold of one of the bars and gave it a good shake, but the construction was so solid that even after so many years, it hardly moved at all.

"This is wild stuff," said Eamon as he fingered the heavy iron padlock that hung by the door, the thing dripping with rust and left open and useless for decades. But while the cage itself was interesting enough, it was the army of chessboards that had been set around it like numbers on a clock that made the scene truly bizarre.

"Chess?" asked Mark, running his hand over a freestanding checkerboard table that was carved from a single piece of granite. There were twelve of them in total, each placed just close enough to the edge of the cage for whomever was inside to be able to reach through and play.

Caroline picked up a rook on the board closest to her and turned it over in her hands. It was heavy and resolute and finely carved, but it wasn't a castle like she had seen before . . . it was a great spire like the one that crowned Addington's mansion. The king and queen appeared to be visages of Addington and his wife, Elizabeth, he in a tuxedo and top hat and she in an evening gown with pearls about her neck, and oddly enough, the rest of the pieces looked to be plucked straight from the book that made him famous. The knights were busts of great bears baring their teeth to the wind and the bishops were sinewy foxes with their noses turned upward toward the heavens, and while the pawns on the white side were rabbits perched on their hind legs, their counterparts in black were frogs stretching to snag their next meal with their tongues.

"I don't know if this is the right word, but this is all a little . . . kinky, don't you think?" Caroline said as she returned the rook to its square.

"I know what you mean," replied Eamon. "It's like a chess orgy or something." He walked the entire circumference of the cage, looking at each board just long enough to get a sense of the games that were still frozen mid-gambit, and though Mark and Caroline didn't understand them much beyond their aesthetics, Eamon did. Chess had been a nightly indulgence when he still lived with his father—a continuous lesson in strategy and tactics that had been cleverly disguised as little more than a game. It seemed innocent enough at the time, but as Eamon grew older and the angle of his lens skewed wider, he realized there was almost nothing he did at his father's behest that wasn't some thinly veiled at-

tempt at preparing him for some fight that would never come. No minute he lived that wasn't somehow in service of his father's fears.

Eamon had quickly become quite the player, and even though he
hadn't touched a board in years, he was still savvy enough to understand
that while twelve different people were playing from outside the cage,
there was only one player within. The players on the perimeter were am-
ateurs at best, their strategies surely marred by a night of drinking and a
lack of experience, and it showed in the chaotic remains of their games,
but the caged player was incisive, aggressive, and practiced . . . and as
far as Eamon could see, he or she was no more than three or four moves
away from declaring checkmate on every board.

"Twelve games at once?" Eamon said to himself.

"What?" shouted Caroline from the other side of the cage.

"Nothing. This is just . . . I've never seen anything like this," he replied as he trudged through the ruins of revelry. There were cigarette
butts and discarded filters littering the ground like a healthy layer of
sod as liquor bottles and champagne corks and tobacco packets played
flowers among the rubble. The leavings of excess were ankle-deep in the
darker corners of the place, but it all seemed more sediment and less fossil in value until Eamon stumbled over a martini glass and took it upon
himself to wipe away the grime that had come to coat it over the better
part of half a century. "Check this out," he said as Mark and Caroline
gathered around to gawk at the frosted crystal vessel with "EBA" etched
onto its side in beautiful script.

"Whoa," Mark exclaimed. "Now *that* is worth taking." Eamon couldn't
disagree, but he didn't even have time to think about stuffing the little
treasure into his pocket before the first few drops of rain spattered its
dirt-stained surface. The downpour came fast and heavy, and this time
around there was no time for one last look at anything no matter how
interesting or divine or otherwise beguiling it appeared to be. There was
only time to run, and as the heavens made known their decision to hold
nothing back, not even a chorus of the island's sweetest sirens could've
convinced the three of them of anything different.

There was no friendly banter as they rumbled across open fields
where the storm battered them from every angle and ran through dense
forests where the heavy raindrops pitter-pattered the canopy above their
heads. There was no good-natured ribbing as they slipped up and down

the otherwise innocuous hills, and there were no quips as they skirted the once-quaint brooks that were already overflowing with runoff, but by the time they had covered several miles, their clothes were soaked through and their feet were swampy and already pained with blisters. They understood then the price they were meant to pay for breaching a paradise that wasn't theirs and breathing air they weren't meant to breathe, each of them feeling the balance of it all with every tortuous step. Each of them busied from the calculations of regret.

When they finally stopped for a rest, they were surprised at how dark it had become, being that the sun hadn't set more than an hour ago, but they were so far removed from anything resembling civilization that there wasn't even a whisper of artificial light, and the stars stood no chance against the thick clouds that they knew to be overhead. It was maddeningly black, and the fact that they might as well have been any-where else on earth where the sun wasn't shining only made the taste of the night's air more bitter.

"Okay, where the hell are we?" Mark asked, his hands on his knees and the whole of his being heaving in a desperate attempt to catch his breath.

"We've gotta be close," Eamon replied as his chin streamed with fresh rainwater. "The broken fence was on the east side of the isle, and we've been running away from where the sun set for half an hour now."

"We're gonna miss our ride," added Caroline, pacing back and forth with her hands on her hips like she had just finished a hard four hundred meters. "There's no way they're gonna wait for us. There's just no—"

"We gotta keep going. Can't be much further, okay?" After sharing a silent glance, Caroline and Mark both nodded their agreement and waited for Eamon to take the lead again, but he didn't take more than two steps before his foot landed on a machined piece of slate. "Wait," he said as he took a few more strides and found a set of stairs that led to a patio so large that its edges were still hidden in the dark. "I think . . . I think we're at the house. I mean *his* house."

"That's not good," said Mark as they all walked toward the center of the landing. "I mean, we're close, but how are we gonna get through the gate to the boat? That iron is like twenty feet high."

"We just have to keep heading east till we find the fence and trace it to the tree and then we're home," said Caroline. "Right?" She and Mark turned to Eamon for confirmation, but he was already gone. "Eamon? *Eamon!?*" They scoured the darkened patio until they finally found their friend standing near a window at the base of the towering mansion, his hands cupped around his face to shield his eyes from the rain and his attention firmly conscripted to something other than their journey back to the mainland.

"Hey, I know you wanna see this, but we really have to go," said Mark as he put a hand on his shoulder.

Eamon didn't answer immediately, but when he pulled himself away from the big bay window, he had the strangest look about his face. "There's a light on," he whispered. "Inside. It's flickering like a . . . lantern or something. Look."

"I don't care, man, we really gotta—"

"There's not supposed to be anybody here."

"*We* are also not supposed to be here. So unless you wanna spend the rest of the night in the freezing rain, we need to—" Mark's urging was interrupted by the sight of another lantern being touched to life, this one close enough for them both to see it without having to strain, and for the most fleeting of moments . . . Eamon was sure he saw a shadow dart away from the flame as it found its stride and bloomed into a proper, vibrant orange.

Caroline took up a place over Eamon's other shoulder, and despite her pragmatic misgivings keeping pace with the storm still raging around her, she allowed her curiosity to be piqued. "I saw that. I saw it too."

"Hey. Hey!" shouted Mark, clapping his hands in front of their faces in an attempt to snap them out of their daze. "There's a light on. So what? Look, I know what's his face is super dead, but I'm sure there's like . . . a caretaker or something that probably stops by once in a while to make sure there's no squatters or whatever living there, right? I mean, doesn't that make sense? Guys . . . let's . . . *go!*" It was a marvelous thing for Mark to be the voice of reason, but Caroline and Eamon still didn't seem intent on paying him any mind. He may have been fueled by a clarity that rarely graced his logic and a gusto that typically fueled his tongue, but those things were no match for the abject wonder of feeling lost in a favorite story . . . and as both Eamon and Caroline were awash in the fantasy of finding some brand-new chapter, neither of them registered a word he said.

The whinny of a creaking door cut through the rain like a thunderclap. They all turned to see only shadows, but the strange shuffle-and-click of what sounded like strained footsteps made it perfectly clear that someone was approaching. They wanted to flee, but they couldn't, all six of their feet firmly anchored to the slate by the searing regret of their own curiosity as some dark figure inched toward them along the wall of the house. The stranger took care to stay sheltered under the shallow overhang of the roof lest he fall victim to the same deluge that they had been battling for the last hour, and in a matter of breathless moments, he was standing in front of the bay window before them, silhouetted against the flickering light of the lantern. Eamon's heart began to beat double-time when he saw the shadow's shape, but his mind simply wouldn't allow him to process it as anything other than madness. Even his big, broad heart wouldn't let him believe it until the scrape of a match breathed purpose upon the wick of the oil lamp the stranger was holding . . . and all of a sudden, before him stood one inarguable answer and a hundred burning questions. One mighty rope and a thousand loose ends.

He was an old rabbit. His fur was gray and ragged, his whiskers spindly and overgrown, and it was clear from his delicate posture that his frame had seen more miles than the three of them put together. He was just as tall as Eamon, and though his aesthetic was leporine through and through, his presence and grace seemed undeniably human as he adjusted his spectacles and looked his three guests up and down. A tweed vest was buttoned about his midsection and a matching ascot was tied loosely around his neck, and while his left hand was still busy with the oil lamp he was carrying, his right was clutching the head of an old walking stick that had been carved from a single piece of wood. It certainly didn't seem out of place for a creature his age to be using such an aid, but there was a more immediate reason for him to be sporting a cane as his right leg had been replaced by an unwieldy wooden prosthesis that looked as if it had been plucked from some century past. And as Eamon's eyes ran from his missing leg to his vest, up to his kindly face and all the way to his ears, one of which was wrapped in a plaid scarf as if it were some wooly bandage, he still couldn't believe what he was seeing.

"Good evening," the old rabbit said to the abject astonishment of everybody present. "Runnymeade Rabbit, at your service." Runny tried his best to offer them a bow, but his tired body allowed him only the faintest dip of his head. It was an inarguably simple gesture, but it was still enough to make the edges of Eamon's reality bleed white and beg his vision to pulse with his still-racing heart. Surely this was madness. Surely this was anything but real. He wanted to believe those things for the sake of faith in his own perspective, but he wanted to believe their inverses for the sake of so much more. For his past. For his present. For John. But as Eamon looked to his friends for some whisper of encouragement or warning, as either would have been welcome, madness spoke again. "And a fine Barley Day to you all."

Part Two

The Frog's Feast

Flackwell had a knack for flavor, a talent the whole village savored
A way with pies and roasts and tarts that brought them to their knees
A passion, see, for feeding others, a yearn to cook and please his brothers
A hand with leeks and spuds and quince and pumpkin, rice, and peas

It was magic to the rest most times, a trick he played beneath the pines
A sorcery of sorts, just him, the cauldron, and the flame
And once a year, his greatest show, the one that took him weeks to grow
Was Barley Day, a meal for which he'd garnered modest fame

Flackwell sped off toward the mill, armed with glee and page and quill
And noted all the things he wished to fix up for the feast
I think we'll have a pastry, yes, of peas and onions, sage and cress
I think we'll have an egg soufflé or tartlet at the least

I think we'll have a roast of squash, full of flavor, nothing posh
I think we'll have a soup of greens with warm and toasty bread
A meal of oats to warm the heart, I think would make a lovely start
And jugs of wine with berries spiced the perfect shade of red

As Flackwell tumbled up the hill and reached to open up the mill
Wherein the food the Hollow stored was surely still at hand
He found it odd it was unlocked and looked to see a single stalk
Of celery lying bare between the front door and the jamb

He slowly opened up the door and to his horror there before
His feet lay not a single bit of parsley, rice, or beans
Barren as the snow it was, unburdened by some selfish paws
The cruelest joke that Flackwell Frog had truly ever seen

I'm sorry, said a shameful Runny, sometimes I'm such a stupid bunny
And Flackwell turned to see his friend approaching from the hedge
It wasn't me, I swear, it was the buffalo I found out there
They followed me back home after my time beyond the edge

I told you not to go there, Rabbit, wanderlust's an ugly habit
And now without this feast before the winter we will starve
Look what you've done, look what they took, the beasts that live beyond the brook
Look what you've brought upon us all with all your disregard

FOUR

Eamon breathed a savage breath of reawakening, and as he gulped the stuff of life into his lungs, he felt the warmth of a real fire on his skin before he even thought to let his eyes flutter open. He had never been unconscious before, and so he had never felt the strange bewilderment that comes with returning to the world from the big, black nothing. It was a sensation that was sublimely new to him and soon he found himself retracing every step he'd ever taken in hopes of squaring where he was. Every last one from the cabin that defined his childhood out into the world beyond his father's umbrella, from one foster home to another and on to the boundaryless terrors of high school, and west from his squalid little apartment to the Washington coast and across the waters to where he was sure he had found himself—somewhere in E. B. Addington's supposedly shuttered manor house.

Eamon wasn't sure how long he had been out, but it was long enough for his clothes to have been dried by the heat of the fire, and as he rose to find that his shoes had been set carefully just in front of the hearth, he got his first glimpse of the character of the room that surrounded him. He was sure it was a study of some sort as the walls were lined with shelves stuffed with old, leather-covered volumes of this and that, their titles and authorship inlaid in gold and silver etching and their bindings regal and proper. Eamon ran his fingers across their spines and drank in their rubrics like the desert dog he was. *Paradise Lost, Hero and Leander, The Canterbury Tales, Robinson Crusoe, Gulliver's Travels, Frankenstein, Ivanhoe,* and countless others—all timeless, inimitable jewels of the written word stowed away in a vault that he felt was most likely built for the same purpose. A pantry for a feast of pages.

Eamon made his way to the far wall where he found a window with a muntin of thick iron running through the glass, which itself was so old that it was sagging at the bottom of each pane. He strained to see through it in hopes of understanding which side of the property he was on, but it was so perfectly dark outside that the only thing he could discern was his own form silhouetted against the gentle glow of the fire. It was no secret that the Addington family had found wealth long before Edward ever put pen to paper, and the mishmash of furniture in the study only seemed to echo the historical depth of their status in its stylistic breadth. Truly the only thing holding the room together at all was the fact that each piece looked just as expensive as the next, as apart from the ornate Victorian sofa on which Eamon had awakened, there was an Elizabethan cabinet to hold strong drink, a comfortable leather Shaker chair next to which sat a hopelessly outdated globe, and a William and Mary rolltop desk that was set against the wall opposite the hearth. It was a strange and meandering history, but it still felt correct. It was jumbled and uncatalogued and piecemeal, but its bones still clattered with honesty.

Eamon's mouth ran dry with the possibility that Addington himself might have parked his being at the very desk that he was now standing over, and as his curiosity eclipsed the bewilderment of his reawakening, he rolled open the covering to reveal the very thing he'd hoped to find in-side—handwritten pages. The parchments were perfectly yellowed and brittle with age, and although the script was sublime and graceful and restrained, the ink was the kind of wild and stormy that only a real foun-tain pen could produce. The writings were old, to be sure, and that only made Eamon more hopeful that they were wrought by the same hand that had penned the book that saved him. And as he gently lifted a page from the pile and began to read, he could have powered London itself with the electricity that flooded his fingertips . . .

I have always been aware of my poorer nature, but over the course of my life I have learned to embrace it as a friar embraces his call from the heavens. Who am I to deny the gifts that he has given me, and further-more, who am I to define such yearnings as anything other than gifts? It seems to me that it is precisely the question of that very definition which determines whether one is tortured or otherwise emboldened by such things. It seems to me that it is the lens rather than the specimen that determines what we see . . . what we fear . . . what we pine for . . . what we try to kill or otherwise hold ever dear. It seems to me that . . .

Eamon was so lost in the presence of his hero's prose that he didn't even notice the commotion at the study door until it had already clicked shut. He wheeled to face the entrance, and only upon seeing the darkened outline of his host did he finally recall the *last* few steps that had brought him to this place—the rain, the run, and the rabbit. Eamon's pulse began to thump against his skin and his breathing turned desperate as he faced, for the second time that night, the reality of having to swallow what was so recently an impossibility. But Runny was a conscientious host and this was old hat to him, and so he was careful to linger by the entryway long enough for Eamon to come to terms with his presence before he stepped into the light carrying a tea tray steaming with fresh brew. "If you need to sit down, I promise I won't be insulted," he said.

Eamon fumbled for the chair that was tucked under the desk and sat the whole of his uncertainty upon it as the rabbit limped his way across the room, pulled open the top drawer, and set the tea tray down. It didn't take particularly long, but it was enough time for Eamon to look him over without seeming too forward and refresh his understanding that this was an old thing . . . a broken thing. Eamon's heart wept at the sight of his ragged fur, crooked back, and scarf-wrapped ear, but still he reached out to touch him if for no other reason than to feel the warmth of his existence against his skin. He simply had to be sure it was all real, and the moment he grazed the edge of the fur around Runny's hip with the barrel of his finger, he knew his eyes had been nothing but honest . . . and in some maddening way, that made the rabbit's circumstance all the more pitiful.

"Are you feeling alright?" asked Runny, stepping back to give Eamon some breathing room.

"You . . . you can talk?" Eamon whispered, ignoring the steaming beverage at his side.

The rabbit let out a sigh and shifted the bulk of his weight onto his cane and added, "Yes, we spoke out on the patio earlier this very night as a matter of fact. Well, one of us did. And by the way, why is that always the first question asked by every anthropomorphic monkey who finds themselves in my presence?"

"Anthropomorphic monkey?"

"That was a joke," offered Runny. "You were supposed to laugh and then I was supposed to say something along the lines of 'see, you and I aren't so different,' and then we were supposed to proceed getting along like fountains and filigree. But it would seem my joking days are about as far behind me as my dancing days," he said, rapping his good leg three times with his walking stick. "I could cut quite a Charleston when I had two of these, I'll have you know."

The rabbit pulled an ottoman to the center of the room and sat himself down, resting his paws on the head of his cane and allowing a casual slump to wash over his posture. "Forgive the monkey comment, it's just disheartening to always be the sideshow and I am an old rabbit and have grown patently tired of it." Runny waited for his guest to offer something in the way of an acknowledgement, but all Eamon managed was a nod of his head and a tentative swallow of stale study air. "This will be much easier for you if you try to relax," Runny continued, "I know your kind is fond of your gifts, but you would do well to stop thinking yourself Prometheus and every little thing you do the gods' own fire . . . or this may prove to be a long night for the both of us."

"I'm sorry," Eamon finally eked. "It's just . . . this is all a little unexpected."

"Understandable. Perhaps a few swallows of tea will help loosen up that bundle of nerves. My very own recipe. Alder bark, spoiled wheatberry, pickled worm silk, and raccoon leavings."

"Oh," said Eamon, doing his best not to seem uninterested.

"That was also a joke," Runny mused, nodding to the porcelain teapot where the strings from several bags of store-bought tea were still hanging over its edge. "It's Earl Grey. Lipton." Eamon chuckled and snagged the steaming cup from the tray and gave it a good whiff just to be safe. "I'm not gonna, like . . . shrink down to nothing when I drink this, am I?"

"Why Alice, what you choose to do after you've had your tea is entirely up to you." Eamon smiled and immediately felt more comfortable after Runny picked up on his reference. Comfortable enough to take a hearty sip, in any case.

"Are my friends okay?"

"Quite! They're in the parlor, as a matter of fact. Having a ball last I checked, along with the rest of your comrades."

"The rest of . . . who?"

"Your sightseeing party or what have you," replied the rabbit, taking a moment to scratch at the scarf that was covering his floppy ear.

"*They're* here?"

"Indeed. Our fencing is not as secure as it used to be, and you all seem to share similar curiosities."

"Can I see them? My friends, I mean."

"Of course you can. You're not imprisoned here, I just thought after the fall you took following your . . . spell . . . you might do well with some peace and quiet."

"Oh, well thank you," said Eamon, now suddenly aware of a bump on the back of his head which he explored with his free hand. "How long was I out for?"

"A few hours or close enough to make no difference. Long enough for the pies to brown and the soup to come together," the rabbit replied with a grandfatherly drawl.

"Pies?"

"Dear boy, don't you know it's Barley Day?" A smile graced the bend of Eamon's mouth as any skepticism that was still clattering about in his skull quickly melted away to nothing. "Wouldn't be the same without a rutabaga pie or three, now would it?"

"Barley Day is . . . a real thing?" he beamed, wrapping both of his hands around his cup of tea and leaning into his host.

"I suppose that all depends on your perspective. But as for mine, it has been a real thing for as long as I can remember. It's a very special day, you know. The day we say goodbye to summer and hello to the cold. The day we say goodbye to friends and hello to a long and peaceful slumber. A very special day indeed." Eamon could do little to stop himself from grinning like fortune's favorite fool as he gulped down the last of his drink, leaned back in his chair, and shook his head with the sweetest disbelief. "Is everything quite alright?" asked Runny.

"Yes. I mean . . . yes. I just can't believe it's really you. *You* from the book. *You.* I mean, that book is seventy-some years old. How—"

"I am an old rabbit, as you can see. Older than most. I have been on this earth longer than even the oldest of *your* kind as a matter of fact, and spirit willing, I will be here for a good deal longer. We are the tortoises of our genera if you will . . . and a stubborn bunch to boot. Hard to kill and even harder to live with," Runny said with a wink.

"We?"

"Those of us that are left. The last of us. We."

"We *who*?" Eamon asked as Runny chuckled quietly to himself and rose with a dignified groan, clearly content with the air of mystery that he had bred.

"Perhaps it's time we joined the others," he said with a tilt of his head. The rabbit turned and hobbled back toward the entrance, the shuffle-and-click of his steps echoing off the old hardwood floors and his form fading back into nothing but a shadow as he distanced himself from the fire. He swung open the heavy door and looked behind him expecting to see Eamon hot on his tail, but to his surprise, his guest was standing by the hearth and staring up at a large oil painting hanging above the mantle. It was done by an experienced hand, and even though the colors were faded and the details clouded by years of woodsmoke and soot, it was nonetheless a striking portrait of some young British lord seated with a pack of hounds at his feet, his boyish gaze fixed directly at the artist himself. He was all but expressionless, but his eyes seemed somehow alive as they bloomed in a vibrant, fiery blue against his auburn tailcoat and burnt-orange hair. Eamon reached out to touch a spot on the frame where it looked like a nameplate had once been affixed, but Runny piped up from the other side of the room before his fingers could find their mark.

"It's not him, if that's what you're wondering." Eamon withdrew his hand and spun around on his heels feeling a bit sheepish to have been caught in a moment of curiosity. "It's quite alright. He's an Addington, of course, just not *your* Addington. Not Edward. Some great-great-great-uncle or cousin or some such nonsense. Bit of a tradition of theirs, all the portraiture. Famous families and their quest for immortality and all that," said Runny before giving Eamon another moment to breathe it all in. "Well, time to carry on, I'm afraid. Our time is fleeting." And with a few hearty raps of his cane against the floorboards, he turned and led Eamon toward the door.

The great hall to which the study was attached was endless and grand and looked as if it ran the breadth of the entire estate. It was dotted with oil lamps and doors to countless rooms and the ceiling was gallery high, which was appropriate considering the walls were covered with hundreds of paintings that seemed to span the whole of the Addington family's post-medieval history. There were landscapes of the sprawling grounds they called home, renderings of their towering castles and English countryside manor houses and getaway cottages, representations of beloved pets and lavish parties and the many factories they had built, and of course there were portraits of the family themselves. And every fifty feet or so, standing watch over them all were suits of armor posed against the walls like guards in a proper palace, some of them clutching pikes and others with their gauntlets wrapped around jousting lances. They were all plenty covered in dust, but there wasn't so much as a dent or a scuff anywhere to interrupt their clean, artfully turned lines, which prompted Eamon to wonder if they had truly ever had the chance to serve their purpose.

Eamon took it as something of a timeline as he followed his furry host toward the center of the mansion and watched as the brush-and-palette clothing on the walls changed from Elizabethan frocks to Victorian gowns to Edwardian suits and threads with more modern sensibilities. It was the family's whole history, and even though he wanted desperately to know who each and every one of them were, Eamon was unable to put a name to any of their faces as the plates on their portraits had been removed just like the painting in the study.

"Where'd all their names go?" he asked, lagging a few steps behind the hobbled rabbit.

"Wartime sacrifices, I'm afraid," answered Runny. "Brass was in short supply during your first World War and Edward's father, being something of a patriot, though not quite enough to enlist his actual family . . . shocking, I know . . . stripped his possessions of the shiny stuff and sent it to the munitions factories. Offerings of the rich in brass and offerings of the poor in blood. Something of a theme in the history of your kind, or so I've been told."

"Guess they didn't feel like sending these suits of armor off to be melted down though, huh?" Eamon mused, flicking a pikeman's breast plate with his fingernail.

"I'm quite sure they *said* they did, but as a matter of course they sent them here instead. I'm sure there was much fanfare when they were being packed up and shipped off, but that was really the point, now wasn't it?"

"You know a lot," said Eamon. "I mean, a lot about us."

"There is little in this house but books to read and pictures to admire, and I have done more of both in my day than I care to admit. Always did like this one," Runny remarked, tapping his walking stick on the frame of a painting of some young, well-privileged lad seated cross-legged with a bunny in his lap. "*That* one is Edward." Eamon grazed the screw holes that once held Edward's bit of brass as he trailed his new friend toward the center of Addington's home where the great corridor emptied out into a cavernous atrium.

Eamon couldn't remember ever being in a place with so many dead things. It was unexpected and pointedly perverse and even Runny knew it was worthy of some note as he made a point of stopping in the middle of the room as if this was the main attraction on the tour. They were hung on every inch of wall and cluttered every corner—zebras and baboons and tigers and gazelles, elephants and mountain lions and moose and bears of every type—the rarest birds of prey and the heads of so many rhinoceros, deer, and giraffes that Eamon couldn't even begin to count them all. And the largest of all the carefully preserved corpses were set in the middle of the space like exhibits in Addington's own natural history museum, posed in ferocious fashion as if to make their hunters seem somehow braver for having felled them. It was all Eamon could do to sidle up to the regal husk of a white tiger and feel the substance of its fangs before thinking himself cross and withdrawing his touch . . . before understanding that the awe he was feeling was the very reason such a thing was taken from the world in the first place.

"He was a hunter?" he asked of Runny, suddenly conscious again of the bullet casing in his pocket.

"Does that surprise you?"

"I don't know." Eamon was no stranger to hunting, and as such, he didn't think it an inherently cruel practice if done the right way with the right respect for the life that was taken, but these things . . . these were trophies . . . body, meat, skin, and all. "I guess it does, yeah. Should it?" he finally conceded.

"If you knew his family, it shouldn't. These aren't all his, of course," said the rabbit, motioning to the hundreds of souls around them. "Was one of the traditions they were fondest of. Foxhunts and pigeon shoots and the like. Suffice it to say, the textile business brought them endless opportunities to travel, and they weren't ones to return home without a souvenir or two or . . . several dozen. As I said, offerings of blood from the poor. Edward was a complicated man," Runny said, moving closer to Eamon until there was but a few tails' space between them. "The good, the bad . . . the generous, the cruel . . . the hermit, the teetotaler . . . the black, the white, and the endless gray in between. You know, it's been said that you should never meet your heroes, but I say better to know whom you place on that pedestal, don't you agree?"

Eamon looked down at his feet as if the answer was written on his laces, and it was only then that he noticed the two of them were standing on an oriental-style runner that extended from the center of the room to a large pair of double doors cut into the back wall, a decorative crest painted across them both from hinge to hinge. "What's in *that* room?" he asked, nodding toward the entrance.

"More of the same."

"Can I see them?"

Runny allowed a moment to pass as Eamon looked him in his big, brown eyes, saying only, "This is a night for celebration. Better to keep it light if we can, don't you agree?" Eamon nodded, and while the shake of his head said one thing, his searing curiosity said something silent and completely different.

"What's the crest mean?" he asked, pointing to the decoration on the doors which was a shield split into four parts, each quadrant filled with a carving of either an arrow, a loom, a shepherd's staff, or a ship. The colors were blue and white with a bit of yellow here and there, and on either side of the shield was a lion clawing at the edges, one male and one female, but it was surely the inscription at the bottom that Eamon was questioning. *Honora Familiam.*

"Honor thy family. What, your kin don't have their own crest?" Runny joked. "Shameful!"

Eamon's chuckle tailed off to a somber, downward stare as he added, "I don't really have any kin, to be honest."

"Yes, well, sometimes it's better that way, believe me. In any case, we really should be going," the rabbit said with three more raps of his cane. "I do apologize, but there's only so much time I can spend in this room without my blood pressure rising to levels that are inadvisable for a rabbit of my age. I do hope you understand."

"I . . . of course."

"Good lad."

"How old *are* you, anyway?" he asked with a childish innocence as he followed Runny toward the other half of the great hall.

"Old enough to remember this land before it was scarred by endless asphalt. Old enough to remember these skies before they were beset by great metal birds. Old enough to know there are many, many things I miss that I shall never see again and old enough to know better than to answer that question," he returned with an impish smile. "Suffice it to say that I am an—"

"Old rabbit. I get it," Eamon offered, mimicking his host's delivery in gentle fashion.

"Couldn't have said it better myself."

They traipsed past the corridor that led to the main foyer and into the last leg of the great hall where they found the walls hung not with portraits but with maps of seemingly every ilk. Layouts of Britain from centuries past and renderings of the new world from a time when nobody knew to call it by any other name, drawings of endless seas with serpentine monsters swimming among the whitecaps and early sketches of Africa, Asia, the Western Isles, and everything in between—all of them emblazoned with the now familiar letter "A" to mark where their family's factories and trading posts had once stood. It was startling to see their once titanic reach mapped in such graphic detail, as there were even several dozen A's scattered about the United States and one of them, in fact, sitting just outside of Boise.

Although the endless clutter of maps was a feast for Eamon's eyes, it was his nose that took the next turn at the vanguard of his journey as the unmistakable smell of fresh bread wafted through the hall. It was like some warm, nourishing memory that he was recalling for the very first time, but it wasn't more than a few steps later when his ears took up the mantle as the din-and-clang of pots and pans began to echo off the walls. Runny didn't even notice that his companion had fallen off until he turned to see that he was walking by himself, and when he finally clocked Eamon standing in the door to the kitchen with his nose in the air, it served as a rather unsubtle reminder that age had ravaged his once-keen senses.

The kitchen was big and broad and outfitted with everything that a chef would need to feed a host of a hundred guests let alone a few wayward sightseers. There were half a dozen ranges and two stately wood-fired ovens, a flat-top griddle and several standalone fryers as well as prep stations for salads and cold starters and desserts and a litany of ice-boxes and hot plates and warming lamps. Pans of copper and cast iron hung from hooks on every available easement and most of the surfaces that weren't used for cooking were stacked with stock pots and baking trays and plates upon plates upon plates. The glory of the kitchen's build was more than worthy of Eamon's awe, but it was the graceful, nuanced movements of the chef that was hoarding his attention . . . and the character of the cook himself that set his heart alight. Every frog in his own little bog, and not a worry to weigh.

Flackwell Frog was a head shorter than Runny, but even from the way he shook a pan and flicked a whisk, Eamon could tell that he was far less reserved. There was a little theater in everything he did—a flair in the way he folded his oven-roasted corn into his pudding base and an unbridled joy in the way he pressed his pastry into the sides of his pie tins so that it was just the perfect thickness the whole way around. Even his dress was bolder than his furry friend's. His white, grease-stained apron wasn't quite long enough to cover his gentleman's tights, which looked to be tailored for exactly his frame, and his button-down shirt, royal blue vest, and patent leather shoes were starched, pressed, and shined as if there was some manner of inspection looming just ahead. And as if all of that wasn't quite flamboyant enough, Flackwell was filling in the blanks between the clang-and-scrape of his handywork with a song . . .

And on that day the miller found a badger in the wheat,
And on that eve the baker thought a pie would be a treat,
And on that night the miller was too drunk to wonder why
There was half a badger in his leek-and-pumpkin pie!

"He's quite the hand in the cookhouse, but I'm sure you knew that," said the rabbit as he sidled up to Eamon. "But truly, what would Barley Day be without a feast?" The frog's voice was powerful and dynamic and unrestrained, and Eamon could only imagine the treat he was in for if his passion for performance carried over into his cooking.

"I know this song," Eamon said wistfully. "I've read it a thousand times, but . . . but I've never heard it before. Not like this anyway."

"It's an old song. Our kind have sung it for generations. It was Edward's favorite. I suppose that's why he put it in his book. It seemed too personal a detail for him to borrow at the time, but the more I thought about it, the more I appreciated having something of ours immortalized like that. Not that he would've cared, mind you. Always *was* stubborn as an ox, that one."

Eamon was well aware that he had asked his share of questions in the short time he had been awake, but with every answer that fell from the Rabbit's lips, he only found himself feeling like there was more he wanted to know. These histories—they felt like fire in the frozen tundra to him. They felt warm and nourishing and sublimely necessary, and he would gladly have surrendered his coat or his snowshoes or even the very pages of his favorite book to add fuel to its flame. Eamon would have given anything to know them all . . . to drink of their substance and lay about the manor's grounds fat and happy and deliriously drunk on their charm. Without a moment's debate, he would've traded the sum of his current knowledge for the promise of what was to come, but his host had thus far seemed happy to accommodate his curiosities, and so the possibility that he might be allowed both flashed ripe and ready through his mind.

"How did you end up here?" Eamon asked without taking his eyes from the culinary ballet unfolding in front of him. "Here in this house, I mean. Edward's house. The way you talk about the old days and how things have changed it . . . it sounds like you miss home or something, but aren't you already home?"

"*That* question, I'm afraid, does not exactly have a simple answer unless you'd care to further define your terms," Runny stated with a politician's tact and a veteran's reticence.

Eamon turned to face his host just as Flackwell began the ritual of running his chef's knife along a honing steel to straighten the edge. "I don't understand. Define what—"

"It *is* a lovely little story, though, isn't it?" interjected the rabbit. "Very interview-ready, or what have you. A writer so inspired by the beauty of his surroundings that he couldn't help but put pen to paper. A man so pure and gifted that he simply couldn't help but turn vessel for the sheer bounty of nature, that about the measure of it?" Runny could see that Eamon's constitution was beginning to run cold with the fear of disillusionment, and in the very same moment, Eamon could tell that there was some amount of pain in what the rabbit was about to say, but he could also tell that his words would be gentle for the sake of them both. "We are indeed from the Hollow, as you've always believed. As you've always been told. But that place is not here. That place is not on this isle. *That* place . . . is hidden away by great mountains and swaddled in endless fields of wild grass and tucked into the earth a month's hop from the ocean's embrace. Not too far from where *you* live, believe it or not."

"How . . . how do you know where I live?" asked Eamon with a surreptitious glance.

"I spent some time with your friends while you were still asleep in the study," he answered. "You get a few cocktails in the big one you call Mark and you can hardly shut him up."

"Ain't that the truth. Sorry, I didn't mean to—"

"Perfectly alright." But Eamon could tell that Runny was far from alright as the old thing leaned more of his weight against his walking stick and bowed his head toward the tile to let the tears welling in his eyes ring more dignified. "We're from a place very much like the one described in Edward's book," continued the rabbit. "It was peaceful and private and complete, and filled with the spirit's most blessed creatures. It was wondrous and wild and provided for us in so many ways that even now I could hardly count them. We had everything we could ever want there, and if I'm honest with myself, which seems to get harder with each passing day . . . I miss it dearly. More and more every time its memory graces my thoughts."

"Why would you ever leave a place like that? It sounds like paradise. I don't—"

"A ferocious and unimpeachable storm," said Runny with the kind of gravitas that only comes with deep and irreversible wounds. "There was nothing that could be done to stop it. At least *we* couldn't stop it."

"A storm?" Eamon's gears began to turn, but it wasn't more than a moment or two before he understood that Runny's cryptic response was born more of grace than deceit, and by the time the rhythm of Flackwell's knife against the cutting board faded away to nothing, he already knew the answer to his very next question. "You mean *us*, don't you? When we moved west?"

Runny picked his head up from the floor, his tears having receded as the years had made those spells less lengthy and easier to swallow with some amount of decorum. "We all have our own buffalo, I suppose. In any case, somewhere in the middle of that storm was Edward, looking to expand his family's holdings . . . and to make a long and tiresome story short, that's how we ended up here. It's peaceful enough, but it's not home. Hollow has a different meaning than it once did to those of us that remain."

Eamon's head was aflood with a cannonade of feelings, memories, sympathies, and questions—there was so much about Runny's story that rang pointedly familiar and so much more that he desperately wanted to know, but the only words that came to his lips were, "I'm sorry that happened to you." They seemed blunt and unnuanced at first, but the more he let them marinate in the kitchen air between them, the more Eamon thought them appropriate and honest.

"I should hope so," the rabbit fired back as the frog's song filled the air once again . . .

> And on that morn the miller felt a quake upon his head,
> And on that noon he shirked his job to stay and rest in bed,
> And on that day he knew not of the pain that was in store,
> When he woke to find a pack of angry badgers at his door!

As soon as the verse was over, Flackwell popped his head into the oven to check on whatever was roasting before whirling back around to a bubbling pot and dipping a spoon into the orangey puree within to give it a considered taste. "Unacceptable!" he said to himself, placing his hand on his hip and shaking his head before giving it a second try. "This, this is unacceptable! What has happened to the squash around here!? What has *happened* to the produce in this . . . Runny! *Runny!*" he yelled before wheeling to find his rabbit standing in the doorway alongside Eamon. "There you are!" Flackwell traipsed across the kitchen with saucepan in hand and shoved it under Runny's nose with a sneer. "Look! Look at the texture of this mess! Thin and mealy and gritty! Just *look* how gritty it is! What is this rubbish squash that you brought me!? Did you get a deal on old war rations or something?"

"It looks fine to me," replied Runny with an exasperation that was clearly familiar to the both of them.

"Does it!? Does it look fine!? To *you*!?" barked the frog, pulling the spoon from the mash and letting the mixture drip back down into the pan. "It doesn't even taste like squash for spirit's sake, it just tastes like . . . like orange. The color, not the fruit. Horrible! And who is *this*?" Flackwell asked, noticing Eamon for the first time.

"This is Eamon."

"Hi," said Eamon awkwardly, feeling himself thrust into the middle of some otherworldly lovers' quarrel.

"Ah. Eamon, the light-of-head," chuckled Flackwell. "How's the noggin?"

"Feels okay, I guess."

"Good, good." Flackwell took a moment to look Eamon up and down as if he was trying to determine exactly how marbled and tender his flesh might be. "Say, you look young and spry enough for your taste buds not to have shriveled down to nothing," he said, giving Runny a sideways glance in the process. "Taste." He held a mouthful of puree at arm's reach for Eamon to sample, which after a slight hesitation, he did.

"Oh my god, that's delicious!" Eamon, the light-of-head, exclaimed after finding the mixture soft and buttery, nutty and perfectly seasoned.

"He forgets that we all were not gifted with a frog's tongue. His standards make him . . . difficult even on his best days," Runny mused, rapping Flackwell in the leg with his cane as if to remind him of his manners.

"That's honestly one of the best things I've ever tasted," continued Eamon.

"Well, at least *somebody* appreciates my cooking around here."

Runny rolled his big, kind eyes nearly into the back of his head. "I appreciate your cooking, and you *know* that I appreciate your cooking."

"Oh, do I? Do I *know* that? Do I know that considering you haven't said it in half a century?"

"I eat everything you serve me, surely that's *some* indication."

"You're a rabbit. You would eat my shoes if I served them to you under a cloche."

Eamon inched his hand a little closer to the pot of mash Flackwell was still holding. "Maybe just one more taste?"

"Asking for seconds. See that? Appreciation," said the frog proudly, allowing Eamon to have another spoonful.

"Yes, well, do try to keep in mind that he's fresh off a concussion before you throw your haunches out patting yourself on the back." Runny turned on his wooden leg and hobbled out of the kitchen, shouting over his shoulder, "If you need me, I'll be taking care of this absurdly large house all by myself without so much as a thank you!" And as the clack of his gait faded into the distance, Flackwell and Eamon found themselves alone for the first time, the latter blissfully unaware of the frog's probing eyes as he was still too preoccupied with the silky mash in front of his face.

"You really do look the part, don't you?" Flackwell said, his theatrics giving way to something more genuine and heartfelt.

"I'm sorry?" asked Eamon, unsure of what had just been said.

"*Eamon!*" Runny's voice echoed from the end of the hall, and while there were questions to be asked and food to be savored, Eamon left his new acquaintance in the kitchen where he felt like he belonged and disappeared back into the corridor.

FIVE

If Addington's study was the brain of his manor, then the ballroom was surely its beating heart. A place that was once host to countless revelers and socialites, it was now just host to their memories, frozen in time in preparation for a celebration that never came and buried under the dust of its own uselessness. The chandeliers were still stocked with fresh candles and the tables around the dance floor were still draped in white linen and set with silver utensils and fine crystal glassware, and while the flowers that made up their centerpieces were long dead, their stems still stood petrified and unmoved like spindly little headstones.

The orchestra pit at the head of the room was stocked with enough chairs for a full philharmonic and the conductor's stand was carved of smoky mahogany to match the molding where the walls met the ceiling, which itself was covered in seamless frescos as if to paint the place some latter-day Sistine Chapel. And while their hues were faded and dulled by half a century of neglect, the memory of their vibrant greens and deep blues, sunny yellows and fiery oranges still danced from corner to corner. But there was no tribute to the Christian heavens in these murals like the great Italian masterpieces that inspired them—instead it was only Diana who was honored here. It was only the hunt that was given the glory of this space as foxes fled from packs of earnest hounds, pigeons dipped low over the brush, great bears stood tall in the face of death with its bow drawn taut, and bucks and does and fauns alike leapt for their very lives as the specters of those who knew no better swayed and mingled beneath them.

And though Addington's more cerebral fascination with life and death may have been dripping from the ceiling, his love for all things carnal was in no short supply against the far wall where a bar the size of two trolley cars set end to end was stationed. Its backing was a glorious collage of dark-stained wood and mirrors and copper inlay, and its shelves were stocked with an endless supply of liquors and wines from all over the world . . . no two of their finely pedigreed, artfully printed labels the same. Even in the low light of an evening when the chandeliers weren't lit and there were no candles flickering on the tables, the ballroom bar still sparkled like the crown jewel it was. Some priceless piece studded with stones of every shade of amber, caramel, and auburn. Some black-tie broach for a belle unbound.

The rear of the room was host to a small casino's worth of tables for blackjack and poker and craps and roulette, and there were even several rows of vintage slot machines running along the wall, their arms beset with cobwebs and their patinas a sad and striking collage of rusty browns and cloudy silvers and unhealthy wood. It was even rumored that Addington, while awash in family money his entire life, used to pay for his legendary parties on the backs of his less gambling-savvy guests, but those accusations were typically explained away as nothing more than sour grapes on the lips of those whose stature had fallen by the wayside and simply weren't invited back. But there was also plenty of entertainment for the tight-pocketed as shuffleboard courts and little nooks for checkers, chess, backgammon, billiards, and snooker dotted the floor. It was like a carnival for anybody too precious to be concerned with the gritty peasant reality of barkers and sideshows and acres of mud pockmarked with the prints of cheaply made boots. And whereas people once flocked there by the hundreds to notch their provenance by sheer virtue of having been let inside, now there was only the fortunate few.

"I think this scotch is like eighty years old or something," said Mark, popping his head up from behind the bar with a bottle of something expensive looking in his hand.

Caroline, who was settled into one of the leather-backed stools on the other side, cradled it, and after a cursory glance, seemed no more certain about its age or pedigree than he did. "It sure *looks* old. Is that good or bad?"

"Isn't old booze always better than new booze? You always hear people going on and on about old wine and stuff."

"Yeah, but *this* old? I mean, isn't old wine just vinegar at a certain point?"

"Is it?"

"Pretty sure. I think *good* booze might get better with age, but I think you have to take care of it a certain way or something like that," she said, trying to make heads or tails of the faded script on the label.

"Well, don't you think this is expensive stuff?" asked Mark, taking the bottle back from her.

"How would I know?"

"Just look at where we are," he replied, gesturing broadly at their surroundings. "You really think this guy was out here serving cheap liquor to millionaires and senators and . . . other rich people or whatever?"

"You might actually have a point there."

"It looks like it used to have wax or something over the top . . . *that's* fancy as shit . . . plus the label's in another language, so you *know* it's gotta be good."

"That's just cursive, Babe," Caroline said with a gentle smile.

"What?" Mark held the bottle up to the light of the chandelier only to find that his girlfriend, as usual, was completely correct. "Macallan private reserve . . . from the Addington family's . . . personal barrels . . . with our gratitude for a lifetime of patronage. May the angels' share be . . . forever in your glass," he read. "I mean, come on, we *gotta* try this!" he said as he placed two glasses on the bar.

"Do you even like scotch?"

Mark disappeared below the horizon again only to emerge a moment later with a wine key which he screwed into the cork amid a useless protest from his partner. "I don't think that's how you—"

"How bad could it be?" he interrupted. "Isn't it just like whiskey or bourbon or whatever, but for annoying people?"

"Are we annoying people?"

"Well," he said, slowly loosening the cork, "we're in the ballroom of the mansion of a world-famous author, drinking his personal brand of booze and hobnobbing with actual characters from his book, so . . . I think we kinda are, yeah." The cork came loose with a wet pop and Mark poured them each three fingers of the golden-amber liquid. He gave his glass a quick sniff and shrugged a disinterested shrug and raised his tumbler to Caroline who lifted hers in return. "To you, my love."

"To *us*," she replied as they both took a tentative sip only to recoil in horror at the taste of spoiled sugars and rancid mash. "Oh my god, that is . . ." she coughed a heinous cough and pushed her glass out of reach. "That is *awful*."

She looked up at Mark who was frozen in disgust with the sour scotch still sloshing around on his tongue. It took all of his strength just to choke it down, and when he did, he exhaled from the very soles of his feet to the hairs on his head. "We are *not* annoying people," he said, stuffing the cork back in the bottle posthaste. "Maybe there's a case of Miller Lite hiding around here somewhere."

"Just as well, I guess. We haven't really done much hobnobbing either." The two of them looked around at the others who all seemed positively at home in the ballroom, the lot of them playing games and soaking in the sights and feeding off the romanticism of it all like there was nothing the least bit strange about where they were or the company in which they had found themselves.

"Yeah, sorry about that," Mark murmured. "I know this is like, pretty much a dream come true for you, I just . . . I don't know, there's just something weird about it."

"You *think*?" she replied with a good-natured wink.

"You know what I mean. These . . . *things* . . . alone in this big old house. Seems like somebody would've found out about this by now, that's all."

Caroline reached across the bar and took his hand with both of hers. "Well, he *did* write a whole book about them. It's not his fault that everybody assumed he made the whole thing up."

"I guess."

"You know, my grandmother was half Blackfoot and she—"

"Oh, was she?" he smirked. "I had no idea. You've only mentioned that like a thousand times."

"Anyway," she continued, "she used to talk about spirit animals all the time. Animals that reflected certain personalities . . . animals that spoke the same truths that some of us do . . . animals that embodied our nature, for better or for worse. Think about it. Bigfoot, the Easter Bunny, werewolves, frogs turning into princes, foxes eating sour grapes . . . maybe they've been there this whole time and we've just been too wrapped up in our own human bullshit to believe that there was anything else out there on our level." Caroline took one of her hands from his and grasped his chin, gently turning his head until his gaze met hers. "Or maybe this is a gift so few people are given that once they have it, they know better than to cheapen it by gossiping about it."

"Or maybe they tell every person they can, and everybody just thinks they're out of their goddamn minds," replied Mark, taking her hand from his face and stroking her fingers with his thumb.

"See, you get it."

"You know damn well that I do not get it."

"That's just part of your charm."

"Well, in that case, I am very, *very* charming."

"*That* we can both agree on," said Caroline just before Mark reached across the bar, grabbed her under her arms and lifted her over to his side as she squealed with an adorable combination of surprise and delight.

"Now," he said, "help me find something back here that doesn't taste like actual death, because this place is starting to creep me out and I *really* need a drink. The fox has had a flask with him the whole time, so there's gotta be something around here somewhere."

The fox in question, of course, was Phineas, who was currently seated at one of Addington's poker tables with his legs kicked up on the felt as if he just couldn't be bothered to pay attention to the game that was unfolding in front of him. Finn was just as old as Runny, but he seemed much younger in spirit—less concerned with being worldly and wise and more wrapped up in his own graces as if he was still a young man who had yet to learn that bravado was no ringer for substance. He was wiry without seeming weak and sleek and svelte and sturdy, even as his red fur had begun to rust around the edges and the gray of his nose had long since crept above his blue eyes. The only piece of clothing he cared to wear was a brown leather jacket from the turn of the century—an old and well-battered thing that looked to be more of a utility than a statement as it hung carefree from his bones, and while his left hand held all five of his cards, his right clutched a pewter flask from which he drank in between bets as his eyes wandered in a desperate search for something more interesting to beg his attention. Even the twenties-era jazz blaring from the record player behind the bar was old news to Finn as he had heard it all a hundred times, and though the faces around him were fresh, he felt like he had seen them all before too.

"What's the word for a group of humans?" Finn asked of nobody in particular, his gaze drifting back to the poker table where he was holding a commanding chip lead in a game of draw with Gareth, his chum, Thomas, and Thomas' girlfriend, Paige.

"What do you mean?" asked Thomas as he slid the remainder of his checks into the center of the table.

"You know," continued Finn, "like a gaggle of geese or a flock of sheep. What's the word? A hazard of humans? A plague of people? An infection of folk? What is it?"

"I don't think there is one," answered Gareth as he also pushed whatever chips he had left into the pot followed by Paige who did the same.

"Well, there *should* be." Finn took a swig from his flask and sat up straight and surveyed the table to see that everybody else was all-in. "Oh, thank the Spirit," he said, turning over the cards in his hand to reveal four jacks. "Anybody beat that? No? Great."

"Well, good game," said Gareth. "That was fun."

"Was it?" barked the fox. "Draw isn't even real poker and nobody paid anything for their chips, so . . . was it fun?"

There was a moment of awkward silence before Thomas asked Paige to join him for a game of checkers, leaving Gareth alone with Finn, much to the fox's chagrin.

"Sorry about that, they're not big gamblers," said Gareth, nervously fingering his leather-bound copy of Addington's book which was resting next to him on the table.

"Poker isn't gambling," Finn fired back.

"What?"

"*Poker* . . . isn't gambling. There's no house to play against, there's no odds in anybody's favor. Gambling is for people who believe in luck and hate holding on to money. Roulette is gambling. Craps is gambling. Poker is sport."

Gareth felt himself a little out of his depth but did his best to keep the conversation moving forward. "Well, in that case, I'm sorry the *game* was boring, I guess."

"Well, I'm sorry that you're sorry the game was boring, but in my own defense, I was cheating the entire time, so I suppose I have nobody to be cross with but myself."

"You were?"

"I was." With that, Finn riffled the deck of cards with astonishing dexterity, shuffling them half a dozen times and cutting them over and over in his capable palms before casually dealing four hands face-up around the table—four jacks, four queens, four kings, and four aces.

Gareth's jaw slacked. "How did you do that?"

"Sharp eyes and capable hands. And practice," replied the fox. "Not much else to do here in this big empty house. Never been much of a reader," he offered, sharping his brow at Gareth's copy of *Winterset Hollow*. Finn gathered the cards and again began to shuffle, his blend so precise that Gareth was almost hypnotized by the perfect interlacing of the corners and the soothing flick-flick-flick of the cardboard.

"But . . . why'd you cheat?" he finally said, looking from the fox's hands back up toward his eyes.

"Beg your pardon?"

"If you enjoy the sport of it so much, doesn't that kind of defeat the purpose of playing? Cheating?"

"Well," said Finn, fanning the cards out on the table before him in perfect fashion before picking up his flask and continuing, "If you *are* just playing for sport, then I suppose you're right, it wouldn't make much sense, would it?"

"Why *else* would you be playing a game?"

"Now *that* is a very telling question, but one that's not particularly surprising given your . . . species."

"My species?" asked Gareth. Finn didn't answer, instead he only nodded and looked up at the ceiling long enough for his counterpart to follow his gaze to the fresco depicting a foxhunt above them.

"Half a dozen men on horseback and twice as many hounds and *one* terrified fox running for dear life. Now, even if those *brave* men with all of their trained dogs and all of their tireless mounts and all of their perfectly oiled firearms somehow fail to kill that fox . . . they haven't really lost, have they? It's not like they're going to be put to death for not playing the game well, now is it?"

"I suppose not," answered Gareth who was undeniably intrigued by the sermon unfolding in front of him.

"So then why play at all? Why waste your energy? Why do it in the first place?"

Gareth looked deep into Finn's eyes as he considered his response and saw earnestness, guile, and ruthlessness dancing hand in hand. It was a bedazzling ballet that seemed to have no designs on an intermission, for the fox simply returned Gareth's gauzy stare and let him know with the slightest cock of his head that he wouldn't be breaking his gaze anytime soon. "Because it feels good to win," the rotund lad finally said, his answer immediately followed by a heavy blink.

"That's exactly it," the fox returned. "It feels good to win . . . even if there's no chance of losing." Finn turned the cards face-down and began to swirl them about the table, a process so patently random as to eliminate the possibility of any deck stacking in both of their minds. Once they were appropriately shuffled, he swept them into a neat pile and again fanned them out in front of Gareth. "Pick one." The portly young man was hesitant to engage in any further games given the brand-new feeling of strings lashed about his wrists being pulled from the heavens, but he was also still drunk on the fox's charisma. "Go on," encouraged Finn. Eventually, Gareth reached out and selected a card at random and brandished it so only he could see that it was the ace of spades.

"Now," continued the fox, "If I told you that you wouldn't leave this place with your life if that was an ace in your hand . . . would you say that I cheated? Or would you say that I was simply better at this game?" Gareth was lost for words, a solemn swallow of breath the only response he offered. "Of course, your answer isn't really the point," said Finn as he rose from his seat and sauntered around the table until he was close enough to lean in and whisper into Gareth's ear. "The *point* . . . is that your answer doesn't matter to me . . . and it doesn't really matter to *you* either," he stated, taking the ace from his hand and slipping it between the pages of his copy of *Winterset Hollow*. "Feel free to keep that. May it help you mark your place in that wretched little book you all love so much."

Phineas clapped him on the shoulders and trotted off toward the bar, and as soon as the fox was out of earshot, Gareth exhaled a fearsome breath that felt as if it had been trapped in his throat for hours. He was shaken by something impossible for him to articulate but at the same time beguiled by an experience he never thought he would have. Half of him wanted to turn tail and run, but the other half wanted more of whatever strange feeling was washing over him, and as if he knew just how to sate that need, he turned over the rest of the cards to reveal nothing but aces—fifty-one of them—and all of them spades.

The fox settled into a seat at the end of the bar where the leather cushion was worn as if it had cradled nothing but his weight for the better part of a century. It was the seat closest to the phonograph, which was set on the back counter still pumping out jazz for nobody in particular, and as Finn drank from his flask, he stared into the giant horned speaker with his eyes glazed and his mind wandering to days past and places he used to know. Mark and Caroline, who had both loosened up after a few cocktails inspired by a drinkable bottle of Wild Turkey they found under the bar, were silently debating whether they would be intruding on a private moment by talking to the fox when Mark took it upon himself to be the decider. "Not your favorite day?" he asked.

"Pardon?" replied Finn, still fixated on the record player in front of him.

"I thought this was supposed to be your favorite day or whatever, but you don't seem super into it."

Finn didn't answer immediately, and he didn't make any bones about hiding the exasperation he was feeling at being questioned so readily in his own house. "I'm sorry," offered Caroline, "he's just had a few drinks, he didn't mean to—"

"Don't apologize for him," returned Finn, swinging his stool to the side to face the couple. "If he's sorry, then let him say so."

Caroline shot her beau an expectant look, but still he didn't quite take the hint.

"What? I'm just making conversation. It's not like I insulted him or anything. I don't know, he's just sitting there staring off into space like he doesn't wanna be here and I—"

"As a matter of fact," interrupted the fox, "this *is* my favorite day. The only day I look forward to at all, actually. I love it so much, in fact, that if it wasn't for our Barley Day traditions . . . I fear I would've left this place long ago."

"What? This house?! This house is awesome, why would you want to leave?" asked Mark, finding his glass to be empty and taking a sip from Caroline's instead. "I mean, sure, it's a little creepy, but—"

"Not this house, you dolt. This earth. This life. You see, it's our celebration of this day that keeps me going. Well, that and my little friend here," said Finn, sloshing around the little liquor that still remained in his flask. "I love this day . . . I just hate this part of it. The babysitting the monkeys while the frog does his cooking part," he said, gesturing around the room at the others who had crossed the channel with them.

"Wait," said Caroline, her interest suddenly piqued by the conversation at hand, "There's been others here?"

"Do you really think you're the first of Edward's apostles to come sniffing around this isle on Barley Day? You humans . . . always so eager to claim discovery. It's adorable. Happens every year, if you want to know the truth. Every . . . bloody . . . *year*."

"It's just," she continued, "I would've thought somebody would've said something by now."

"I'm sure they have. Tell you what, when you get back home, you tell as many people as you please and see how many of them believe you."

Mark's eyes lit up with the pride of a prediction proved true and he finished the rest of Caroline's drink in triumph. "See? Told you."

"And while you're at it, why don't you tell them you stopped in Wonderland on the way and had tea with the Mad Hatter? At least *that* book had some real imagination behind it." Finn tipped his flask back into his maw until the last few drops dripped out onto his tongue.

"You don't like the book?" asked Caroline with a genuine curiosity.

"Should I!? Should I like *the book* that was written about me without my permission!? Should I like *the book* that became so famous that everybody under the sun thinks they know me!?" Finn rose from his seat and slowly made his way toward his partners in conversation, sliding his flask along the bar with a sickening scrape. "Should I like *the book* that makes me a disappointment to everybody if I don't crack wise all the time or play their games with them or answer their *awful* questions about the place that used to be my home until their fathers' fathers' fathers razed it to the ground!?" The fox was no more than a tail away from Caroline now, his teeth bared in anger and his hackles up. "Should I like . . . *that* . . . *book*!?" The record had run its course and the silence between Finn and his demons was now only echoed by the crackling of a needle with no groove to follow. "I see you've found my stash of Wild Turkey," he said as Mark refilled his own glass and then Caroline's while chuckling to himself under his breath. "Something funny?"

"I guess," he replied, "it's just funny 'cause a fox *would* like to drink Wild Turkey 'cause foxes eat turkeys and—"

"The fox likes to drink Wild Turkey . . . because nobody else here does . . . and so the fox, therefore, can have it all for himself," Finn said pointedly, slowly panning his steely gaze from Caroline's sheepish expression to Mark's oblivious grin.

"Sorry," eked Mark as he put the bottle back on the bar with an unusual and particular care.

"Apology accepted," Finn offered with a breath of casualness, the sting of his diatribe melting away before their very eyes and his ears falling back against his head in a show of biddability. "Now, why don't you top me off," he continued, sliding his flask over. "And throw another record on and we'll call the whole thing even, sound good?" Mark nodded and filled the fox's vessel for him, the creature still smiling a wicked smile at Caroline, who herself hadn't taken her eyes off of him since he had approached. She was taking him in—his confident posture, his capable glare, the air of adaptability in his persona. He reminded her of a grifter in a way, undeniably charming and magnetic on demand but ready to shift into whatever vein of being suited his situation at the flick of a switch. It was only when Mark left to tend to the music that Finn spoke again. "You're a sharp one, aren't you?"

"I like to think so," Caroline responded, her voice not wavering a whisker.

"Good. Very good."

"Good?"

"Well, I guess we have to be, don't we?" Caroline's demure brow furrowed in confusion as Finn rolled up the sleeve of his leather jacket and stroked the fur on his arm. "Gotta be sharp if we're gonna be different, eh?" Her eyes flared at the surprise of a parallel she was in no way expecting and it set her gears turning with a timbre she hadn't felt since she had left the mainland. Her differences, her struggles, her feelings of miscreation and her constant conflict between pride and opprobrium—they were here now, whereas even just a moment before they were an ocean away. The air was thick and familiar now, whereas just a breath ago it was light and lovely.

She straightened her spine and lifted her chin, steadied her gaze and closed her fists and was careful not to let her breathing stray from its normal cadence. "Funny," she said, "you don't strike me as much different at all."

"Now, now," said the fox, "no need to get your knickers in a twist. Just because you came in here stinking of peaches and lavender doesn't

mean you have the moral high ground." Finn chuckled and took a measured sip from his flask. "I do like this one," he said as the breath of new
music cut the air between them. "Where is your friend, by the way? The
redhead? Would be a shame if he missed the feast."

Caroline didn't even have a chance to craft an answer before the
door on the far side of the ballroom swung open and Eamon and Runny
trotted into the fold. She sprung from her seat and hurried over to greet
them, and for once she felt like it was Eamon's turn to offer her some
escape from her circumstance. "Are you okay? How's your head?" she
asked as she stopped the pair just inside the entrance.

"He just needed a little rest, that's all," answered Runny, painting his
face with a kind smile and shifting his weight to his walking stick. "I
hope you haven't found entertaining yourself too much of a chore."

"Not at all," she said. "Thanks for taking care of him."

"Was the least I could do." Runny bowed as best he could and limped
off to touch base with his other guests as Caroline grabbed Eamon by the
hand and shuffled him off toward the center of the ballroom.

"Can you believe this!?" she exclaimed, pulling him onto the dance
floor.

"I mean . . . no."

"I know!" she yelled before quickly quieting herself. "I know. They're
. . . they're all here and *we're* here, and—"

"I was in *his* study. I saw his writings and . . . and . . . and did you
know that Flackwell is in the kitchen making us a feast!? Like a Barley
Day feast just like in the book!?" It was only then that Eamon took a moment to look around and let his jaw drop to the floor at the realization
of where they were standing. "Oh my god, we're in his ballroom, aren't
we?"

"Yup. Just look at this place! Can you imagine what it must've been
like back in the day?" Caroline twirled a graceful twirl and grabbed Eamon's hand so that she could turn him as she pleased. "The orchestra,
the beautiful people dancing, the captains of industry and the politicians
and the writers and the movie stars and . . . it's like I can still feel them."

"This place is so big I feel like it should have a gift shop on the way
out or something," he said as she spun him to a gentle stop.

"Definitely didn't see one of those, buuut . . . check this out." Caroline pulled a box of matches from her pocket that had *Addington Manor*

stenciled along the top and brandished it like it was a bar of gold.

"You probably weren't supposed to take that."

"Why not?" she returned. "There was a whole bowl of them in the foyer where I left my pack. I don't think anybody's gonna miss *one*."

"It's still technically theft and . . . I don't know, I just always thought you were better than that. Did you get one for me?" asked Eamon, suddenly unconcerned with the morality of it all.

"Actually . . . no," she said with a shameful grimace amid a chuckle from her friend.

"It really is beautiful," mused Eamon, scanning the frescos on the ceiling and the hand-carved molding and scraping his cheap shoes along the perfectly veined marble floors. His gaze darted from the gaming tables where Runny was holding court to the dining area that was still set for nobody and nothing to the sprawling bar where, unsurprisingly, Mark was chatting it up with his furry new friend. "Wait, is that . . . is that—"

"It's Finn." He and Caroline shared the purest smile as if they were having the same wonderful dream. "They're all here, Eamon. All of them. Here with *us*. Here *for* us."

"Not all of them," he returned with an air of melancholy, noticing that Caroline's favorite character was nowhere to be seen and fearing him no longer among the living. "Just like in the book. Do you know what happened to him? Did you ask—"

She grabbed his hand again, this time pulling him toward the wall opposite the bar. "What?" he asked, playfully resisting her urging. "What!?"

"I wanna show you something." Eamon relaxed and let her guide him through the throng of empty tables and over to a set of double doors that were hanging open just a breath. It was just a sliver of space, but it was enough for a familiar flicker of light to leak through—an unnatural play of hues and shadows that could only be from a television screen. It was a strangely comforting reversal from the old-world romanticism that seemed to drape every inch of the place, but it made Eamon feel as if he was about to intrude on some candid moment or step into somebody's den without their consent, and that thought made him more than a touch uneasy. He looked over at Caroline who nodded her approval, and as he tried his best to breathe a bit easier and stepped closer to the door, he was able to recognize the music that was seeping through the narrow opening as well. It was a familiar, jaunty tune that brought an immediate smile to his face, and having no intention of hiding how he felt, there in a quiet corner of paradise with so close a friend, he relaxed and let a smile replace every last one of his worries.

Eamon eased the door open just enough to set one whole eye on whatever was on the other side, and just as he expected, he saw the cartoon adaptation of *Winterset Hollow* playing on the far wall. It was a relic by modern standards, but it still filled him with a nostalgia for a childhood he didn't really have with its masterfully written score, imperfectly handwrought animation, and timeless voice acting. He had seen it hundreds of times, but as it was released decades before he was even born, this was his first time seeing it in a theater, and that irony was not lost on him as he carefully swung the door open another few inches. The big screen stretched from wall to wall and the sound system was powerful and seamlessly integrated into the darker corners of the room, which was easily large enough to accommodate an audience of a hundred . . . but Eamon was so absorbed in the glory of finally seeing his favorite story play out in proper fashion that it took him the better part of a minute to notice who else was watching it.

Binghamton Bear was a mountain of a thing, and even at a distance of thirty yards, Eamon could see that he was just as solid. His ears were easily eight or nine feet above the ground even though he was seated on the bare floor with his legs crossed and a large blanket covering his hulking shoulders like a shawl woven for some kindly giant. The space around him had been cleared of the chairs that were once bolted to the cement floor, and while his powerful form was singularly imposing, his posture was somehow sorrowful as he sat there with his spine slumped, quietly watching some cell-shaded version of himself alive and well in the most beautiful version of the Hollow he once knew. Even his breathing lamented the things he had lost—each powerful exhale bringing with it a low, pitiful groan as if the wheel inside him was slowly squeaking to a horrible halt with every push of his lungs.

"He looks so sad," said Eamon.

"I think he *is*," replied Caroline with all the empathy she could muster in a whisper. "It's like that was really his home or something."

"It *was* really his home. They fled here or . . . were brought here, I think. Runny told me that the place they're from was just like this," he lamented, nodding toward the endless green and bright blue skies on the screen. Caroline's heart fell at the notion that they had all been so displaced, and it fell further at the realization that Eamon wasn't so different and that perhaps, when he was alone in his little apartment with the shades drawn and the television shining, he was just another broken bear slumped on the theater floor. Bing reached over to a pile of earthenware jugs and wrapped his paw around the neck of whichever one was handy, and when he raised the thing to his maw and emptied it down his gullet with a single pour, Eamon could see that his arm was spotted with naked patches of skin that were ragged with scar tissue.

"His arm," said Caroline with a piteous lilt. Eamon had skinned enough deer carcasses to recognize the wake of a bullet when he saw it, but he thought it better to steer away from any morbid reality to which he was privy so as not to spoil everyone's magical evening.

"Look, he's got his hammer," he said as he noticed the mighty, oversized sledge that was resting on the floor next to the clutter of empty jugs.

"No way," chimed Caroline as she leaned in for a closer look. But just as she moved to ease the door open another inch, she was reminded that she had not come to this place alone.

"What's up, losers?" bellowed Mark from not more than a foot behind them. Eamon and Caroline jumped in surprise and turned to try and quiet him without raising any more racket.

"Would you shut up?" shushed Caroline under her breath.

"Don't tell me to shut up," he fired back coyly.

"Just shut up for a second, okay."

"I will do nothing of the—"

She put her hand over Mark's mouth, and while he playfully tried to swat it away, Eamon turned back toward the theater only to see Bing staring back at them with his giant head cocked over his shoulder and his empty eyes squinting to see what the commotion was all about. Startled by the bear's attention, Eamon swung the door shut with a noticeable click and quickly wrinkled his nose at the ruckus.

"Ugh, that was loud," said Eamon regretfully. "You're an idiot, by the way."

"Oh, *I'm* an idiot?" barked Mark.

"There's an *actual* bear in there and I'm pretty sure he didn't want to be disturbed, so it would probably be a good idea to, you know, *not* disturb him."

Mark rolled his eyes and took a sip of his cocktail. "But it's not like, a *real* bear, right? Like he's probably not gonna rumble over here and *eat* you. He's probably just gonna politely ask you to keep it down or something." Eamon and Caroline just looked at him and shook their heads. "I mean, am I wrong? *Am I?* Wait, is there an *actual* bear in there!?"

"You're an idiot," repeated Eamon.

"I'm not an idiot, I just came over here to see if you guys wanted some food. The . . . frog one . . . cooked a bunch of stuff," he said, motioning to the back of the ballroom where everyone else was busy stuffing their faces with a selection of treats that Flackwell had brought in from the kitchen.

"So, let's get two things straight," Eamon continued. "First, if you're not an idiot, you're at the very least a rube. And second . . . yes, I would like some food please."

If food was an art, and surely nobody who had ever tasted his cooking would deny that it was, then Flackwell Frog was a once-in-a-generation master. It didn't hurt that he had been allowed several human lifetimes to hone his flavors and sharpen his techniques, but it was also perfectly clear that he truly enjoyed feeding others and watching them swoon over his savvy as he brought silver tray after silver tray of delicacies in from the kitchen. There were pastry tartlets filled with squash puree and roasted nuts, freshly picked mushroom caps stuffed with artichoke hash and sheep's milk cheese, and toasted slices of freshly made bread capped with asparagus, pickled onions, and fig jam, among other ingenious creations.

There was, of course, also plenty praise, which Flackwell took with the grace of a seasoned and consummate host, even going so far as to offer some insights into his craft along the way. "You have to keep the butter cold when you roll the pastry or else you just won't get it to puff like that," he said after Gareth remarked that he had never tasted anything so flaky. "The trick is to put a bottle of wine in the freezer and use *that* to even out your dough instead of a rolling pin. Saves you from having to stop what you're doing and pop it back in the cooler every few minutes," he beamed, grateful for a stranger's admiration of his craft after so many months of feeding the same mouths. "Fold and roll and fold and roll again. The more layers you create, the higher the rise and the better the pastry, in my humble opinion. It's a labor of love, but I do believe it's worth it in the end, don't you think?"

Gareth simply nodded in agreement as his mouth was still full of pickled tomatoes and olives en croûte. This was all a far cry from his daily dealings at the Portland comic book store where he and Paige both worked, and though he would typically feel sorely out of place in such a situation, there was something about Flackwell's warm, natural demeanor that put him at ease. Neither he nor Paige nor Thomas wanted their host to leave, but they understood that there were other guests to tend to, and by the time the frog bid them farewell and left an entire batch of delectables in their care, they all felt better for having sampled both his camaraderie and his cooking.

Rowan and Patrick were about as dissimilar as a pair of friends could be, but they certainly both seemed to enjoy the fried oysters with chive vinaigrette and cress when the frog swung by with a tray of fresh bites and a few kind questions. Patrick was long and lean and confident, and Rowan was anything but all of that, seeming quite antithetical to his pal with his stocky frame, rounded posture, and perpetually floor-cast gaze. But even after just a few minutes in their company, Flackwell could see why they had been so close for so many years as they seemed to balance each other perfectly with every word and every flinch of their bones. They were affable and kind, and to the frog's delight, keenly complimentary of what they had been served, proving themselves just as eager to fill their bellies with his creations as they were to oblige him with interesting discourse. Flackwell was genuinely loathe to leave their company when he felt their conversation nearing its end, and it didn't help his separation anxiety that he could already hear the storm of mindless biblio-babble that he knew he had to brave next.

"Do you feel he captured the essence of your character or did you feel at all . . . I don't know, stereotyped in any way?" asked Percy as he shoveled some fire-roasted sardines with spicy marmalade into his maw without even a nod toward the chef.

"Do you see yourself whole on those pages or do you feel one-dimensional? I guess what I'm trying to say is, were your flaws mapped out as they should be?" added Talia without giving Flackwell a chance to answer the first question.

"Mmhmm, yes," continued Percival, unabated. "Your journey. Your passage. Do you think it served your arc?" It was all Flackwell could do not to turn and make a mad dash back to the kitchen. Barley Day was about many things for him and his fellow creatures at the castle, but it was never really about Edward's book, and the feeling of being reduced to nothing more than somebody else's words on somebody else's pages sent a bitter shiver up his spine that he was keen to shake.

Eventually, the frog was able to break free of their stocks, and as he hurried away for a breath of anything other than hot air, he brushed past Finn who said in typically prickly fashion, "I see you've met the monkeys."

"I have indeed. Not particularly fond of *those* two, if I'm honest," he replied, nodding toward the tiresome pair of academics he had just fled.

"Well, I'd be more than happy to take care of them for you," added Finn with a gleam in his eye.

"Yes, I'm sure you would. But if we let you have *your* way, the rest of us wouldn't get to have any fun at all, now would we?" Flackwell grinned at the fox and shoveled a squash tart into his mouth with a glee that only seemed to tug at Finn's poorer nature.

"You really do love all this fanfare, don't you?"

"I am a simple frog with simple needs."

"Well, I'm inclined to agree with exactly half of that," said Finn with a sneer as he leaned in and whispered, "Do enjoy yourself. Just don't forget what this day is about, because I promise you I won't." He put a firm hand on Flackwell's shoulder and left him to his own devices, skirting the hungry crowd and sipping from his flask and growing envious of the beaming smiles and full hearts around him, for Finn knew he had left those things behind in a place that no longer was. He also knew the things he had taken with him in their stead had twisted him into something he barely recognized anymore, but as the last of his kind, there was no one left to tell him any different and that, it seemed, was validation enough.

There were hors d'oeuvres of the highest caliber, but there was also drink equal to the task—mulled wine laced with cinnamon, juniper, clove, and fortified with just a touch of fresh grape juice to take the edge off of the hard spices. It was complex and layered, but it was still undeniably drinkable and the fine crystal glasses that had been set out were emptied and refilled time and time again from a parade of earthenware jugs that streamed in from the pantry. In Addington's book, the hours just before the Barley Day feast were a time for the nightingales to sing their songs and the owls to read their ancient histories and the foxes to wow the rest with their sleight of hand, and while Flackwell's edible wonders had been in keeping with the spirit of those offerings, it was Runny who gave of himself in the most unexpected way.

The clang-and-clatter of glasses and plates was so thick that nobody even noticed when the rabbit hobbled over to the record player and replaced the swinging jazz with something entirely different . . . and the wine was so ready that nobody paid him any mind when he hopped over to the orchestra pit, eased open a weathered case, and took from it an old viola of divine craftsmanship. Nobody saw him unscrew the head of his walking stick and pull from within a horsehair bow, and nobody saw him rub it red with rosin and tuck the beautiful little instrument under his hairy chin. Nobody noticed a blessed thing he did or heard so much as a rustle of his paws, but once Bach's *Come Sweet Death* began to fill the room and Runny played the first sweet, soulful note of his accompaniment . . . every single one of them paid him the whole of their heed.

It was as if the ballroom had been built to carry that song alone, and there wasn't a corner that Runny's gift escaped or an ear or a heart or a conscience that it didn't touch. The arrangement itself was sublime and sorrowful, but it was the rabbit's punctuation that made it all the more touching. It was the way his shoulders drooped and his head swayed, the way his ears softened and his whiskers jumped with the rise and fall of it all. There were tears from some and long stares from others, and for a moment, Eamon even thought he saw Mark wipe something from his eye when he was sure nobody else was looking. Flackwell parroted the timbre of the music, dipping his head toward the floor and clasping his hands about his waist while Finn played predictably unaffected as he propped his feet up on the bar and wagged his finger about like he was conducting every movement. There was no applause when Runny played his last note—in its stead bloomed only the sad shuffle of his fiddle falling from his chin and the echo of his haggard frame slumping forward in his chair. His effort had run roughshod through his entire being, and though it had been a proper and heartfelt goodbye, he seemed almost sorry for having played it . . . almost mournful for what he had added to the story.

After an eternity of quiet crackling, it was Bach himself who decided to lighten the mood as the phonograph needle found its groove along a decidedly upbeat aria. The change in atmosphere was just enough to remind everyone that they were at a celebration, and it wasn't long before conversations were rekindled and spirits began to lift and the wine began to flow again. Even Finn seemed to fall into the feeling of things as he took on all comers at one of the hand-carved chess tables that were set by the doors to the patio. He was a considered and cunning player to nobody's surprise, and as Eamon stood on the sidelines and watched his fellow revelers fall one by one, he couldn't help but marvel at the fox's command of the game and his talent for trapping his opponents time and time again. At one point, he made a show of taking on three players at once without so much as breaking a sweat, and as if that wasn't spectacle enough, he allowed Percy to remove two of his pieces before their game began and still managed to whip him in four deft moves.

"Do you know why that's called the Scholar's Mate?" asked Finn as he picked up Percy's king and reset the pieces amid an embarrassed silence from his opponent. "Oh, that wasn't rhetorical, I just thought you might know," he added with a grin. Mark had been nudging Eamon for the better part of an hour in a bid to get him to sit down across from the fox, but when his turn to try his mettle came around, Eamon's head began to ache and his ears started to ring and it was all he could do to step back from the crowd as his concussion finally caught up with him.

"You okay?" asked Caroline, rubbing the dimple between his shoulders with a caring hand. "Maybe you should sit down or—"

"It's just a headache."

"Too much wine maybe?"

"Maybe," replied Eamon, running his fingers over the still-tender spot on his head where it had met the slate. "I think . . . maybe I just need some fresh air or something. I'm just gonna step outside for a second, okay?" His head did ache something terrible, but the prospect of having some time to collect himself and process the day's events was also enticing, if not necessary.

Eamon quietly excused himself from the gathering and made his way to the row of doors that abutted the patio, and not wanting to inconvenience his hosts with his meager traumas, he was glad to find the first exit he tried unlocked. It was cool and crisp now that the clouds had passed and the moon was left to light the isle as it saw fit, and the brisk evening breeze gave Eamon a much-needed shot of clarity. He breathed deeply as he strolled about the sprawling veranda, which like the ballroom, was built purely for the art of celebration—each corner adorned with an elaborate gazebo and the slate marred by stanchions fit for party tents that once housed rolling bars, chamber orchestras, and sideshow performers that once served at the pleasure of so much American royalty.

Eamon walked the entire breadth of the manor and looked through every window before he found one that was filled with something other than darkness and disuse, but even through the dusty glass that kept him from the dining room, he could tell that Flackwell had no designs on being anything other than meticulous as he set the table for their feast. He folded every napkin edge-perfect and polished every bit of silverware again and again until they all sparkled like jewels, and only after every glass had been wiped clean of fingerprints and every ramekin had been filled with precisely the same amount of butter did he stop to pull his pipe from his pocket and look over his labors. It wasn't lost on Eamon that he was lucky to be a part of all of this, and as he took another gulp of sweet September air and thought back to his exchange with Runny in the kitchen, he wondered how much of what he had come to know as Addington's fiction was truly history, and in the same moment, he wondered the reverse.

The land just beyond the patio still rang with the echo of something finely manicured, but its edges were rough and wild and the weeds were strong and thick among the thistle and vines. There was a fountain just past the main staircase to the veranda—a concrete basin thirty feet or so in diameter with a tiered piece in the center that Eamon was sure once flowed with a grand waterfall, and while it was plenty full from the recent storm, there was just no life to the thing after so many years. Eamon traced the perimeter with his gait and watched the breeze ripple the leaves that were floating atop the rainwater until something in the near darkness caught the moonlight just right, and when he strolled close enough to see what was shining in the night, he found a statue of white marble towering above his head.

It was a visage of a man set atop a plinth not unlike the one Mark had claimed as his own not even several hours earlier—a remarkable replica of somebody whose features appeared to be from good stock and whose clothes looked to be of expensive thread. He was standing with one hand in his jacket pocket while the other was busied checking the time on a pocket watch, and while Eamon thought he looked a bit like Edward at first glance, he didn't understand the full measure of the resemblance until he cleared away the brush that was crowding the thing and saw the inscription that was etched there. *James Addington. Beloved brother. Fiercely may he hunt and far may he travel.*

Eamon scoffed at the thought of such a grand tribute, but after a moment's consideration, he understood it to be not all that different from a headstone and felt himself a bit callous for the sentiment. After all, it was a fine rendering and seemed an honest memorial, but Eamon knew that Edward had two brothers, one older and one younger, and it didn't take more than a cursory glance at the other side of the fountain to find the rest of the litter. *Theodore Addington. Beloved brother. May his broadheads be as sharp as his wit.* Theodore's statue was no less finely made, even though the man who stood atop it was a good five or six inches shorter and his features far more homely. He was posed with both hands clutching the lapels of his jacket and his chest puffed out like some longlost Roosevelt, and Eamon couldn't help but mimic his form by grabbing ahold of the sides of his coat as he drank in the beautifully carved lines and layers of white stone.

It was only in the silence of his satire that Eamon heard a rustling in the trees overhead, and when he glanced up into the night to see what the commotion was all about, he saw a shadow sitting high above him with black holes for eyes. It had feathers about its frame and grappling-hook talons which were wrapped around the branch upon which it was perched, and even in the low light of the evening it looked to be a strong and stately thing. Eamon squinted into the darkness to better see his company, but before his vision could catch up to his curiosity, the specter among the branches took it upon itself to satisfy its rather similar interests.

"And who might *youuu* be?" said the shadow. No answer came to Eamon's lips. He took several steps backward toward the patio as the darkened form flapped its wings and floated down to a lower branch that was naked to the moonlight, revealing herself to be an owl about three feet tall. She was a handsome creature of black and brown spotted feathers with a kindly face, a breast as white as the driven snow, and eyes that flashed ever-fiery with the incessant need to know. "And who might *youuu* be," she repeated, tilting her head in curiosity.

"E . . . Eamon. I'm Eamon," he answered, doing his best to regain his breath.

"That's an odd one, yes? Hmmm."

"Is it?" he asked, this time stepping closer to the bird for a better look. She was truly beautiful, regal and elegant and decidedly unferocious, which put his suddenly raging anxieties at ease.

"Quite," she said. "But youuu should be glad of that. Youuu should know the worth of being unlike the others."

"Are you . . . from the Hollow?"

"We are of the Hollow, yes. We are of the owls, yes. Long have we watched."

"Like in the book?" he managed between raging heartbeats. "Like . . . historians?"

"We know not of this book. We are of the eyes to see and we are of the ears to hear and we are of the mind to remember all, but we know not of this book. For we are of the land and not the manor, youuu see." The owl unfurled her wing and scratched her brow, and as Eamon took several steps to his left to see her from a better angle, she sidestepped right along with him.

"Do you have a name?"

"We have been called Olivia by many. By many whom youuu think your friends."

"*Think*, my friends?"

"Kindness is as kindness does, but so tooooo does duplicity, youuu see. Long have we watched. Much have we seen." She scratched her brow again and Eamon began to understand it as something of a nervous tick, and so he was unsurprised when not a moment later, she did it a third time.

"What are you trying to say? I don't quite understand," he said, moving a few steps closer.

"We are not of our kind anymore," she said with a sweet sadness. "We are weaker than our foremothers. We are a foul thing and we wish to change that, youuu see?"

"No, I . . . I don't see. I'm sorry."

"*Youuu* must *fly* this place!" she bellowed, jutting her head toward Eamon and flaring her brow.

"You want me to leave?" asked Eamon, almost a little offended at the notion. It had been a night of revelations to say the very least, but the momentum of all that discovery was so blinding that he hadn't for a moment stopped to consider that there might be a reason for all of the questions and all of the answers, and above both of those things, a reason that he was allowed to be there in the first place. It wasn't until he felt the great bird's energy clash against the spirit of the rabbit and the generosity of the frog that he even bothered to consider that perhaps his place within the manor wasn't the universally perfect fit that he felt it to be. It was a worthy consideration, but there in the sweet September air among the brothers of the man that taught him so much, Eamon felt it to be little more than his mainland anxieties trying to worm their way across the sea and onto the shores of his beautiful new frontier.

"Look, I know I don't belong here," he said after a moment to himself. "I know I'm not like them or . . . or like you. But I like it here. I feel at *home* here, and I don't really ever feel that way, so—"

"*Fly!*" she said again as a rustling nearer the patio stirred Eamon's attention.

"Is everything quite alright out here?" queried Runny as he hobbled down the stairs and settled near the statue next to which Eamon was still standing.

"Yeah, everything's fine," he replied, checking the tree out of the corner of his eye and seeing no trace of Olivia. "Just . . . these are really beautiful," he continued, running his fingers over the marble. "This was his brother, wasn't it?"

"Quite right. Quite right." The rabbit adjusted his bifocals to better see the sculpture and took a silent moment to admire it. "Marvelous work, if I do say so myself. There are many throughout the property. Fifty-eight of them, I believe."

"Fifty-eight?"

"Honor thy family. Easy if you have the means," said Runny as he rapped the plinth with his walking stick, a harmless exclamation that begged a separate question altogether.

"Where'd you learn to play the violin like that, by the way?"

"It's a viola, actually . . . and I learned it during my time here at the manor. Edward fancied himself something of a musician, though he never really had an ear for it. I think it just . . . seemed to him to be something he *ought* to be good at. Of course, he filled an entire room with the finest instruments money could buy, and of course he couldn't play any of them worth a lick. But you didn't hear that from me," he said with a wink. "In any case, there was a time when I found myself laid up for a spell and hadn't much else to do, and so I took up the fiddle and found it came quite naturally to me. And spirit, was I ever glad to finally figure out what these *ridiculous* ears are for." Eamon chuckled at the notion, but as his gaze drifted from Runny's oversized ears down to the space where his leg once hung, he began to read a little more into the rabbit's story, and his suspicions only seemed bolstered by his host's candor. "Something lost and something gained, but such is life."

When he was moved to do so, Runny had a stately way of phrasing even the most precious words so that they were whitewashed of their gravitas and stripped of their otherwise brilliant edges, but just as Eamon was about to chuckle away his speculation on the heels of the rabbit's folksy musings, he noticed a subtle change in his demeanor. It wasn't anything outrageously pointed, but it was enough to keep Eamon's mind latched—just a slight grimace of pain and a shift of his weight onto his good leg as if Runny could somehow feel those scars fresh and unfamiliar again. But Eamon wasn't the only one keen on reading the situation, and just as he could feel the change in his host's manner, the rabbit seemed as if he could sense the lad's searing curiosity bubbling up through his skin and decided to see just how bold he would be in the face of sudden silence. Eamon felt the night breeze riffle his hair and looked down to see a school of leaves cartwheel past his shoes as he mulled exactly what part he was meant to play in an evening laced with so much serendipity and party to so much unmasking. It was a confounding struggle between the need to know and the desire to remain benign enough to be accepted . . . between being the beast for once or remaining a mouse for the moment. It wasn't until Runny, tired of the stalemate they were breeding, opened his mouth to speak that Eamon made his call and said, "I wanna know what happened to your leg."

It was hard to tell exactly who was more taken aback by the young man's forwardness, but after they both took a few unsteady heartbeats to recover and realigned their respective roles, Runny replied only, "No, you don't." He let his answer hang between them until it was spent ringing its tone, and only then did he venture to unpack the slick speech that he'd stowed away for the time being. "My tiptoeing days may be long over, but at least it keeps me from hopping past the hedge. Now, we should get back to the celebration, don't you think? If we're the reason Flackwell's roast gets cold, I will never hear the end of it, believe me." The evening breeze gusted its goodbye and Eamon took one last glance at the moon before he and the rabbit sauntered back toward the embrace of Addington Manor.

"What was that song you played, by the way? The sad one?" Eamon asked as they rounded the fountain, glad to feel the familiar graces of his host and more than happy to play the grateful guest again.

"Bach's *Come Sweet Death*. A true classic. A bit over-sentimental, but I hardly think you can blame a man who lived through more plagues than he could count on one hand."

"Huh."

"Not a fan of the baroque?"

"No, I mean . . . yes. Actually, I honestly don't know. I just . . . why would someone write an ode to death?"

"Well, perhaps it wasn't *his* death he was longing for. Or maybe it was. Or maybe in a pinch, any death would do." Climbing the deep slate stairs proved a bit troublesome for Runny, but he was too proud to accept any aid, and as he waved off Eamon's outstretched hand, he looked back over his shoulder at the tree in which Olivia had appeared as if he knew her to be there all along. She, of course, was gone, and with her went the history of so many things that some ached to know and others ached to forget . . . and if it hadn't been for the comfort of the statues' permanence and the pain of his own weight on his only good knee, Runny might not have turned back around at all.

SIX

The formal dining room was big enough to seat a hundred diners though the table was fit for no more than twenty. It was a single stately slab of redwood, and while it had been sanded smooth and heavily lacquered and cut to an exacting rectangle, its grain was wild enough to color the whole space as if it were an ode to nature as well as a fine space in which to feast. Stunning landscapes wrought in oil hung on every wall and the floor was left bare as a tribute to the character of the planks, which were hidden only by the myriad hutches and credenzas that had been purpose built to house the endless collections of priceless china, silver, and glassware that sparkled against the candlelight of the chandeliers. It was a priceless space—a room in which it was impossible to have anything less than a feast, no matter the meal.

The table itself was set with professional care thanks to Flackwell's irascible eye for detail, and the centerpiece was a stunning collage of brightly colored autumn leaves and burly pinecones and snow-white birch branches set around a beautiful antique hourglass. Heralds of change guarding their keeper. Nobody could recall a reference to an hourglass in any of Addington's writing, but it seemed fitting given Barley Day's history as a tradition to mark the shifting of seasons and an opportunity to take stock of one's perspective amid the ever-flowing sands of time. It was a testament to the spirit of the holiday that so much care had been given to the substrate upon which community would be formed, and all of the guests felt positively welcome upon taking their seats along its edges and sprinkling themselves between Runny and Flackwell, who were seated at the heads of the table, and Finn, who was seated plum in the middle of the north side.

Everybody expected a speech by the rabbit or the frog prior to the meal, but there was surprisingly little fanfare before the wine glasses were filled and a delightful flight of soups was served for the first course.

There was, of course, a barley broth laced with dandelion greens which was followed by a corn and leek chowder, and to finish, a pureed pot of carrots with cinnamon and nutmeg. Each bowl was more delicious than the last and all of them served with fresh bread, hand-churned butter, and a spread of herbs, sunflower oil, and toasted pine nuts. The conversation flowed into little pockets as the table was a bit large for everyone to hear each other from end to end, and while the pots of soup were passed down the line, they all took their turn to speak about their own little Barley Day traditions and various recipes from the book that they had tried to both great success and abject failure. It was shallow banter for the most part, but it was more than enough to fill the empty spaces between the food and drink, and given the lateness of the hour and the exhaustion that the day had brought them all, it was banter enough and plenty sweet.

The second course was a grand salad of peppery greens, walnuts, cranberries, and goat's cheese dressed with homemade vinegar and grapeseed oil, and by the time it had been brought in from the kitchen, the chatter had turned to the beauty of their surroundings and how refreshing it was to spend some time away from the hustle and bustle of modern life. There was true gratitude flowing from every guest amid the shuffle of serving trays and jugs of this and that—gratitude not only for their hosts and the meal they were being served, but gratitude for the book that had brought them all together as well. It was as if the love that each of them felt for Addington's timeless collection of verse had been validated in the most searing manner, and it buoyed every one of their spirits and made them all feel a little less miscreated.

They were all patently well lubricated by the time the roasts of cauliflower, pumpkin, and squash were served with rutabaga pies and charred asparagus and butter-browned potatoes. All of them, that is, except for Eamon who had opted for water instead of wine on account of his headache and was lucid enough to notice that despite the wealth of good-hearted conversation, neither Runny nor Flackwell nor Finn had really said anything at all. They seemed oddly somber in fact, their heads buried in their food and their eyes fixed on the table and their words confined to terse, tortured answers to questions about the feast or the history of the manor or the makeup of the isle. It was a strange and weighty affectation as if they were eating their last meal before heading off to war and they were still hiding their conscriptions from their families. It was an odd air, and although most of the party was too preoccupied with delicious food and endless wine to take note, Eamon felt it in his very bones.

"What's wrong with them?" he whispered to Caroline who was planted at his side with Mark just another seat down the line.

"They're probably drunk," she replied, waving her wine glass at Percy who was on his metaphorical soapbox crowing about the rhythm of Addington's prose. "Or did you mean that in a more general sense?"

"No, not them . . . *them*," Eamon said, nodding to Runny and Flackwell who had both lost the shine of their kindly graces. And while the two of them looked decidedly melancholy, Finn just seemed rather annoyed by the whole ordeal, leaning back in his chair and glowering about the table as he forked little bites from his plate into his scowling maw.

"I don't know," Caroline said after nudging Mark into their conversation. "You hate holidays too, maybe . . . maybe this isn't just a great day for them?"

"Didn't seem that way a few hours ago."

"Or maybe you're being overly dramatic and they just miss their home," chimed Mark in typically casual fashion. "I can tell you this much, though . . . this is the best goddamn meal I've ever had and we're for *sure* coming back next year."

"Really!? You wanna come back!?" Caroline's eyes lit up like oil lamps and she cozied up to Mark with a surprised smile on her face. "Really!?"

"Are you kidding? I would drive to the literal ends of the earth for this food," he continued, helping himself to some more fire-roasted pumpkin drizzled with maple and vinegar. "I might even read that stupid book, who knows?"

Caroline turned to make sure Eamon had heard Mark's proclamation, but he was too busy studying Runny who was aimlessly moving his last bit of cauliflower about his plate with his ears drooped down to his shoulders, and although the rabbit's mood gave him pause, it was his next glance around the table that begged a more important question. "Why isn't there anybody here that's been here before?"

"What do you mean?" asked Caroline, stealing some pumpkin from Mark's plate.

"Mark's not wrong. This is the best food I've ever had . . . and this place is *amazing* and even Runny said that we're not the first ones to show up here on Barley Day."

"So?" Mark managed with his mouth full.

"So, where's everyone else? Seems like there should be dozens of people here, no? What fans of his book would come here and meet these wonderful characters and stay in this house and eat this food and drink this wine and not want to come back? Where *is* everybody?"

"People have lives," offered Mark. "Just because we don't have important stuff going on all the time doesn't mean other people don't. I mean, it's not like this is a real holiday and everyone gets the day off work or whatever."

True as that may have been, it didn't satisfy Eamon, who out of the corner of his eye noticed Runny pawing at his scarf-wrapped ear like somebody clawing at a fresh scab. But there was barely time for his thoughts to come together before Gareth cleared his throat, rose from his chair, and raised his voice to the rafters. "Well, I just wanted to say that this has been the most wonderful day that I've ever had. And on behalf of everybody here, I would like to thank our hosts for their hospitality . . . and their food . . . and their wine," he said, taking a sip amid encouraging chuckles. "I'm not much for toasts, and I'm admittedly a terrible writer, but I know a good book when I see one and I think I know some words that would do. So, if I may," he continued, opening his leather-bound copy of *Winterset Hollow*, "The table was set and all were met with barleywine and beer, there were kin abound and smiles all around as Barley Day was here. Glass-blue skies and pumpkin pies and bellies full of bread, stories of old about glory and gold and the paths the elders tread. The Hollow was never so peaceful amid—"

"Oh, for Spirit's sake, *must* we do this!?" interrupted Finn.

There was a moment of the most uncomfortable silence before Runny challenged him. "Now, Finn, he's just trying to be—"

"Must we!? Must we sit here *again* . . . and listen to those words from that book *again* . . . and pretend like it doesn't drive us mad?! Why don't we just get on with it, eh? Haven't we had enough of this nonsense tonight?!" he exclaimed, slamming his fist on the table and flashing a fearsome look the rabbit's way.

"Traditions are traditions, Phineas," the rabbit said, baring his backbone in return. "And soon enough, you will have yours. But for now, why don't you just—"

"Are you not angry anymore, Rabbit!? Because I'm still angry! Do you not miss your kin!? Because I still do!"

"You know that I do, Fox."

"Then let's just get . . . on . . . with . . . it," Finn growled, grabbing his flask from the table and gulping it down.

"What's happening?" whispered Eamon.

"Maybe this is why nobody comes back," retorted Mark under his breath.

"I'm sorry for that," Runny stated, leering at Finn as if he were speaking for him. "We've all had a bit to drink tonight and today is a day for fond memories, but for us it is also a day for foul ones. There is much we miss . . . and much we know we'll never see again. I'm sure you all understand."

There were nods from everyone around the table except for Finn who seized on Gareth, still frozen in mid-sentence and holding his beloved book. "Sit . . . down!" Gareth sat amid the searing silence of uncomfortable shuffling, and it seemed like an eternity before somebody broke the stalemate.

"Well," said Runny, "there's trifle in the kitchen, perhaps that will lighten the mood."

"I'll get it," offered Flackwell from the other side of the table.

"No, no. Allow me," replied the rabbit, staring hard at Phineas as he rose from his seat and limped from the room, the click of his leg against the ballroom floor playing his way out.

"So," said Flackwell, taking up the mantle as host in Runny's absence. "Have I ever told you good people about the time I invented corn pudding?"

Runny's eyes welled with tears as he traipsed across the ballroom and down the great hall, breezing past the entrance to the kitchen and instead opening the door to the washroom. He leaned his rickety frame against the porcelain sink and stared into the mirror only to be horrified at the raggedy old rabbit glaring back at him. "What animal are you?"

he said, slowly unwrapping the scarf covering his right ear. "What *are* you? What thing are you?" Runny unwound the last of the wool and let the scarf fall to the tile, revealing his ear to be a mangled piece of meat scarred through and through, misshapen from infection, and almost bare of fur. He leaned into his reflection and stroked the edges where there were dozens of bits of flesh missing like teeth on some putrid saw, and in that moment, he shivered with pain and release and pride and punishment all at once.

"Do you not miss your leg?" he said, echoing Finn's sentiments from their earlier exchange. "Do you not miss being whole, you awful thing!?" he challenged as he opened the cabinet and took from it an ivory-handled straight razor. "Tell me what you are, for once!" But the rabbit looking back at him said nothing as he unfolded the razor and ran the blade along a honing leather that hung from the edge of the sink. "You awful, voiceless thing."

Runny brandished the sharpened steel so that both of them could see it and there were no more secrets between them. He took a few measured breaths to steady his hand, and once he was calm enough to know that it would properly hurt, he cut deep into his flesh so that fresh, hot blood ran into the corner of his mouth and he shuddered at the bitter taste of his own worthlessness. He watched as the old thing in the mirror sliced into itself a second time and he heard it scream and growl as it dug the blade about until a piece of its being fell into the basin with a sickening thump. The razor clattered to the tile and he turned his head to the heavens and clenched his jaw, leaning into the white-hot burn of the musty manor air licking his insides amid some strange chemical rebalancing. It felt like water in the desert to him, and once he had rightly quenched his thirst, he looked one more time at his sad, bloody reflection and whispered, "Say something."

Runny slipped back into the hallway with his scarf once again wrapped about his ear, and with a renewed vigor in his step, he hurried past the kitchen where the trifle sat and dipped back into the ballroom where he limped his way to the theater's entrance. He breathed a deep, desperate breath before he swung open the double doors and hopped inside to find Bing still sitting in the same spot . . . still staring at the big screen which was now flickering with an endless white nothing. The rabbit hobbled over to the projector and clicked it off and let it whir to a gentle stop as the only light in the room faded to black, and knowing it was only he and the great bear in the darkness and that the beast before him had never been much for words, it was only Runny who spoke. "I believe it's time, old friend."

Flackwell was doing his best to keep everybody occupied as they picked through what was left of the feast, though his heart clearly wasn't in it. He seemed distant as if he was lost in some painful memory or perhaps some equally painful future sight, but his guests were doing their best to keep a positive momentum around the table so as not to end their once-in-a-lifetime evening on a sour note.

"So, are you all vegetarians, then?" Talia asked as she helped herself to another serving of wild ramps that had been singed in the oven and dressed with pickled garlic. "Percy and I have been meat-free for years," she said with a beat of self-satisfaction.

"Absolutely shocking," jabbed Mark.

Flackwell shifted uncomfortably in his chair and took a moment to straighten the lapel of his vest as he chose his next words. "I have cooked my share of meat in my time, but we don't do that anymore."

Finn chuckled to himself as he picked at his nails with the silver knife that was left at his table setting. "Well, Flack, why don't you *tell* them why you don't cook meat anymore? Hmm? Surely, they would like to know, yes? Lovely story."

There were agreeable shrugs and nods around the table, but Flackwell only grimaced at the prospect of having to dance around whatever the answer truly was. "I haven't cooked meat since . . . since Edward left us."

"Oh, yes, that must have been it," barked Finn. "Surely, that's the whole story! Must feel good to get that off your shoulders, eh, Frog!?"

"Perhaps *you* would like to tell them?"

"Perhaps I would."

"Well, then be my guest. Please," the frog said as he leaned back in his chair and crossed his arms, but Finn didn't even have time to open his mouth before Runny entered the room and made a beeline for his place at the head of the table without so much as a word. He didn't even seem to notice the air of confrontation that was hanging heavy between his two friends as he slumped into his seat and stared at his empty plate. "Well, did you bring the trifle?" asked Flackwell.

"The what?" said Runny, lifting his head for the first time since he sat down only to feel a drop of blood trickle from his scarf and fall to his napkin.

"His ear," Eamon whispered, nudging Caroline who leaned over in time to see several more drops stain the white cloth with an obscenely gentle pitter-patter.

"Oh, god," she quietly muttered. "Poor thing." And as if Runny's nerves knew that the silence of her sympathy would have been too much for him to suffer, his leg began to thump against the floorboards. *Click-click-click-click*. Every pair of eyes at the table was now fixed on him, his consternation beating a metronome for their uncertainty which was rising as his rhythm quickened. *Click-click-click-click*. He could feel their focus even though his gaze was still on his empty plate, and just as they all started to wonder what had turned him so dour, they heard the first rumble in the distance. *Boom. Boom. Boom.*

"The hell is that?" Mark asked amid the thunder of war drums slow and steady.

"I don't know," answered Eamon, glancing at his wine glass only to see the water within rippling with each crack of the storm. *Click-click-click-click. Boom. Boom. Boom.*

Eamon's breathing quickened, and just as his internal alarm bells began to sound, the doors to the dining room flew open and Bing, the great bear, squeezed his hulking frame into the space, his jaws dripping with vitriol and his giant hammer in hand.

"Jesus," muttered Caroline as her wind fled her lungs. Bing was a singularly frightening thing and not at all the kindly giant she had so often envisioned any time she saw fit to sink herself into Addington's pages. He was twice as tall as any man in the room and almost as wide as the entrance itself—big and brawny with paws the size of dinner plates and a head that was easily as broad as Mark's shoulders. He was wearing a leather cuirass that looked like something out of an old Greek myth, and although his barrel chest was covered, his limbs were left naked so as to bare his scars to the world, pockmarked as he was from head to toe.

Bing was seething, his eyes darting back and forth between the guests and his great chest heaving in anticipation of a storm nobody else knew was coming, and in the midst of the starkest silence that Addington Manor had ever witnessed, he loosed a war cry that shook the very rafters and rattled even the rabbit's bones nearly to dust. No one moved a muscle except for the beast who brushed past Flackwell and moved along the length of the table, stopping only when he arrived at Finn's seat which was properly in the middle. The fox smiled a broad, unapologetic smile as he felt the cool of the brute's shadow swallow him, and as Bing leaned in toward the centerpiece, everybody stiffened with horror only to see him grab the antique hourglass with his kingly paw and turn it over to set the sand moving.

The great bear stepped back from the table with a huff and settled in for a wait. Bewildered looks began to fly and a dull murmur rose from the crowd of feasters, and as Eamon turned to see that Runny was still staring down at his empty dinner plate, he felt it wise to ask him, "What happens now?"

"My dear boy, don't you know it's Barley Day?" answered the rabbit cold and unaffected, his ear still running red with blood and his eyes still somber and sunken. Runny turned to Eamon with a glare that spoke of the trials of some history he wasn't privy to, and as he reached down with his paw to stop his nervous leg from stuttering against the floorboards, he said only, "You run, Eamon. You run."

Part Three

The Fox in His Orchard

Finn, he flashed a wily smile, he bared his teeth and gnashed his guile
For news of the outsiders' theft had reached the orchard trees
And though the rest were fraught with woe and all his kin were feeling low
The idea of a caper oddly put the fox at ease

And so he rustled up his pack and filled it full of barley snacks
And opened up his trunk to find his knife the elders made
A handle carved of ancient oak, stained with blood and alder smoke
And the sturdiest obsidian to give the perfect blade

He felt it was a part of him, an ever-sharp and ageless limb
He felt it was a talisman to keep him strong and wise
He felt its weight along his hip, it balanced him from toe to tip
And so alone he ventured out beneath the autumn skies

Through the trees he crept at night, careful to stay out of sight
Of anyone who'd dare to raise a question to his whim
He snuck around the orchard's edge and slinked his way across the hedge
And soldiered toward the prairie and the buffalo within

Their scent was strong, to say the least, and soon he found the bloated beasts
Tucked in for a slumber with their bellies full of crops
They snored and snored and tossed and turned, but clearly none of them had learned
To leave a watch awake in case a fox approached their flock

Finn, he showed himself around, and careful not to make a sound
He rifled through their trunks to find the treasure from the theft
But all he found were scraps and rinds, vittles of the meekest kind
And soon his blood was boiling at the thought of what was left

How dare these brazen beasts, he thought, how dare they come and take our lot
How dare they leave us scared and starving for an evening's fill
How dare they steal what's rightly ours, how dare they leave us cold and sour
How dare they ruin Barley Day and empty out our mill

Ripe with rage, he drew his knife, and knew that should he take a life
He might set off a fray and have to tangle with the rest
But Finn felt someone had to pay and here the fattest bison lay
And so he snarled and sunk his blade head deep into its chest

SEVEN

There's no town around here worth a visit, not even for a second. There's nobody worth talkin' to but me, and there's no land worth crossing except for ours and God's. You understand me? You are here . . . and you are here forever . . . and that's the only way you're gonna get through this life. I won't have you end up like the rest of them.

Those were the last words Eamon ever heard from his father, and while he had heard them countless times before, the timbre of uncertainty in his voice on that particular day was enough to make the wispy hairs on his arms stand on end and his young mouth run dry with worry. He had seen his father pack his bag before as well, as he would often venture into the wilderness for days at a time to check his traps or empty his fish wheel, but it didn't escape his notice that he took more food than usual this time . . . and it didn't slip Eamon's attention that he retrieved some items from the cast iron safe in the cellar before he left, the combination to which was a secret that even he, his father's only anything, wasn't privy to.

The things he took with him were telling, but the things he left behind in the days before he disappeared were in some manner even more worrisome. The way he chopped enough wood to last them through the winter even though the first snow was months away, the way he smoked enough fish and canned enough vegetables from the garden to bulge their little cellar at the seams, and the care he took to make sure Eamon was buttoned up on how to clean his rifle, treat his own wounds, and make the stars his compass—these were practices that had come and gone for years, but the sudden urgency surrounding them made them seem like some awful living will. *This is all I know, and now you know it too. This is the sum of my experience. This is all I am.*

There were so many questions in the weeks that Eamon waited for Jack to return. There were questions about where he went and if he was ever coming back. Questions about how long to wait and where to go if he never came home again. Questions about how to feel and whether this was really just a way to make sure his father's mad prophecies were finally fulfilled . . . whether he was truly crazy enough to take that ingrace into his own hands. So many questions for the now-and-future John that never was. *How are you doing with all of this? How are you coping? Do you want to verbalize what you're feeling? Would you care to draw something instead? John?*

Eamon was there now, even though he wasn't. He was being called by someone else's name and gawked at through frosted glass as if he was some newly discovered species, certain that he knew nothing of the world and that the world knew nothing of him. He was there again, even though he wasn't. A boy swimming in his father's boots while he waited for somebody to bring him a reasonably sized pair of sneakers and knowing that no matter the fit, they simply wouldn't feel right. Knowing none of it would feel right. "J" for Jack. "J" for John, and nobody else.

It was deadly quiet in the dining room save for the drunken, bloated breaths of the great bear and the crystalline whisper of the sand filtering through the waist of the hourglass. Eamon, whose every trauma had been triggered by what the rabbit had said to him, was a moment away from asking for some clarity in hopes that it might bring his reopened wounds some salve when Runny took it upon himself to enlighten the table. "This day is a day of traditions. And while some are tender and warm and pluck at our heart strings even all these years later . . . others are dark and unwelcome. Necessary, mind you, but unwelcome. It should be no surprise to any of you at this juncture that Edward was not above conscripting our history into his own. Borrowing from our past to bolster his future. Taking what was ours to further what was his."

"What did he say to you?" Caroline asked Eamon with a whisper, noticing that his face had turned a shade whiter, but there was no answer from her friend as he turned to meet her gaze with a heartachingly distinct mix of betrayal and bewilderment slathered across his face. There was no clarity for her, just as there was none for him. There was only the contagion of lightning-strike stress and an unexpected entropy that wormed its way from his body to hers as Eamon's eyes darted about the table.

"This day is not what it once was, and for that my heart breaks," continued the rabbit. "But it is *because* of that we carry on with these things . . . these rituals. Even those that are new to our history. Even those the buffalo brought." There was a distinct reverence woven into the silence that followed, and as another drop of blood fell to the table from Runny's bandaged ear, his eyes began to well with the stuff of life.

"The debt must be paid!" barked Finn, emptying the room of every last bit of romanticism and sparking a parade of raised eyebrows and confused glances.

"Indeed, it must be," Runny sniffed. "And after tonight, after all this time . . . it will be paid in full."

Finn bared his teeth and snarled, "Bloody right. In *full*."

"What are they talking about?" asked Caroline, glancing at Mark who had nothing to offer her but a shrug and a pair of upturned hands. She was but a breath away from begging the same question of Eamon when Bing chimed in by slamming the head of his hammer against the floor—a feral and unapologetic exclamation that spoke volumes along the spines of everyone at the table.

"It's time for the hunt," said Runny without an ounce of theater. "Hurry now . . . time is fleeting," he continued, shifting his gaze until it was firmly fixed on the hourglass, a subtle maneuver that prompted a sudden flurry of uncomfortable chatter from his guests. Caroline and Mark joined in the chorus, hoping that Eamon's knowledge of Addington's text might offer their confusion some quarter, but he could hear nothing above the tide of the sand and the nerve-crushing stutter of Runny's wooden leg against the floorboards . . . so there were no answers at all for them. Eamon's mind was awash in the deafening din of all of the things that were and all of the things that could be fighting for the same space. The chaos of all of the things he loved and all of the things he feared circling each other with sour intentions. And when he opened his mouth to speak, he could only swallow his words because he was unsure if even the most honest among them were true. Say something. Please.

It was the most wretchedly familiar moment when the sand stopped. A moment Eamon had lived more times than he ever cared to count. It was the moment he toed the edge of the road that would lead him into town for the very first time and it was the moment he realized his father was never coming back. It was the moment he first shook hands with the strangers who were assigned to be his new family and the moment he first found himself in a proper school among a thousand aliens who were slated to be his peers. Every piece of him wanted to jump through his skin and run back to the woods and live a life full of nothing again, but his gears were so firmly seized that he couldn't even will himself to breathe. Breathe. Please.

It was the look of surprise on Runny's face that gave the game away to the rest of them, the nervous chatter slowly bleeding out as they all wheeled in turn to discover that the flow of the hourglass had been stymied by a few grains of sand that had lodged themselves about its waist. Not even the rabbit's leg was shaking now. Not even the great bear's chest was heaving. There was only a wild and ferocious nothing for a string of breathless moments, and though everybody else's lips were pursed with uncertainty, Finn couldn't help but smile.

"Well . . . isn't that something? It's a Barley Day miracle," he said as he quietly wrapped his hand around the knife that was set next to his dinner plate. Finn sprung from his seat in a flash of fur and launched himself across the table, thrusting the blade square at the middle of Eamon's throat amid gasps from the rest of the party. Eamon, frozen to his chair, could only close his eyes as he felt the silver tip pierce his skin just below his Adam's apple, and to his own surprise, there was little but calm and the wretched stench of inevitability as the whole of his meager life flashed before his mind. He judged himself a human nothing in that instant—a tumbleweed in the desert of the world that had gone largely unnoticed by anyone or anything that might wish him well or harm or something stranger in between. *John? John, is there anything you'd like to say? Would it be easier to write something down instead? Can you hear me? Don't you think you should run, John?*

Surprisingly, Eamon opened his eyes to see that the knife hadn't traveled much further into his flesh. Finn was growling and stretching with all his worth to push it in up to the hilt, but Bing was having none of it, his great paw holding the fox by the scruff of the neck and his strength keeping him just inches away from spilling Eamon's being all over the table. But it was clear from the searing rage on the face of the bear that his actions weren't born of charity, and when he flung Finn clear across the room and let loose a terrifying roar, it was plain for all to see that he simply wanted the day's prize all to himself.

Bing brought his fist down upon the table with a pointed rapture and buckled the old, thick wood along its center to a chorus of shattered crystal and clattering porcelain that sent the entire room into a panic. The throng of dinner guests leaped from their seats, each of them grasping for their friends and feverishly glancing for the exit as their uncertainty was quelled in the most terrifying manner imaginable. The brute grabbed ahold of the broken table, which was still lying between him and Eamon, and with one mighty flick of his arm he sent it flying clear across the room, the once-sturdy redwood landing with a crash not far from where Finn was still trying to shake the discourtesy from his bones.

The rush for the ballroom was wild and chaotic, and while most were keen to stay clear of the fray, it was only Gareth, lost in a terror-stricken fog, who bowed to the instinct to cut in front of Bing on his way to the door. But before the once-jolly lad could even reconsider his folly, the bear swung his hammer and landed its heavy head plumb in the middle of Gareth's chest, crushing whatever was inside. His portly, crumpled frame slid backward along the floor and hit the wall with a horrid, fleshy thump that made Runny and the frog cringe as if the sounds of battle were somehow more disgusting to them than the sight of it.

"Gareth!" screamed Paige as she reached out for her friend, the shock of seeing real violence for the first time dripping from every pore. The instinct to come to his aid was strong, but Thomas wasn't about to let her make the same mistake as her chum, and as she leaned into the fray to try and be of some help, she instead felt only the sturdy pull of her beau leading her toward the exit.

Eamon was the only one still seated. Still frozen to his chair. Still shell-shocked and staring up at the great beast before him as blood from the shallow hole in his neck pooled at the intersection of his collarbones. The builder bear was close enough for Eamon to smell his fetid breath and feel the floor bend under his weight, and as Runny crossed his arms and averted his eyes, the rabbit said only, "Make it quick."

Quick, thought Eamon. *Yes, thank you. I would rather it be quick.* Eamon wondered if this was charity. He wondered if this was kindness or if it was grace. He wondered if this was a deal he considered fair—a moment of unspeakable pain in exchange for a reprieve from the slow bleed of the years that were sure to follow. *Quick*, he thought again. *Yes, make it quick.*

Eamon braced for the end, but as he watched the bear reach his weapon to the sky, he felt the familiar weight of a heavy arm around his shoulders. Mark ripped him from his seat and dragged him away not more than a moment before Bing's hammer shattered his chair and smashed clean through the floorboards, adding, "Let's go, *let's go!*" as he dragged Eamon to his feet. Mark wheeled toward the door, but Caroline was already a step ahead and grabbed him by the hand to usher them both into the ballroom, leaving Bing alone with the shame and frustration of having to pull his hammer from the floor still unbloodied.

"Haven't lost a step," mused Runny sarcastically as the bear ripped his sledge upward in a shower of splintered wood. Bing growled his displeasure as the rabbit shook his head at the gaping hole in the once-perfectly finished sea of solid hickory boards.

"That should be easy to fix," said Flackwell, who was still in his chair looking rather nonplussed about the whole ordeal.

"I believe you have something for me?" barked Finn, rejoining the others near the ruins of their feast. Bing scowled at the fox before reaching into his cuirass and handing him the gleaming obsidian dagger that had been made famous by Addington's prose. Finn felt the comfort of its weight and groaned in pleasure as if a long-forgotten piece of himself had finally been fit back into place. He balanced it on the ridge of his hand and flipped it between his fingers and ran his thumb over the diamond-sharp edge, admiring its craftsmanship and fantasizing about its capability in the same moment. It was an old knife made by a people who no longer existed, and as the very last of his kind, it gave him an extra sense of purpose to use a weapon of their design. It gave him courage to know that he was not alone in the debt he felt he was owed and it gave him permission to be free of the moral quicksand that might otherwise poison his appetite for revenge. "You grab me by the neck again, it'll be the last time you use that paw for anything," he snapped at Bing who just chuckled and gently jabbed him with the head of his sledgehammer.

Knife in hand, Finn scampered toward the door and the bear turned to follow only to have his foot brush against a jug of wine on the floor that was still sloshing about with nectar. He snatched the vessel up and held it above his maw, emptying whatever was left into his gullet with a fiend's abandon.

"Oh yes, more wine . . . that should do the trick," said the rabbit amid the judgment of his brow.

"Can't say I blame him. It was a particularly good batch," added Flackwell. "I *do* wish you would have brought that trifle, though. Raspberries, crème patisserie, and homemade ladyfingers. Your favorite."

"Sounds lovely," Runny returned with a forced and fleeting smile. "Perhaps later when everybody's dead."

"Yes, well . . . that'll be just fine if you like soggy trifle," lamented the frog, sinking deeper into his seat and tipping his chin to the rafters with a palpable indignation. "Just fine indeed."

"We can get out to the patio from the ballroom," huffed Eamon as he and his two comrades sprinted out into the lavish party space only to find Paige, Thomas, Talia, and Percy already huddled around the back doors and patently stymied by thick chains that had been looped around the handles.

"There's no way," said Thomas with panic in his throat before giving one last desperate tug at the metal shackles and surrendering. "We've gotta find—"

"Front door's chained too!" They all wheeled to see Patrick and Rowan stumble in through the opposite entrance with sour news hanging from their faces. "Padlocked," said Patrick as he and his friend rushed to join them in their huddle.

Caroline scanned the room for another option. "There's gotta be a window or something we can—"

"Now, *what* is the rush?" asked the calmest voice in the room. Finn strutted toward the gaming tables where Eamon's trio was trying to formulate a plan, flipping his knife about his hand with ease and never taking his eyes from his prey. "Not sure where you'd be going anyway. We *are* on an island in the middle of miles of open water, you know. Might as well relax and enjoy the time you have left," he said as he sprung atop a billiards table and brandished his blade with a searing snarl. The three of them turned to run, but Finn was far too quick and equally nimble, and in half a heartbeat he leapt from table to table and grabbed the nearest chandelier to swing himself back into the middle of their path like some uncorked, vulpine Achilles.

"And as for *you* and your lovely little friend," said Finn, pointing the tip of his knife at Mark and then Caroline, "you'd be wise to leave the other one here with me and give yourselves a nice head start. I just wanna have a little quality time with him, that's all. Chat about the weather, shoot some pool ... open him up from stem to stern and watch him melt into the tile." Finn slowly backed them down until the three of them turned to run again, but the fox took off with whiplash speed, sliding under the first snooker table with a dancer's grace and vaulting over the next to block their escape for the second time in just as many moments.

"Oh, come on now ... no need to get all worked up," sneered Finn. "Just think of it as a game. Isn't that what you all came to see? A fox in his orchard, so to speak? A night of tradition? Everybody loves traditions, don't they? I know Edward did," he added, nodding up at the fresco on the ceiling above them. They turned their gaze to the heavens to find that they were standing underneath the fox hunt, and although the three of them were far too terrified to spend any energy on the synesthesia of it all, there was enough of a connection to give them the briefest moment's pause ... which was all the opening Finn needed.

He gripped his knife by the blade and loosed it at Eamon's chest, the seamless obsidian cutting a silent path through the stale manor air, but Eamon's instincts for survival proved a stubborn tail to shake and something in his lateral mind moved him to feint like a boxer, dipping his shoulder to the side and turning his body so that Finn's dagger flew past without incident. But the knife was so well balanced that it carried past the three of them and toward the far wall where it buried itself deep in Percy's back as he followed the rest of the guests toward the great hall. The impact sent him stumbling forward, but the adrenaline was coursing so readily through his veins that he felt little more than a scratch, and like the others he was tailing, he was too lathered with hysteria to have any semblance of perspective, even with a dagger shunted between his shoulder blades. Talia turned to make sure he was okay, but seeing nothing amiss from her spot in front, she only grabbed him by the hand and rushed him into the corridor to rejoin the pack.

"Hmm," murmured Finn as he watched his prized possession hitch a ride out of town in the back of some unsuspecting buffalo. "Why don't the three of you just stay *right* here, make yourselves comfortable, and I'll be back in a moment to finish our little chat, okay?" There was, of course, no answer from Eamon and company who were busy slowly backing themselves away from their furry would-be assailant. "Great," said the fox, "be back in a flash." And with that, he zipped across the room and disappeared through the front entrance to cut the rest of the pack off at the pass.

Eamon's head was swimming with the most perverse and unwelcome possibilities, and holding his head in his hands, he collapsed into a squat as soon as the fox was out of sight. "What the hell is happening!?" he moaned. "What is this!? What . . . what—"

"I don't know. I don't know," said Caroline, crouching down to his level with tears in her eyes as Mark broke a billiards cue over his knee and brandished the thicker end like a club. "I don't know what's happening, but . . . but all that matters right now is that we find a way outta here, okay? We gotta go, you understand? Eamon!?" He didn't seem moved at all by her words until she gently pulled his hands from his temples and turned his chin so they were eye to eye. "You hear me?" A nod was all she received in return, but it was enough to get them all back on the same page, and as she helped Eamon to his feet amid the expectation of a snarl from some great beast behind them, it was instead the sound of a viola being tuned that piqued their senses.

Runny and the frog had made their way to the orchestra pit, the former holding his good ear to his instrument as he tweaked its tuning pegs and the latter lounging with his bare feet propped up on the empty viola case, casually stuffing his corn-cobb pipe with something green and leafy from his vest pocket.

"Your A is sharp," said Flackwell, tamping down the stuff in his bowl with a little metal tool made strictly for that purpose.

"Oh, is it?" asked the rabbit with a familiar exasperation. "Is that what those pinhole ears of yours are telling you? That my A is sharp?"

"My ears may be tiny, but at least I have two of them. Maybe you should take that scarf off so you can hear how out of tune you are." Runny let a scowl leak from the side of his mouth and strained to better hear his fiddle to little avail. "You're sharp half a step," said the frog as he struck a match and touched it to his pipe, giving it three hearty puffs to set it burning before exhaling with a particular gratitude. "*Spirit*, that's good."

Runny, mumbling under his breath as he was wont to do any time his pride was tarnished, slacked his A string a bit and played a smart little run to ensure that indeed everything was pitch perfect. "Fine," he said. "So, what'll it be? Something to lighten the mood a little? Something jaunty? What say you?"

"Mmmm," mused the frog between puffs. "Something to drown out the madness would be just lovely."

"Wouldn't it *just*, though?" seconded the rabbit, cocking his head to the side for a moment of pause as he picked through the catalogue within until he set his chin to his fiddle and began to play. The first few notes of the fourth movement of Mozart's *Symphony Number 40 in G Minor* cut through the stale ballroom air like the opening volley of some great war, but while the carefree blitz of Runny's viola set a wide and welcome warmth across Flackwell's face, Mark's chest heaved with rage at the condescending stench of it all. He squeezed the broken cue in his hand and shifted his weight toward the orchestra pit with every intention of ending their concert in an encore of blood and fur, but he didn't take more than half a step before Bing, as if charmed from his cave by the sweet science of the melody, lumbered out of the dining room and wiped his still-dripping jaws.

The brute set his bottomless eyes on Flackwell, who was waving the stem of his pipe in the air as if he had been tasked to conduct, and gave him a contemptuous snort before turning to see Eamon, Caroline, and Mark standing frozen not more than a dozen yards to his north. The builder bear's gaze narrowed as he choked up on his hammer, and as they began to backpedal toward the great hallway, trembling and grabbing at each other for any whisper of security, Bing opened his maw to the sky and screamed war.

They fled into the grand hall and raced past the collage of maps, crossing over the corridor that led to the front door, knowing it to be barred, all the while hearing the strides of the brute in their pursuit growing longer and more purposeful at their heels. Bing's gait sounded like the gods' own timpani—a deep and terrible thrum that echoed through the whole of the manor—its dark crescendo prompting Eamon to glance back over his shoulder to see the bloodthirsty giant was but a few thin moments behind him, his silhouette filling the breadth of the hallway like the front of an untamable storm.

"There!" said Caroline, pointing to the door at the far end of the throughway, the window cut into the upper half looking out onto the wilderness just on the other side. She quickened her pace and the other two followed suit as they flew past the kitchen, the portraits that Eamon had stopped to admire not more than a few hours earlier now nothing but a blur in their peripheries. But as they drew near enough to the exit to allow themselves some measure of hope, the chains that were looped through the handles came into focus and they shared a silent panic, for there was no turning back and there was no stand to be made. Certainly not here. Certainly not like this. The moment they felt the shade of Bing's shadow on the napes of their necks was the same moment they understood there would be no more running, and as they glanced behind them to see the brute flying through the air with his jaws agape, the need to stay together gave way to the instinct to survive, and without another thought, Eamon dove through the study door to his left while Mark pulled Caroline into the room on the opposite side.

Bing hit the ground with a raucous boom, the momentum from his leap enough to send him sliding along the floorboards until he crashed into the doors at the end of the hall, buckling them at the hinges and letting the crisp night air leak through to lick at his fur. He staggered to his feet and looked back at the empty passage behind him, and as he crept closer to the two rooms into which his quarries had fled, he quieted his rage and turned his nose up into the jetstream of manor air.

Mark and Caroline found themselves in a space filled with harps and cellos and xylophones, kettle drums and double basses and woodwinds of every ilk, and while it was anchored by a lavish grand piano and an antique harpsichord at the center, they thought it best to flatten themselves against the wall and take refuge behind a bookshelf stuffed with sheet music.

"What do we do?" whispered Mark between desperate gulps of wind. "Is Eamon out . . . is he still in the—"

Caroline clamped her hand across his mouth as a shadow cloaked the light filtering in from underneath the door, her eyes wild and her chin trembling. There was a rustling from the other side followed by a creaking of floorboards and a series of hearty sniffs that they could hear even halfway across the room. They closed their eyes and squeezed each other's hands and thought about all the things they wished they had room to say as they waited for the surefire rattle of the doorknob, but the knob never turned and the door never opened. The hinges never whined and the latch never lifted, and as the creature's shadow left the company of their only egress, the rush of freedom that washed over them was quickly poisoned by the realization that if they were safe . . . Eamon surely wasn't.

"I don't think he cares about us," Caroline said as she choked back a surge of relief and put her hands on her knees, allowing herself to breathe freely for the first time in what seemed like hours.

"What do we do?" asked Mark with real desperation in his voice.

Caroline could only glance around the room for an answer, and finding none, turned back to look him in the eyes. "I don't know," she said. "I don't know."

EIGHT

Bing inhaled deeply around the edge of the study's entrance, and feeling fine that his prey had fled that way, he tried the handles and found them both locked before giving the spot just below a hearty tap with his hammer, cracking the mechanism and pushing open the double doors. But when he stepped inside, he found only the things he already knew to be there—the books, the desk, the globe, the fireplace still glowing with embers clinging to their charge, and the portrait of some ruddy-haired son of privilege hanging above it. They were familiar visions, but they were different than Bing remembered as they were laced with a new scent. A scent that had crept into the theater to disturb his requiem earlier that same evening. A scent that made his very mouth water and his hackles come alive and a scent that, it seemed, had already escaped through the narrow, low-ceilinged door that led into the next room.

Just on the other side of the threshold, Eamon finally allowed himself a breath. He quickly realized that the door he had just taken was far too small for the great bear to squeeze through, and so he welcomed the chance to stop and think, though the only thing that was racing through his mind was the question of whether Mark and Caroline were safe. He listened for anything that might paint some picture of what was happening elsewhere be it the crash of a hammer or the scraping of claws against the floor, but there was none of that. There were no desperate screams from his comrades or menacing growls from his hosts and there were no sweet songs from the rabbit's viola or sinister diatribes from the fox. In fact, Eamon could hear nothing at all from the tearoom in which he found himself except the silent song of the fossils that surrounded him.

There were dozens upon dozens of porcelain and silver tea sets displayed on every surface and in front of every blank bit of wall, but it was a family of foxes sitting on a nearby table that caught the corner of Eamon's eye, and while there were far more pressing things at hand, he couldn't help but give himself over to the need to digress. There were twelve of the creatures in total—one painted on each of the eight cups and the other four adorning the matching kettle, milk boat, sugar bowl, and biscuit box—all of them finely drawn and brightly colored and looking rather happy to be in each other's graces. They were so lovely and pure that Eamon was drawn to them even in the middle of all the madness, but as he reached out to pick one up and cradle the sweet little thing in the palm of his hand . . . it jumped at him.

The rattle of the cup against its saucer startled Eamon so readily that he leapt back a full stride, and as the rest of the room began to clamor and clink in kind, his pulse began to race and he glanced wildly about the room for an answer to any one of the hundred questions that were ringing in his ears. But it was only the timpani's muffled booming that turned him back toward the little door that led to the study, and it was only the drums of war sounding from the other side that sent him backpedaling out of pure instinct. These were indistinct harbingers at best, but somewhere in the corners of Eamon's frazzled mind, he knew what was coming, and still he couldn't help but stay for the spectacle of it all.

Bing thundered through the wall in an eruption of wood and plaster and stone, his frame throwing shrapnel to every corner of the room as if he was a cannonball and every last precious tea service some poor, itinerant soldier. When the dust cleared, Eamon and the great bear found themselves not more than a body length apart, each staring at the other and wondering if this was the end, and for just a moment, Eamon considered standing his ground and taking his medicine. He considered falling at the hands of a thing that had meant so much to him during his struggles . . . accepting death from an idea that had previously given him life, but the lack of blood on Bing's hammer and the still-foul smell of spiced wine on his breath told him that Mark and Caroline hadn't yet met their end, and so there was but one thing to do.

The beast could barely even flinch before Eamon darted out of the tea parlor and flew across the front hall to the gallery come sitting room. It was a beautiful space that ran from the house's exterior all the way to the front door—a place studded with period furniture and draped in timeless works of art—its corners filled with beautiful sculptures and delicate vases and busts of historical figures from no era in particular. It was a shocking and unrepentant display of wealth, and while under any other circumstance Eamon would've been more than happy to lose a day gawking at the merits of the treasures and feeling ill amid the vanity of it all, at present they were little more than priceless obstacles.

Eamon weaved around the heirlooms and darted between the vintage furniture, wasting not a moment to look behind him at the tempest he knew to be on his tail as the sound of breaking glass and splintering wood was enough for him to know that Bing was somewhat waylaid by the hurdles that lay every few feet. He burst into the grand foyer, and finding that the front door was indeed chained shut, Eamon turned back toward the great hall to see Paige, Thomas, Talia, and Percy barreling toward him with panic dripping from their every pore. It felt good to see them. It felt like a step toward freedom to find himself among peers again, but as he took a stride in their direction, he saw Finn round the corner behind them and flattened himself against a depression in the staircase that led to the floor above.

He tried to make himself invisible and turned his feet and chin sideways so that he wouldn't be noticed, but as the hysterical shuffle of his fellows closed in from the hall and the clatter-and-smash of Bing's dogged pursuit grew louder, Eamon only felt more trapped. There was simply nowhere to go. Nowhere to run. He played the pointless game of deciding if it was better to fight the fox or the bear first, but as he mulled his two equally unsavory options, he pushed himself further against the wall only to feel the handle of a hidden door dig into the small of his back.

There were two sets of stairs that led to the second floor, one on each side of the grand foyer that curled up the walls in opposite fashion to a landing flanked with mahogany bannisters. Finn was but a few strides behind Paige, Thomas, Talia, and Percy when they decided to split and take their escape to the upper level, having exhausted all the ground floor had to offer in terms of both fight and flight. Paige and Thomas took to the steps along the left wall and Talia and Percy took to the right, but Finn was unfazed, and with a startling spring in his step, he launched himself from a credenza, grabbed the bottom of the landing, swung himself over to the other side and vaulted up over the railing.

He landed in the middle of the footway just as the two pairs of terrified guests skidded to a stop on either side of him, and for just a tick of their racing hearts, the five of them shared the strangest silence.

"Would you two give us a moment?" the fox said to Thomas and Paige, the pair of them struck dumb by his sudden appearance before deciding to flee through the door at the very end of the hall. "Very good," he offered with a satisfied smirk, turning back to Percy who was trying to shield Talia behind him. "Now," he continued, "If I could just have a moment alone with Percival here, I would *very* much appreciate it." Percy was quaking now, his face white as the pages of the book that had brought him to this place, and Talia, noticing for the very first time the knife that was hilt-deep in her partner's back, began to back away from him at the sight of the crimson stain that was overtaking his cardigan.

"T?" asked Percy as he turned to face her, but she could only swallow her horror and point with a quivering hand.

"Yes, run along," said Finn. "We'll only be a minute."

"T, don't . . . don't . . ." stammered Percy as he reached out, but she was already halfway down the stairs and fully on her way to anywhere else by the time he could finish his thought.

"Now that it's just you and me, I believe you have something of mine," said the fox as he gripped the handle of his knife and removed it from its place just to the side of Percy's shoulder blade. Percy grunted as the blade slid free and felt the pain of his wound for the very first time now that the adrenaline had waned.

"Look what you've done," lamented Finn, showing him the blood that was covering his prized blade and wiping it along his college-boy sweater until it was clean and black and gleaming once again. Percy looked down at the deep red streaks striping his chest before reaching over his shoulder to explore the burning sensation that was coursing through his back, his fingers coming away damp and dripping with the stuff of life. He held his hand before his face as the pieces finally began to fall into place, his eyes growing wide and black and his chin and spirit trembling at the same harrowing frequency. "Don't worry, it's only a flesh wound. Nothing vital back there, I promise."

"Vital? Nothing . . . vital?" eked Percy as he watched the viscous, red stuff run down his palm and drip from the ball of his hand.

"Not at all. If I wanted to stick you somewhere meaningful, I would've hit you in the chest where all the organy bits are." Finn tapped his knife on the center of Percy's sternum just above the spot where his heart was beating a country mile a minute. "Surely somebody of your academic standing could've put that together. Or maybe you'd prefer I do you like I did Edward. Would you like that? To pass on from this life the same way your hero did?" Finn stepped closer until they were almost chest to chest . . . the fox's calm, controlled energy colliding with Percy's boiling mortal anxiety in a strange, brackish aura. "Do you know why you're having trouble speaking now? It's because you've hung your whole life on words. Your words, Edward's words, words of authors and words of those who taught you about them. But now . . . now that the end is so close you can see it and there's nobody around who cares to hear you speak . . . you realize that all of those words don't mean a thing, don't you?"

Percy opened his mouth, but all that came out was fetid, horrible breath and the sour stink of fresh bile. It was only then that he looked down to see that Finn's knife was buried deep inside his gut, and as the fox slid it a few inches to the side and withdrew the blade, Percy clasped his hands about his midsection and let out a long and sickly moan. Finn laid a paw on top of Percy's hands and rather gently helped him to the floor, setting him on his back and once again wiping his prized weapon clean on his shirt. "You know, you remind me of Edward," he said as Percy began to gurgle and choke on his own misfortune. "Building a life on the stories of others. Always waiting for everyone to be awed by your prowess or whatever other garbage you've convinced yourself is important." Phineas stood and admired his newly clean blade before turning back to his prey. "Took him the better part of ninety minutes to bleed out. I guess we'll see how much you two really have in common in an hour or so."

"Talia? Talia!?" Percy begged, his hands struggling to contain the flow from his gut. He tried to sit up but was immediately set back down by the weight of Finn's foot on his shoulder.

"I wouldn't do that if I were you. Best not to sit up. Breathe. Just breathe," said the fox, demonstrating slow breaths in through his nose and out through his mouth until Percy picked up the cue and joined in. "There. Just like that. Anything you want me to tell her when I see her? Talia? I'd be more than happy to pass along a message or two," he whispered with a grin, but all that Percy could manage in response was a crude and indecipherable murmur. "Sorry, I didn't catch that." Finn hovered his ear above Percy's mouth, giving him another chance to speak, but there was nothing but a desperate last gasp for life. "Have it your way," he said with satisfaction. "Well, this has been lovely, but I'm afraid I must go. Would be rude to keep the other guests waiting. I'm sure you understand." Percy grabbed at Finn's ankle, but the fox simply shook him off with a flick of his foot, and without another word, he traipsed toward the door through which the others had fled.

Finn turned the pitted knob, and finding it locked, he slid his knife into the space next to the jamb and lurched the handle upward, popping the mechanism free of its hold with a clank. The room smelled stale and musty, and while it was pitch dark, the fox's eyes quickly adjusted to the lack of light, and soon enough he could see it all in near-daytime detail. He was in Edward's master suite—a lavish chamber set into the corner of the second floor with a four-post bed against the far wall and all of the other trimmings requisite to the place where a couple might sleep sprinkled about the space. There was a leaf-patterned dressing screen for his wife, Elizabeth, and old safari trunks filled with family treasures and an endless walk-in closet stuffed with dresses, ballgowns, tuxedos, leisure wear, and shoes upon shoes upon shoes. There was art here, too, as there was in the other rooms—an eclectic collection of works that included a Monet, a Van Gogh, a Rembrandt, and even a Picasso, which was a simple line sketch of a fox drawn in nightmarish cubist fashion that made Finn chuckle at the implications it forced him to dismiss.

It was all exactly as he remembered it, from the boxes of pre-inscribed *Winterset Hollow* pressings to the crates of jet-black hair dye to Elizabeth's collection of broaches that she kept arranged just-so on the vanity. It was all just as he had left it, which was more cause for concern than comfort, for Thomas and Paige were nowhere to be found. It wasn't until Finn poked his head into the bathroom and saw the night breeze billowing the curtains that he knew where they had gone, and as he tucked his knife into his belt, climbed out of the window, and descended the trellis that carried the honeysuckle and ivy up the south wall, he knew where *he* was going as well.

Finn hit the ground running with purpose and sliced his way along the edge of the manor toward the drive that led down to the waterfront.

He was clearly on a course to somewhere else, but before he left the homestead proper, he hooked sharply around the front of the house and stopped at a cluster of oleander bushes, where after a moment of digging, he emerged holding a bow and a quiver stuffed with arrows. The bow had a fairly short throw to it, the wood hand-carved from one piece of timber and the arrows tipped with obsidian just as his prized blade was, and while he wore the quiver slung over his shoulder as most hunters would, he also kept several arrows in his draw hand in order to avoid fumbling behind his back during a critical moment. His strides were lithe and athletic, his feet almost looking as if they never touched the ground as he darted between the trees with his bow ready and his knife sheathed about his waist. He was truly where he belonged now, holding tight the things that were dearest to him with his nose to the wind and his eyes trained on the task ahead, nothing less than a fox in an orchard not of his own choosing . . . and nothing more than a tree born of a wind-blown seed.

The coat closet was seamlessly cut into the space just below the staircase, and as such, it offered the strange solace of a place that didn't exist to the outside world. It smelled of old, dry leather and crumbling rubber soles, and as Eamon was stuffed against the furthest wall behind the stash of down jackets and fancy overcoats, the sound of the manor's madness was muffled just enough to give him the feeling of retaining some distance from it all. Every piece of him wished that he could stay there forever—that he could grow old there and wither and die behind his fabric shields and that he would never have to open that door again to see what awaited him on the other side. It was folly, but he wished it anyway. It was folly, but still he squeezed his eyes shut and held his breath when the floor beneath his feet began to warp under the weight of the beast trolling the hallway just outside. It was folly, but still he prayed to a thing he didn't believe in, there in the darkness. There in a place that offered no escape but silence and seclusion.

Bing's nose told him that Eamon was close, but his eyes couldn't hang a lantern on where he might be as he stood in the middle of the foyer and surveyed his surroundings. It wasn't until he caught a whiff of stale cowhide that he remembered the closet was there at all, and as his brow bent in satisfaction, he knew that the thing he sought was surely trapped inside. The builder bear's hammer exploded through the wall like the first shell falling on the Ardennes, leaving Eamon stunned and certain of his own demise as a shower of splinters bloomed through every corner of his little sanctuary. The creature shoved his giant arm through the opening and slashed about the space, his fearsome claws cutting down everything in their way until there was nothing left hanging between Eamon and his talons except space and time and the most visceral existential terror. Eamon flattened himself further against the back of the closet, every heavy swat of Bing's paw getting closer and closer to tearing through his flesh but landing just short of his mark. The bear loosed a frustrated roar and grabbed at the sides of the hole he had left in the wall and began to tear at its edges to widen his point of entry. The paneling came away in his hands like papier-mâché, and when he snaked his arm back inside to have another go, his claws shredded Eamon's shirt and scratched the skin on his chest deeply enough to draw blood.

Eamon could do nothing but wait as Bing began to tear at the paneling again, knowing it was just a matter of seconds before the gash in the wall was large enough for the creature to be able to cut him to pieces. He tried not to think about how painful it would be—about how long he would be left alive once it began and how much he was sure to suffer, but as he reached up and felt the dampness of his shirt, he heard something wholly unexpected—agony.

Bing reared to find that a spear from one of Edward's suits of armor had been sunk into his haunches and wheeled to see Mark staring up at him. Mark took a hard swallow of manor air as Caroline tugged at his shirt and begged him to turn and run, but he was so hypnotized by the aura of the beast that he barely heard a thing, and when Bing raised his hammer to deal with him, he simply stood and watched. "*Mark!*" she screamed as she grabbed him by the shoulder, but he was too absorbed in the sheer spectacle of something so perfectly unique and wildly monstrous. "*Please!*" she yelled, pulling at his arm as Bing began to swing his great hammer to end them both with one mighty swat. But for the second time that night, the builder bear's intentions fell short of his actions, and he loosed another painful roar as Eamon, newly freed from his confines, twisted the spear to sink it even deeper into his flank. The brute growled and flailed his bludgeon as he turned, snapping the pike in two and leaving Eamon holding nothing but a splintered wooden handle.

"Get outside!" yelled Eamon as Mark and Caroline backpedaled toward safety.

"What about you!?" returned Caroline. "What are—"

"Just get outside!" he shouted again, locking eyes with the bear to ensure that he would follow him when he ran—and run, he did. Eamon broke toward the front door, taking an abrupt turn and bursting back into the ballroom to the sound of Mozart still echoing through the space. Runny looked surprised to see him and raised an eyebrow as he continued to fiddle, and Flackwell nearly choked on a mouthful of smoke at the sight of him scurrying toward the center of the room with his shirt soaked in blood.

"I must say, I wouldn't have put money on seeing *him* again," said the frog between coughs. "Maybe old Bing *has* lost a step or two." It wasn't but a moment later that the great bear followed Eamon through the doors, his gait stunted and angry and his desire to cut a quick pursuit causing him to toss aside every last table and chair in his way. "What a mess," Flackwell chided amid a disappointed shake of his head. "Shame."

Eamon glanced over his shoulder to see Bing parting the ballroom décor like the red sea. He was nearing the doors to the patio, which were still locked down in chains, and there was no room to double back with the creature so near his heels, so Eamon knew a quick decision had to be made or he would not have the chance to make one again. Bing slowed to a limp when he saw Eamon disappear into the dining room, and when he rattled the handles to find them locked from the inside, the beast huffed in frustration and readied his hammer to clear his path.

"Now, just wait one moment, old boy," said Flackwell, already halfway across the ballroom and jangling a set of keys. "You already owe me a dining room table and spirit only knows what else, judging from the clatter I've been hearing. No need to go ruining a perfectly good door. We all still have to live here after the debt is paid, you know." Bing grumbled his displeasure but relented, lowering his hammer and backing away from the entrance. "Good gracious, what happened to your leg?" said the frog, pointing the stem of his pipe at the wound in his friend's haunches. "You let that little rat get the best of you?" The bear just growled and pointed at the doors and Flackwell, reading he was in no mood to be ribbed, obliged him by unlocking them with his key. "Make it quick . . . and *clean*, if you can. Terribly messy business, all this vengeance."

Bing eased open the door and slipped inside with his weapon at the ready, but it seemed that the only other soul in the room was Gareth, who was still slumped against the far wall struggling for the slightest sip of air. The space was infected with the strangest silence—an incongruous quiet that rang disingenuous among the porcelain rubble and fractured furniture and still-swaying chandelier. Eamon was nowhere to be seen and the builder bear could no longer pick up his scent through the leavings of Flackwell's delectable creations that were hopelessly scattered about the room . . . and even after the brute had checked every window to make sure they were all unbroken, every hutch to be certain there was nobody hiding inside, and every dark corner, there was nothing but the wake of the night's madness . . . and the hole left in the floor by his hammer.

The basement was dark and dank and appropriately musty, and just from the sound of his own footsteps, Eamon could tell that it was cavernous and concrete from wall to wall. He staggered forward with his arms outstretched like a man whose sight was newly failing and felt about for anything that might aid him, but all he managed to find were boxes of this and that and shelves stocked with tins whose contents were impossible to discern in the unyielding black that surrounded him. Eventually, he came upon a metal structure that he assumed to be a boiler, and as he stumbled his way through the cobwebs and around to the other side, he saw a pair of flickering lights a few dozen yards ahead. He inched closer and soon he could tell they were lanterns by the way their flames trembled, but it wasn't the lights themselves that piqued his attention as much as it was the strange and unexpected scene unfolding in their glow.

Each lantern was set inside an iron cage about the size of a modest prison cell. They were awful looking things in form, but Eamon was surprised to find them outfitted with an unexpected array of creature comforts—sturdy beds made up with expensive linens, decorative rugs that looked as if they had been plucked from the sitting room, and exquisite wardrobe closets that seemed wasted in the black of the basement. Eamon poked his head inside to sate his curiosity and found they weren't lacking in things to help pass the time either, as seemingly every corner was stuffed with cookbooks, sheet music, classic adventure novels, and plenty of pens, pencils, and paper for when the already-printed words got stale.

The cages were set a few feet apart and their entrances were cambered toward one another so that their doors spilled out onto a common area where Eamon found a breakfast table and a matching pair of chairs carved into the darkness. It was a shockingly domestic sight that reminded him of something out of an old homewares catalogue, and Eamon's heart melted when he saw the little collection of salt and pepper shakers, ketchup bottles, whole-grain mustard, and HP sauce that was cozied up next to the napkin holder. There was a radio, too, which was sitting atop a stack of yellowed newspapers that was tall enough to stretch from the floor to the table itself, and Eamon couldn't help but think that it all looked like home to him. A strange and solitary home buried under the surface of everything that anybody else could ever want, but home nonetheless . . . and he was riffled with a twinge of jealousy at the prospect of a life that simple, even if it meant being caged.

Eamon reached out to turn on the radio in hopes of tasting this existence a little better, but before his finger could even touch the dial, he heard a great crash from above as Bing began to bash himself a bear-sized hole in the dining room floor. He snapped back to his current predicament and grabbed the nearest lantern and began searching along the wall for a way out, but by the time he hit the first corner, he'd found nothing but rusty piping and cold concrete. The thumping from above was growing more earnest by the moment, but as Eamon found himself halfway down the next section of wall, the clamor suddenly stopped . . . and so did he. Eamon tried to quiet his breathing, but his fears required too much air. He tried to stop the lantern from rattling, but his free hand was quivering just as badly and did little to help silence the clamor. He felt like a pawn without a move to be made . . . a jetty stone just waiting to be swallowed by the tide. Not knowing how to proceed and not wanting to take a step in the wrong direction, he squinted into the endless black to see what the intermission was all about, but all he found staring back at him was a pair of enormous, blazing-brown eyes . . . and Eamon knew he was no longer alone.

Seeking refuge in the dark, Eamon dropped the lantern at his feet and began earnestly feeling for anything that might resemble a way out as the clatter of shelves being knocked aside and boxes being crushed swept toward him like a storm. Eventually, his hand found a turn in the concrete that led to a narrow passage, and after stubbing his foot on what felt like a step, he glanced behind him to see the bear's silhouette eclipse the lantern's glow and knew there were mere seconds between him and the beast on his tail. Eamon pressed forward and was buoyed to feel a second step and then a third beneath his feet, and knowing a staircase could only mean one thing, he charged up the rest of the flight only to find himself trapped by a pair of bulkhead doors. He tried to push them open as his chest pounded with the promise of salvation so close at hand, but when they refused to budge even a whisper, he was gutted to find they were made of heavy iron and all but frozen shut with rust.

He lunged at the center seam with his shoulder in hopes of break-ing something free, but the doors gave only a breath before they came thundering back down on top of him. He was well stuck, but Eamon didn't realize he had been truly cornered until he heard a ferocious roar from the mouth of the stairs and felt a claw dig into the sole of his shoe. Before he could even brace himself, his leg was pulled from underneath him and he crashed down onto the steps, the back of his head whipping against the concrete and the echoes of his demise im-mediately beginning to crash about inside his skull. His ears were ring-ing and his vision was pulsing with pain, but he could still hear Bing growling and gnashing his teeth as the beast tried to pull him from the narrow passageway to tear him to ribbons. Once Eamon's senses began to refocus, he saw that the brute's frame was too hulking for him to squeeze into the corridor and he gave a desperate kick that knocked the creature's claws free of his shoe. Eamon wasted no time in flying back to the relative safety of the bulkhead and tried to push it open again and again . . . every fiber of his being firing with every bit of strength he had left, but still he could see no moonlight on the other side. Still he could taste no fresh air. He screamed for help with all the voice he could muster, but he knew there was nobody there to hear him, and as his shoulders slumped with the inevitability of defeat, he felt a thunderbolt split him in two.

The head of Bing's hammer struck him like a freight train, sending him lurching forward with an uncompromising violence and introducing his face to the grit of the iron dripping from the doors before him. The builder bear had taken it upon himself to extend his reach, and Eamon could only turn to try and swat away the jabs as they mounted like the most unyielding hail, battering his body and crunching against his bones. Eamon was sure that it was only a matter of time before there would be nothing left of him but dust, and it was in the midst of that certainty that a well-placed stab split his guard and hit him square in the chest, driving every last bit of wind from his lungs. It was a hopeless and pitiful defense without any air to stay his strength, and as Eamon felt his will give itself over to the determination of the bear's bludgeon, he reached for the doors one last time only to feel a sturdy pair of hands pull him to safety.

"Sounded like you could use some help with that hatch," said Mark before noticing the welts pockmarking Eamon's limbs and the blood that was smeared across his frame as he writhed on the ground and begged for breath.

Caroline covered her mouth with her hand, aghast at the crimson streaking his clothes. "Oh my god, are you okay?"

"No . . . I'm not . . . okay," Eamon replied between grateful gulps of wind.

"What happened to—"

"Close . . . the . . . door! *Close it!*" he pleaded.

Mark straddled the open hatch and looked down into the darkness only to see two giant eyes throwing moonlight back his way, and without a second thought, he swung the iron doors shut and left Bing to languish in the dark where he belonged.

"Jesus, what happened?" asked Caroline, crouching down to try and be of some assistance.

"I got mauled by a bear . . . like . . . twice."

"Well, let's try to keep that number under three, okay?" added Mark as he helped Eamon to his feet.

"Hold on, let me see your head." Caroline took her pack from her shoulders and dug about inside until she found a package of tissues.

"You went back for your pack?"

"Grabbed it on the way out," she said as she carefully blotted some of the blood from Eamon's head. "Are you sure you're okay?"

"You can keep asking me that, but I'm just gonna keep telling you no," he replied, wincing at her touch. "How did you guys get out?"

"Bing knocked one of the doors off the hinges. We slipped out with two of the others . . . the redhead and the tall one."

"Look, I'm . . . we don't have time for this," Eamon moaned, gently pushing Caroline's hand away. "We gotta get off this island *now*. I can get patched up later. Let's just—"

"They said they were heading down to the dock," she interjected.

"Then we should probably do the same."

"Do you really think our ride is still gonna be there?" huffed Mark.

"Gene was passed out pretty hard," added Caroline. "Still might be."

"Even after the rain?" Mark's logic gave them all pause, and for a string of directionless moments, they shared only tentative glances instead of words.

It seemed like hours before somebody spoke again, but it was Caroline who finally took it upon herself to try and turn their spirits around. "Maybe he waited it out in his boat. I'm sure he wouldn't just leave us in—"

"I would've," interjected Mark. "If I had the choice between waiting out a thunderstorm until a bunch of kids got done getting lost in the woods or coming home to you . . . I'd be gone. And you probably would be too. Am I wrong?"

Eamon put his hands on his hips and began to pace. "Look, even if he's not there, maybe . . . maybe there's a rowboat or a canoe or something in the boathouse on the landing. Maybe there's—"

"But what if there isn't?" Mark questioned, looking them both in the eyes in turn.

"Then I think it's still our best bet to find the others. But if you have a better idea, now would be a pretty good time to share," said Eamon as the uneasy haze of being a piece of somebody else's game washed over him.

Mark tried to will a better solution to his lips, but when he opened his mouth, the only thing that came out was, "I don't," and Caroline only seconded his notion with a defeated shake of her head. Eamon wanted so badly to speak to the gravity or the extraordinary nature of their circumstances, but he felt he would be able to say little that would matter more than the things they had already seen or the terror they had already felt or the blood that was still soaking through his shirt and matting his hair. He wanted to tell them that they were just wasting time by arguing about whose ideas were savvy and whose ideas were untenable, because reality was a realm they had departed hours ago . . . and none of them had any context in any of their histories for anything this far beyond the pale. Eamon wanted many things in that moment, but most of all he wanted to be home—home in Boise, home in the country, home with a set of foster parents that he hated with every bone in his young being—anything would do. Anything would do, but he knew all too well that none of it would come to him, and so as he had done countless times before, John Eamon Buckley put one foot in front of the other with the hope that the next step might make it all worthwhile.

NINE

Patrick slammed the rotted door to the boathouse only to have it spring back open far enough for everyone to see that there was nothing inside but a small forest of weeds that had pushed their way up through the floorboards. "No boat. No nothing," he exclaimed as he paced back to where Rowan, Thomas, and Paige were waiting by the edge of the landing. All of them were understandably wracked with anxiety, but Thomas looked a little more broken than the rest with his arms crossed and his head down and his cheeks stained red with panic.

"Your friend . . . Gareth . . . is he . . ." Rowan thought it better not to finish his sentence, knowing they didn't have any more answers than he did, and silently chided himself for giving in to the instinct to ask.

"I don't know," Paige replied. "I wanna go back, but—"

"No way," said Thomas, bursting with emotion and barely managing to swallow his hysteria between syllables. "Back!? We can't go back there! We have to *go!* We have to . . . we have to swim or *something!* Those things are gonna kill us. They're gonna fucking *kill* us and if we just stand here all night, they're gonna—"

Paige stroked his arm to calm him. "We're gonna get out of here, I promise. We just . . . we just gotta figure out—"

"Figure what out!?" he screamed, pushing her away and slamming his fist against his chest. "Figure . . . *what* . . . out!? Did you really think there was gonna be a . . . a *boat* just waiting here for us to use!? We're on an island! We're on an island, so let's just *swim!*"

"We can't swim," she said as Thomas moved toward the edge of the water only to have her hurry in front of him to block his path. "Tom, we can't—"

"Get out of my way, Paige, I swear to god!"

"It's three or four miles of freezing ocean water, you'd never make it . . . or I'd go too," added Patrick. "There's no way."

Thomas tried to push past her again, but Paige held him back until he folded himself to the ground with his head in his hands. "I just . . . just wanna go. I wanna *go* and I don't wanna be here and I just wanna fucking *go!*" he sobbed.

"I wanna go too," said Paige, crouching down beside him and stroking his hair. "But I can't do it without your help. So I need you to be strong . . . and I need you to be smart like you always are. Can you do that for me?" He nodded and wiped the tears from his eyes and swallowed the violence of his nerves, but even as Paige helped him to his feet, she wasn't sure that she believed him, though she was certain she had little other choice.

Eamon, Mark, and Caroline had found their way to the fence that ran along the coast and traced it back to the gap that was gifted to them by the fallen tree, and after a desperate sprint along the footpath that followed the sea, they felt they were almost at the landing as the trail began to widen. Their instincts were only confirmed when they rounded the last bend to see the others gathered by the dock in the distance, but as they slowed to a trot and took a moment to survey their surroundings, their hearts fell hard when they saw there was no boat in sight.

"I knew it," snorted Mark. "We're stuck here. We're stuck here on this goddamn island and—"

"Well, at least we're not alone." Caroline raised her arm to signal to the others that they had arrived, but as she looked to greet them, Eamon grabbed her wrist in protest.

"Stop," he said as his instincts began to fire.

"What? I was just—"

"The gate." Eamon nodded at the towering gate in front of which they had all left their offerings of thanks earlier that day, the doors to which were hanging wide open. "It was chained shut earlier."

"So, they cut the chain. I don't—"

"Cut it with what?" Eamon challenged, looking behind them as if he was expecting a surprise any moment. "Those chains were heavy. They left it open on purpose. They must have."

"Why would they do that?" asked Mark. "Wouldn't they want to keep us *inside* the fence?"

Eamon scanned the area from the manor to the sea, hoping to feel something in his subconscious click. "I don't know. Maybe . . . maybe they knew we'd all come down here if we got out of the house. Maybe they *want* us here."

"I don't understand," questioned Caroline. "Why would they want us out here in the open?"

"That's exactly why," offered Eamon, nodding toward the space between the gate and the dock. "It's a clearing. There's no trees to block the moonlight. It's the lowest point on the island and there's water all along one side. You heard what Runny said, this—"

"This is a hunt," added Mark, nodding as he began to pick up Eamon's train of thought.

"Exactly. This is a hunt . . . and that's the perfect place for a clean shot."

"Shot of *what?*"

"I don't know," Eamon replied. "But if we're all herded together down there, they could just pick us off like—"

"Like buffalo," said Caroline.

Eamon's voice trailed off to a careful whisper. "Like buffalo." He put his finger to his lips and crept into the brush, encouraging Mark and Caroline to do the same, and once they were all comfortably hidden behind the thicket, Eamon threw a stone toward the others in hopes of grabbing their attention without drawing any unwanted notice. His first attempt fell well short as did the second, but Mark was quick to pick up his slack and gave the next stone a mighty heave, and together they watched it land not more than a yard away from Rowan's feet.

"What was that?" said Patrick as he wheeled and threw a desperate glance in every direction.

Rowan joined him in his search, but neither of them thought to look far enough down the trail to see Eamon and company peeking out of the brush. "I don't know, sounded like a rock or something."

"A rock from where?" he asked as he looked first at the sky and then at his three comrades who all seemed to know just as much as he did and nothing more.

"We gotta get outta here," offered Paige. "We can't stay—"

"*Ow,*" barked Patrick as he flinched in pain and swatted at his leg.

"What's wrong?"

"I think something just bit me," he replied. But as he looked down at his ankle where he expected to find the leavings of some nasty bug, he saw instead a gash that was starting to run red with fresh blood. "What the—"

The second arrow flew close enough to his face that he felt its wake on his skin, but the whistle from its fletching was so unfamiliar that even after he heard its shaft split the shallow water just beyond the shore, he still couldn't parse what was happening. The next two shots fell in rapid succession, the third landing several feet shy of where Thomas was still sitting and the latter missing him by no more than a hair's width. Suddenly, they all felt themselves awash in a hopeless tide of confused unease, and by the time both of the bolts had buried themselves in the earth and soaked up enough moonlight to be recognized, the entire party was mired in an undeniable flood of panic.

"Let's go!" Patrick yelled to the couple, eager to join Rowan who was already a dozen strides away and making for the cover of the trees. Paige pulled Thomas to his feet, but as she tried to lead him by the hand, he broke free of her grip and made a dash for the water. "Let me go!" he screamed as she grabbed him from behind, not yet ready to let him float off into the night.

"Tom, we have to go! Goddamn it, we have to—"

He turned and knocked her to the ground just as another shot landed close enough to her face to kick a few wayward pieces of gravel into her eye. She pulled herself up, brushing the dust from her face and feeling utterly defeated, and as she scanned the hillside where she thought the arrows to be coming from, she saw nothing but shadows and knew they were well trapped. She turned back to the sea and wanted so badly to run after her partner, sweep him up in her arms, and carry him away, but her legs were too wobbly and unsound to listen and Thomas, as always, was too stubborn to make things easy.

"Bloody swirling winds," Finn muttered to himself from his position a hundred or so yards toward the house. He wasn't accustomed to his arrows missing their marks, but he had given himself a challenging distance from which to shoot and it was almost impossible to know which way the breeze was blowing down on the landing from his tree-lined haven on the hill, for even the leaves closest to the shore couldn't seem to agree on which way to sway. It wasn't until Thomas stopped just shy of the water and the moonlight caught his hair billowing in the breeze that Finn knew he had a solid read, and as a grin grew across his jaw, he nocked another arrow, drew back his bow, and slowly emptied the breath from his lungs.

Paige had stopped screaming by the time Thomas waded in up to his knees, her nature somehow resigned to watching him swim away to what would surely be his end amid the hope that it would be less painful than what might otherwise befall him on the island. It was a crude and unwelcome thought, but in light of everything she had seen that night, nothing seemed too perverse, so she let it linger in her head as long as it wished. By the time her partner was up to his waist in the surf, she had already said a silent goodbye, and by the time Paige heard a sharp whistle just above her head, she had already blamed him for cutting their time together even a minute shorter than it should have been. Her grim meditations would've echoed to the mainland and back again if it hadn't been for the sickening thump of the arrow striking Thomas just to the left of his spine, and though his end broke her completely, it was hardly a long way to fall as there was barely a stitch left holding her together as it was.

Thomas fell in one crash of the waves and Paige was glad that it was quick. She found herself alone for the first time since she had left home, and as Patrick and Rowan had already cut their ties and fled, there was no need for strategy and no impetus to think quickly or consider the safety of anybody including herself, so she felt free just to sit by the shore and let the waves bring her Thomas back to her. She stayed with him until she heard the whisper of stealthy footsteps on the gravel behind her, and though Paige knew to whom they belonged, she didn't even turn to acknowledge him.

"Aren't you going to run?" said Finn with his bow in one hand and a clutch of arrows in the other.

"No," was all that Paige could muster in return.

"Are you sure? I would *very* much like you to run."

"I know," said Paige as strangely dignified tears streamed down her cheeks. "Why are you like this?" she said, finally turning to look Finn in his steely eyes.

"Like *this*? Like what?"

"We didn't do anything to you. You didn't even know us before today."

"But I know your *kind*," said the fox, slowly circling Paige until he was standing right in front of her. "It's as if you thought I've never met a human before. Well, I've met plenty. Plenty." She looked up at him with the blankest of stares as if he was speaking some strange tongue. "I've been taken from my home by them. I've been hunted by them. I've been made to dance for them as they thrive off of the fruits of my land and I've seen the last of my kind disappear under their boots. You may not think I know you, but I know you *all* too well. Having *met* you is hardly the point."

Finn crouched down to meet her eye to eye and continued, "I suppose you think I'm twisted . . . ruined by the things I've done. Well, you might be onto something there. I've done worse than what I just did to Thomas in my day, I can promise you that. Maybe I am twisted. Broken. But just between you and me," he offered as he stretched to his feet and his voice faded to a sinister whisper, "I've made my peace with that."

Finn loosed two arrows so quickly that it seemed like the same motion, both of them striking her square in the heart. She took only two more breaths before she passed, her eyes frozen open in surprise and her tears already drying in the ocean breeze, and as she crumbled to the gravel beneath her, Finn thought himself clever for taking the two of them so close to one another. He felt himself the keeper of their nature and a stronger creature for having done so . . . keen as they come and a bellwether breeze among the branches.

"And what of the others?" said a voice from the hill. Finn turned to see Runny limp through the main gate and stop just in front of the entrance. He, of course, had his walking stick to his right as he always did, but tucked under his other arm was a lever action rifle that was gleaming like some surf-polished stone in the low light of the moon. It was a strikingly elegant weapon made of darkly figured wood and blued steel, the action plated with etchings of filigree that were trimmed in gold, and even the stock had a vein of the yellow stuff running up the middle of it like some priceless river. It was a weapon of royal caliber, and though it looked strange in the hands of the old pauper who now carried it, there was also something serendipitous about that disconnect as if the rifle itself didn't care a whit for its own stature. "Where have they gone?" the rabbit continued.

"Scattered," replied Finn, still looking at his catch and drinking in the calm that always came after the final moments of a hunt.

"Hmm. Unfortunate. So, what now?"

"Now we have some proper fun." Finn raised his gaze to meet Runny's, his eyes gilded with the sweet certainty of a fix on the horizon.

"Very well," returned the rabbit. "I shall watch the house while you have your fun." Runny turned and began to hobble back up the drive toward the manor, adding over his shoulder, "Give my regards to the hounds."

The stable was set a few hundred yards to the northwest of the house, and in the shadow of the opulence of the manor, it looked a decidedly modest structure. It was built in typical Tudor style and adorned with almost nothing that wasn't strictly utilitarian—in fact, there was hardly anything on the exterior to take note of at all except for the two A's that were branded onto the front doors and the heavy lock that was looped between their handles. Finn slotted his key inside and the thing fell open with a dull clank, and as he tossed it to the ground and eased open the doors, he recoiled at the fetid stench that escaped from within.

There was no neighing or whinnying or stomping of hooves as Finn entered, and even in the gentle light of his lantern it was clear that there were no bales of hay stashed in the lofts or saddles on hooks waiting for their mounts. There were no stirrups or bits or brushes of any kind adorning the walls, no horseshoes cluttering the corners, and no anvils or hammers with which to shape them . . . and in place of the stalls that would typically have been set along the building's length, there were only cages similar to the two that sat alone in Addington's basement. There were thirteen of them in total—six on each side and the largest one placed against the back doors as if it were seated at the head of the table, and as Finn casually strolled to the center of the space, it became plain that this wasn't a stable for horses at all, but a home for a different sort of beast altogether.

There were five of them left—all housed in their cages along with the bones of the hounds that came before them, ragged and pitiful and hopelessly broken. They were still human in makeup, but it had been a lifetime since any of them had felt that way in spirit, their clothes now nothing but rags and their beards just as knotted as their foul, rotten hair. It had been ages since they had stopped fighting the mites and the lice that flocked to the place in droves for a feast they knew couldn't escape. It had been ages since they stopped fighting anything really, and they wore the countless layers of dirt caked upon their skin like the bark on the trees that stood just outside, that resignation being somehow easier to swallow than the torture of having to peel it away and count the rings inside time and time again.

Finn swung his lantern around to each of their cages, and in turn they all recoiled from the shock of the light and scrambled to the rear of their confines, shielding their faces as the flame flickered off their water bowls, each of which was painted with a name—Queeny, Sir, Rooker, Bishop, and King. "Are you ready to work tonight, rats?!" bellowed the fox, kicking their cages and ringing their bells like cluster bombs, their chorus of awful moans and grotesque clicking sounds landing wholly welcome upon his upturned ears. "Tonight is the most important night of your worthless lives, do you know that? Today is Barley Day, an anniversary of sorts for you all. And on this day, the debt will finally be paid . . . and as it happens, so might yours." The hounds spoke no words, but they whistled in response, the prospect of some fortune shining upon them, however grim, lifting their hobbled spirits.

"Tonight, this all ends. And if you perform as a hound should . . . if you do as I say, you'll never see the inside of these cages again. I'll let you live out your worthless lives here on the isle . . . free to do as you please. But if you don't," he continued, running his knife along Bishop's cage and letting the blade clang off of every iron bar, "if you don't . . . if even one of you runs . . . I'll open you all from end to end and bleed you into your water bowls until there's nothing left. Is that clear?" He looked directly at Bishop who gave a low, agreeable whistle as he ran his hands over the myriad scars that covered his skin and felt them burn as if they were fresh cuts again. "Alright then," he said as he opened the locks on their doors.

The hounds crept out of their cages and stretched themselves and their joints cracked like kettle corn, and although they were all rather slim from their years of captivity, they weren't necessarily gaunt as they had been kept just healthy enough for the purpose they were meant to serve. They looked like five broken things from the same twisted litter as they stood there leery of the lantern's light—all of them bent into the same crooked posture and painted with the same putrid brush. All of them deathly afraid of what may come and rightly calloused by what had already passed.

"Grab your gear," said Finn, nodding to a collection of five wooden spears and a pile of just as many lengths of rope which the hounds slung over their shoulders like sashes. "You can be free rats or dead rats. Choice is yours."

Finn ushered them out of the stables, but as he turned back to close the doors, he gave in to the impulse to take one last look at the cage at the head of the table—the one fronted by the water bowl that read *Finn*. He had been free of it for ages now, but he could still hear the incessant barking of the dogs from dusk till dawn till dusk again. He could still smell their foul breath and feel their dander thick in the air, and even though their bones were strewn about the place and his were not, it didn't seem to make his ears ring any less and it didn't calm his blood from boiling. He would kill them all again if he had the chance. Human or hound, it made little difference to Phineas Fox. They were all rats to him . . . and all the world a maze.

TEN

The wind was beginning to whip and had already turned everyone's cheeks crimson by the time Caroline and Mark noticed that Eamon was no longer running beside them. They had just passed the fallen tree and were making their way back up the coast in a sheer sprint after witnessing the demise of Thomas and Paige at the fox's hands, and when Caroline looked back to see that Eamon had stopped by the broken fence, it seemed that even she could find no room for patience.

"Eamon!" she yelled. "The hell are you doing!? Keep running!"

"Stop," he said, his head turned up at the trees. "We've gotta go back inside."

"What?" huffed Mark as he and Caroline marched back toward their friend until they no longer had to shout to reach him. "Are you out of your mind? We need to keep this fence between that thing and us and that . . . that bear."

"This fence might as well not be here. You think Finn can't climb this? You think Bing can't fight his way through it? You think it'll stop an arrow?"

"We need to keep *running*," Caroline barked. "We need to—"

"We do," Eamon interjected. "But we need to run to the other side of the island." He looked up at the canopy above him and watched the leaves turning belly-up in the breeze. "The wind is blowing in from *this* coast. That means anything on this island can pick up our scent right now, and if we stay near the shore, we're sitting ducks. Nowhere to run when they find us. We need to get in *front* of the wind or it's just a matter of time before we're dead."

"Our scent?" questioned Mark. "He's not a bloodhound, he's a—"

"He's a fox. A predator. And he may not be a bloodhound, but he's not far off." Eamon turned back to his two comrades and closed the distance between them so as to have their full attention. "You guys need to understand the disadvantage we're at here. It's not gonna be light out for a while, and not only can that thing smell us from a mile away and hear us from just as far . . . he can see in the dark. Foxes are nocturnal. I mean, he hit a shot with a bow from god knows how far away . . . in a cross-breeze . . . in the dead of night. Hit Thomas right in the heart. One shot. I can't tell you how impossible that is, but I *can* tell you that if we keep moving along the water like this, we're gonna catch an arrow just like he did." Neither Caroline nor Mark said a word, but the gravity hanging from their brows told Eamon that they understood. "We need to find somewhere to spend the night. Somewhere closer to the west shore and in the morning, once it's light out . . . well, at least we can see him coming. That way we've got half a chance."

"Half a chance at what?" said Mark. "You think we're gonna be able to kill that thing or that . . . that monster of a bear . . . out *here* . . . in the middle of these goddamn woods that they know like the back of their hands?" Eamon didn't even need to verbalize the fact that he didn't know, because it was written on every pore.

"Wait," said Caroline, a light flickering behind her eyes. "There's a lighthouse."

"A lighthouse?" asked Mark rather dubiously.

"On the tip of the island," she exclaimed, sloughing her pack from her shoulders and rummaging around inside until she produced the copy of *Addington's Hollow* she and Eamon had fawned over during their trip across the waters. She flipped through the pages until she found the black-and-white picture of the old lighthouse overlooking the sea, and as she held the book open before the two of them, Eamon's memory caught up to his instinct.

"That's right," he said. "His inspiration for the barley mill. Maybe there's a way to signal somebody or . . . a . . . a radio with a generator. I mean, it's there for emergencies, isn't it? Gotta be *something*."

"Maybe there's a boat," said Mark, chiming in from the sidelines. "Wouldn't they need a way to get out to sea if a ship wrecked?"

"Yeah," Eamon agreed. "Yeah, they would."

"Does it say where it is?"

She skimmed the text before glancing back up at them with a look of disappointment hanging from her face. "No. Just that's it's here somewhere."

"It's gotta be on the north end," said Eamon confidently. "We would've seen it coming over from West Rock if it was anywhere else."

"That makes sense," Caroline replied with a nod.

"So we find somewhere safe to lay low until dawn, then we head for the lighthouse. Unless anybody has a better plan."

"I sure don't," returned Mark. "But if we can't follow the coast, how do we know which way is north?"

Eamon pointed to the sky and traced the shape of a ladle with his finger. "That's the little dipper. Now, see that bright star at the very end of the handle?" That's the North Star. Just gotta follow that."

It was an odd bit of knowledge to have so right and ready, but while Mark was never above poking fun at his friend's eccentricities and the unique history that had bred them, a pall washed over him as he wrestled with the realization that if Eamon's upbringing was truly of value in their current situation, they must be so far off the reservation that they might never find their way back. "Do you really think we'll be able to make it all the way across without running into them again?"

Eamon hesitated for a moment, unsure whether honesty or encouragement was the best remedy, or even if a remedy was in the cards at all, but he had never seen a breath of the world through rose-colored glasses and so he felt there was no good reason to start pretending otherwise. "No," he said. "No, I don't."

Patrick had never seen anybody die before, let alone witness an acquaintance of his be killed in gruesome fashion mere yards in front of his face. It was a particular and potent fuel and it had given his powerful legs license to endure a lengthy sprint during which he heard nothing, felt nothing, and saw nothing but the curtain of the night into which he was fleeing. When he finally stopped somewhere in the middle of the endless black that hovered below the island's canopy of trees, it took him the better part of a minute before he remembered that Rowan had been with him when they left the landing. It was a jarring recollection that brought with it some additional measure of panic, but no matter how intensely he listened, how hard he squinted into the dark, or how loudly he yelled, there was simply no sign of his friend anywhere.

"Rowan!" he screamed, his voice already hoarse with the shame of having left his friend in the dust amid a panic he had no index for. "*Rowan!*" he bellowed, but again there was no answer except the whistle of the wind through the pines. Patrick squatted and held his head in his hands, torn between the desire to find his chum and the searing urgency to fly as far away from danger as his stamina would take him. It was a cowardly conundrum, but he fell victim to it nonetheless, and as he thought himself free of it at the sound of a twig snapping, that hope quickly crumbled when he saw the silhouettes of three strange, ragged men pull themselves from the shadows with spears readied about their hips like forgotten Spartans. Patrick backpedaled to buy himself some time, but with every step he took, they each took one to match him. The moonlight washed over their crusty skin as they crept forward, but with each bit of horrid reveal he began to understand that these were beastly things that meant to savage him, and suddenly there was no longer any decision to be made.

"*Rowan!*" he screamed as he crept backward, glancing side to side to try and put an eye on his exit. "If you can hear me, I need you to run away from my voice as fast as you can!" The hounds shared a glance and Sir quickly peeled off and disappeared back into the shadows as Patrick understood that his warning may have done his pal more harm than good. "*Rowan, run!*" Queeny and Rooker hunched their backs and thrust their spears in front of them, the former slowly circling to Patrick's left and the latter to his right, and when they stepped in to make their move, he made himself a promise that he would come back. A promise that he would find his friend again. And as the salve of that oath cooled his shame and set his mind at ease, he dug the balls of his feet into the earth and prepared himself to be hunted.

"Well, this is *just* delicious," said Runny as he dipped his spoon into his glass for another helping of trifle. He and Flackwell were sitting in a pair of rocking chairs on the patio, enjoying dessert while keeping an eye on the manor and feeling rather fine about the whole situation despite the spectacles they had witnessed earlier in the night. The rabbit's rifle was laid across his lap and a rather menacing looking slingshot, which belonged to the frog, was resting on the little table between them along with an expensive bottle of champagne that seemed as if it had long been waiting for the right celebration to be of use. "And you know, it's not even the berries that make it—it's the crème. What did you put in it this time?"

"Cardamom," said Flackwell proudly. "Really gives it some body, don't you agree?"

"I do agree. It's *just* lovely. And, you know, the ladyfingers aren't even a whisper soggy."

"I candied them in caramel. That way, they can sit and aren't at all the worse for wear."

"You . . . are a genius, have I told you that, lately?"

"As a matter of fact, you haven't, but that doesn't mean I don't love hearing it," said Flack, polishing off a heaping spoonful of his own. "I'm just glad you're enjoying yourself." They both seemed to be of more chipper disposition now that the hunt was in the hands of their comrades, a welcome shift that allowed them license to relax a bit and enjoy the peace of the night for what it was. "What shall we do when this is all over, eh? What say you? When the debt is paid, you know?"

Runny scraped the bottom of his glass for the final bit of cream and berries and made a show of savoring the last of his dessert before setting it down and propping his good leg up on his viola case. "Well, I should think we retire to the forest on the north side of the isle. Build ourselves a little home in the middle of nowhere. Somewhere we can't be found."

"Yes, yes," replied Flackwell agreeably, "somewhere past the lake . . . near the rye patch perhaps."

"Yes, the rye patch! Near the forest and the water. The best of both worlds."

"I shall miss this kitchen very much, I must admit."

"And I shall miss the food, but there is something to be said for a meal cooked over an open fire and the fruits of an endless garden."

"I'm certain we can rummage up enough stone to build an oven and there's no rule saying we can't take a pot or two with us, now is there?" said the frog as he dug his pipe from his pocket and jammed it full of twisted greens.

"No rule at all," Runny concurred. "I'm sure Finn will be over the moon to have the house to himself. More room for him to brood."

"Oh my yes. *Plenty* of brooding space." They shared a chuckle as Flackwell's gears began to turn and his gaze wandered off into the distance. "Maybe we'll bring a few knives, as well. A large whisk and a small one. We'll need a spatula . . . oh, and an oyster shucker, a zester, a hearty set of tongs, a garlic press, a—"

A wild snort from behind them cut short the frog's musings and they both turned to see Bing lumbering out from the ballroom with hammer in hand. "Bing, old boy! I would've expected to see some blood on that hammer of yours at this point in the night. What seems to be the hold up?" questioned Runny. The great bear, of course, gave no answer. Instead, he snatched the bottle of champagne from the table, broke the neck clean off with the head of his bludgeon and went about emptying the perfectly aged bubbly down his monstrous gullet.

"I've been saving that for decades," said Flackwell with real contempt.

"Yes, how . . . brutish and unexpected," added Runny with a roll of his eyes. But Bing cared not a whit, wiping his maw with the back of his hand and throwing the empty bottle clear into the woods. And as if the woods were keen on answering back, a sharp whistle in the distance split the late evening silence. "Well, it seems the hounds are out and about."

"Awful things."

"Quite," said Runny as he opened his viola case. "Who needs champagne tonight, anyway? I believe it was Napoleon who said, 'In victory, one deserves it . . . in defeat, one needs it.'" He set the fiddle under his chin and began to tap a thumping rhythm on the slate with his wooden leg, adding, "Allow me to play you out, old friend. Happy hunting."

The first few soulful bars of *Bonaparte's Retreat* cut a smile across Flackwell's face, though it was quickly hidden by a thick cloud of smoke. "Who needs it, indeed," crowed the frog, sinking back into his chair and allowing himself to melt into the song's graceful melody as if the night was nothing but warm and sweet and free of the things he knew it all too well to carry. It was a dishonest and guilt-laden bliss, but it was bliss nonetheless. And no matter how temporary and how perverse Flackwell knew it to be, he was determined to enjoy it until he could enjoy it no more, for though the night was lovely and lithe from his place on the patio, he was certain that elsewhere it was dark as death itself.

Binghamton Bear would never have been confused for nimble, but that didn't mean he wasn't fast. Once he had picked up a full head of steam, he flashed across the isle like a hurricane, and it wasn't long before he came upon Sir who was standing by the trunk of a tall spruce with his spear at the ready and his length of rope uncoiled on the ground. It looked as if he was guarding something, though there was nobody else in sight, and when the bear stepped toward him, Sir thrust his weapon in his direction and gave a horrid, garbled scream in a meager attempt to ward him off. But Bing was no stranger to challenges of dominance, and when he opened his jaws and roared war in the hound's face, the pitiful thing's knees buckled and his spear shook and even the lice that clouded his skin quivered in terror. But death's role as certain scapegrace was less harrowing to Sir who had seen his life stripped away time and time again, and so despite the devil bellowing in his ear and serendipity proving itself absent as ever, he stood his ground. Bing thought him a dog with a bone freshly buried. He thought him mad with possession and irrational, and while he couldn't quite put his paw on what the prize was, the sour smell of urine wafting down from the treetops gave the game away with the next kick of wind.

Thirty feet above the ground, Rowan was certain that he had seen his last sunset. The moment that thought had entered his mind with any real gravity was the same moment his body lost the will to hold back its fluids for the proper time and place, and soon his jeans were soaked through and his face was glistening with tears and spittle. He had never held anything so tightly as that tree, and while his eyes refused to look down at whatever terrors were unfolding below, it was his ears that betrayed him . . . and at the sound of Bing's war cry, he began to sob uncontrollably in the way that the true prospect of the end moves a man to pieces. He tried to focus on anything but the inevitability of his circumstance—the sandpaper scratch of the bark on his fingers, the sweet smell of sap, the boyish freedom of being up in the wind without anything resembling a tether—but it all seemed so moot. His thoughts soon drifted to his greatest regrets, and there was none more searing than his decision to come to the isle to chase Addington's ghost with his best mate in tow. It was as innocent a decision as either of them had ever made as there was nothing even resembling a reason for the pair to have been cautious or canny or otherwise vigilant, and that, in a way, made it all the more painful.

Bing raised his great hand and pointed a finger into the distance as if to give Sir one last chance to abandon his post, but the hound knew what awaited him if he failed, and so he gave one last desperate whistle just before the brute's hammer flashed across the night and struck him clean in the chest. Sir crashed against the tree and fell to the ground limp and breathless, and as if Bing was relieving himself of some bothersome louse, he grabbed him by the heel and flung him a dozen yards into the shadows, leaving nothing between him and his prize but thirty feet of spruce. The next thing Rowan expected to hear was the scraping of the bear's claws as he scaled the tree, but the silence that followed proved equally as terrifying, and just as he opened his eyes to see if by some miracle the great builder brute had left him be . . . Rowan felt his whole world quake.

Bing's shoulder hit the tree like a freight train, rattling Rowan's bones and breaking several of his teeth which were clenched together so tightly that they were chattering from the sheer force of his own bite. At the next impact, he heard the trunk begin to fracture, and at the unmistakable crack of splintering wood, he cried out into the night for a savior he knew wasn't coming. "*Patrick!*" he yelled as the bear rammed the evergreen again and again, the creaking of the spruce buckling under the pressure growing more and more desperate with each strike. Rowan knew it was almost over when he felt himself begin to lean, and though he could picture the tree tilting toward the ground with terrifying clarity in his mind's eye, he refused to look as the distance of that ignorance still offered a whisper of hope. But there would be no divine intervention, and as the thundercrack of the spruce giving way echoed through the forest, Rowan could only hold on for dear life . . . and call out for his friend one last time.

The pain was incomprehensible. It was a feeling he had no baseline for, and when he finally opened his eyes upon hitting the ground, Rowan could see nothing but bright white light and hear nothing but his own desperate gasps for air as his punctured lungs refused their charge. Bing grunted as he lifted the tree and put it aside to free his quarry from its crush, but even without its weight on his chest, there was no reprieve from its legacy. The brute waited until he saw Rowan's eyes pull themselves back into focus amid a rush of deathbed adrenaline, and even though he hadn't the wind to speak, the beast imagined the desperate pleas that his prey otherwise would've made for his survival. It did Bing good to hear them even if they weren't real, and he took a blessed comfort in knowing that the last thing Rowan ever saw before he was taken in pieces from the world . . . was the sincere, brawny smile wrapped around his maw.

ELEVEN

"Where are we?" whispered Mark as they hurried through the woods. They had been on the run for some miles now, all the while being careful to keep a low profile and stay inside the edges of the shadows as best they could.

"Almost halfway across, I think," Eamon replied.

"And that's . . . that's good, right?"

"It's better than being where we were," said Eamon, slowing to a trot and checking which way the trees were swaying to make sure they were still ahead of the wind. Mark and Caroline followed his lead and throttled back, happy to take a few moments to regain their breath.

"Do you think the rest of them are dead? The others?" asked Mark.

"I think it's best if we assume it's just us now," replied Caroline. "Won't do us any good to wait for help that's not coming."

"She's right. Even if they're not dead, it's not like they're gonna be looking out for *us* at this point." Eamon tried to get a peek at the stars to try and affirm that they were still heading due west, but the canopy above them was thick and a scattering of clouds had started to roll in from the sea. "I need to get a better look at the sky," he said, nodding toward a hill just past the edge of the forest they were skirting. The cloud cover seemed to be growing thicker by the moment, and even once they were atop the knoll, it was difficult for Eamon to parse whether or not they were on course. "Guess we'll just have to trust the wind," he said with an air of resignation. "Doesn't seem like it's shifted much, right?"

"You're asking *me*?" scoffed Mark as something in the distance piqued his attention. "Wait. Is that . . . who is that?" He pointed to a dark figure who was traipsing along the ridge of the next prominence, and while it was hard to make out any details in the low light, it was clear from his gait that he was human.

"Is that . . . Patrick?" asked Caroline, squinting into the night.

"Looks like him. I wonder what happened to his friend, uh . . ."

"Rowan," chirped Eamon. "His name's Rowan."

Mark waited until the silhouette turned in their direction to throw a wave his way, and to his delight, the shadow waved back. "He's coming over," he said, happy to have a firm enough grasp on what was happening to justifiably narrate. The stranger started down the hill, but it wasn't long before his jaunt turned into a purposeful sprint, and once the night sky had deigned that a little moonlight should be allowed through, the three of them noticed that his hair was long and his face was covered in a heavy beard . . . and whatever he was holding was being cradled like a weapon.

"Wait, who is that?" asked Mark, his voice beginning to tremble.

"Run," said Eamon as the stranger put his fingers to his mouth and loosed a sharp whistle.

"What . . . what . . ." stammered Mark.

"*Run!*" Eamon shouted, this time loud enough that there would be no mistaking his intentions. They turned on their heels and dashed back toward the woods, but as they neared the bottom of the knoll, another strange figure emerged from the trees with spear in hand and a savage gleam in his eye. He, too, gave a whistle that rattled their eardrums, and thinking he might be signaling to even more of his kind, Eamon felt it wise to abandon the tree line altogether. "This way!" he yelled as he pivoted, leading Caroline and Mark further out into the grasslands, and as they crested the top of the next rise in the earth, Eamon glanced back over his shoulder to see that both of their pursuers were splitting out to their flanks like two sheepdogs trying to corral a herd.

King's strides were long and athletic and inarguably graceful, and while Bishop's gait wasn't nearly as fluid, there was a tenacity in his carriage that spoke volumes about his nature—something vitriolic in the way his soles slapped the dirt that made each scar stitched across his body a thing to fear rather than a thing to pity. But even though both hounds looked capable of overtaking them, neither seemed very keen on moving in for the kill, and whereas that might have been a relief to most, to Eamon, it was only a sign of things to come.

"They're keeping us in the open," he said, doing his best to stay at a dead sprint.

"What?" huffed Mark, his big chest heaving and his face flushed.

"Cover. We need . . . to find cover." Caroline was the first to top the next hill, and when she stopped and pointed toward something in the distance, she barely had enough time to raise her finger before Eamon's ears picked up a wheezing in the wind. He surged toward her and hit her with his shoulder, knocking his friend to the ground and sending them both tumbling down the hill with their arms entangled and their spirits bruising a deeper shade of purple with every lick from the earth. When they finally rolled to a stop, they turned to see Mark looming over the spot where they had been standing, and as they watched him stoop down to pluck an arrow from the ground, Eamon was shattered to see that his instincts were as keen as he feared.

"*Don't stop!*" yelled Eamon. Mark heard the whistle of another bolt echo about the little valley, but before it could split him, he heeded his friend's advice and rumbled down the hill, scooping Eamon and Caroline from the ground mid-step. Their impulse was to zig, but the hounds were within a few strides of their heels, and they knew that if they were overtaken it would certainly mean their end, so they thundered straight ahead in a mad dash for the cover at which Caroline had been pointing—the hedge maze.

Eamon could hear the arrows edging nearer to their mark with each shot, and knowing the fox was dangerously close to dialing in his aim, he was certain it was only a matter of a few more strides before one of them found themselves on the wrong end of a broadhead. His legs were burning and his teeth were grinding each other to dust as the entrance to the maze drew near, but the shriek of Finn's missiles was motivation enough for him to draw level with Caroline in a final push for safety. Eamon kicked and kicked and bled his battered body for all the stamina it had left, and just as he felt his legs begin to seize and his wind set fire to his lungs, he heard Finn's final shot ripple the night and knew it was meant squarely for him. It was an act of pure desperation when Eamon left his feet, but these were desperate moments and little else mattered but the cover of the hedges . . . and though validation was of no concern as he threw himself through the air, he felt it through and through when the fletching of the fox's arrow tickled the nape of his neck just before he hit the ground.

The hounds slowed to a trot outside the entrance to the labyrinth, both of them huffing in exhaustion, and not a moment after Bishop looked to King for some direction, they were heeled by a sharp whistle as Finn stepped out of the tree line. They bounded up the hill to greet him as the fox gazed out over the hedges with utter distain and compulsively stroked the knife in his belt as if he wanted to cut every last vine, bush, and thistle to ribbons. "You just *had* to chase them into that bloody maze, didn't you?!" he said as he leered at King. "I suppose it's my fault . . . leaving you to your own devices like that. Useless rats."

The two of them shared a look of displeasure that was pointed enough to raise Finn's eyebrows and he drew his blade to let the moonlight glint off the edge just so. "Something you need to say? Go on then, spit it out!" But there would be no further protest from King nor Bishop as they hung their heads in a show of fealty, knowing all too well that any disobedience would surely mean their death. "That's what I thought. Now go flush them out. Leave the little one alive and do what you must with the other two."

"You guys okay?" asked Eamon as he and the others wound their way through the knot of hedges.

"What the hell *were* those things?!" said Mark, barely able to gather enough breath to speak.

"I don't know, they were like—"

"Feral or something," added Caroline as she felt something wet on her cheek and wiped it away to see fresh blood running down her finger.

"Your face," Mark lamented, gently grabbing her chin and finding a surprisingly clean cut running from her ear to her nose. "Looks like he got you pretty good."

"I didn't even feel it," she said. Mark gathered a handful of his shirt to wipe her face, but she was having none of it. "Later. We can't stay here."

"What direction was the arrow pointing? The one you picked up?" Eamon asked.

"That way," Mark replied after some consideration, pointing north.

"Then that's the way we go. Better to keep this maze between us and him if we want a chance of getting out of here. It'll give us a head start anyway."

Mark added his approval with a nod, and without further debate they hurried past the chess boards and the bamboo cage and carefully waded through the slew of champagne flutes, wine bottles, and cigarette filters that littered the ground. They were halfway through to the other side when Eamon heard a rustling in the hedges and knew it was something other than the wind whistling between the vines . . . something accompanied by the soft crush of grass under foot and the subtle rustle of cloth.

"Stop," he whispered, holding his arms out to freeze his friends in place. In short order, they heard the shuffling too, but it was only another heartbeat before it stopped, and soon there was only the silence of apprehension to needle their senses. They were all so fraught with trepidation that none of them even dared to breathe, and it wasn't until Mark finally opened his mouth to drink some air that a spear flashed through the hedge and stuck him square in the thigh. He growled in pain as he felt the steel tip burn his flesh, but he was still keen enough to grab the hilt with both hands before whomever was wielding the thing could pull it back. He unstuck it from his leg and blood streamed down his haunches, but still he kept an iron grip on the handle and did his best to match the dogged determination of whichever hound was trying to rip their weapon free. Caroline and Eamon both sprang to action, splitting off in opposite directions to try and find their way around to the other side, but as soon as they left Mark's company, a rope fell over the hedge and quickly found its way around his neck. The sturdy loop of twine closed around his throat and pulled him back against the thistles, and finding himself suddenly alone in a vicious battle for his very life, Mark had little choice but to let go of the spear and fight to keep his air.

Eamon slinked through the labyrinth's sinewy corridors and darted around corner after corner, but as he made the turn that he was sure would put him on the other side of Mark, the butt of a spear flashed through the darkness and struck him in the face, shattering his nose and sending him hard to the ground. It was difficult to see and nigh impossible to breathe with his sinuses full of blood, but there was a part of him that was glad he couldn't fully witness Bishop standing over him with both ends of his weapon now wet with crimson. The hound spit on the earth as he began to walk away, and while Eamon was relieved to see him depart, the thought of one of his friends being the first to die struck such a sour chord in his heart that he lashed out and dragged Bishop to the dirt by his ankle.

The maze was proving difficult for Caroline to navigate in the midst of her understandable panic, and after a series of wrong turns and dead ends, she wasn't even sure if she was heading in the right direction at all anymore. "Eamon!" she yelled, but there was no answer. "*Eamon!*" she screamed again, but nobody called back. "*Mark!*" she bellowed at the very top of her lungs, but the silence she received in return led her to fear the worst. She abandoned her plan and backtracked to where she had started, but to her horror, she arrived just in time to see Mark being pulled through the wall by King, the rope now wrapped around his neck several times over and his face an alarming shade of purple. Mark struggled to wedge his fingers under the sturdy twine, but the whole of King's weight was now leaning on the other end, and as they fell to the earth and the hound gave the rope one last mighty tug, Mark's body went limp and his hands fell motionless at his side.

Bishop's rage flooded his allegiance as he hit the dirt. Shirking Finn's request, he blindly swung to plunge his spear into any piece of his prey he could find, but Eamon mounted him with surprising speed, and as he held the hound's weapon at bay, he rained fist after fist down upon his head. Eamon was unhinged, and with blood pouring from his nose and his vision blurred, he grew just as savage as his enemy as he growled and roared with every gust of his will, but Bishop was no stranger to struggle, and in a flash, he let go of his weapon and plunged his thumb deep into Eamon's eye. The world went white and Eamon howled in pain. He collapsed to the earth and immediately felt Bishop's weight on top of him, the thing wasting no time in jamming his horrid digit deeper into Eamon's skull.

There was nowhere for Eamon to go now—firmly locked against the dirt in a struggle for his very life as the beast on his chest snarled and screamed and refused to relent. He tried with every piece of himself to wrest control of the hound's arm, but his efforts seemed entirely hopeless until his flailing feet brushed up against something glassy and unnatural. He began to shift his hips, turning the pair of them like two embattled hands of a clock until he spied an empty champagne bottle settled under the hedge out of the corner of his good eye. A beacon in the darkness. Eamon knew it would be a gamble, but fearing the fight for his vision was already lost, he released Bishop's wrist, wrapped his fingers around the neck of the thing, and crunched the bottle against his attacker's skull.

The hound let loose a terrifying scream as the glass exploded over his temple and Eamon soon felt the peculiar warmth of another being's blood cascading down his face. He found his chest suddenly free of Bishop's weight and crawled to his knees, blindly slashing into the night with the jagged edge of the bottle in hopes of feeling it drag along the beast's grimy skin or sever something vital inside him. But after an eternity of lashing out at the shadows, Eamon could find nothing into which to sink his glassy teeth and stumbled to his feet, drained some blood from his eye, and coughed up a mouthful of red horror. The world around him began to come back into focus, and to his surprise, he found himself alone amongst the hedges . . . rightly exhausted, newly scarred, and unsure if he had just tasted victory or defeat.

King stood over Mark's breathless body and raised his spear to finish the fight, but as his muscles fired to loose his weapon, Caroline leaped through the hole they had left in the hedge and threw herself on the hound's back, wrapping her arms around his neck and squeezing as she had seen him do to her partner. King flailed as he tried to fling her from his shoulders, but she was resolute and plenty strong, and with every attempt to buck her, Caroline only squeezed tighter until she could feel his windpipe flex against her forearm. He backed her up against the thistles in the hope that the thorns would come to his aid, but they proved themselves a useless ally, and as he grabbed her hair by the fistful and tried to wrench her from his being, he could see little but her grit shining in the low light of the moon.

It was a welcome shock when Mark's eyes fluttered open and he drew the first of several savage breaths. He rolled about the ground in a haze of confusion, completely unaware of where he was or what was happening around him, and while Caroline was plenty relieved to see her partner alive and well, King was just as pleased to see him kicking for entirely different reasons. With his air supply waning and Caroline still wrapped about his neck, the hound saw an opportunity to force her to choose her fight and centered himself over the still-struggling Mark. He was well stuck and knew it, and as he felt his lungs begin to burn between hopeless gasps for a decent gulp of wind, it took every bit of strength that King could summon just to raise his spear as he looked to deliver Mark a bitter end.

"*No!*" screamed Caroline as she grabbed for the hound's weapon, throwing them both off-kilter and sending the pair stumbling to the ground. There was a scrap for the spear once they hit the earth, but King had regained enough of his wind to fight her doggedness with his size, and after a series of elbows to her face, he was free to wield his pike as he pleased.

He felt sorry for her, lying there in the grass and writhing in pain and wondering if she would ever see home again . . . for he was there once too. But that was so far in the past and there were so many callouses between that feeling and his yearning to be free again that he could barely even feel it burn anymore. He could barely even feel the sting of captivity or the ingrace of servitude anymore. Truly, King could barely feel *anything* anymore, which is why he registered a distinct and euphoric gratitude for the sensation of his own effluence warming his grimy skin as he postured to run Caroline through. And by the time he looked to see Eamon twisting the broken champagne bottle into his side, he was so wistful for the normalcy of pain that he couldn't imagine wanting anything else at all . . . and there in the darkness bred by a maze not of his own choosing, King sat down in the dirt to relish it.

Eamon pulled Caroline into his arms and asked her, "Are you okay?" She nodded and wiped her face, and when Eamon left to tend to Mark, Caroline plucked King's pike from the ground and stood over him as he had so recently done to her. She tried to make sense of his distant gaze and the ecstasy that seemed to be blooming through his being as he was being bled, and for just a moment she thought that she even saw him smile through it all. It was a big, brilliant grin that he flashed at the night around him, and save for the rot in his gums and the holes in his teeth, it would've been welcomed by them all under any other circumstance.

It was Mark who first noticed Bishop's form emerging from the shadows, and though he didn't yet have the strength to speak, he managed to gather himself enough to point at the ragged figure standing at the end of the corridor. His head was caked with blood, his eye was cut open, and his ear was hanging from his scalp by a thread, but his grip on his weapon was still strong . . . and his rage was still unquieted. He charged the three of them, screaming as he ran with his pike readied for war, and while Eamon and Mark were caught on the ground with little recourse, Caroline let her reflexes speak to her will to survive. She growled as she loosed King's spear through the darkness, her arm in perfect rhythm with her hips and her leg balancing her form just so as she followed through, and before the hound could even take another step, he found himself impaled by his comrade's pike and fell hopeless and defeated to the earth.

Finn had grown so impatient from his spot on the hill that by the time he heard King trumpet a desperate whistle from the labyrinth's depths, he was already several steps toward the entrance. But the fox wanted no part of parroting the ritzy revelers that had spent so many hours wandering the maze's twists and turns, so instead he scurried up the outer wall and bounded across the tops of the hedges like the gifted hunter he was. His bow was drawn at the ready, and as he swept his broadhead over each shadowy corridor that appeared beneath him, he was more than prepared to dispense with the theatrics and loose an arrow or three straight into somebody's heart. He neared the source of the whistle and pulled his bowstring taught, but to his dismay, the only humans he found within the knot of vines were King and Bishop who looked like two halves of the same foul and bloody mess.

King had torn his shirt to ribbons and tied it around his midsection to stem the flow from his wound, and while he seemed lucid enough, Bishop, who was curled up in the dirt with a pike still lodged in his gut, was struggling to hold on to what he had learned to call a life. King looked up at the fox with tears in his eyes as Finn hopped down from the hedge top, shaking his head in exasperation and sighing a disconcerted sigh as he slung his bow back over his shoulder.

"Did you let them do this to your friend?" asked Finn as he crouched over Bishop. "With *your* spear, no less? For *shame.*" King's embarrassment was as palpable as his anguish, and though he was clearly heartbroken to see his friend in such pain, Finn offered him no quarter. "Worthless cur. Have you said your goodbyes?" he asked as King gave a solemn nod. "Very well." The fox grabbed a hold of the pike when he saw King turn his head toward the hedge. "Don't you dare turn away, you hear me!? You let this happen, now you watch it end." The hound knew he had no choice but to obey, and with a profound despondence, he righted his gaze and watched Finn pull the pike from Bishop's gut in a torrent of blood and bile. He let out a low, ghastly growl as the fox rolled him onto his back, and even in the haze of his final moments,

Bishop seemed to know what was coming. The hound barely flinched as the slick obsidian blade pierced his neck just above his shoulder, and as it slid through his musculature and severed his life with ease, his last gasp seemed more like a sigh of relief than an expression of pain. Finn wiped his knife on the grass and slid it back into his belt, and after the deed was done and Bishop was dispatched, he stood and took his bow from his shoulder once again. "You should have done that yourself," he said to King. "A better friend wouldn't have let him suffer."

King began to gather Bishop up in his arms when Finn made his objection known. "Leave him be. He's not going anywhere, I promise you. We have work yet to do and you owe me a hound, wouldn't you agree?" But King did not agree, and as he hoisted his dead friend onto his shoulder, the despair on his face was so thick that Finn thought he might prove more of an anchor than a rudder and made a rare concession. "Fine. Go find some hole to throw him in. I'll deal with you later." And with that, the fox scampered up the hedge and leaped to the top of the bamboo cage, and while he saw no trace of Eamon, Mark, or Caroline anywhere, he caught a shift of the wind and turned his nose to the sky . . . and felt the spirit might finally be smiling down upon him.

It was only when they arrived at the river that Mark noticed the tears streaming down Caroline's face. "Stop," he said as Eamon began to wade across the water.

"We can't stop. The wind's changed. If we stop, we'll—"

"*Stop!*" bellowed Mark, unafraid of being heard. He took Caroline's chin in his hand and studied her face. It was bloodied from Finn's arrow and swollen from her tussle with King, and it didn't take more than a glance before he too began to cry. They were dignified tears, but they spoke volumes of their circumstance, and without a word between them, he drew her into his chest and let her sob without the pretense of having to appear stronger than she was.

It was a brief exercise, but it was necessary for them to be free to focus on the task at hand, and as Eamon waded out of the river, all he could think to say was, "Where'd you learn to throw that thing like that?"

Caroline wiped her eyes and even chuckled under her breath a bit. "I don't know," she said. "Felt like a javelin when I picked it up, I guess. How's your nose?"

"I'll let you know when I can feel it again," replied Eamon.

"That eye doesn't look so hot either."

"Yeah, well, it's not all that bad. Looks like I've got *four* of you with me, so at least we've got numbers on our side now," he said as he rubbed his grotesquely swollen socket.

"Do you think there's more of those things?" asked Mark. "The wild ones with the beards and—"

"And no tongues?" added Eamon.

"No *what?*" said Caroline with a bend of her brow.

"They had their tongues cut out. I saw it when he was on top of me. That's why they were whistling the whole time. And I don't know if there's more of them, but if we wait here any longer, we're probably gonna find out."

"Well, where do we go?" said Caroline. "I mean, if we can't stay here, then—"

"I don't know," he answered. "The wind is coming from the north now."

"And that means . . ."

"That means . . . that assuming he's faster than we are, one of us is gonna catch an arrow in the back regardless of how far we run."

"So, we stay here and fight," said Mark. "There's three of us and it sounds like it's gonna happen no matter what so . . . we fight. Right?"

"I've only got one good eye and you've got a hole in your leg . . . and he's got a long-range weapon and knows how to use it." Caroline touched the gash in her cheek at the reminder of how close she had come to tasting one of Finn's broadheads. "We won't even see it coming before it's over. Not an option. Not now, anyway."

Caroline turned to the water, grateful for a few moments to watch the river bubble by and center herself amid the sound of the current cresting the rocks. "Might as well leave this here," she said, slipping the backpack from her shoulders. "Just dead weight at this point." She set her pack on the ground and took from it the paperback copy of *Winterset Hollow* she had brought with her. It was old and yellowed and dogeared again and again, and as she turned it over in her hands and weighed the merits of leaving it behind, it was clear that it held some gravity that neither Mark nor Eamon was aware of.

"Do you really need to take that with you?" Mark asked as delicately as he could. But there was no answer as she flipped through the pages . . . there was only reticence and the pain of a decision she thought she'd never have to make.

"Hold on," said Eamon, the glimmer of an idea washing over him. "Let me see your pack."

Caroline shrugged as she handed over the satchel. "There's nothing in there but a blanket and my—"

"I know," he said as he rummaged around inside before unrolling the blanket along the ground. Eamon found a stick nearby and used it to punch a hole in the quilt, digging his finger into the puncture and tearing a narrow but lengthy section of fabric free. "Use this to bandage yourself up," he said, tossing the scrap to Mark whose leg was still bleeding through his clothing. "And I'm gonna need half your pants."

"Half my what?"

"The bloody half," he said as he took off his jacket and began to unbutton his overshirt. "And make it quick. We don't have much time."

By the time Finn had his legs underneath him and his muzzle in the wind, he had all but forgotten about his frustrations with his hounds. There was something about a hunt that behooved him to narrow his focus and block out the usual distractions that would otherwise peck at his nature and that, just as much as anything else, was why he cherished these nights, few and far between as they had become. He was driven by a rage he could never seem to quench and a history that still made him weep, and as much as he still used these things to fuel his survival even all these years later, that didn't keep him from feeling useless most days. He had become well tired of sitting in that cavernous house, listening to Runny and the frog babble on like fishwives and playing games he had grown bored of half a century ago. It was only when he was on a trail that he felt truly useful. It was only with his bow in his left hand and his bolts in his right that he still felt like he belonged . . . and it was that sentiment that always made the kill pointedly bittersweet.

He chuckled to himself when he hit the river, waved his nose in the breeze, and pegged his prey's position as half a mile or so downstream. Finn was ever amused by the comfort that water seemed to give humans on the wrong end of a hunt, as he had all but lost count of the number of witless sapiens he had found scurrying down the river's bank or traipsing along the coastline throughout the years. He imagined there was something about the life of the current that made them feel less alone, but as a tracker born and bred, he knew that to be folly as water cools the air around it and heavy air holds a scent even in the face of a stiff wind.

His poise was unshakeable as he darted through the trees that flanked the shore, being careful to stay within the shadows and keep his bow just below level so it was only a flick of the wrist away from being true to a target. He felt utterly in control as their scent grew stronger, for he knew there was no way that a group of three so injured and exhausted could possibly outpace him in his element. He knew it was just a matter of time. Just a matter of staying his focus and keeping his senses sharp. Just a matter of the formality of pursuit before he had them in his sights. Before the debt was paid.

Finn could tell they were moving with the current as their scents shifted direction when he approached the big bend the water had carved in the earth—a rough-and-tumble section where the rapids broke heavy against the rocks. And thinking it wise to try and catch them in a spot where it would be impossible to hear him coming, he leaned into a run and headed for an outcropping not more than a hundred yards ahead to cut them off at the pass. He could almost see them running along the shore while looking back over their shoulders every few moments, wary of what was behind every tree and around every corner but never thinking to look up. Never thinking to look above them on the bluff where he would be waiting.

When Finn arrived at the overlook, he couldn't find their scent and knew he had beaten them to the spot, and so there was little to do but wait for the sound of stones crunching beneath their feet and the tell of fearful whispers leaking from their mouths. He crawled into the brush, nocked his truest broadhead, and watched the waters below with a sure and steady focus, but after a parade of expectant moments, there were no footsteps at all. There was only the rush of the rapids and the creak of the trees, and as the sound of nothing began to grate on his nerves harshly enough for him to scamper down to have a look upstream, the only thing Finn saw was a backpack being carried along by the current. It floated toward him and caromed off a rock, eventually coming to rest in the eddy just below where he was standing, and though he couldn't yet see what it held, he already knew what he would find inside . . . for he could smell the peaches and lavender clear as day.

The pack was punched full of holes like a sponge, and as the fox emptied its contents onto the shoreline, he felt like a terminal fool for underestimating his quarry. "Clever little runt," he said as he looked over the items at his feet—a swath of bloody jeans, an overshirt stained red with the stuff of life, and half a blanket covered in Caroline's hand crème. Finn had no sooner cursed himself for being so brash when the skies opened up with a thunderclap and a flash of fire, and in a matter of moments he was soaked from head to toe with the feeling that on that night, he had lost and they had won. The feeling that on that night, he was but a shell of a fox . . . and they were the rarest rabbits.

TWELVE

The rains had driven Flackwell and Runny inside, and as they sat at the ballroom bar sharing a decidedly less expensive bottle of champagne and waxing poetic about their future, they barely even paid a glance to the three bodies that were lined up on the dance floor. Paige, Thomas, and Percy had all turned a ghastly shade of pale yellow and were stiffening by the moment, and though they were but a stone's throw away from their former hosts, anyone within earshot would have been hard-pressed to guess as much from the timbre of their conversation.

"I have half a mind not to clean any of it up at all," said the frog between sips. "We won't be here forever and those two will have to learn to look after themselves sooner or later. I do hate the place looking a mess, though. Rubs my more obsessive proclivities the wrong way, you know."

"Yes, well . . . do yourself a favor and don't go into the tearoom then."

"Why? What happened in the tearoom!? You know what? I don't care. See, this is me not caring about what happened in the tearoom . . . to all the vintage matching services . . . that I love so much." He smiled a disingenuous smile and clumsily fumbled his pipe from his pocket to find it already packed. He struck a match and puffed it to life but could only pretend to be unaffected for so long before his act wore thin. "Okay, I need to know what happened in the tearoom."

Finn stomped through the patio doors a sopping wet mess. He breezed past Runny and Flack without a word before hopping over the bar and refilling his flask with a fresh batch of nectar, downing whatever was left in the bottle with one long swig before unceremoniously throwing it in the bin.

"You seem . . . less than enthused," said the rabbit.

"And wet. You seem wet," added Flackwell.

"Rain has a way of doing that to a fox."

"I see you've returned unburdened," the frog continued. "Did you leave them out in the storm?"

"Them?"

"Yes, them. The bodies. The dead ones. The deceased. You know."

Finn dabbed at his face with a bar towel and wrung it dry over the basin. "The little one and his friends are more cunning than I had given them credit for. We leave tomorrow at first light."

"We?" asked Runny with a flick of his brow.

"First light?" added the frog.

"Yes, we. As much as I hate to admit it, I believe I'll need the bear for this. And you two as well."

"I . . . I . . . I'm not sure we're really in any shape for a proper hunt," blustered the rabbit as he and Flackwell shared a furtive glance. "It's just that . . . it's been so long and I—"

"It's just like riding a bike, except bloodier," Finn mused. "Besides, after it's over, the debt will be paid in full. Fitting that we all go out together, no?" It was a question that required no answer as there was really no decision to be made once it had been asked, but Finn paused for one to drive the point home before continuing, "Is your rifle in working order?"

Runny hoisted his gun from his side and laid it on the bar top, patting the action with his hand. "Far as I know."

"And what about my sling?" asked Flackwell, feeling a bit left out. "You . . . you'll need that too, no?" The frog received nothing but a blank stare in return, but he could only stand to be unappreciated for so long. "It's a fine weapon, you know. Just as accurate as any firearm and completely silent. And in the olden days, it was prized for its—"

"What is that noise?" asked the fox with a cock of his head and a twitch of his ear. Neither Runny nor the frog heard a thing, but as they shrugged off his suggestion, Finn leapt from behind the bar and trotted over to the dining room to investigate, sticking his head just inside the door to have a look around.

"What is it?" yelled the rabbit.

"Nothing. Just the house settling. Anyway, enjoy your drinks. Like I said, we leave at first light." Finn slipped inside the entrance and pulled the doors shut behind him, but when he turned to face the maelstrom of broken furniture and shattered china, it was clear that the noise he had heard wasn't the house settling at all, but rather Gareth who was still slumped against the wall, visibly broken and hopelessly struggling to breathe.

His moans would have read pitiful and nauseating to most, but they were a salve to Finn's woes. The fox picked up Gareth's leather-bound copy of *Winterset Hollow* from the floor and strolled over to the beleaguered young man before crouching down to his level. "Do you want to read a little now that we're not in the middle of dinner? Give us a show? Go on, read," he said, shoving the book into Gareth's sternum which resulted in a horrid gasp. "Oh, I *am* sorry," he continued, "I forgot you took a lick to the chest from old Bing. Here, I'll hold it for you." Finn opened the book and held it in front of Gareth's face, but he barely had enough strength left in his being for his eyes to focus, and when he tried to speak, all he could muster were wretched, unintelligible whispers. "Sounds like you're having some trouble. Allow me," he offered, leafing through the pages until he found a suitable passage and began to read aloud . . .

> *What is it that you thought you'd see? What is it that you thought I'd be?*
> *What is it of my nature you can't fathom, said the fox*
> *They stole from us, you saw it, too, they took our food and left us blue*
> *Is that not worth a beast or two in cages or in stocks?*
>
> *That is not how we live, said Runny, and you elected me head bunny*
> *I'm sorry, there will be no battle raging past the hedge*
> *I find it rich to think, said Finn, that you would let the monsters win*
> *Lest we forget that it was you who ventured past the edge*
>
> *I care not that they're big and fierce, I care not what their horns have pierced*
> *If no one else will go, then I shall take them on alone*
> *It's fine to be afraid of war, but there are things worth fighting for*
> *And if you lot won't fight with me then I'll fight them on my own*

"Seems to me old Edward hit that nail square on the head, don't you think?" he said, setting the book to the side and drawing his blade. Finn slipped the tip of the knife underneath the first of Gareth's shirt buttons, and one by one he popped them all free of their thread, letting his garment fall open to expose the nightmarish bruise that covered his entire midsection. "You did take quite a thumping, didn't you? Tell me, how does it feel to have your own ribs puncture your lungs? Does it hurt?" Gareth's lips moved, but nothing in the way of words escaped.

He reached up to swat the knife away but couldn't even gather the muscle to keep his arm off of the ground, and as if to hang a lantern on his helplessness, Finn stuck the point of his weapon under the young man's chin and used it to raise his head. "I'm sorry, I didn't catch that. You'll have to speak up."

There was no voice to accompany the movement of his lips, but their form was clear enough. "Help . . . me."

"Oh, that's why I'm here," replied Finn. "See, I plan on opening you up a bit . . . get that air circulating inside you again. Now, I'm no doctor, but I've seen my fair share of dissections, so I wouldn't worry. My hands are steady. And lucky for you, I know *just* where to cut." He traced his knife down from Gareth's chin until it came to rest in the center of his chest. "You know, you remind me of Edward," he said, echoing his comments from his dealings with Percy on the stairs. "Living your lives in service of somebody else's words. Maybe I should do you like I did—"

Finn didn't even flinch when the back of Gareth's skull exploded against the wall. It was an unexpected and violent impact, but when he saw the crisp, circular hole in the middle of his forehead begin to well with blood, the fox didn't even need to turn around to know what had happened. "Always there to ruin my fun, eh Frog?"

"As I was saying . . . a fine weapon," Flackwell boasted from the doorway as he lowered his slingshot to his side. "Besides, I rather liked that one. Said my squash tartlets were the most delicious thing he'd ever tasted, so I'd rather not see his entrails scattered about my dining room if it's all the same to you."

"You don't know what you're missing," Finn replied as he stood and sheathed his blade.

"I'm sure I don't." Just then, a clamor from the ballroom begged their attention and the three of them turned to see Bing dragging a decidedly dead Rowan and an equally lifeless Sir across the floor by their shirt collars.

"Gracious," remarked Runny, recoiling at the sight of Rowan's throat which was torn clean open. Bing dumped them on the dance floor next to the others, but as he turned to make his escape to the theater, Finn hurried over to have a word.

"Is that one of my hounds?!" he exclaimed, receiving only a shrug of the bear's mighty shoulders in response. "Did *you* do that? You did, didn't you? You big, dumb mutt, you just can't help yourself, can you? Years and years of training all for nothing now. I hope you're happy with yourself." Bing flashed a rare smile directly at Finn before he turned and made for the theater doors. "Fine . . . go and watch your cartoons!" the fox yelled after him. "Go and hide away in the dark!" But the bear just waved off his comments with a flash of his paw, and soon after he disappeared through the entrance, the score from the only film he ever cared to watch began to leak into the ballroom. "Goddamn mutt with your stupid goddamn movie!" Finn screamed across the room, the night's frustrations boiling over between his lips. "You better be ready to hunt tomorrow! And that goes for the two of you as well," he added, pointing to Runny and Flackwell before traipsing over to the bar and grabbing several towels along with a bottle of clear liquor.

"Where are *you* going?" asked the rabbit.

"To get some air before I do something you'll regret."

King was fighting a losing battle as the rains pounded the dirt. He was a few dozen yards behind the stables he had learned to call home and digging furiously with an old, splintered spade as his dead friend lay on the ground beside him. The hound was putting in an admirable effort considering his injuries, but the walls of the grave he was trying to flesh out were crumbling under the weight of the storm and the pit seemed to be growing no deeper no matter how earnestly he toiled. It wasn't anything resembling a proper graveyard as there were no headstones or markers of any kind, but it was clear from the subtle mounds of earth scattered about the space and the lush greenery that crowned them that Bishop wouldn't be the first to be buried there. It was a place King loathed to visit, and every time he had the displeasure of passing through, he tried to resist the temptation to count the number of unfortunate souls that had come before him, but time and time again he counted them anyway.

"For your wound," said Finn as he placed the bar towels and the bottle of alcohol on a barrel just outside the barracks, prompting a nod of acknowledgement from a beleaguered but focused King. "And for a good night's sleep. We have a long day ahead of us tomorrow. Have the others returned?" The hound pointed to the stable, and seeing there were no bodies lying about save for Bishop, Finn could only look to the heavens and shake his head in frustration. "They came back alone, I take it?" There was no answer from King but the morbid rhythm of his spade and the shower of raindrops against the canopy overhead, but his dogged-ness spoke volumes and Finn didn't blame him for wanting no part in what was coming.

Rooker and Queeny were already in their cages when the fox opened the stable doors, and with the first mighty flash of lightning he could see that they had both pushed their way to the back of their confinements and balled themselves up like frightened pups. "There were supposed to be two fresh faces in these cages and yet I see only old, tired dogs," said Finn as he marched toward them. "Well, what do you have to say for yourselves?" Rooker made a walking motion against his arm with two of his fingers before shielding his face. "You let him run away? Even after I told you what would happen to you if you failed me? You . . . *useless* . . . *runts!*" he bellowed as he kicked their cages. Amid their pitiful moans, Finn's gaze wandered to the corner where he noticed there was only one spear leaning against the wall, and as he plucked it from its place, he asked, "Which one of you left your pike behind?" There was no answer of course, but as he caught a glimpse of Queeny's blackened eye and bloodied nose, he knew he had his culprit.

"Did you let him take it from you?" he queried as he crouched down in front of the cage. "You know, maybe Bing had the right idea after all. Maybe there's just too many of you. Perhaps the herd needs to be thinned. Too many runts in the litter." Finn threw the spear to the ground be-tween the two hounds, adding, "When I come back here in the morning, I expect to see only one of you alive. And if I don't . . . I'll kill you both myself. Happy hunting," he offered with a wink as he left them shrouded in the same darkness in which he had spent so many nights.

Finn closed the stable doors behind him and felt immediately grate-ful for the rains, for he was glad to have something to wash the stench of his past troubles and present failures from his fur. He was a hunter through and through, but he was no machine, and so he was pleased to have an excuse to eschew his responsibilities and skirt his identity if only until the storm passed. He was happy to be soaked down to his bones . . . for his silhouette to look gaunt and ragged and patently unlike himself as every snap of lightning framed his shadow against the door. But that did seem to be the way things had become. Flashes of light and ages of darkness. Silhouettes and shadows instead of sinew and soul. It was hard to get a read on the world with so limited a perspective—a handicap not lost on Phineas Fox who had chosen to embrace his stunted view of it all rather than weather the sting of change. But stasis is not without its own brand of pain, and as if he felt that equivalence in every sopping wet fiber of his being, Finn tilted his head toward a still-toiling King and instructed, "Dig another one."

The manor's kitchen had always been something of a Zen garden for Flackwell, particularly at the end of a long Barley Day when there was a mountain of dishes to clean and pots to scrub. It was the perfect outlet for his nervous energy, and when all the work was done and every handle had found its hook, he always felt centered and useful in a way that had escaped him in the days since he left the Hollow. It made him feel like he had done his part amid the hunts from which he had gradually removed himself, and that night was no exception as he slotted the serving trays back in their appropriate spots and polished every last silver spoon and took a rag to the countertops. And when he was finished and the sum of the leftovers had been tucked away in the cooler along with the remainder of the spiced wine and whatever trifle was still in the bowl, he ran his finger over his cutting board to make sure it was free of grease, sighed a satisfied sigh, and took stock of his perfect little garden only to notice that his chef's knife was missing from its block.

Flackwell was sure he remembered stowing it away, but even after checking every drawer and every cupboard, every tangle of tools and every gap between the counters, it was nowhere to be found. It wasn't until he heard some uncomfortable shuffling from behind the still-smoldering stove and turned to see a puddle of sweat pooling around a pair of shoes that he knew he had been robbed, and after accounting for all of his guests in his head and noting the slender cut of the culprit's feet, he was sure he knew who had robbed him. "You may as well come out of there before you roast to death. I assure you there are less painful ways to die."

"Stay away from me!" yelled Talia in between sobs, brandishing the missing knife while keeping the bulk of herself hidden behind the cast iron appliance.

"No need to yell," replied the frog. "I'm right here."

"What . . . what happened to Percy? Where is he!?"

"He's in the ballroom. On the dance floor, as a matter of fact. I imagine you'll be seeing him soon one way or the other."

"What did . . . what did you do to him?"

"*I* . . . did nothing to him except serve him the meal of his life. I'm sure you remember. It was exceptional. May I have my knife back?"

"No! No, you can't," she said as she wormed her way out from behind the stove while holding Flackwell's blade at arm's length with a horribly shaky hand. "You just . . . you just stay where you are. You just stay right there!" she commanded as she inched toward the door.

But Flackwell just raised his hands in the air and calmly offered, "I'm not going anywhere. I promise."

Talia broke into a run for the exit, but she didn't even take half a step before she stopped dead in her tracks at the sight of Finn leaning against the door jamb.

"Evening," he said calmly. She screamed and backed herself up against the wall, and while the fox stayed put, Flackwell slowly made his way toward her.

"You know, you must've been hiding here the entire time I was tidying up. Plenty of time to stick that knife in my back, and yet you didn't. Curious, no? I have a feeling that if it was Finn who was distracted with his duties, you wouldn't have thought twice about it. Is that because I seem harmless to you? Ineffectual? Good-natured? The fox who's always looking for a fight, the bear who won't give anyone the time of day, the rabbit who's too curious for his own good . . . and the frog who likes nothing more than to please everybody? The one without all the issues? That about the measure of it?"

Talia waved her knife wildly back and forth between Flackwell and Finn, and as the frog began to inch toward her, she thrust the blade at the air, yelling, "Don't come any closer!"

"Well, I have plenty of issues," he uttered, continuing his advance. "And yes, I love to please, but I also love to be recognized for it. Adored for it. Lauded and praised and validated. It gets my veins twitching in a way that's . . . I don't know, it's hard to put into words," he said with a shiver. "And even after I spent a week preparing a meal fit for royalty for you and your *insufferable* fiancé, neither of you even bothered to say thank you—not even once. Not a compliment or a rave review or an ounce of acclaim . . . even after all the wine you drank and all the hors d'oeuvres you ate and all the main courses you stuffed into your ungrateful gullets. Not one."

"I'm . . . I'm sorry," she said tearfully. "It was all just so overwhelming and I—"

"It's a little late for that now," said the frog as he stopped within arm's reach of her. "There are no second chances when it comes to saying thank you. Not in this house. Not anymore."

"I'm sorry! I'm sorry and thank you and—"

She swung her blade at Flackwell's person, but he was composed enough to catch her arm and pull his chef's knife from her grasp, and without another word he turned and slotted it into the wooden block where it belonged.

"This one . . . this one you may have," said the frog as he stepped past Finn and exited the kitchen, adding over his shoulder, "Do try and clean up when you're done." He was a long way from the Hollow and ever aware that each passing day made those memories grow fainter, and although it was getting harder to spackle those gaps with his time at Addington Manor, there were nights when it was almost enough . . . nights when it almost mattered as much. There were nights when he almost felt like his old self again and nights when he swore he could feel the life of the stars warm and lovely like days when they all had different names. There were good nights and bad and sour nights and sweet, and while both of those scales seemed to grow more unbalanced by the season, on that night at the very least, Flackwell Frog felt well useful.

THIRTEEN

They followed the river west as far as it would take them before Mark's leg began to fail him. It was as good a reason as any to stop and find somewhere to hunker down as the rains showed no signs of slowing and Eamon's face had become so badly swollen that he could hardly see at all anymore. The two boys were sheltered under an outcropping of rocks not far from the water, and though there was barely enough room for them both in the graces of the shallow overhang, the respite from the storm was nothing but welcome. The bandage that Mark had tied around his thigh was soaked through with blood, and even with the tempest still raging, Eamon could hear how carefully he was trying to control his breathing so as not to focus on the pain. But even Mark's hardships were a welcome distraction from his own, for the miles they had run since their time in the maze had been rugged and hard on their bodies, and now that the adrenaline was wearing off, they were all starting to feel every step.

"Jesus Christ, I'm freezing," said Mark, the whole of his being shivering and still sopping wet from their journey. "It's not even that cold out."

"It's plenty cold. I'm freezing too," Eamon fired back as he dabbed at his swollen face with a damp corner of his shirt.

"You look terrible, you know that?" joked Mark. The jab made Eamon chuckle, but even that was a more painful process than it should have been, and soon he was both laughing and crying—a fit he thought an appropriate spot on his emotional barometer given their circumstance.

"I found as many as I could," said Caroline as she joined them, the hood of her jacket bulging with a cache of pinecones. "You said to get the big ones that stand upright on the branches, right?"

"Douglas fir, yeah." Eamon took one from her stash and smelled it as best he could. "They look right anyway."

"How's your head?"

"I don't know. It sounds like the wind is whistling around in there or something. Probably just a massive concussion though. Nothing to worry about," he quipped.

"No, actually . . . I hear it too," she offered, quieting the rustle of her jacket-turned-satchel to better listen. "Sounds like someone left a window open."

Eamon's eyes lit up, and suddenly it seemed as if he was lifted by the prospect of some modicum of good news. "And where would you say that window is exactly?"

Caroline led them from their meager shelter, and though it was exhausting to be out in the rain again, they were rewarded for their efforts when they came upon the mouth of a cave cut into a sheer face of rock fifty or so yards down the line. "It sounds like it's big," said Eamon as he listened to the timbre of the wind whipping in and out of the entrance.

"As long as it's dry, I don't really care," snorted Mark, wincing as he tried to keep his weight off his injured leg. They stepped inside just far enough to be safe from the deluge and Eamon wasted no time in snatching a stick from the ground and tying a scrap of blanket he had been careful to keep dry around the end.

"Still have those matches?" he asked. Caroline looked surprised as if she had forgotten they were in her pocket at all, but after a modest moment's digging, she handed the box of Addington Manor matches to Eamon who struck one to life and set flame to the fabric.

The makeshift torch bathed the entrance in yellow light, but as they took another step toward the belly of the cavern, they were surprised to find that a barrier had been built across the entire breadth of the entrance—thick bars of steel which were seated deep into the mountain and latticed together like the front of a cage. There was a door fashioned into the middle much like a prison cell, and though it had been removed from its hinges some time ago, the opening was wide enough to fit all three of them through shoulder to shoulder and tall enough to accommodate two of Eamon stacked head to foot. Mark couldn't help but tug on the bars which were coated with rust and laced with cobwebs, but even though they had clearly seen their share of seasons on the isle, they were built so soundly that there wasn't even the slightest bit of give.

"Jesus, how many weird cages *are* there around here?" he asked.

"I saw a couple in the basement as well," said Eamon. "Much smaller, but it looked like . . . like one was for Runny and the other was for the frog."

"You think they were kept in cages?" said Caroline with a distinct sorrow.

"Looked that way. There was furniture and all sorts of stuff in there. Sheet music and cookbooks and radios and things and it . . . it kinda looked like they still slept in them. Like the sheets were fresh and the beds were made. I know they all have the run of the house now, but I don't think they were always here as guests, you know?"

"Like prisoners?" asked Mark as he gave the steel bars another tug.

"I mean, they sure seem pretty worked up about *something*. Maybe more like . . . trophies. You saw all the taxidermy and priceless art in his house, it's all just status symbol stuff. Look what I have that you don't have. Look at all my shiny things, look at all—"

"The rare and beautiful items I have locked up in this castle," added Caroline. "Look at my conquests."

Eamon waved his makeshift torch about the cavern's mouth and mused, "At this point I'd be surprised if that was even half of it. All this talk about hunts and traditions and debts . . . feels like it's deeper than that."

"Honestly, considering what we've been through . . . I kinda hope you're right," jabbed Caroline with a sincerity that gave them all pause enough to silently agree with her. "At least that way I'd understand all of this a little better."

"And we just happened to swing by on the one day of the year they like to take their anger out on the rest of our species?" questioned Mark.

"Lucky us," returned Caroline as she peered into the dark of the cavern. "You think this was for Bing?"

Eamon waved his torch about to cast a light on the scale of the steel. "Why else would the door be this big?" he said as he began to recite a passage from the book . . .

And with the building season passed, the bear could rest his paws at last
Looking toward his long and silent slumber in his cave
A chance to let his blisters heal, a proper feast for his last meal
And months without the need to live the hammer and the trave

"That's great and everything, but can we go inside now? I really need to sit down," said Mark, his voice shaking from the pain. Eamon and Caroline each took one of his arms around their shoulders and soon they found a dry patch of earth on which to let him rest, and as Caroline emptied her jacket and balled the husk into a pillow for his head, Eamon took his torch and began to look around the cavern for anything else that might be of aid.

"Look at *this*," he said as his light hit the wall. Caroline was preoccupied with Mark's soiled bandage, but when she glanced up to sate her curiosity, she was so taken by the sight of it all that it was hard for her to look away.

"Are those . . . are those—"

"Bones," said Eamon. An endless mural of bones. It was a breathtaking effort that covered every inch of the cavern's walls from floor to ceiling—a striking and seamless image that was equal parts beautiful and morbid and spoke to a lifetime's effort.

"Jesus. Are they . . . human?" asked Mark, his jaw agape at the sheer scope of what surrounded them.

"Deer," Eamon remarked as he ran his fingers over a femur that was mounted into a depression that had been carved from the rock wall. It was a forest scene played out in macabre but stunning detail—trees with vertebrae trunks and spindly antler branches, flowers with clavicle petals and shin bone stems, ribs masquerading as reeds beside a river studded with cloven rocks, and even a flock of gulls soaring through the sky, each of them fashioned from a pair of jawbones set joint to joint. "This goes on forever," he said as he traced his torch along the wall to discover rolling hills, a quaint little pond, a quiet valley, and a patch of tall grasses that could have passed for a rye field.

"That's a lot of goddamn deer," said Mark, wincing as Caroline unwrapped his sorry excuse for a bandage, the puncture in his leg gnarly and discolored and still flowing with blood.

Eamon nodded in agreement. "I mean, if Bing was in here for this long, they had to feed him something, right?"

"Do you think this is the Hollow?" posited Caroline.

"Makes sense if you think about it. If I were locked away in a cell or a . . . cave or whatever . . . I'd probably wanna see home too. No different than having pictures of your family up on the wall, I guess." No sooner had those words left Eamon's mouth than he came across the only portion of the mural that wasn't hewn from bone. It was a relief carving etched directly in the rock—a visage crafted with inarguable care and painstaking attention to detail and the sheer size of it made him wonder how many months, seasons, or even years it had taken to finish.

Under a sprawling oak tree sat two grown bears and one cub, and though it was hard to tell if one of them was Bing given the years of wear, the feeling of it had yet to be washed away by the trickle of rainwater soaking through from the ceiling. Even at just a glance, Eamon was sure they were a family. There was something about the posture of the adults and the way they doted on the little one that spoke volumes about how they were connected, and in that moment, he felt a surge of sympathy worm its way through his being as he thought about the things *he* had left behind to venture out into the world. The simplicity of a life removed, the agonizing luxury of solitude, the innocence of a world where the rules were easy to follow—Eamon knew these weren't perfect things, but he was sure they would be there in his cave of bones, forever etched into the rock.

They built a meager fire with some kindling that had blown far enough into the mouth of the cave to stay out of the rain, and though it wasn't much, it was enough to dry their clothes and keep them warm and they were glad for the comfort as they sat under the strangest night sky that any of them had ever seen.

"Which one is that?" asked Mark, pointing to an arrangement of vertebrae on the cavern ceiling.

"That's Orion," Eamon answered. "They call him the Hunter. See, those three stars in a row there are supposed to be his belt . . . and the ones to the right of it are supposed to be his bow." It was an odd and beautiful rendering of the cosmos, but it all somehow seemed correct. The back bones really did make for perfect little stars, and as far as Eamon could tell, they all looked to be in their proper places as well.

"And that one's the Little Dipper, right? Like you said earlier?"

"Actually, that's the Big Dipper. And if you take the bunch of stars next to it and try to look at it as one big picture . . . it's Ursa Major, the Great Bear. See, that's her tail and her head and her legs," said Eamon, tracing the lines with his finger.

"I don't know, seems like a stretch to me," mused Mark.

"Well, it's a bunch of deer vertebrae trying to recreate a cluster of stars a billion lightyears away, so you gotta suspend your disbelief a little."

"Right, I'm just saying . . . bears have four legs last I checked, not three."

Eamon was glad to see that Mark was in better spirits now that his injuries had been tended to. He had shown Caroline how to extract the sap from the cache of Douglas fir cones and how to use it to coat an open wound, and to her credit she quickly found herself to be quite the hand at Eamon's brand of makeshift medicine. It was an old trick his father had taught him to stave off infection and help the blood to clot, and now that the three of them had their traumas wrapped in fresh bits of blanket and were allowed a few moments to convalesce around the fire, they all looked to be feeling a little less bedraggled. But after all the dry kindling had been scavenged, their little blaze began to wither, and as they watched it die down to almost nothing, Caroline reached into the back of her waistband and removed the copy of *Winterset Hollow* she had rescued from her pack back at the river crossing.

"You kept that?" asked Mark.

"I had my reasons," she replied, tearing out the title page, balling it in her fist, and throwing it onto the embers. "But damn if this fire doesn't feel good." The boys looked on as she ripped several more pages from the spine and added them to the blaze, and while it was cathartic for them to watch the words that had brought them all to the brink of disaster turn to ash, the issue was a bit more complex for Caroline.

"This was actually my mom's copy," she said, ripping out an illustration of Finn and tossing it on the pyre. "When she was young, she and her friends used to trade books with each other and they started this tradition of making notes in the margins at parts they really liked or things they thought were sad or passages they found exciting . . . that kind of thing. Then, when it was their friend's turn to read, it was almost like they were reading it together. When my mom passed, her best friend gave me a whole box of books she had kept—*Alice in Wonderland, James and the Giant Peach, A Wrinkle in Time, Charlotte's Web.* Dozens of them."

Caroline pulled another leaf free and held it close enough to the flames for Eamon and Mark to see that indeed there were handwritten words and little drawings crowding the parchment. "And now, every time I find myself missing her, I just pick up one of those books and pore through a few chapters and it's almost like . . . almost like she's right there. Like I'm just a kid again and she's sitting on my bed reading to me."

"You don't have to burn that if you don't want to," said Eamon. "My clothes are pretty dry."

"It's okay. Like I said, I've got a whole box of them at home. Not like I'm gonna be reading *this* again anyway," she asserted before letting the page she was holding fall into the flames with a pointed finality.

"Guess I won't be either, now that I think about it," Eamon pondered. "Did I ever tell you guys that I ran away from home the first time I read it? Well, I guess I ran *back* to home. I was with my first foster family and it was just . . . sitting on the kitchen table one morning. A nice hardcover version too. They said it was for me and I asked them where it came from and they said they didn't know. I thought maybe it was from my dad, but the return address was just some bookstore and there was no name on it, so I just figured maybe my social worker had sent it to me or something."

Caroline threw some more fuel on the fire and they all watched as the flames swelled and the night sky sparkled back at them from above. "I read it cover to cover that night and it . . . it just reminded me so much of home," he continued. "The peace and quiet, the simplicity, the woods and the bog and everything. So, of course, I stole my foster dad's bike and rode until the sun came up. It had been a few months, so a lot of what we left behind had been looted already, but I stayed there anyway. I was there for like two days before they found me and took me back to the city, but I knew I'd come home again at some point. Every time I went back, there was always a little less of it there though. Last time it just looked like a . . . a shell of what we had. I guess that's what this book always was to me. A way to fill in that shell. But I suppose I don't even have that anymore. And I guess *you're* never gonna read it at all, huh?" he said, throwing a glance in Mark's direction.

Mark was still flat on his back with his head on Caroline's jacket and his hands folded behind the nape of his neck. "I've read it," he finally said.

"Wait, what?" gasped Eamon.

"You have?!" Caroline exclaimed. "When!?"

"Couple of years ago. That week you had to go to your sister's wedding and I couldn't get off of work. I was bored and maybe a little lonely, so I thought I'd read your favorite book and see why you loved it so much."

"Aww, that's kind of sweet actually," she said. "Did you like it?"

"I did," he continued, rolling onto his side and propping himself up on his elbow. "I liked it a lot. I mean, I like it considerably less *now*, but—"

"Why didn't you ever tell me?"

"It was gonna be a surprise, but when you got back from your trip, you were so exhausted and . . . and I could tell it was a tough week without your mom there . . . and you just picked that book up off the table and buried yourself in it for the rest of the night. So I figured maybe that was your thing that you need to have just for you, you know? I didn't wanna take that away from you. Plus, I kinda like when you tease me about it. *You*, not so much," he quipped, nodding toward Eamon.

"Understandable," he replied. "So, who was your favorite? I mean, if I had to guess, I'd say it was—"

"Bing," said Mark without a moment of hesitation.

"Really?" Caroline's eyes lit up as if they were just getting to know each other for the first time.

"There was something about the way he went out. The sacrifice he made for his family and for everybody else. He just seemed like good people. Honorable or something."

"What is it they say? Never meet your heroes?" Eamon asked with a smirk.

"To be fair, there's been a few times I've wanted to crack your head open with a hammer myself, so—"

"Again, understandable." They shared a chuckle before the gravity of their situation brought a familiar pall down upon them, and it wasn't long before there was nothing to fill the cavern but the whistle of the wind and the crackle of the fire and the hesitant beating of their hearts. Caroline's head dipped low, and Mark, feeling her spirits sinking, grimaced through the pain and shuffled over to find a spot right next to her on the bare earth.

"You okay?" he queried, knowing full well the question was far more important than the answer . . . and knowing the answer before the question was even asked.

"No," she replied, lifting her gaze from her mother's pages and meeting his stare with a shake of her head. "Are you?"

A dozen answers flashed across his lips as he considered what to say, and although he wanted to be strong for her as she had always been for him, he wanted more so to be present. "Not even a little bit," he said. Caroline took comfort in his genuine candor as she always did, and as she laid her head on his shoulder and let a few dignified tears roll down her cheek, Mark took her mother's book from her grasp and assumed the burden of burning her sweetest memories to keep them all warm. He tried to be silent as he tore each page from its binding, but still he felt her shudder with every pass of his hand. She glanced up to see him choosing only the pages that were unmarked in hopes that they would be enough, and when he felt a squeeze of gratitude on his arm, he was happy to be graced with something so warm and so familiar.

Mark hoped that maybe Caroline might find a few moments of sleep now that he could feel the bulk of her weight against him, but as he turned to see if Eamon had found the courage to rest, he saw that his brow was furrowed and his ear was cocked toward the cavern's entrance. "You hear that?" Eamon said.

"Hear what?"

"Scratching. Like something—"

"We are pleased to see youuu are still among us," said Olivia as she stepped out of the shadows and into the light of the fire. Mark and Caroline were startled to their own defenses, but before they could even scramble to their feet, Eamon set them at ease with a wave of his hand and a confident tone.

"No, no. It's okay," he said as he stood. "Her name's Olivia."

"You know that thing?" asked Mark incredulously as he looked her over from her spindly feet to the tufts of feathers above her eyes.

"We are not a thing!" the owl shot back, hopping toward them and staring down her beak as she admonished Mark. "We are of the owls. We are of the watchers. Long have we watched, I'll have youuu know!"

Eamon did his best to diffuse the tension with a word of context. "I talked to her when I stepped outside for some air earlier. She tried to warn me. I mean, I'm pretty sure she did anyway."

"And you didn't think to mention this at any point?" challenged Caroline.

"I don't know, I was kind of already in emotional overload and I just didn't think to say anything."

"Well," said Mark as he relaxed his posture until he was looking decidedly nonplussed, "we've already had a frog cook us dinner and a fox try to hunt us for sport, so why *not* a talking owl? Makes perfect sense."

"We told him to fly this place!" boomed Olivia. "We told him he does not belong here! But he did not heed us. He did not—"

"I didn't really understand what she was saying. She talks in riddles."

"We do not speak in riddles!" sneered the owl as she moved close enough to the fire for the white about her face and breast to shine back at them like misshapen moons. "It is not our fault that your tongue is so horrid. It is not our fault youuu have never learned another. We are of the Hollow where we speak clearly of the things we have seen. Much have we seen. Much do we remember. Long have we watched, youuu know."

"Yes, we know," said Mark with a roll of his eyes as he lay down on his side and turned away from it all, tired of talking beasts and their histories. Tired of characters and their realities.

"This one does not believe us?" asked Olivia as she spied the fire dwindling out of the corner of her eye and breathed new life into the blaze with a few healthy flaps of her wings.

"It's not that. We've just had a long night and we're very tired. I know you can understand that, right?" Olivia offered an understated empathy with a quirky cock of her head, and as she scratched her face with her wing as was her wont to do, Eamon carefully made his way over to where she was standing and crouched down beside her.

"Can you help us?" he asked. "They mean to kill us and . . . and we need to find a way off this island."

"Yes, we know," returned the owl. "This is why we are here, youuu see? We aim to be of service. We know much about the isle and we aim to—"

"Oh, you wanna help us?" Mark bellowed, suddenly awake and itching to get involved. "I'll tell you how you can help. You can fly yourself back to town and tell somebody what's going on here. How about that?"

Caroline could see that Olivia had not taken kindly to Mark's gruff tone, and as she quieted him with a gentle wave of her arm, she did her best to inject some much-needed finesse into his intentions. "Actually, that's not a bad idea. There's a man named Gene. He owns a boat called, uh . . ."

"*The Standard*," interjected Eamon.

"That's right. *The Standard.* He brought us here yesterday and he said he usually hangs out by the pier waiting for charters. Do you think maybe you could find him and tell him to meet us at the lighthouse?"

Olivia hung her head, and with a distinct timbre of sadness, she whispered under her breath, "We cannot."

Mark threw up his hands in frustration, but Caroline persisted in her measured approach. "Look, he left us here for whatever reason, and I'm sure he'd be willing to—"

"I am sorry, but we cannot." Olivia paced over to the fire, and after losing herself in its glow for a moment, she gave the flames another boost of wind and turned back to explain herself. "We cannot leave this place. We have been banished here for the things we have done. Clipped our feathers, they have. Burned us to stop them from growing back, they did. We would never make it across the waters," she lamented as she unfurled her wings to show them the scar tissue that she had been careful to keep hidden. "We can still fly a whisper, but . . . we would surely die over the sea."

"Who did this to you?' asked Eamon, hoping to build a bit of rapport. "The fox?"

"Was our own kind," Olivia replied. "The watchers. We are many, youuu know. Punished us for things we did. Spiteful deeds, we committed. We are a horrid thing." She hung her head in shame, but her tick was growing more frequent and Eamon and Caroline shared a glance as if they knew that their window for keeping her stable was growing thin.

"I'm sorry that happened to you," said Eamon. "It doesn't seem—"

"It was not right!" she shouted, her vitriol erupting to overshadow her indignity. "It was not right what they did to us! It was not right to shun our children! To loose them from the chain of knowledge!" Her eyes flashed with anger and a savage bend formed in her brow. "It was not right to punish us like this! To do the same to us as that which they decried! It was not fair to our . . ."

Caroline crouched down next to Eamon and did her best to soothe the fiery beast. "It's okay. Just breathe a little. It's okay." She took several deep, measured breaths, and before Olivia knew what was happening, she was doing the same, and though she seemed less agitated after the exercise, her grudge was no less apparent.

"What is your word? Your word for *them!?* Your word for those who do what they preach evil!? What is—"

"Hypocrites," said Caroline.

"Yes! That!" she shouted. "They are that in spades! It was not right what they did to our children! But we are a horrid thing . . . and now we understand . . . and we are here to atone. We are here to untie our sins."

Olivia settled down on her haunches, and feeling it was time for a more civil chat, Caroline and Eamon each took a seat on the bare earth as the forest around them suddenly came alive with a flash of firelight. The great bird turned to see that Mark had resumed feeding the flames with more pages from the old book, and as fortune would have it, it was just enough fuel for her to be able to see the forest of bones that surrounded her for the very first time. She spun her head from side to side in the way that owls do, and after she had seen the towering pine trees and listless rivers, rolling hills and breeze-swept grasses, she said, "If only we knew we would die for such a thing."

The grisly prospects of how the three of them might die had run through each of their heads too many times to count since their feast had turned folly earlier that evening, but the question of what they might be dying *for* was a debate that they had yet to internalize until that very moment. Caroline and Mark each snapped to each other's attention as if to make clear that they would both give their lives for the other without so much as a thought, but Eamon's brow only wrinkled in confusion as a whirlwind of possibilities danced through his head, though none were singular enough for him to read them with any clarity. *How far did you walk to get here, John? Are you hungry? Can I get you a pop? Would you like to lie down for a bit before we talk?* Eamon thought it a fool's errand, but still he couldn't help but give himself over to the question of whether there was truly anything in the circle of his existence that he would happily give his life for. He knew it to be poison, but still he tasted it.

He longed to have a concrete and immediate answer to that consideration, but even after he scoured the more unreachable corners of his heart and cast his emotional net beyond boundaries he thought wise, there was nothing . . . nothing but a name that wasn't his and places that never felt like home and people that rang unfamiliar and put-upon by his presence. Not a partner, not a child, not a country, not a king, and not a creed. Nothing. And in the middle of that mire, Eamon was unsure if he was really without such an attachment or if perhaps he was just too damaged to see it, but he knew his only chance at survival was to play the part of a man who was less uncertain. A man with more to die for. A man with more to live for. And as he scanned each wall that stood draped in the bones of so many things that had perished so another could survive, he wondered if they fought like more vicious beasts before succumbing to the builder bear's whims . . . or if they simply saw the beauty that surrounded them and rolled belly-up in the breath of his cave.

FOURTEEN

Runny couldn't help but remark to himself what a brilliant morning it was as he stepped out onto the patio and gulped a noseful of dewy-fresh air. He was glad to have a moment alone to mull things over, as Finn and Bing were nowhere to be seen and Flackwell was busy in the kitchen packing sandwiches to keep them all fueled for the day, but still he couldn't shake the knowledge that some unsavory brand of commotion was but a breath away. Runny was looking the part in his hunting jacket and galoshes and with his rifle slung under his arm, and as if he wished to shake the weight of those things, he closed his eyes and did his best to focus on the tittering of the squirrels and the jawing of the birds. Life as it once was. Life as it would surely be again. He leaned his walking stick against the jamb of the door and took a few steps out onto the slate to test his steadiness, and to his surprise he was feeling rather rough and ready without anything latched to his side. In fact, he would have thought himself a spry young rabbit again if it weren't for the creaking of his wooden leg and the intermittent pitter of his own fresh blood dripping from his bandage onto the patio tile.

"Cursed thing," he whispered to himself as he leaned his gun against the half-wall and wrapped the scarf a bit tighter around his mangled ear. "Should just save myself the trouble and take it off altogether." But as he made sure the knot was snug and winced at the pleasure of it all, he heard a rustle on the roof and turned to see Finn scurrying down from the spire with his bow slung about his shoulder and an old brass spyglass clutched in his paw. "Lovely morning, eh Fox?"

"Clear as a bell," said Finn as he skillfully slid down the roof tiles, swung himself from the gutter, and landed next to Runny with barely a sound. "You can see for miles up there."

"And what did you see, pray tell?"

"An old friend of ours with a big mouth and crippled wings. She's a ways off, but I'm sure it was her. Flies like a drunken guinea fowl."

"Meddlesome owl," sneered the rabbit. "She was outside the manor last night, you know. I managed to scare her off, but spirit knows what she said before I got there."

"Should've put a bullet in her beak."

"If I had my rifle with me, I might have done just that."

"Yes, I'm sure you would've," jabbed Finn.

"And what's that supposed to mean?"

"Let's face it, Runny . . . your anger has gone the way of your ear. I just hope there's some meat left on that carcass, because we just might need it today."

Runny sighed as he gazed out into the forest, and though he knew it to be a far cry from the Hollow in so many respects, he was well aware that it was as close as he would come to seeing it again before his days were over. "I have no love for these beasts either," he said. "They've taken everything from me that a creature can take. But the older I get, the more I feel the desire to let it all go or I feel as if I'll never be happy again. And I do wish to be happy. So, while I understand your inclination to rage at your past until you just can't rage anymore, I hope you understand my wish to find a quiet place by the lake and let it all fall away from my bones like rotten fur."

It was clear from the crease of the fox's brow that he did not understand, and it was plain from the quiver of his lip just above his canines that there was no small amount of disdain attached to the notion that a grudge as savage as theirs could somehow mellow with age or even be forgiven for the sake of some peace of mind. Finn was maddened by the prospect of such an idea in so many ways—roiled by the thought of such grace being born of their common trauma and incensed by the knowledge that he was incapable of that very thing. And as if to be sure that he was still the same creature he had always known himself to be, he slid his tongue along the sharpest of his fangs until he tasted the character that was flowing through his veins.

"Sandwiches! I've made sandwiches," shouted Flackwell as he plodded through the patio door with his slingshot in one hand and a shoulder bag in the other. "Fresh chopped eggs, rémoulade with tarragon and chives, and baby greens. Oh, and there's some capers and a bit of shallot in there for good measure!" The frog brandished his pack with pride but received only silence in return from his two friends. "Did I interrupt something? I don't know if you heard me, but I made—"

A sharp whistle from the direction of the stables cut him off at the knees and the three of them whirled to find King and Rooker carrying a large wicker basket fit with shoulder straps up onto the landing. "I thought you had more hounds than that," said the frog.

"Yes. I did," replied Finn as he made his way over to his dogs and went about inspecting the contraption they had fetched.

"What's the basket for?" asked Runny.

"For you."

"Excuse me?"

"It's for you. We need to be fast. And I don't mean to be insulting, but fast isn't exactly your forte these days," he said, nodding at the rabbit's wooden leg.

Runny looked to Flackwell to share his exasperation, but the frog seemed surprisingly bullish about the whole ordeal and simply shrugged. "What? Looks like a fine basket."

"It is!" shouted Finn from across the patio. And as if cued by the fox's endorsement, Bing finally lumbered through the doors with hammer in hand and shooed the hounds away with a growl and a flash of his teeth. The two of them waited expectantly by the basket until Runny's pride gave way to his pragmatism and he shuffled over and climbed inside the contraption. The great bear slipped his arms through the straps and hoisted the thing onto his powerful back, and all too quickly the rabbit found himself with a bear's eye view of his surroundings for the first time he could remember. "There, now that's not so bad, is it?" asked the fox.

Runny found his new ground a bit wobbly as Bing adjusted to the weight, and as he steadied himself against the side and leaned over to take his rifle from Flackwell, he whispered, "I will be glad when this is all over and I can be left to suffer my indignities in private as an old rabbit should."

"Over?" said Finn, his ears as keen as ever. "My friend, this will be over when I am dead and buried beneath the rye field. Only then will this be over."

"Duly noted," replied Runny as the fox gave a whistle and his hounds fell into place behind him. They were a motley bunch and looked nothing like the fearsome war party that Finn had envisioned when he first freed them from their cages and sent them out onto the breadth of the isle. King was understandably hobbled by his wound and Rooker, while appearing unscathed, was all but shattered by the trial he had weathered the night before and felt the weight of it with every single step. They were old dogs now—tired and displaced and stripped of everything the world had to offer save for the companionship of a single, silent friend. But even old dogs still yearn for fresher meat and sweeter drink, and even the most hopeless stray still hopes to find home around the very next corner. And so with Flackwell, Bing, and Runny in tow, they went about blessing the beautiful, late summer morning with a proper hunt . . . and dreamed of something better on the other side of it all.

"This would've been a lot easier if you had just let us follow the owl," said Mark as he gracelessly leaned against a towering statue of some Addington from a generation past. Heeding the instructions Olivia had given them the night before, they set out at sunrise and traced the river upstream until the hills mellowed into a grand meadow where they found a statue garden set among the grasses.

"Yeah, it probably would've," replied Eamon as he placed a rock on the ground to mark the point where the shadow of the statue's forefinger fell along the earth. "But a bird that big would just give us away. You can probably see her up in the air for miles. She'd be more like a vulture than an owl to anybody looking for us. Besides, her directions were pretty simple—take the river until you find the statue garden, then hike four miles due north until you find the hunters cabin. I mean, she wasn't quite that direct about it, but we should be able to find the place okay."

Mark glanced up at the marble visage above him and shook his head at the perfectly coiffed old man who was frozen in time with his hip cocked, one hand slipped inside his vest, and the other in the air as if he was pointing the way to the stars. "What is it with these people and the need to surround themselves with dead things all the time?"

Eamon glanced up at the sun then back down at the shadow to see that it had moved away from the rock a whisper. "I don't know. It's like even their relatives are trophies to them. Like it was some great conquest to have been born into one of the wealthiest families in Great Britain and they spent most of their time just high-fiving each other."

"This guy looks like a general or something. Albert James Addington," he said, reading the inscription on the plinth. "True as a cannonball and sharp as a saber."

"He might have been. I know some of his family were in the military at some point. Of course, I'm sure that means he sat in a tent and told a bunch of poor people to go march in a straight line toward a row of artillery or whatever."

"Maybe that's what he's pointing at," quipped Mark. "Walk toward *those* cannons, assholes! I'll just be over here getting my wig powdered."

"Would you wear one of those wigs? Like, if it was still the style?" asked Eamon, his attention still fixed on the statue's shadow.

"Oh, hell yeah."

"Really?"

"What, you don't think I can pull off curls? Dude, I would have the biggest, gnarliest wig. Would be down to my waist like a horse's mane. It would be . . . beautiful," he said with a surprising tenderness.

"You've really put a lot of thought into this, huh?"

Mark shifted his posture uncomfortably, and looking suddenly a little sheepish, folded his arms about his chest. "No, I haven't." It was a subtle denial, but the breath of casualness that it injected into their situation was like rest to the weary. It was refreshing to have a conversation that revolved around something other than survival or escape or how to treat any one of their myriad wounds, and it only reminded Eamon of his friend's worth as he waited for the sun to show them the way. It reminded him how grateful he was to have somebody by his side who was always game to relieve him from his world of mirrors and memories, and as his smile faded away at the sight of Mark's injured leg, it tugged at his heart to imagine a world without him. It was a sobering thought, but Eamon welcomed it as he knew that being drunk on distraction would be of no service to any of them, and as he closed his eyes and braced himself for the coming consideration of a life without Caroline, she once again came to his rescue.

"Some of these are really breathtaking," she boomed from across the garden, her hand tracing the leg of another effigy, this one a rather spry-looking girl no more than thirteen or fourteen years of age. The young lass was seated on a rock with her nose buried in a book, and while under other circumstances Caroline would've been positively charmed by such a thing, she wanted nothing more than to break her from the stone and gather her in her arms and let her know that it was all going to be okay. "I wonder what happened to her. She looks so young," she bellowed.

"Can we try not to shout?" said Eamon.

"Sorry," she replied, this time much more quietly. She looked down at the husk of her mother's book which she had kept with her since their night in the cave of bones. It was just a ghost of a thing now—gaunt and war-torn and empty, but it still felt just as heavy in her delicate hands. It still felt like it meant something to her, and although she knew that even her mother would forgive her the impulse to leave it behind, she still craved the comfort of the cover's rub as she ran her thumb over the rabbit that lived therein. But it wasn't until her gaze found the inscription beneath the lass's feet that Caroline's thirst for the solace of all the words that were now ash began to fade. *Isabelle Jane Addington. No less in this world now, and none the worse for it.* She leaned against the plinth as a wave of understanding about somebody who was just a stranger a moment prior battered her and set her tumbling and kept her beneath the surface until she could barely breathe at all.

No less in this world now, and none the worse for it. She read the words again and again and tasted nothing but salt water and heard nothing but the world spinning around her . . . and when Caroline finally scratched her way above the fray for a sip of air, she was sure she knew the little girl in front of her like a sister. She saw the earnestness in her eyes and the cross of her fingers hidden beneath her book and understood that she simply wanted to be somewhere else, and whether it was a story or a memory or even a vision of how things ought to be . . . she was sure it mattered little to her. She was sure because she knew her so well, and as her heart sank at the thought of Isabelle Jane Addington carrying the mark of a miscreant until the weather saw fit to wear her down to nothing, she set the husk of her mother's book at her stony feet . . . and turned back toward her comrades without the weight of all the nothing that remained between its covers.

There were fifteen statues in the garden, each of them set a few dozen yards apart and interconnected with winding pathways that were just whispers of what they once were, their clean lines now beset with weeds and their borders blurred from the years of wind and rain. In a way, it reminded Caroline of the portraits hanging in the manor's great hall as some of the carvings looked like they'd seen centuries of wear while others seemed not more than a few decades old to her untrained eye. And while the subjects varied in age and era and gender, they all had the same thing in common—the name Addington etched somewhere below their likenesses. It was a history of the family just like everything else on the isle, and it didn't escape Caroline's train of thought that even the cave of bones and the gash on her cheek were now part of that tale—a tale far darker than she ever imagined. And as she rejoined her party on the far side of the garden and carefully wiped the leavings of her silent musings from her expression, she wondered how much of that untold history would ever make it back to the mainland.

"All these statues are pretty creepy, right?" said Mark as she joined the two of them.

"I don't know," replied Caroline. "Considering we just spent the night in a literal forest of bones, I'd say this is pretty tame by comparison. How goes the orienteering?" she asked as Eamon placed a second rock on the shadow's point, a marker that had moved a good few inches given the travel of the September sun.

"I know this is taking a while," he said. "But if the cabin is four or five miles away and we're off by a few degrees, we might never find it."

"And you're sure this is worth the trip?"

"No, I'm not," he replied. "But Olivia said it's not far out of our way to the lighthouse. And if we can find something there to help us defend ourselves, all the better. It *is* a hunting cabin, so there's gotta be something."

Caroline and Mark shared an uncomfortable glance as if they were silently deciding who was going to ask the next question, but it was Mark who eventually took the burden upon himself and said, "You think they're gonna catch us before we make it to the coast, don't you."

Eamon looked up at his two friends, both of them battered and bandaged and starving for any inkling of hope or encouragement, and as he let a sigh slip through his broken nose, he said only, "I'm sure of it." It wasn't the answer they were hoping for, but it was the one they needed to hear, and as if they had just been roused by a speech from the general whose effigy was pointing the way, they straightened their spines and steeled their courage and prepared themselves for the trek ahead.

"So, which way do we go?" asked Caroline.

Eamon tapped the two rocks with his fingers. "East . . . and west," he said as he plucked two small sticks from the ground, using the first to connect the two stone markers and laying the second on top to form a cross. "South," he offered as he touched one end of the stick and then the other. "And north."

The ground turned more rugged and unforgiving the further they walked, and though they were plainly surrounded by boulders and trees and rocky rises in the earth, all that Eamon saw as he led his friends toward an oasis they knew by reputation only . . . were bones. It was hard to cut a straight line north with the more impassible sections of terrain forcing them to take several small detours, so Eamon had taken to picking a marker every few hundred yards to serve as a waypoint—an outcropping of clavicles here, a shin bone spruce there, or a prominence capped with spindly little ribs swaying in the breeze. They were all fossils of the death he now understood was woven into the isle's fabric, and whether they were real or imagined made little difference at this point because their provenance was unimpeachable. The trio trekked from bone to bone until the sun showed noon, and just as Eamon was beginning to think that he must have fallen off course somewhere along the line, they heard the welcome rumble of a steady current.

The river crossing was the owl's last marker before they were supposed to arrive at the hunter's cabin, and they all felt a renewed sense of confidence in her words as they waded across the waist-deep water and mounted the far bank. It was the same river to be sure, but its flow was more powerful and the crash of its tide was far more violent than they remembered . . . almost as if the waters themselves were fleeing right alongside them.

"Why didn't we just follow the river the whole way instead of guessing our way through the woods like that?" asked Mark as he grabbed Eamon's hand and helped him up onto the bank.

"It's flowing the other way."

"What do you mean? Which way is it supposed to be flowing?"

"It's flowing north," said Eamon as he reached down to the water and helped Caroline out of the current. "It was flowing east back by the cave which means that somewhere along the line there was a big bend that probably would've taken us a few hours out of our way. Birds think in straight lines just like they fly, I guess . . . which is fine by me considering we're being hunted and all."

"No, I know," said Mark sheepishly. "I was just, uh . . . making sure you were paying attention."

"I wouldn't have it any other way," Eamon offered with a grin as he led them away from the rustle of the rapids and up the tail of a ridge covered in towering trees. They were halfway up the hill when Mark decided to ask another question, this time certain it was worth the breath that he so desperately needed this far into their journey.

"What did she mean when she said it was the others like her that clipped her wings?" he said. "Other owls? Are there more? I mean, she said they banished her here as if they have rules or laws or something."

"That's what it sounded like to me," Eamon replied. "In the book, each of them watches a different tribe. It's sort of their calling to observe and remember . . . just like the foxes are good at games and the frogs are good at cooking and the bears build. And every time they cross paths with each other they share what they've learned, and I guess the idea is that given enough owls meeting other owls, eventually they all know everything. It was his way of explaining the mythology behind their wisdom, although it seems it wasn't really his idea at all . . . just like everything else in that book, apparently," he said before clearing his throat and recalling a bit of Addington's work . . .

> And so the owls sang their tune, above the earth and 'neath the moon
> Knowing what they'd seen was worth a whisper and a word
> And as the council gathered near and soaked their beaks in barley beer
> They spoke of all the secrets they were careful to have heard

"You know, my mom used to use that to keep me from telling lies when I was a little girl," Caroline said as she braced herself on the trunk of a tree to navigate a particularly slippery section of slope. "There's no lie the owls won't hear. We never went to church or anything, so it was like . . . her way of guilt tripping me in the context of something I loved, you know? Worked pretty well actually, now that I think about it. I remember lying in bed at night listening to them hoot outside my window just *sure* that they were watching my every move." She chuckled to herself at the childish simplicity of it all. "I guess maybe they were after all."

Eamon's history was laced with owls as well, just as it was filled with countless other creatures that roamed the same countryside that he once did, and as he listened to his friend wax nostalgic about her childhood, he could almost hear them calling to each other under the thick blanket of stars that greeted him each and every night. His father always said that owls were good to have around the cabin because they kept the mice from worming their way into the cellar, but the thought of them being charged with something greater and more human sent an eerie shiver up his soul, even though he couldn't recall ever seeing one that was any bigger than a breadbox.

"What do you think she did?" Caroline asked as her chest began to heave from the climb. "Olivia, I mean."

"I don't know," said Eamon. "I just hope it wasn't giving bad directions." It was a treacherous last few yards up to the top of the ridge, but when they arrived, their efforts were rewarded with a sweeping view of the valley below, and as if Olivia herself had overheard their misgivings and sought to set them straight, nestled among the canopy of femur firs and sacrum spruces was a cedar-shingled roof.

The cabin looked every bit the part from its log-and-thatch walls to its cobblestone chimney to the wooden shutters on the windows, each of which was well rotten and warped from the countless storms it had no doubt weathered over its tenure. It wasn't nearly as grandiose as they expected given Addington's penchant for making a statement, but it wasn't a simple dwelling either in that it was fitted with two stories and a porch that ran the breadth of the front wall. And although it wasn't quite resplendent enough to have its likeness hanging in oil and canvas in the great hall of the manor, it was clear that it was still finely built on the heels of wealth. Eamon carefully turned the knob only to find it locked, and as he stepped back to case the exterior to look for another way in, Mark wasted no time in putting his shoulder through the door and granted them instant entrance.

"I guess that works," Eamon mused as they stepped inside to find a great room that was predictably musty and rightly caked with dust and cobwebs. There was a kitchenette built into the far wall, a cast iron stove tucked away in the corner overlooking a dining table, and a set of particularly uncomfortable looking couches . . . and the only door apart from the rear entrance led to a room of bunks that sat below a loft fit with a rickety set of stairs that could've passed for a ladder in low light. They were miles from Bing's cave, but there was death dripping from these walls too—deer skulls and antlers nailed to every beam, bear pelts draped over every chair, and skin after skin after skin under foot. It was equally morbid but decidedly artless, and Eamon couldn't help but think that if he was given the choice, he would probably have preferred the cavern.

They didn't speak a word to each other before they split off and began to search for anything that might be of aid, and as luck would have it, Eamon hadn't even opened the first kitchen cabinet when he found a pitted old skinning knife atop the counter. He snatched it up and scanned the haggard old blade from tip to tail, and thinking it useful enough, he slipped it into his pocket and stepped toward the stack of drawers when his foot brushed up against a bit of cloth on the floor. He could tell from where he stood that it was bloody, which wouldn't necessarily have been cause for alarm, but as he bent down to retrieve it and found it heavy and damp, Eamon knew they weren't alone.

Caroline wheeled when she heard him whistle, and when Mark exited the bunkroom carrying a cricket bat to find Eamon holding his finger to his lips and pointing to the loft, they both stiffened in steely fashion. Eamon cautioned them not to move with a wave of his hand as he crept across the floor. He was careful to stay atop the skin rugs as he slipped the knife from his pocket, but when he let his weight fall on the very first rung of the rickety staircase, an explicit creak from deep within its bones gave him away. He knew it would only be another step or two before he could see into the second story, and deciding surprise was a deadlier weapon than prudence at this point, he stormed ahead until his eyes cleared the landing only to find Patrick stuffed into the far corner. His shirt was well bloodied and his eyes were frozen wide with fear, and clutched in his quivering hands with its point leveled squarely at Eamon . . . was Queeny's pike.

The relief in both of their hearts was matched by their twin sighs, and as Eamon extended his hand and helped Patrick down the steps, the only thing the long, lean college boy could think to say when he saw that Mark and Caroline were along for the ride was, "Is Rowan with you guys?"

"Rowan? Last we saw he was with you," Caroline replied, looking Patrick over from the arrow wound in his leg to the sizeable gash in his side. "Down at the dock."

"You guys were at the dock?"

Eamon grimaced as if to let Caroline know that she had opened an unwelcome can of worms, but he quickly decided that the truth was the best way to get everyone back on track. "We were close enough to see, but not close enough to—"

"To help? Is that what you were gonna say?"

"Hey, you ran too," added Mark. "You *and* your friend, so I'm not sure where you left him, but don't take that out on—"

"I didn't mean to," Patrick said with real pain in his voice. He hobbled over to the kitchen area and resumed dabbing at the wound on the side of his ribs with the cloth that had given him away. "I just . . . I just ran . . . and by the time I stopped to see where he was, he was gone. Next thing I knew, I was being attacked by two . . . I don't know . . . two *men*? Men, but they were . . . wild. Beards and dressed in rags and—"

"We know," said Eamon, pointing to his fractured nose. "One of them got Mark pretty good. Got *all* of us actually. The fox was using them like . . . dogs or something to try and box us in." Eamon sidled over to Patrick, and seeing he was about to tear the rag into ribbons for a bandage, handed him the knife. "They had their tongues cut out."

"Well, that's just lovely," Patrick offered as he tried to slice the cloth in two only to find the edge of the blade too rusty to cut through much of anything and threw the rag back on the counter in frustration. "One of them was pretty fast. Caught up to me at one point and sliced me open. Got the better of him, though. Knocked him out and took his spear and . . . I just ran all night."

"You should've killed him," Caroline said with a cold glare.

"Yeah, probably. Should've done a lot of things differently, but I was scared. And I've never killed anybody before, but I sure know how to run."

That was a sentiment Eamon could properly relate to, and suddenly less concerned with their timetable and more open to his own sympathies, he nodded to Patrick's wound and said, "If you can find some fir cones outside the cabin, I can help you get patched up." He pulled open his shirt to brandish the strips of blanket that were neatly adhered to the scratches on his chest, but Patrick seemed preoccupied with the opportunity to emote to another human again.

"This is all so fucked," he said with a bow of his head and a rush of moisture to his eye. "One minute I'm thinking to myself I can't believe this is actually happening to me and the next I'm—"

"Thinking I can't believe this is actually happening to me," added Caroline, finishing his thought for him. "You should really let him treat that cut. You'll be thinking about it less and that'll be good for everybody when they catch us. *If* they catch us, I mean."

"I don't have time. I'm going back to find Rowan."

"You can't go back there, man," Mark boomed from across the room. "You've got no chance all by yourself."

"Neither does Rowan," Patrick said with a guilty heart. "I'm going back to find him . . . because I left him out there all alone . . . and he's my best friend."

Eamon drank of Patrick's persistence and found it sweet and satisfying, but still he knew their party would be stronger for having him among their numbers, so he decided it best to press him. "Look, we're going to the lighthouse. It's not more than six or seven miles and there might be a boat there or a way to call for help or something. It's our best chance of getting off this island. You should come with us . . . and we should all get off this rock and then we can come back here with the police or something, and *then* we can find your friend. There's a lot of ground here and plenty of places to hide. I'm sure he's just waiting it out somewhere. He wouldn't want you to die either. Think about it."

"I've done nothing *but* think about it," responded Patrick with a grim immediacy. "What are you gonna tell the police? Huh? You gonna tell them that a talking fox, a one-legged rabbit, a fancy frog, and a bear with a sledgehammer hunted you for fun? That what you're gonna say?" He looked to all three of them for something that resembled a reply, but their silence was all they were keen on offering in the face of logic that sturdy and terrifying. "You really think that blood on your shirt is gonna make a bit of difference? I don't. This is between us and them . . . and there's not a goddamn thing we can do to change that." Patrick picked up his spear and took a moment to inspect the dried blood that was still staining the tip before saying, "Good luck finding that lighthouse. And if you do get off this island . . . just go. Just go home . . . and don't say a word to anybody about any of this . . . and be glad you still have your friends." He moved for the front door, but as he swung it open and took a step toward the waiting woods, Mark stopped him with a question.

"Any guns in here? Any anything?"

"If I found a gun, don't you think I'd be holding it?" answered Patrick. He dug around in his pocket and withdrew an old, brass-cased compass disguised to look like a pocket watch and tossed it to Eamon. "Place was empty other than this. Just a waste of time. Lot of help that owl turned out to be."

"Wait," barked Eamon, his face suddenly awash in a wave of concern. "*You* talked to Olivia?"

"She found me up by the falls, told me about this cabin. Followed her all the way here for nothing. Should've known better," Patrick remarked over his shoulder as he turned to leave, but Eamon had to be sure of what he had just heard.

"You followed her *here!?* When did—"

The sound of the arrow splitting Patrick's eye was so grotesque that all three of them immediately knew they would never forget it as long as they lived. He fell to the floor amid a sudden and devastating silence with the bolt buried deep in his skull like some stalky weed. His death was nothing like it was supposed to be . . . nothing like anything they'd ever watched on the silver screen or seen scratched out in big, bright colors in a comic book. It was anything but immediate and Patrick fought it the whole way, his limbs flailing and his throat pumping out the most horrid, confused moans that any of them had ever heard. It was all so ghastly that the young blood pouring over his face and pooling at the nape of his neck proved to be the most palatable part of his last moments. Even the scent of him soiling himself as his life wriggled from his clutch was far more bitter. It was all so incorrect . . . and each of them knew they would never be able to wash away its stain.

FIFTEEN

Eamon peeked through the front window to see Finn, Bing, Runny, and Flackwell standing on the crest of the hill overlooking the cabin while King and Rooker hustled down the ridge to their flank. "Shut the door!" he barked with wide eyes and narrow breaths.

"Wh . . . what?" asked Caroline in return, her eyes still locked on Patrick's body which had finally stopped moving after what seemed like an eternity of rudderless twitching.

"The door!" he shouted again, this time forcefully enough to snap his two friends to action. Caroline grabbed his spear and Mark, being careful to stay hidden behind the wall, was able to get ahold of Patrick's shirt and pull him out of the way as Eamon swooped in to slam the door closed, but the lock had barely even clicked against the jamb when the first bullet ripped through the wood. They had weathered several storms on the island since their arrival, but none was quite as fierce as the torrent of steel and lead that blew through the cabin's windows that day. They dove to the ground and covered their heads as rifle shots smashed the old glass panes to pieces and ball bearings from Flackwell's sling lodged themselves in seemingly every inch of wall.

It was a full minute before they knew silence again, but it seemed like a season in itself, and as they all took their hands from their heads and looked to each other to make sure everybody was okay, the only thing that Mark could think to say was, "Oh, they've got guns now?"

"Are you all in there!?" yelled Finn from his perch on the high ground. "That would sure make things easier! As much as I love a challenging hunt, I'd really prefer more of a short chase followed by a long massacre at my age! Go on, why don't you all come on out and we can talk this through!"

"I've brought sandwiches!" added Flackwell with a sincere grin.

"Not now, Frog," the fox snapped with a whip of his head.

"I'm just saying, they won't be good forever. The rémoulade is a little temperamental and the cress will wilt and—"

"Not now!" Finn turned his attention back to the cabin and boomed, "I *am* sorry that there aren't any firearms in there for you all to scavenge! If I remember correctly, the first batch of hunters that we had the pleasure of murdering took them all when they ran off into the woods! I don't want you to feel like you're missing out though . . . they didn't seem to do them any good either!"

Eamon and company scurried to their feet and pressed themselves flat against the front wall. "Are they all up there?" asked Mark as he carefully peeked one eye around the edge of the window only to be met by the echo of a discharge and the wake of a bullet that missed him by the thinnest of margins. He jumped back into cover only to eke, "Yup."

"You missed," said Flackwell as Runny took the stock of his rifle from his shoulder.

"Perhaps I should have thrown a sandwich at them," sneered the rabbit in return.

"Honestly, there's no need to be crass."

"I really don't know what all the fuss is about!" continued Finn. "Being hunted is a Barley Day tradition! You *love* Barley Day, don't you!? Of course, I was never caught, so my memories may be a bit sunnier than others'. Maybe you should talk to Bing about it!? Spirit knows he's been on the wrong end of a large caliber a time or two!" Bing let loose a roar that shook every fir, spruce, and redwood in the valley, his maw dripping in anticipation and the scars that pockmarked his fur plain for all to see. "You can come out . . . or he can come in! Up to you!"

Eamon crouched low and scampered through to the bunk room where he peered out of the side window to see King and Rooker making their way down into the shallow of the valley. "They're gonna have us surrounded in a minute," he said as he hurried back to his friends in the great room. "We gotta go. And we have to split up."

"What? No way," urged Mark. "Let's just all go out the back and—"

"They'll catch us if we don't. Finn may be fast, but he's got nothing on that bear at full speed . . . and *you've* got one good leg . . . and if we're all trying to stay together, then—"

"We're all dead," said Caroline with a sorrowful resignation.

"Back at the manor, Bing came after *me* for whatever reason. So, I'll go out the front and head east and you two go out the back and head west . . . and the best we can hope for is that he follows me."

"And then what?" asked Mark with real reservation. "What, we just run until—"

"Yeah," said Eamon. "We run. We survive. And then we meet at the lighthouse and get off this island." He took the compass that Patrick had given him from his pocket and popped it open to make sure it was still functional before placing it in Caroline's hand. "Run west for five minutes, then north-northeast until you hit the coast. Should be pretty close to where we need to be. If we both follow the shore, we'll run into each other eventually." Eamon glanced at the cricket bat in Mark's hand. "Mind if I borrow that?"

"Well, what's it going to be!? Shouted Finn from the hilltop as he nocked a broadhead and steadily drew back his bow. "Surely, you wouldn't begrudge an old fox his Barley Day fun!?"

Eamon eased open the front door with a creak that could've doubled as a thunderclap. He waited until Mark and Caroline slipped out the back and reached out into the threshold to feel the warmth of the sun before squaring up to see the silhouettes of the four things he loved most in this world waiting to tear him limb from limb. *How are you doing with all of this, John? Are you okay? How long have you been on your own? John?*

"Attaboy," whispered Finn as he pulled his draw to his cheek and gave one last look to the leaves fluttering in the breeze. "And a fine Barley Day to you."

Eamon heard the whine of the arrow cutting a clean path through the air plain as day, but he resisted the temptation to look up into the blazing sun, knowing it would only harm his vision. Instead, he focused on Finn and watched as the creature let his bow fall gracefully from his face in the way that only someone who had loosed a thousand arrows would, and as the fox's gaze shifted from the heavens to the doorway in which he was standing, Eamon threw the cricket bat in front of his heart and let the arrow bury itself in the old wood.

"Clever little runt," Finn jeered as he plucked another arrow from the ground only to hear his hounds whistle their alarm. He wheeled to see Caroline and Mark disappearing into the woods, and though any man would've set his bloodlust boiling, he quickly decided them the plainer prize. "You two," he said to Runny and the frog, "see if you can't slow them down." Flackwell and the rabbit obliged him and marched along the crest of the hill to find a position where they might have a clearer shot, and as Finn drew another missile to his furry cheek and emptied his lungs of breath, Eamon snapped to action, ripped the fox's first arrow from the cricket bat, and darted off to the east.

Eamon didn't need to glance behind him to know the great bear was charging, for he could feel the very ground tremble as he made his dash for the trees. He didn't need to call out to his friends to see if they were still alive, for he could hear the rabbit's rifle shots booming in the distance . . . and he didn't need to look over his shoulder to be sure that Finn was getting ever closer to putting an arrow through his back, for he could feel the whizz of his bolts stinging his ears. It wasn't until Eamon reached the relative safety of the forest's edge that he allowed himself a moment to peek back and make sure that death was still hounding his heels—and indeed it was.

Finn was firing from the hip as he ran, deftly cycling arrows from his clutch to his bow between pulls, and though this was old hat for him and his aim was true, Eamon's move to the trees had resulted in the fox wounding wayward firs instead of the runt in his sights. Growing more frustrated with each miss, Finn stopped at the edge of the woods and thought it wise to ground his stance, raising his bow to his cheek and giving himself enough time to track his prey until he was sure he had the timing to catch him in a gap in the foliage. He could see the broadhead's path before he even let it fly—six inches over Eamon's shoulder and a foot in front of him—the perfect drop and the perfect lead to strike him square in the back, but just as his quarry cleared the next big redwood, Bing thundered in front of him in frenzied pursuit. "You mutt!" barked Finn as he tried to find a shot around the great bear, but the eclipse of his frame was too much to navigate and he was forced to take up the chase on foot once again.

Bing was an unstoppable force at full clip, and while Eamon was proving himself fleet of foot and deft at weaving between the trees, the bear had no need to bob and feint, for anything but the sturdiest trunks simply shattered to splinters as he plowed through the forest with his hammer in hand and his teeth bared to the wind. But no matter how fast he ran, Eamon knew this was a race he was sure to lose, and hearing the snap-and-crash of the trees growing ever louder behind him, he was sure he had to make a change of plans or face his fate at the end of the builder bear's bludgeon. It wasn't but a few footsteps later that he felt the shadow of the brute swallow him, and as he saw the silhouette of his hammer rise above his head, Eamon threw himself to the ground and rolled behind the safety of a thick pine which the creature split to kindling with one swing of his sledge.

What was left of the trunk fell between them, and Eamon could do nothing but crawl backward along the earth and watch the beast flick the tree from his path like it was some windswept twig. Bing stepped toward Eamon slow and steady, sliding his hammer into the back of his cuirass as if he wanted nothing more than to feel the life drain from Eamon's being with his naked paws. As if he wanted this, the surefire end of it all, to be as personal as the spirit would allow. The brute bared his claws and swiped at his target's chest, but Eamon was quick enough to thrust the broadhead he had been carrying into the path of the bear's strike, and before the thing could sink his talons into his flesh, Bing found himself recoiling with the pain of an arrow clean through his palm. He reared and growled at the heavens, but though his injury was bothersome, pain was nothing but a sparkplug to a creature who had experienced so much of it, and without a second of hesitation, he pulled the bolt through the other side of his hand and tossed it on the forest floor.

Eamon took advantage of the distraction and scrambled to his feet. He wheeled and sprang forward with all his body had to give, but instead of welcoming the promise of open ground, the only thing he saw before him was the familiar visage of Finn nocking an arrow and pulling it to his cheek. There was nothing to be done now. There was nowhere to go with the great bear to his back and the fox to his face, and as Eamon let his shoulders slump, he felt a heavy flood of sorrow break through his levees. There was nothing to be done now, there in the forest of bones . . . there among the sacrum spruces and femur firs. It was a familiar mire and just as dark, even though the sun was high on its hill, and while Eamon was sure that he would see no more of the island and hear no more from his two friends, the thought that they might find their freedom on the heels of his sacrifice proved to be no modest comfort so close to the end. It relaxed him in a way. It gave him a substance that felt honest and worthwhile and he was rightly glad to know it even for just a moment, and as he took one last breath of the air he had been waiting his whole life to breathe, he watched the tip of Finn's arrow sway back and forth until it settled on a course to his heart. Even Bing seemed resigned to letting it all end this way, standing his ground and huffing a satisfied huff and being content just to have a seat for the show. The only beast on the isle, in fact, that had any idea to the contrary at all . . . was the owl.

Olivia bombed through the canopy with a searing screech and sunk her talons deep into the fox's eye, and when he loosed his arrow in a fit of reflex, it soared past Eamon's head and buried itself deep in Bing's shoulder. Finn cried out and covered his face with his arms, and as the owl continued to tear at him with her hooks, he drew his blade from his belt and slashed wildly at the air in hopes of a piece of the great bird. "Fly!" she said as she left Finn to his pain and zoomed over to the builder beast, diving at his head in a flurry of feathers and wind. "*Fly!*"

Eamon sprinted away with uncommon speed, vaulting downed logs and shouldering aside saplings and thanking whatever semblance of grace he felt was left in the world for another chance at life. But his panic blinders were so thick around his bid to flee that he didn't even notice when there were no longer any trees to his flanks, and it was only the sound of raging water that cued him to stop before there was no longer ground beneath his feet. The cliff in front of him was sheer and rocky and high enough above the river that jumping was simply out of the question, particularly with the tide looking as shallow as it did. Eamon looked back to see Olivia struggling to escape Bing's fury with a broken wing hanging from her frame, and just as a surge of sorrow wormed its way up his spine and into his throat, a flash of red and black fur overtook him and he felt his feet come unstuck from the earth. It was only some blessed instinct by which Eamon managed to grab ahold of the fox's arm as he swung his knife, but it was that same instinct that saw them hopelessly tangled in a knot of flesh and fauna, tumbling through the brisk September air with two good eyes between them . . . and nowhere to go but down.

Caroline and Mark found themselves tailed by an endless volley of gunshots and a gathering storm of sling steel as they fled deeper into the forest, the showers of shrapnel stinging their skin like crazed hornets after every thwack of lead against wood. Their intentions were fixed firmly to the west, but prudence begged them to keep one eye to the south where King and Rooker were quickly closing as Mark's leg was proving more of a liability now that his wound had been given enough time to swell and riddle him with unspeakable pain.

"The big one doesn't seem to be much of a runner," said Flackwell from halfway up the hill as he slotted another ball bearing into his sling.

"I wouldn't know what you're talking about, I'm sure," the rabbit replied as he threw the lever action on his rifle, set it against the crook of his shoulder, and squeezed the trigger only to savage another tree. It wasn't nearly the shot he was hoping for, but it was enough to throw a flurry of splinters into Mark's eyes, causing him to stumble to a halt and furiously paw at his face.

"*What's wrong!?*" boomed Caroline as she tried to pull him up from his knees.

"I can't see! I can't . . ." He pulled his hands away as she helped him to his feet, and when he finally swallowed enough of the sting to try and open his eyes, he was greeted by a dazzling display of white flares and dark spots that refused to stay still enough for him to navigate. "I can't see anything!" he exclaimed as another boom echoed through the valley and another bullet screamed in between them.

"Come on!" she yelled as she took his hand and led him through the thick twist of trunks, clocking the two hounds who had easily halved the distance between them out of the corner of her eye. After another few desperate yards and amid the endless pop of gunpowder in the distance, Mark's vision slowly began to return, and just as he was able to recognize the vague shape of the woman leading him by the hand, he heard a sickening, fleshy thwack and saw Caroline clutch her side. She growled in pain and felt the wetness of blood on her palm, but still she had the wherewithal to wait until they were behind the cover of a great redwood to stop and collapse, her eyes welling with a troublesome cocktail of strain and resignation.

"Let me see. Let me see," said Mark as he rubbed his eyes once more, the world around him pulsing and bleeding light as it reluctantly came back into focus. He pulled up the side of her shirt to find a hole about the size of a quarter just below the turn of her ribs, and as he wiped away the fresh blood that was flowing from within, more only seeped out to replace it.

"Goddamn it, it hurts," she moaned as she gritted her teeth and looked down at the puncture. "It *hurts*."

"You're gonna be okay, you hear me? Just..." Mark cut short his words of comfort as he noticed that the thing embedded in her side was smooth and round and nothing at all like he imagined the shape of a bullet to be.

"Oh, I think I got one!" exclaimed Flackwell with glee.

"Did you, now!?" added Runny. "Well, I should see about getting the other or I'm never going to hear the end of it." The rabbit took a few steps forward and carefully raised his weapon to his eye, and as he spied Mark reaching for something around the edge of the tree, he pulled the trigger only to hear the disappointing click of an empty chamber. "Oh, for the love of the Spirit," Runny said as he dug about the pockets of his dapper hunting coat to the jingle of loose rifle cartridges from within. "Always something, isn't it?"

It was a piece of plaid cloth on the forest floor that Mark was reaching for, but when he tried to pull it toward him to help with Caroline's wound, he was met with the rattle of something dry and hollow like the song of some tangle of strange wind chimes. He looked to see what was tethered to the other end and brushed aside a littering of dead leaves and forest floor to find a pile of boots and clothing and bones, this time undeniably human. They had been there for decades by the look of them— picked clean by the elements and the scavengers that any healthy wood should house, and as he freed the flannel shirt from their clutch, Mark couldn't help but wonder if they had been the hunters that Finn had mentioned during his sermon on the hill. Wolves sent to the slaughter. Trailblazers of tradition.

He wiped her side clean once more and pulled her wound open with his fingers as she howled in pain. "Deep breath, okay?" he said as she replied with a nod, her eyes bloodshot and yellowed and her cheeks well drenched with sweat and tears. Caroline knew what was coming, but she also knew they would both be the better for it, and as she braced herself and looked away, Mark dug his fingers into her side and pulled the stainless-steel bearing free of her being.

She gasped as if she had just returned from the dead and the wave of relief she felt from being free of the thing gave her hope that they might find a way out of their trap, and when Mark pressed the flannel shirt to her side and showed her the shiny slug, she remarked, "That's not a bullet."

"Nope. Now, let's get outta here, huh?" Caroline tried to stand, but the motion only stretched her wound and begged a fresh tide of blood and a stab of pain so sharp that it brought her right back to her knees. Dogged and determined to rise, she reached for Mark's hand, but it wasn't there. Her world slowly vignetting from the sting of her injury, she felt about in the crisp autumn air for the sturdiness of his leg or the texture of one of his shoes, but those things weren't there either. And in the throes of her agony and the mire of her understandable panic, she feared herself alone and crippled and ill equipped for the battle bearing down on her, but a firm hand on her shoulder set at least one of those anxieties at ease, and a voice she knew nearly as well as her own sought to erase the others.

"Just stay down," said Mark as he plucked Patrick's spear from the ground, widened his stance as much as his ragged leg would allow, and thrust the point in front of him like some wayward legionnaire. The hounds were no more than twenty yards away and Caroline knew it would be mere moments before they were swarmed, and even with her adrenaline surging, she couldn't stop herself from wondering if they too would end up just another pile of bones in the middle of somebody else's wood. But it was within that same pile of bones that she saw the promise of deliverance, for wrapped around somebody's desiccated waist was a belt . . . and on that belt was a holster . . . and in that holster was a pistol.

Caroline scrambled for the gun, but only when she freed it from the tangle could she see that it was rusted and pitted and caked with forest floor. Her spirit fell, for she knew she had no time to shake it clean before the hounds would be upon them, but she felt that even a solid bluff might buy them enough time to turn the tide of their predicament, and so Caroline played her hand as if it was a surefire winner. At the sight of her stepping in front of Mark with her weapon raised, the hounds broke from their straight run and began to zig in and out of the trees, but they barely slowed themselves even a whisper. She hadn't bought them more than a moment or two, and once that calculation clicked in some distant corner of her mind, a resignation wormed its way across her lips, and she felt the searing need to know if she was holding freedom or folly in her hand. Caroline tracked them both with her pistol outstretched and surprisingly steady, and King's larger frame quickly outed him as the wiser target as they slithered between the trees and darted in and out of whatever cover was clever. The big hound's head didn't flash across the bead of her barrel for more than the slightest sliver of a moment, but it was enough for her to feel fine about testing the mettle of the miracle she hoped she had been blessed with, and as she thought she saw him smile for the second time in as many days, Caroline pulled back on the trigger.

The sound of nothing was as deafening as it was expected. She could feel the years of grit and rust holding the chamber back from turning as she tried to will the ancient thing to fire again and again, but even after thumping the gun against her thigh to shake loose the disease, the trigger simply wouldn't budge. The hounds were within striking distance now and emboldened by her weapon's impotence, both of them flashing fresh and fearsome looks through the shadow of the canopy as they reversed their grips on their spears and readied themselves to pounce. Mark tightened his grasp on his pike and backed himself up against his partner to tuck her away behind his hulking form, but Caroline wanted no part of a sacrifice that might mean even a minute on this earth without her other half, and so she gently pushed him aside and stepped forward until they were shoulder to shoulder . . . and together, with little between them but blood and the still-buzzing steel from high on the hill, they waited for it all to unfold.

It was Rooker who was first to strike—dashing in from behind a tree and pulling back his pike to sink it deep into Caroline's frame, but as his muscles fired to take his kill, she rattled the old revolver against her leg one last time, pulled back on the hammer . . . and squeezed out of sheer desperation. Rooker's chest exploded in a storm of blood and he fell limp and lifeless to the ground before the promise of a yelp could escape his throat.

"Well, you got one," sneered Flackwell.

"Oh, damn it all," the rabbit said as he lowered his rifle. "I would've had her plain as day if that . . . that stupid cur hadn't jumped in the way. Listen," he said, turning to the frog, "we don't have to mention the particulars of this to Finn. I'm sure if we just say that they got the better of one of his hounds, he'll be none the wiser. What say you?"

"I say you better keep shooting, that's what I say," replied Flackwell as he slipped another bearing into his sling.

Mark and Caroline stood breathless and stunned as they watched King abandon his charge to try and pull his only friend back from his final moments. He kneeled next to Rooker and took him in his arms and moaned a horrid and sorrowful moan as he watched his eyes roll back into his skull and his chest grow still. He looked up at Caroline, who was processing a stark return to her own pain now that the frenzy of the fight had subsided, and in place of the unflagging look of menace on his face just a few seconds prior, there was only powerlessness and grief . . . loneliness and wretched resignation. There was loss and there was fear, and as he opened his mouth to loose some ghastly, garbled nonsense upon them, she heard him clear as anything. He was asking for help . . . for kindness. For somebody to breathe grace into his life again. And as much as she felt for him in a strange way, she would also have understood if Mark wanted to pin him to the earth forevermore with his pike. These were delicate and complicated considerations, and though Caroline would've welcomed the time and space to think them through, the ricochet of another rifle round reminded her of more pressing matters, and with their wounds open to the wind, she and Mark limped off into the western woods.

Finn and Eamon hit the water with a deafening crash, and as they plummeted to the bottom with their arms entwined and their legs flailing, the crimson tails leaking from their wounds fused together like some awful ink blot as they faded into the current. Soon enough, they bobbed back up to the surface, and after both of them had taken a desperate gulp of air, Finn tried to force his knife into some fleshy part of Eamon's person, but with his adversary still holding back his arm, it seemed they were locked in a tangle of grit and grudgery until one of them offered to be the first to come untied.

"Why won't you just lay down and die!?" yelled the fox as the heavy current carried them along. Finn looked over his shoulder to see what trials lay ahead, and though there were plenty rocks and rapids, there was also a horizon after which there was simply nothing at all. "You hear that?" he said amid the crescendo of the crash of heavy water just ahead. "That's the falls. A hundred feet. Rocks at the bottom. That how you wanna go?" Just as the question left his maw, they were swept into a swell and slammed against a stony outcropping in the riverbed. "I'll make it quick if you let me. I hear that drowning is nasty business," he snapped. There were countless comments spinning themselves up in Eamon's throat, but still he said nothing. He was rightly exhausted and equally terrified, and it was all he could do just to hold on to the fox's arm, and therefore his very life, as the river washed them toward a danger that might prove more equitable than Finn's blade. It was the most pitiful brand of hope, but it was hope nonetheless, and even if Eamon still had the strength, there would have been nothing else to cling to at all.

A moment later, they were swallowed by a wave of current, and when they broke back into the island air, Eamon saw the fox's blade inching ever closer toward his chest, and feeling his own arm begin to give from the strain, he grabbed Finn's knife hand with both of his to try and buy himself a few seconds of precious time. The fox sensed that Eamon's strength was beginning to wither and flashed his fangs, leaning into his dagger with the whole of his weight as they were sloshed from rock to rock and dipped into the depths of the water again and again. "Just let it happen," said the creature as the tip of his blade just pierced the fabric of Eamon's shirt. The young man growled and clenched his teeth and pushed with everything he had left, but even with the sum of his will billowing his sails, he felt the fine black blade enter his skin and begin to burn whatever was underneath. "Just let yourself go," continued Finn, his every sense heightened by the sight of fresh buffalo blood. "Don't you want this to be over? Don't you—"

It was a wild wave born of a large boulder in the middle of the river that saw the water consume them once again. It was only a heartbeat of distraction, but it was enough for Eamon to glance downriver and see that the drop was but a few narrow moments away. He could still feel the point of the fox's knife biting at his chest and knew it was only a matter of time before it was buried in his heart, and as he saw Finn's fangs begin to lust for a brief and bloody end to it all, Eamon felt another inch of flesh was well worth his life . . . and let go. The fox was surprised as his blade began to slide into his enemy with such a sudden ease, but that sensation was quickly equaled by the feeling of Eamon's thumb slotting itself into his already-ailing eye, and amid a growl of pure pain and a flash of white light . . . Finn began to feel the island air nipping at his naked fur.

They tumbled over the edge and into the sweet embrace of nothing, spiraling hand in hand as they fell free through the spray and shower of the great falls, and even in their wild and weightless descent, Eamon refused to let go. It wasn't until they hit the water that their knot came undone from the sheer force of the impact. The jolt to their systems was sudden and staggering and strong enough to knock Finn's knife from his grasp, the precious blade taking a stone's journey to the riverbed as the creature was forced to scramble to the surface for a gulp of air. But while the fox felt the panic of being awash in an element unfamiliar to his kind, Eamon simply emptied his lungs and sank to the bottom, and for a moment, he found a whisper of tranquility. For a moment, he was back in the woods of his youth playing possum under the lake to the tune of his father's booming voice. For a moment, he was anywhere else and there was no crazed fox on his tail and no monstrous bear waiting to bludgeon him to bits with his hammer . . . there was only the respite of the water and the nagging honesty of the promise that it, like everything else, was temporary. It was far from a trustworthy peace, but that didn't mean it wasn't sweet, and before it began to sour as he knew it would, Eamon drank of it with a grateful gusto.

Finn was a cunning hunter as his breed allowed, but by that same token, he was anything but a strong swimmer, and as he struggled to dive deep enough to reclaim his blade, he could feel the burning in his chest blooming fiercer with each paddle of his paws. The fox was nothing without his knife as the bear was lost without his hammer, and so there was no decision to be made but to take it back from the deep, but as he heard the call of the surface growing sweeter, he stretched himself further and kicked and kicked only to feel the churn of the falls pushing him away time and time again. The blade was almost within his reach by the time he felt himself take a breath, but Finn was dogged even in the face of death, and as he sensed his lungs filling with water, he made one final push and almost smiled at the familiar feeling of his fingers wrapping themselves around the handle. Even when it all went dark, he felt vital and powerful with the thing in his hand. Even when it all went silent, he felt his decision worthwhile, for even the most treasured pieces of Finn's life had proved themselves to be fleeting, and the knowledge that at least something had remained permanent to the very end made it all seem a bit less grim.

SIXTEEN

Eamon's shoulders felt a bit less weighty now that the river had washed his musk from his clothing. He knew he was surely a little harder to track after his impromptu swim and that set a sliver of his anxieties at ease, but that didn't mean he wasn't still riled by misgivings about his present and the existential madness that defined his near future. As he trekked north and felt the myriad fresh wounds now covering his body begin to scar, Eamon couldn't help but tend to his more emotional injuries as well and wondered if he would ever see his friends again. He wondered if he was going to make it to the lighthouse in one piece, and if so, how long he would wait for them before deciding it was in his best interest to carry on with his own salvation, however that might be realized. He wondered if he would ever feel the relative comfort of his little apartment back in Boise again and he wondered, to his own distaste, how he would ever get on without the pointed relief of Caroline's kindnesses and the refreshing simplicity of Mark's candor. But above all of those things, he wondered about the hows and whys of it all, and the endless gray that shrouded those questions was still plenty thick enough to choke him with each breath of the breeze.

Eamon felt like a soldier in a war he didn't understand—like a boy in a uniform he didn't recognize who'd been conscripted in a language he didn't speak. It was maddening to feel the vital nature of it all with each step while having no grasp on where he was marching, what his orders were, or even what flag was flying above his ranks. It was survival for survival's sake, and though he had felt that instinct through and through for what seemed like the sum of his days, it seemed somehow less potent in the face of an enemy that clearly had the fuel of some history to keep their fires burning. Eamon was well aware that impetus was a double-edged sword and rightly sharp, but as he dragged his bones away from the river and toward the coast, just the thought of the taste of it made his mouth run wet with a craving that rang hauntingly familiar.

"We are pleased to see youuu are well," said a voice from above as Olivia stumbled out of the sky and landed next to Eamon, her wing hanging gimpy from her side.

"I am *not* well," he replied without so much as looking in her direction.

"But youuu are alive," she pointed out, hopping along beside him with a rather chipper disposition despite her injury.

"Go away."

"Don't you wish to thank us?"

"Do I wish to *thank* you?" uttered Eamon with a disdain that felt as if it had been brewing for hours.

"We intervened on your behalf," she boasted. "We tried to make up for the things we have done, don't youuu see?"

Eamon stopped and leered down at the great bird who looked back up at him with a pride that boiled whatever of his blood hadn't been left back at the hedge maze or beneath the falls. "You led those things *right* to us," he barked. "Patrick . . . Patrick is *dead* because of you and my friends probably are too, and we would be at the lighthouse by now if you hadn't insisted on *helping* so much so, sure . . . thank you . . . now go away!" He broke back into his stride and stepped across the forest's edge and into a clearing where he saw another statue of some Addington awaiting him not more than fifty yards ahead. Eamon rolled his eyes at the mere sight of the thing but thought it better company than the bird and soldiered on.

Olivia's bushy brow furrowed in confusion as it often did when she stuck her beak into the world of humans, and as she waddled along until she was nipping at Eamon's heels again, she said, "We do not understand."

"What don't you understand?"

"You are free, but still youuu are melancholy. You are alive, but still youuu wear that grimace on your face. Long have we watched and much have we seen and—"

"Stop saying that!" Eamon yelled as he stopped near the backside of the statue. Olivia flapped her burned and broken wings and struggled to fly her way up onto the sculpture's scalp, cocking her head to the side as she landed.

"We are sorry. Meant to offend you, we did not. We are simply trying to atone. Foul things have we done and—"

"Stop! Just . . . stop it! I don't know what that means, okay!? I don't know what *any* of that means!" he shouted as he began to pace back and forth. "I can't understand your riddles and I don't know what you did, and at this point, I don't really care either! I don't know why I'm being hunted on this *goddamn* island, I don't know what debt was supposed to be paid last night, and I don't understand what any of this has to do with me or Mark or Caroline or *whoever!* So unless you feel like *actually* helping instead of talking in circles about shit I don't understand . . . leave me alone!"

There was nothing but silence from Olivia as her eyes grew wide like saucers. "That's what I thought. Now, go away!" But Olivia didn't move, and not knowing what else to do, Eamon plucked a stone from the earth and hurled it in her direction, but she just stood just as still as the statue she was perched upon and let it bounce off her sturdy frame. "Fuck *off!*" he yelled as he stooped down to snatch up more ammunition, but before he could loose another round, she stopped him with a question of her own.

"Did you say the debt was to be paid?"

"Oh, for Christ's sake," he wailed, throwing his arms up in frustration as his eyes welled with tears of madness.

"Then you are the last. If the debt was to be paid . . . then youuu are surely the last. And we have surely failed." The great owl hopped down from the statue's head and landed on the plinth and said with a stark gravity, "Will you tell them what we've done? My children. Will you tell them what we have sacrificed?"

"You . . . you mean your wing? I don't—"

"When you get back to your world," she said. "When you get back to your world, will you go home to the woods of your youth and tell the owls there what we have done? So they may know their mother did not die a horrid thing?"

"My youth?" said Eamon as he stepped closer to her.

"Will you tell them!?" she pressed. But as she looked to Eamon and hoped to meet his eyes, Olivia noticed that his gaze was fixed on something else entirely, and as she glanced behind her at the statue's feet, she couldn't understand why such an unimportant part of such an unimportant thing was proving such a draw. But what seemed so ordinary to the owl was anything but unremarkable to Eamon, and as he reached out and touched the perfectly realized marble boot, his fingers traced the shape of the figure that was carved into its heel. "J" for Jack. "J" for the now-and-future John that never was. "J" for so much and "J" for nothing at all.

Finn looked a sorry and sallow thing slumped over the great bear's shoulder like a fresh kill. Bing's expression was decidedly dour as he carried his friend along the riverbank, and though the fox's bones were limp and useless and his body was haplessly rising and falling with each of the brute's giant steps, his prized blade was still clutched in his paw which seemed somehow rusted shut. The builder beast's gaze was distant and his direction seemed unfocused in the wake of all that had happened. His posture had taken on a timid slump and his blazing brown eyes were locked to the ground as if he was traveling for traveling's sake alone, and while he was unsure of his destination, he nonetheless felt compelled to keep moving as if each step had the chance to deliver him somewhere better. Somewhere sweeter. Somewhere he fit.

In a strange twist of serendipity, it was the ungainly rhythm of Bing's gait that finally flushed the water from Finn's system. The fox's eyes darted open and immediately his entire being was overcome by a torrent of heinous coughs laced with river runoff and a chorus of desperate gasps for unsullied air. The bear set him down and let him retch until he could retch no more, but Finn's wits were slower to return than his instincts, and the moment he felt himself able to move with any real sense of purpose, he turned and bared his blade at the still-blurry creature before him. He lunged and slashed and sliced through the air between them, but Bing was unfazed and equally unafraid of his diminutive comrade, and with one gentle tap of his hammer's head, he sat Finn back down on the dirt and coaxed another bit of water from his lungs.

The fox shook the cobwebs from his senses, and once the world around him began to come back into some manner of focus, his first thought was to try and clock the position of the sun to parse how long he had been unconscious. He craned his neck to better see through the canopy of trees, but the attempt only served as a stark reminder that one of his eyes was all but useless, and as if that recollection was enough to hang a lantern on his exhaustion, he collapsed before he could determine anything other than the fact that he was still alive.

The particulars of where he was and how he had arrived there slowly came trickling back from the big black beyond, and as Finn let his head roll to the side and saw the river still raging not more than a few dozen yards to his flank, he began to recall the frenzy of his recent pursuit and the terror of his plunge into the river. He began to recall what day it was and exactly what that meant to him and his history, but perhaps most importantly, he began to recall precisely with whom he was entangled when the waters pushed him over the great falls.

Bing stood over his comrade and shook his big, broad head as his shadow tried to cool Finn's suddenly resurgent ire, and though the fox knew the bear couldn't speak, he didn't need to hear any words to suss that Eamon was but a distant memory by now. It was the second time in as many days that a river had helped his quarry escape, and in the same breath that he finally felt his lungs empty themselves of the water that almost took him from this earth, he better understood why humans seemed to flock to the stuff like rabbits to their holes.

"You let him get away, didn't you?" barked Finn as he wobbled onto his haunches amid a chorus of contemptuous snorts from Bing. "Oh, oh *I* let him get away? I jumped off a cliff and got thrown over a waterfall. What did *you* do besides stand there and block all my arrows with your big head?" Bing just huffed and crossed his arms as Finn stood and stretched a mighty stretch and felt himself realigned in more ways than one. "Well, what do you have to say for yourself?" The great brute, of course, had no answer except a series of grumbly, under-his-breath harrumphs. "You thought I was *what?*" sneered Finn. "*Dead?!* You thought I was dead, so you just . . . you just let him go!?" Bing simply shrugged, feeling neither the need to explain nor defend himself from the rain of Finn's judgment. "Well just so we're clear," said the fox, "I am most certainly *not* dead . . . and neither is that little runt that I took over the falls with me. And if *you* would have drowned back there and *I* still had my sights on the last buffalo, well I would've left your carcass on the riverbank and never looked back. Just so we're clear."

"Perhaps you should be a bit more thankful and a smidge less spiteful," said a voice from the edge of the trees. Runny stepped out of the forest and into the light of day with the frog nipping at his heels. "Even the most fearsome hunter needs to beg the ear of grace every now and again, you know."

Finn glowered at the pair of them as they settled by the shore and Flackwell sated his thirst with a few handfuls of fresh water. "If grace himself were standing between me and that runt, I would put an arrow straight through his gut and never think the better of it," sneered the fox.

"How . . . uncharacteristically colorful," the rabbit responded with a gentle roll of his eyes, turning to face Finn only when the deed was done. "Are you alright?"

"Just ducky," he fired back. "What of the other two? The big one and the peach? Dead?" Flackwell and Runny could only turn to each other as the same look of resignation carved twin grimaces across their faces. "*Neither* of them!?" the fox continued, his hackles beginning to bristle.

"Not to worry. Your hounds are on their trail," interjected the frog with a surreptitious glance at his chum who knew better than to breathe more truth than necessary into their exchange. "I wounded one of them, so they should be easy enough to track. I suggest we head back and—"

"There's no time to backtrack." Finn closed the distance between them until there wasn't more than a few whiskers of air separating their auras. "Besides, we already know where they're going."

"We . . . we do?" asked Flackwell with a curious cock of his head.

"Of course we do." The fox slinked over to the river's shore and stooped low enough to spy his reflection leering back his way. His image was skewed and well fractured by the current, but as he tried to get a look at himself to see exactly how much damage had been done since the ambush at the cabin, it quickly became clear that no matter how long he waited, the wind and the water wouldn't have offered him a clean look. "The buffalo are all the same. Herd animals. You know one, you know the rest." He dipped the blade of his knife into the water's surface just below his good eye and watched the stuff ripple and break over the obsidian edge. "We know where the others that have come before them have gone . . . so we know where they will be as well. Perhaps Edward wasn't so daft," he said as he dried his weapon on the fur of his leg and secured it under his belt. "'Twas on the hill the barley mill had stood for all this time."

Eamon wasn't sure how long he had been standing in front of the statue of his father in the clearing, but by the time he looked up at the sky again, the sun had jumped clear across the horizon and a breezy dusk was already falling upon the isle. It was a staggeringly perfect visage. Every feature and every fold of his skin was just as he remembered. Every pockmark and every ragged pore. Everything from the weight of his brow to the curl of his ever-stern grin was perfect, but it wasn't the unexpected reunion that unsettled him as much as it was the inscription that was etched on the plinth. *Jack Buckley Addington.*

Eamon had never felt his heart sink as low as it did when he read those words. Not even on the day that he realized his father was never coming back to their quaint little cabin in the woods . . . and not even on the day he learned his real first name. It was one thing to be lied to, but it was a far darker deceit to have the truth of who he was buried by the very person who was supposed to shepherd him through that weight. Eamon had never wanted to see his father more desperately than he did as he stood beneath his likeness, for there was so much he still wanted to know and an orphan's lifetime of anger suddenly reenergized and aching for release. Jack Buckley Addington was the answer to a question that Eamon had asked himself a thousand times, but it opened a door to so many more that a name alone would never satisfy. He had a feeling the beasts on his heels knew the unfractured truth of the thing, but he thought it folly to offer them the quarter of his curiosity while the lives of his friends were still hanging in the balance, so as he tried not to let the callouses of his past add to the dire circumstance of his present, Eamon pressed on.

As the isle's persona turned to bare and rocky flatland, Eamon thought himself lucky to have not yet been caught by the fox and the bear, for even though the river had washed him of his scent, he was sure the hours he had spent in the shadow of his father had given them time to see to their injuries and take to his tail again. Even Olivia was nowhere to be seen as he searched the skies for a glimpse of the great owl in hopes that she might, as she had done before, give away the game of friend or foe . . . but there was nothing to be gleaned from the heavens and little to be learned from the earth as Eamon walked until his still-damp clothes were well dried by the island winds. In fact, with each step he took, Eamon only felt more uncertain about every last piece of his past, present, and future.

There were no answers as he found the coast and traced it north and there were no resolutions as he watched the sun begin its dive toward the horizon to rest its bones. There were no telling treasures underneath the rocks he kicked and no helpful histories waiting over any of the dunes. There was nothing at all beneath the tide of hairgrass and nothing that had been washed ashore by the sea . . . nothing but a rush of faded memories and the echoes of words like home and family and history, none of which meant what they did even a few short days ago. It was a dangerous time for Eamon to let his mind wander for countless reasons, but as hard as he tried to steel himself to focus on the task at hand, he simply couldn't find a firm grip on his own reins. He tried every trick he could think of to remain present and aware, but nothing seemed to quell the firestorm of questions that was clouding his view and pummeling his eardrums and plugging his throat with thick, black ash.

Eamon's need to know was fast eclipsing his need to survive, and the further he trekked along the isle's shore in search of safe passage from the reach of its secrets, the call of the things he had left behind to rot began to ring sweeter and sweeter. It was a siren's song, the chance to understand after all these years, but it was just that—a chance. It was a chance to find context for his new wounds and a chance to help heal his old scars, and just as Eamon's vision narrowed to nothing but a straight line between his past and his present, he clocked the silhouette of what could only be the lighthouse standing sure against the glow of the young moon.

He felt a familiar urgency course through his veins as he picked up his pace, suddenly conscious again of his journey's trials and the island's horrors and the desire he felt to never see their like again. Those things were fueling his stride now, though the pull of enlightenment was still strong, but as if serendipity herself saw fit to tip Eamon's scales, the bedraggled forms of Mark and Caroline limping their way toward the islet caught the light of the stars. Eamon had to take a moment to make sure he was seeing things as they were and not simply as he wanted them to be, but even after he had rubbed his eyes and shaken the cobwebs from his constitution, they were still there . . . both of them . . . and somewhere in the wake of that reality, Eamon even managed to smile.

Mark's embrace was powerful and desperate and laced with real joy, and as he unwrapped his arms from Eamon's frame and set his hands on his shoulders, he mused, "What a weekend, huh?"

"Are you guys okay?" asked Eamon as he noticed Caroline holding the bloody rag to her side. "What happened?"

"I'm alright," she replied as she dug around in her pocket and produced the ball bearing that struck her down. "Was touch and go there for a second, but once we got out of range, they couldn't catch us. Could just as easily have been a bullet, though."

"Did one of them have a slingshot or something?" Eamon said as he took the bearing from her palm and rolled it between his fingers.

"Lucky for us," added Mark. "What about you? Where's the fox?" he asked, glancing about surreptitiously.

"I don't know. They chased me over the falls and I haven't seen him or—"

"*Over* the falls?"

"Yeah, and if you think *that's* the craziest thing that's happened to me since we split up, you're gonna choke on your french fries when we get back to the mainland."

"That sounds great, but maybe . . . you know . . . a hospital first or something?" Mark joked, wincing and shifting his weight from his injured leg. "*Then* french fries."

"We'll see," quipped Eamon as he scanned the archipelago from the spire to the dock that stretched out into the sea, his eyes eventually coming to rest upon something with clean, manufactured lines nested among the rocks. It wasn't long before Mark and Caroline saw it too, and though it was beginning to get properly dark, the cut of the thing was unmistakable, and its place on the beach just above the fade of the tide smacked of salvation. And with the promise of providence numbing their wounds for the moment, the three of them hurried over to lay a closer eye on their fate, and when they drew near enough for the moonlight to better show what they were seeking, they saw there were three of them lined up along the shore, neat as sand dollars and just as rare.

"Boats," Eamon said as he exhaled for what seemed like the first time in days. They were just simple rowboats by the looks of them, but they were just as welcome as three arks waiting to deliver them from the flood.

"Thank god," exclaimed Caroline as the pain from her injury made a fearsome return and she fell to her knees. Mark and Eamon helped her back to her feet, and once she was standing again, she quickly and confidently waved off their aid, but her collapse was an unsubtle reminder that time was of the essence and that it was folly to wallow in their fortune for even a moment longer.

"I'll get one in the water," said Eamon. "But we'll need oars."

"There's a storage shed on the other side of the lighthouse," added Mark.

"I'll go," offered Caroline. "You two just—"

Mark shook his head so readily that it silenced her mid-sentence. "You're not going *anywhere* alone. Not when we're this close to getting outta here."

"It's fine. Just gimme that spear and I can wedge one of these off the rocks," Eamon said with real confidence as he extended his hand. "And if there's any flares or anything in there, grab those too."

The weight of the pike in his palm was the only reply that Eamon needed, and as he watched his two friends hobble toward the lighthouse, he grinned as if everything was set right with the world again—as if he was back on Main Street nipping at their heels with his hands in his pockets, happy just to see them happy again. It was a warm and wonderful feeling, and it made him hungry for the tiresome simplicity of his life for the first time that he could remember, and with a fresh appreciation for what awaited them all back on the mainland, Eamon hurried over to where the three boats were beached and looked them over with an eye for whether or not any of them would make it across several miles of open water.

The first craft was warped and well rotten and the hull was crumbling from the decades of salt-stained winds and rain, and the second didn't look to be faring much better, as all it took was a gentle tug on one of the cleats for the side of the thing to break away from the rest like candy brittle. It was a concerning pattern, and Eamon's outlook would've quickly soured if it hadn't been for the fresher coat of paint and the slightly different build of the third boat, a surefire tell that it was from a more recent era. It looked to be quite healthy in fact, and as it was a smaller design and visibly lighter, Eamon threw his pike to the sand and gripped the wood with his bare hands and readied his back to drag the thing to the ocean's edge.

He gave it a mighty tug and was surprised to feel the hull slide across the sand with relative ease, but as he began to backpedal toward the coast with the edge of the stern firmly in his grip, Eamon was gutted to notice that the bow wasn't moving at all. The craft was split in two like the ripest of melons, and as his spirit broke for so many reasons and his head began to swim with the most grim and unwelcome possibilities, Eamon turned his chin to the sky and felt the most bitter tears welling in his eyes. All those miles for nothing. All that blood for a mirage on the coast. He looked to the islet to see Mark and Caroline making their way to the lighthouse, but he just didn't have the heart to tell them what he'd found. He barely had the heart to accept it himself. But it wasn't until he let his head fall about his neck like some broken thing that Eamon understood that they weren't the only creatures to have braved the beach that day . . . for in the sand uncovered by his efforts was a footprint so large that it could only have belonged to one beast . . . and it was fresh and unsullied by the night's rains.

Mark wasn't even halfway through the lighthouse door when he felt Finn's knife slip into his gut. It was more surprising than it was painful at first, but as he saw a smile creep across the fox's furry face, the sensation of the glassy blade grating against his insides spidered through his being and he loosed a startled growl. Finn sunk the thing in up to the hilt with a mighty push and a sideways sneer, and all that Mark could think to do was to clamp his hands around the fox's grip and yell, "Caroline!"

"Oh, don't worry. I'll get to her soon enough."

"Caroline!" he yelled again. "Run. *Run!*" The fox tried to pull the knife free, but Mark was too resolute and just as strong, and his powerful arms proved enough to hold the blade in place as he dug deep into his reserves. Finn tried to wriggle his paws free of the handle, but Mark's grasp was iron clad, and only then was it clear to the fox that he had found himself knotted in another impossible life-and-death tangle. "Run!" Mark screamed again, gritting his teeth and growling pure will through his lips as they ran mad with spume. "*Run!*"

Caroline darted from the utility shed only to be chased right back inside by a volley of bullets from somewhere in the bushes, the hedgerow suddenly flashing like a cloud carrying the fiercest of storms. She dove behind a pile of boxes stuffed with boating gear and covered her head as the old wooden walls began to explode in a spray of splinters, and as she pressed herself against the ground and heard both panic and pain in Mark's voice, she wanted nothing more than to run to his side.

Eamon was only a few strides into his sprint for the lighthouse when he took a ball bearing to the leg. It staggered him to his knees, but he was quick to shake off the pain and peer back up over the rocks to see the cannonade of muzzle flare bursting from the cover of the thistles. It was open terrain between him and the islet, but there was really no choice in the matter, for there was precious little that was truly important to John Eamon Buckley, and it seemed the only things Addington Isle hadn't yet taken from that list were but a dash away. There was really no choice at all, and so Eamon centered his courage, took a deep breath of ocean air, and broke for the archipelago amid the incessant buzz of sling steel across his bow.

Runny's rifle was breathing fire as he threw the lever action again and again, the lead from his barrel chunking away at the side of the shed where he knew Caroline was still sheltering. But while Flackwell, who was perched next to him in the thicket, loosed round after round at Eamon's silhouette without so much as a thought toward a respite of any kind, the rabbit was beginning to tire of the viciousness of it all. Truthfully, he just wanted to return to his quiet little routine and live out what remained of his quiet little life, and though he felt in his heart of hearts that he would be just as happy to watch Eamon walk off into the waves as see him fall dead in the sand, he knew there would be no end until the lad took his last breath. His demons were locked in battle with his better nature, but he wanted badly for that to be done with too, so with a silent sigh and a heavy spirit, Runny swung the bead of his barrel until it was square to Eamon's head . . . and pulled the trigger one last time.

The click of an empty chamber was almost a relief to the rabbit, and as he dug his paws into his jacket in a reluctant search for more ammunition, the feeling of nothing but the bottom of an empty pocket was twice as welcome. "I'm spent," he said to the frog at his side.

"I venture to say I am too," replied Flackwell, looking down at the lone ball bearing left in his palm.

"Then I do believe it's time, old friend," said Runny with a pointed hesitation. But it wasn't the frog to whom he was speaking, and as the two of them stepped aside to make way for the coming storm, an endless and unimpeachable shadow eclipsed what remained of the night sky.

The sight of Bing rumbling out of the brush stopped Eamon dead in his tracks. The great bear had no qualms about making an entrance, and as he reared back and brandished his hammer and fired a fearsome war cry across the beach, Eamon looked to the relative safety of the lighthouse and knew he would never make it without being overtaken. He knew then that it was done. He knew then how he would meet his end and that the bear had already won, but if he could at least prove enough of a distraction for Caroline and Mark to shore up their survival, then that, he told himself, would be a worthwhile reason for his bones to be scattered on the walls of whichever cave they found themselves in next. He knew the better course of action was to swing about and lead the brute away from the islet, but Eamon was well tired of running and the fresh hole in his leg was begging him to stand his ground, and so with Addington's fiercest beast bearing down on him, he dug his feet into the sand, tightened his grip on his spear, and waited to greet his grisly end.

Blood was dripping from Mark's hands like he was wringing some oily rag, but still he refused to loosen his grip on Finn's paws. The fox clamped his jaws down upon his wrists and tore at his skin, but still Mark wouldn't let go. "Come on, then," growled Mark as he waited for the fox to come up for air and slammed his forehead into his mangled eye. Finn was clearly dazed, but he was just as stubborn as his adversary, and as he wrenched his arms in a bid to further open Mark's wound, Mark struck him in the eye once again. The third blow from his heavy skull knocked the fox unconscious on his feet, and when he staggered backward only to regain his wits a moment later, Mark collapsed against the lighthouse wall. "Come on, then," he said again as he pulled Finn's knife from his own gut and held it at arm's length. "Take it."

The fox looked at the blood cascading down Mark's midsection and knew the fight was surely won. He yearned to have his knife in his grip again, but with his head ringing and his eye out of commission, he thought patience was perhaps the better part of persistence and declined his adversary's offer. "I'd rather not, if it's all the same," he said. "That'll be far easier once you've bled out."

Mark was exhausted and fading fast, and as if the fox had cued his next turn, he leaned back against the wall and slowly slid his way down onto the floor, landing on the tile with a sickly moan and the creature's blade still ready in his grasp. It was a clear and present struggle to find the grit to keep his eyes open and his lungs full, and Mark's trials didn't escape Finn's notice as the creature casually made his way over to a stack of chairs that were set against the far wall. "You know, I have a habit of telling you people that you remind me of Edward, because most of the time it's true," he said as he slipped a seat from the pile. "But if I'm being honest . . . you don't remind me of him one bit. Frankly, it's refreshing to see that you all aren't so lost, not that it makes me want to savage you any less." Finn gave the chair a shake as if he was evaluating its craftsmanship. It was a bit of theater without the pretense of being disguised as anything else, but the fox could never help himself in moments of life and death, and even though he was certain nobody was watching, he still felt compelled to give his prey a bit of a show before his final breath. "You'll have to pardon me. It's been a long day and I'd prefer to have a sturdy seat to watch you blink your way off this earth."

He was feeling like his old self again even with his blade in somebody else's hands and one eye gone the way of the owls. He was feeling like the same clever creature that had felled the most famous Addington and helped to claim his isle in the name of the Hollow. He was feeling like a proper fox in so many ways again—lithe and lethal and loosed from the shackles of his failures—and as he turned to set his seat in the front row of a grand and august theater of his own design, he remarked, "Why don't we just sit here for a bit and see if any of your friends feel like—"

The fox fell a motionless and defeated thing for the second time that day, his monologue cut well short by the edge of an oar that cracked him just below his ear like Bing's own hammer. Mark's eyelids were growing heavier with each labored thump of his heart and his head was beginning to bob lazily about his neck, but still he knew who had come to his aid for the last little gasp of lavender in the air told him so. "I thought I told you to run?" he said as Finn's blade fell from his grasp and clattered against the floor with a distinct finality. Caroline threw down her oar and rushed to his side, every piece of her exploding with worry at the sight of her partner's ghastly wound and the unsettling tremor in his voice. "Is it dead?" he wondered aloud, motioning to the fox who was laid out on the floor with blood seeping from his head. But Caroline didn't answer, for she knew that Mark was running out of time, and as she removed her overshirt and pressed it against his gut, his wherewithal flickered like a lantern and he asked her again, "Why didn't you run?"

"Because I didn't wanna go without you," she returned, her eyes welling with tears. "And I still don't." She managed to smile in hopes of lifting his spirits and brushed his hair back from his forehead, the shirt covering his wound feeling damp to her touch already. "I just need you to stay with me for one little boat ride, okay? I won't even make you row, how does that sound?" she said as the tears started to come. Caroline wasn't sure how much time they had left together, but she was already endlessly grateful for every moment of it, and hoping she'd be able to look back and measure it in years instead of minutes, she threw his arm around her shoulder and prepared to give everything she had left to get him to his feet.

Eamon could see the fire in Bing's eyes as he drew closer, his powerful legs pumping and his massive frame cutting through the night at full clip. It was all so inevitable as he stood his ground with his pike leveled at the charging beast, but as the brute rumbled to within striking distance and Eamon closed his eyes and waited to feel himself come unstuck from the earth, Bing slowed to a stop and walked the last few yards until the two of them were toe to toe. It was the sour sting of the creature's breath that moved Eamon to open his eyes again, and when he did, he saw the great bear looming over him with more curiosity than rancor about his air. Bing was considering him as if he were some brave new specimen—studying him from head to toe and spear to scalp and back again, and though Eamon was unsure of the reason for the delay, he welcomed it without question. He welcomed the chance to simply be, if for but the most fleeting of moments. He welcomed the chance to just exist in what should have been his Eden, even if that existence was sure to be painfully short . . . to be there with a clarity he never found in life now that death's shadow was darkening his door. He welcomed it all even if it wasn't meant to be his for very long.

The whole of Eamon's being was soothed by the prospect of a purposeful death, and as his fingers relaxed and his spear fell to the sand, the great beast before him cocked his head as if he didn't understand. Bing opened his powerful lungs and screamed war in Eamon's face, but still the young man before him was unmoved . . . still he was unrepentant in his decision. It wasn't until the creature glanced past Eamon's shoulder and out into the great endless sea that he seemed to want to finish the thing at all, and whether it was the substance of nothing or the absence of it that buoyed him, it made little difference to Eamon as Bing raised his great hammer high above his head . . . and swung.

The first three bullets hit the builder beast square in the chest and sliced through his cuirass with ease, the old leather proving of little use against such a heavy caliber. It had been so long since Bing had felt the sizzle of lead tearing through his flesh that it hit him like a warm and unexpected memory. He staggered backward and clutched at his sternum, and as his past collided with his present and both of them painted an increasingly grim portrait of his future, a fourth round struck him in the lung . . . and a fifth in the throat. The giant fell to one knee and looked to be finished, but the legend of his strength proved to be rooted in truth as he used his hammer to wobble himself back to his feet, his cuirass running red with tired blood. He was broken now—his shoulders slumped and his breathing labored, but his spirit was still very much alive, and as he raised his maw to the heavens and growled one last fearsome growl, another round split his armor at center mass, and there at Eamon's feet . . . he fell.

"The hell happened to *you?*" said a gruff voice from the way of the water. Eamon wheeled to see Captain Gene striding across the beach with revolver in hand as *The Standard* idled noisily by the lighthouse dock.

"What . . . what are you doing here?" asked Eamon as he fell to his knees in exhaustion.

"You wouldn't believe me if I told you," Gene replied, looking over the scene before him as his jaw dropped further and further toward the sand at his feet. "Then again, maybe you would," he added, finally grasping that the beast he had just killed was not only armored but wielding a sledgehammer to boot. "It just you?"

"No," said Eamon as he pulled himself to his feet and leaned the whole of his relief against his pike. "No, it's not."

SEVENTEEN

The trip back to the mainland was silent and solemn, and though Gene wanted desperately to ask them all a thousand questions, he understood that there were more important things in process than his curiosity, and so he left them to their own devices as he cut a quick path back to the pier. Mark was laid out on the sleeper bed below deck, the towels from the squalid little galley proving of little use against the tide of blood still pumping from his wound, and Caroline, who was with him hand in hand, could only count the rumble of the waves against the hull as if she knew just how many grains of sand were left in his hourglass. Eamon, however, stayed above with his face in the spray, quiet and content to watch the island disappear into the distance. The captain had given him an old overshirt and a windbreaker to wear over his bloody rags, and while Eamon was set at ease not to see himself so mangled and war-torn, he was still cold from toe to tip for innumerable reasons.

He had often found it a starkly unfeasible task to explain to anybody, even Mark or Caroline, what it felt like not to know who he was, where he came from, or even who had given birth to him. It was an impossibly lonely notion that often made him feel as if he was just some cardboard cutout in a world of living, breathing things, but somehow the cork to that hole in his history didn't make any of that go away. In fact, it only made him feel more adrift as he sat there on the stern of *The Standard* and watched the tree line of Addington Isle sink into the sea. He thought himself a puppet as he let his head hang down toward the wooden rails of the old trawler, the strings he never knew to be lashed to his wrists now choking the wind from his throat. It made little difference that perhaps his father wasn't quite as crazy as he had always believed, for there was no way to go back and live those years through a new lens, and it was impossible to hear his manic ramblings with a different frequency.

And even though the things he had learned in those days had served him well on the isle, Eamon couldn't quite see the point of it all if he was to make the trip back home without Mark or Caroline or even the purity of his reverence for his favorite book. It was all so gray now. It was all so muddled . . . and so much of it was gone.

Mark was still breathing by the time he was loaded onto a gurney and slipped into the back of an ambulance, but if the urgency of the first responders was any indication, there was a far more terrifying forest for him to wade through in the miles ahead. Eamon promised he would take the car and meet them at the hospital, but even as the heavy doors closed behind his two best friends, Eamon was already feeling the weight of that lie. He didn't want to face the questions that were sure to be asked, because truly he had no answers . . . and he didn't want to feel the judgment he knew would come if he told the truth of the thing, because who would believe him anyway? Why should they? It was in that moment that Eamon felt himself caught between a reality he knew to be true and a fantasy he had always hoped to be real, and somewhere in the middle of all of that stood the now-and-future John that never was . . . and nobody else. *Is there anything you want to verbalize? Can I get you a glass of water or maybe a pop? Those boots look a little big for you, can you tell me where you got them?*

"Poor thing dropped dead as soon as he told me where you all were," said Gene. Eamon hadn't even noticed that he was staring at something bulky that had been wrapped in a tarp and set in a corner of the deck until the captain mentioned it, but as soon as he snapped out of his daze, he knew exactly what it was. "Was so exhausted he could barely speak. I mean, I knew parrots and that could talk, but . . . I don't know, this all seems so crazy. He talked just . . . just like a human would. A little off, but—"

"She," offered Eamon as he looked Gene in the eye for the first time that night.

"What?"

"She," he repeated. "Her name was Olivia."

"Of course it was," replied Gene, his compass stuck somewhere between incredulity and fascination. He watched in silence as Eamon crept over to the tarp and gently pulled aside the covering to reveal a scarred and broken wing that was attached to a great bird who was now at peace.

"You doin' okay with all of this?" he asked as he watched Eamon's face crackle with every emotion from grief to gratitude.

Eamon chuckled at the question, and though it was one that he had always answered with silence, he saw no point in dancing around it anymore. "No," he finally said. "No, I'm not."

"For what it's worth, I didn't really mean to leave you all there, just ... by the time I woke up, it was rainin' and everybody was gone and I just figured you were all campin' for the night or somethin'. I even came back the next day, but—"

"It's fine," interjected Eamon, though that was hardly the truth. "I get it." He appreciated the explanation well enough, but it didn't do anything to soothe his darkening sensibilities. It was a hard turn to see the island's history boil over its borders and flow across the sea to leave its stain on fabric he felt familiar. And as the flashing lights of Mark's ambulance finally gave their last gasp and faded away into the night, it sickened Eamon to know that his traumas were no longer just his anymore ... and it gutted him to know that their roots had left their stamp on his friend in the most indelible manner. He had seen their spindly vines and smelled their earthy musk during his time on the isle, and even though he had moved a goodly amount of earth and hacked away at what lay uncovered, Eamon knew they were still hardy and had plenty room to grow. He was on solid ground now, but nothing felt any different. He was an ocean away, but still he felt like he was fleeing through the halls of the manor or floating toward the edge of the falls or waiting for his end to come in the shadow of the lighthouse.

It was an unfamiliar and pervasive uneasiness, and it weakened Eamon's knees and dried his throat and set his hands to shaking. It was wild and woolly, just like the place that had burdened him with it, and as he lifted his chin to the stars and let the aftertaste of new horrors and old grudges drip down the back of his gullet, he wondered if this was how his father felt most days. Eamon almost choked on the answer, for he knew it through and through ... and it was all he could do not to retch his guts out and leave Gene's boat covered in tired memories and forbidden questions and childhood confusions.

"Well, I don't know about you, but I need a drink," said Gene as he stepped up onto the dock and took a long look at the quaint little nothings strung along Main Street. "You comin'? On me." But before Gene could even turn around to extend Eamon a hand, he heard a sharp, metallic click.

"I'm gonna need to borrow your boat," Eamon said as he leveled the revolver at the captain. "I'm sorry, but . . . I need it."

"You know, there aren't any live rounds left in that thing," Gene stated, cool as anything as he turned to face his lone passenger. "I don't even keep any extra on board anymore." Eamon let the gun fall to his waist with an exasperated sigh. "Why in the hell would you wanna go back there anyway? To get tore up like your friend?"

"There's just . . . something there I need," Eamon replied. "And if it kills me, it kills me. But one way or the other I'll be done with it."

Gene seemed taken aback by his candor and oddly sympathetic to his cause, but as somebody who'd spent his life on the ocean, it was hard to shake the pragmatic failings of it all. "I'm not sure there's enough fuel left to make it there," he said after a minute's consideration. "No place open to refill this late either."

"I'll take my chances."

Gene grimaced and looked up to the night sky as if he was waiting for the heavens to rain a reason to say no, but Eamon's longing felt genuine and he had a hard time valuing the use of his old boat over somebody's peace of mind, particularly somebody that he had left stranded to the possible tune of his friend's life. "At least gimme my gun," he finally said. "Won't do you no good anyway." Eamon crept to the rear of the boat and handed the weapon over to Gene who slipped it into the back of his waistband. "There's a stash of flares next to the med kit below deck. If you get stranded, call for help on the radio before the battery runs out and keep one of those things lit till someone comes and gets you. And if you make it, watch the throttle when you pull into the dock, she sticks a little bit," said Gene with an odd affection.

Eamon nodded and turned for the cockpit, and as Gene untied *The Standard* and watched her engines roar to life at somebody else's behest, he hoped she would be as kind to Eamon as she had always been to him . . . for these were desperate times, and there was little else to keep them all afloat.

Part Four

The Broken Bear

You fool, you fool, the rabbit barked, have you not heard the owls, hark!
Have you not heard them say that all this anger was in vain?
The balance of our food they kept, and all this while the king beast wept
For just this morn he woke to find his only son was slain

'Twas youthful folly, nothing more, 'twas but three beasts who took our store
And on this day the king he was to come and pay respect
All this for one empty bin? A life gone for an onion skin?
And now they have no cause to come and bring us what is left

But wrong is wrong, replied the fox, as empty as the onion box
How was I to know that this was folly and not war?
A young beast acting out of frame, a king's command, it's all the same
They'll see my knife again if they don't give us back our hoard

Well, sadly you might have your way, because of your untimely play
The king has offered us a chance to come and claim our yield
Nose to nose and teeth to teeth, the stars above and ground beneath
A creature of our choosing is to meet him on the field

Battle to the death, they will, beside our cherished barley mill
And if our fighter bests him, then our Barley Day is won
But if we lose the bout, you see, then Barley Day is not to be
And we will surely starve amid the languid winter sun

But Finn was bold and unafraid and boastful of the mess he'd made
And so he went to meet the kingly bison on the field
But when he finally saw the beast, five times his size to say the least
His legs, they went to pudding and before the brute he kneeled

Whispers flew among the crowd and all the creatures gasped aloud
For as the fox surrendered, they knew Barley Day was lost
But as the king beast turned and crowed, there's still a debt that I am owed
There was among them one who thought his mettle worth the cost

So out stepped Bing, the builder bear, his courage and his hammer squared
And loosed a fearsome roar, he did, to shake the ogre's bones
And as the bison wheeled to fight and drew his sword and bared his bite
He knew this was an adversary worthy of his throne

EIGHTEEN

Eamon awoke to find *The Standard* beached on a sandbar not more than a few dozen yards from Addington Isle's shores, and though this wasn't some shattering surprise given the way the waves were flowing, it was a welcome sight nonetheless. The old trawler had run out of fuel when the island was still a speck on the horizon, and the moment Eamon took a seat on the deck to curse his luck and overthink his intentions, he made the mistake of closing his eyes amid the soothing rumble of the waves and was taken by a deep and immediate sleep. It wasn't anything he desperately wanted, but rather a need he could no longer eschew given the rigors of the past few days, and now that his eyes were open, he was glad to have had it, for he felt renewed and ready and young again.

The sky was just as dark as when he had left the pier, and Eamon wasn't sure if he had slept for two hours or twenty, but judging by how ragged the hole in his leg had become and how much the swelling around his shattered nose had gone down, he was inclined to lean toward the latter. He was still a little groggy and his edges a bit softened by his slumber when he began to search *The Standard* for anything that might be of aid, and it wasn't until he ventured down into the cabin and saw the bloodstains on the sleeper and the knife that had created them that he remembered what had become of Mark. A shiver of shame ran through his spine when he realized he had left him and Caroline in what was surely their darkest hour, and there wasn't a single piece of him that wasn't wrapped up in wishing they would understand. He hoped they would forgive him. He hoped their arms would still be open as they always were and he hoped he would be able to see them both alive and well when this was all over, but he was sure that things would change between the three of them, because as sure as the tide pulls, he knew *he* would never be the same . . . and he was certain they felt likewise.

He cleaned Finn's knife in the ocean until the obsidian shined with something other than his friend's blood, and when he was done, he turned it over in his hands and took a close look at the relic for the first time. It truly was a remarkable thing with its wooden handle worn to a polish and its perfect edge standing in contrast to the ocean of swells and valleys that littered the breadth of the blade. And as Eamon felt the brilliance of its balance and the finesse of its character, he couldn't help but wonder how many had taken their last sip of air at its behest . . . and in that same breath, he couldn't help but consider the possibility that his father had been among those ranks. There was nothing else of interest aboard Gene's boat save for the aforementioned flares which Eamon stuffed into his back pocket, and so with Finn's prized possession in hand, he threw himself over the bow, trudged through the knee-deep water at the edge of the sea, and once again stepped foot on the shores of Addington Isle.

Eamon's head was so brightly abuzz that he couldn't even find the silence to tell if his footsteps were too loud or his breathing too heavy as he wound his way through the trees that thickened the manor's lawn, but as he slipped through the patio door and into the ballroom, he found the strangest peace of mind. It was the kind of solace that comes with a campaign unburdened by reservations—a focus that follows only a blessed purpose, and Eamon felt it in every bit of his bones as he greeted the ghosts of the manor in a different light than he had just two days ago. There was a time when he was sure they were dancing and playing cards and feeling fine from the sting of the finest liquors, but now he was certain they were clamoring to escape. Now he knew their plight.

The old house was starkly silent in the absence of celebration or catastrophe. It was quiet enough that Eamon could hear the drafts breezing through the hallways and it was all depressingly dark now that the chandeliers had burned down to nothing and the lanterns on the walls had sipped themselves dry of oil. Truly, he would've believed that nobody was there at all if it hadn't been for the frog's pipe smoke wafting up into the dining room through the hole that Bing had left in the floor. There were scars everywhere he looked, from the chaos of the dining chamber to the overturned billiards tables to the bodies of people he once joined in revelry still lying toe to toe on the dance floor. He knew these things would one day be wiped away, but to Eamon they felt as permanent as the island itself. They would always be there, and in a way, maybe he would always be there too.

He didn't know what he was looking for or what he would do when he found it, but he knew his search to be necessary even if it was blurred and amorphous at the outset. He wasn't sure what he was seeking, but he knew it had to be within the manor's walls, and as he tiptoed past the collage of maps that littered the great hall, he heard a pitiful wailing leaking from the lavatory and sidled up to the door. "You foul, awful thing," said the voice from within. "You rotten, useless . . ."

A muffled growl interrupted the sentiment, and though the door was thick and plenty up to its task, Eamon was all but certain that Runny was on the other side . . . and he needed only a peek under the threshold and a glimpse of one furry paw and one wooden leg to be sure. Eamon readied his blade and waited for the cover of another heinous growl before he tried the knob, and finding it turned freely, he eased open the door to the sight of Runny slicing into his ear with a handsome straight razor. The rabbit didn't open his eyes until a chunk of flesh fell into the basin with a putrid thump and he had given himself a few deep breaths to savor the ecstasy of it all, but when he did, he was greeted by the specter of Eamon standing behind him and said, "Give us a moment, will you?" For some reason, Eamon felt it wise to oblige him, and so he simply stood and watched as Runny let the blood drip from his mangled lug and gripped the sides of the sink and felt his chest heave with equal parts regret and relief.

"Is that what happened to your leg?" asked Eamon, finally breaking the silence as the rabbit continued with his ritual and wrapped his scarf around his butchered ear. "You take it off piece by piece? That what you did?"

Runny turned and clocked the knife in Eamon's hand, and after he carefully closed the door to the hall, he answered, "If you must know, *Edward* happened to my leg." The rabbit said nothing more as if his response should have been enough to sate Eamon's curiosity, and though there may have been a time when his manners would've kept him from pressing such matters, it didn't take more than a glance at the unwavering bend in Eamon's brow for Runny to understand just how much things had changed since they sat down to break bread together. "Edward could never stand the nervous thumping," he continued, "and as you might imagine, there was much of it during my tenure here. Well, one day he decided that he just couldn't brook it any longer, so he handed me his razor and gave me a choice," recounted Runny as he wiped the ivory-handled blade clean, folded it away, and returned it to the drawer below the basin. "My life or my leg. Believe me, I thought about both of those options before I took that blade to my flesh, but in the end, I just didn't have the heart to run it over my wrist. Spirit only knows how the frog would've gotten on without me."

Eamon took a few full heartbeats to process what he had just heard before he asked, "But wouldn't your tick just be louder with the wooden leg?"

"Edward was never one to let pragmatics interfere with his pageantry. He was simply making the point that he could have whichever piece of me he desired whenever he desired it. It was proper torture, but I felt a release that night that I had never felt before . . . .as if I was removing the worst part of me. I suppose I've been chasing that ever since, though it's hard for me to find a righteous piece at all these days." Runny glanced to the floor as if he was all of a sudden retotaling the sum of his sins and had come to the end of the ticker. "That night, Edward and his guests had quite the supper. English peas and mash on the side. I was still young, so I'm sure it was tender, particularly with Flackwell in the kitchen. So, if you came all the way back to this place for a portrait of the kind of man Edward Addington truly was . . . there you have it." The rabbit looked Eamon up and down as if he hadn't seen him in years. As if he'd been to war and back. "What on earth *are* you doing back here?" he said with real melancholy. "You were free of this."

"Free?" retorted Eamon with an edge no longer hidden. "My father was five hundred miles away and he wasn't free of this. He raised me like the rest of the world was on *fire* because of this. I hated him my whole life because of this. I was an orphan because of this. This is a part of me just like it's a part of you . . . and even if I never came back here, I would *never* be free of this." Finn's blade began to quiver in his hand as his emotions swelled. "But my children will be. And their children will be. And I guess that's why I'm here."

"Your father?" asked Runny, clinging to his last shred of guile out of reflex. "I'm sure I don't know what you mean."

"I saw his statue. Out in the clearing on the north end. I saw it."

Runny's face fell and he knew there was nothing left to do but tell his truth. It had been what seemed like a lifetime since he had spoken anything other than subterfuge and deceit, and now that those things had run their course, he felt himself useless and hollow. But he was an old rabbit and there was so little meat left to cut, and he always knew that sooner or later the light would surely shine on him too. "Then you know," he said. "Have you come to kill me?"

"I don't know," his guest replied with a convincing immediacy.

"Then what can I do for you besides dying?"

"Help me understand," Eamon said as he inched close enough for the tip of his knife to dimple Runny's jacket. He expected the rabbit to flinch or wince or show some manner of worry, but to his surprise, Runny leaned into the blade until it pierced the fabric of his clothing and sunk its teeth into his skin. He closed his eyes and let the familiar shiver of his blood being let wash over him until Eamon pulled his arm back, not wanting to further confuse his intent with the rabbit's twisted brand of satisfaction.

"Come, then," Runny said as he opened his eyes. He reached for the doorknob but was stopped short by Eamon's hand.

"Where's Finn?"

"He's not exactly the type to check in." After a moment's consideration, Eamon gave him a nod and followed him into the great hall, and once again, they were walking side by side through the manor that had come to define them both . . . only this time there were no wonderful scents wafting in from the kitchen and no friendly faces waiting to greet them at the end of it all. This time, every step they took echoed with a far darker timbre.

"I was excited the first time I heard the owls' rumblings about white men moving west toward the Hollow," said Runny as they ambled through the corridor. "I'd never met one myself, so it seemed like something of a new adventure . . . and I was a young rabbit and easily bored. So I did what all young rabbits do, which was exactly what I wasn't *supposed* to do, and strayed from the safety of home to meet them. My English was quite poor back then, but that didn't stop me from making a fool out of myself. Nothing ever did in those days," he said wistfully as he stopped to gaze at the old map of the Pacific Northwest that hung on the wall.

"Edward was rather taken with me when we first met," he continued, "and I must admit, I was quite taken with him as well. He seemed a fine specimen. Regal and confident, dashing and capable and he had the respect of everyone around him, so I thought it wise to invite him to share our table. After all, it *was* Barley Day and I couldn't see the harm in building some rapport with such a man, so with an open heart and an eagerness to exercise my politicking . . . I asked him to join our feast." Runny broke his gaze from the map and limped toward the atrium and Eamon followed in kind with his knife still at the ready. "I still remember his eyes when he sat down to eat with us," the rabbit recalled, clasping his hands behind his back. "Astonishment of the rarest kind. I was sure that I had done something bold and constructive. Sure that I had weaved an alliance with a creature who would prove a valuable ally. Little did I know that his gauzy stare was just the lust that came with stumbling upon a community of trophies that nobody else had hanging on their wall."

They arrived among the polar bears and jaguars and condors and gazelles and elephants, and Eamon suddenly felt as if he was in the presence of a thousand tragic stories instead of just a thousand fallen creatures. "Edward played the grateful guest until his brothers and riflemen arrived and boxed us in. He took an hourglass from his pocket and set it on the table, and while my friends and family were fleeing in terror, I pleaded with him to reconsider. I was prepared to be the first to fall, but inspiration can be a fickle thing . . . and Edward was so taken with my performance that he decided then and there that the only thing better than a dead trophy . . . was a living, breathing one. He wanted four of us to bring back to his home—myself, the cook, the gamesman, and the builder—and if we agreed, he promised to let the rest of our kind live in peace. And so, after hundreds of miles in shackles, we arrived at glorious Addington Manor," said Runny, reaching out and stroking the fur of a nearby grizzly. "And here we stayed for years. Decades. Serving at his pleasure, cooking, cleaning, entertaining, being brandished to his socialite friends as if we were each some fine Swiss pocket watch. And once a year on our most sacred of days . . . he got the one thing he'd wanted since the very first time we met."

"A hunt," offered Eamon.

"Aye," said the rabbit as he stepped close enough to Eamon to feel his knife against his frame again. "A hunt. The wiliest fox that ever was and the biggest bear the spirit ever saw fit to carve. I'm sure you can imagine how proud he was to have those things at his behest . . . to give his chums the pleasure of hunting such creatures. Such rare beasts. Things even money could never buy . . . and he had them. Edward, the great white hunter. Edward, the noblest king in the court."

"Didn't you ever try to leave?" Eamon asked with an affectation bordering on empathy.

In lieu of an immediate answer, Runny only turned and hobbled along the ornate runner that led to the double doors in the back of the atrium, and as he stood at the crest of the family that had taken him from his own, he uttered, "Edward purchased our land. Not from us, mind you, but that's neither here nor there. Anyway, he wasn't shy about reminding us that if we ever set even one foot toward home, he would bring our kin in by the wagonload and stack their bodies on the patio for us to gut before he had them stuffed. So, no . . . we never tried to leave. We lived our lives as his trinkets and hoped that our families would remember us well."

"How could a man like that write such a beautiful book?" asked Eamon as he reached out to touch the arrow on the crest.

"Edward was never content with people loving him for what he *had*, though he never shied away from it. He wanted them to love him for what he *did*. For what he *was*. So he took from us the only thing we had left . . . our memories. And sure enough, they made him into a god built on the back of unimaginable cruelty. And love him, they did. And celebrate him, they did. And revere him, they did. The great wide open beyond the hedge is far crueler than I ever thought it could be."

"*Honora Familiam*," Eamon said, reading the inscription beneath the Addington crest.

"I imagine that has a different ring to it now that you've discovered the truth," posed the rabbit.

"I never had a family. And as far as I'm concerned . . . I still don't."

"I know the feeling." Runny took a key from his jacket pocket and turned it over in his paws. "One night, after one of Edward's soirees had wound down to nothing, I found him passed out drunk here in the atrium. So drunk that he had forgotten to lock this room, which I had never in my life seen unsecured." The rabbit slid the key inside and the chunky padlock fell open with a clink, and as he eased open the doors, a warm, yellow light filled the entranceway. "It's the only part of the house where we keep the lanterns filled year 'round."

Eamon had never seen the leavings of a holocaust with his own eyes before, but the moment he stepped into the sprawling chamber, he understood it all. The callouses that covered Finn's humanity, the vitriol that Bing spewed with every war cry, the feeling of worthlessness that Flackwell tried so hard to deflect, and the gray between vengeance and grace in which Runny seemed to live—it was all spelled out on every inch of plaster and every square foot of floor. Rabbits and foxes, bears and frogs and owls and countless others frozen in death, their eyes still wide with terror and their mouths agape as if they were slain mid-scream. Eamon felt a quiver in his gut as he scanned the hundreds of heads mounted to the walls and the dozens of bodies posed in grotesquely twisted postures, and as he stepped further into the space, he was unsurprised to see that the floor was covered in skins of every imaginable pattern and color.

"My brothers and sisters," said Runny with a breath of reverence. "My mother and father. Every friend I've ever made. Every creature I've ever quarreled with. Every acquaintance to whom I've ever given a nod of my head and every paw I've ever shaken. They're all here. All of them. Every last one. You came here wishing to see the Hollow . . . and now you have."

"He killed them all?" whispered Eamon, the bigger picture starting to take shape.

"He and his friends and family. Trophies only they would have. Spirit only knows how long they had been hanging here while we were giving Edward our very lives to ensure their survival, but I suppose that's beside the point." Runny stepped forward until he was shoulder to shoulder with Eamon, the both of them gazing up at the breathtaking collage of death and deception in tandem. "Edward woke from his stupor the next morning without his keys in his pocket. He thought he had just misplaced them in his booze-addled haze, but of course I had taken them. And that night, after I freed Finn and the bear from their cages, Edward got exactly what he deserved."

It was only after those words had left the rabbit's mouth that Eamon noticed the chamber's centerpiece—a man sitting on a chair made from twisted gun barrels and broken stocks. His skin was held together with chunky, leather stitching that cut across his body like aimless train tracks on some map of what he once was. He wore no clothes and his face was locked in an expression so horrid that Eamon could only assume it was a portrait of how he died. And as for how he lived, there could hardly have been an indictment as cutting as the beautifully engraved repeating rifle in his left hand . . . and the fountain pen in his right. The pair walked together until they were within arm's reach of the ghastly effigy, and as Eamon reached out and touched his dry, leathery skin, he remarked, "He has red hair."

"Always did," replied the rabbit. "The only one in his family. His father thought it might throw his inheritance into question, so he taught him to dye it when he was just a lad and I guess it stuck. A charlatan in so many ways. Edward always did love his trophies, and to be honest, I never understood the fascination. But I do now. I do indeed."

Eamon had always fantasized about the things he would say to Edward Addington if he ever had the chance to meet him on some far away day in some far away realm. The fawning thank-yous, the endless questions, the confessions about how his book had helped him through his darkest years—but that all seemed so empty as he peered into his hollow, brown eyes and tracked the seams that streaked his naked frame. It all seemed so incorrect. So foolish.

"My father's statue," Eamon finally said. "Was that a trophy like all of these? Would you have made one out of me as well?"

The rabbit considered his words for a moment before speaking, being careful to remain present in the space in which he stood even though there was a knife still meant for his flesh not more than a breath away. "Honor thy family," he finally said, his gaze not wavering from Edward's preserved corpse.

"How did you know who I was? *I* didn't even know who I was."

"Oh, Eamon. Did you never close your eyes at night and listen to the owls? Did you never hear their song?"

"Olivia," whispered Eamon.

"There is nothing they don't see. They have been with you all your life." Those words hung so heavy in the air that Eamon could taste them when he finally remembered to breathe. Breathe. Please. There was confusion as there was clarity . . . and there was rancor as there was sympathy. It was in that moment that Eamon understood Runny in a new and blinding light, for all of a sudden, he wasn't the only one who knew what it was to have his family turned to trophies and to bear the wake of that madness while trying to tread the water of a normal existence. He felt every bit of the rabbit's shame . . . every ounce of his guilt . . . every stitch of his anger and every lash of his weariness, and for just a moment, Eamon even thought he could feel his own ears dipping down toward his shoulders.

"The bulk of your family were all quick to come. A letter baring the promise of money *here*, a document with the lure of inheritance *there*. Like starving dogs to meat. But you and your father . . . the two of you took finesse. Patience. Truthfully, there were times when I thought we would never see the end of Edward's line, but then—"

"Then I suggested we just send you the book," said a voice from the entrance. Flackwell traipsed through the doorway with his slingshot stretched at the ready, and in the shake of a rabbit's tail, Eamon shielded himself behind Runny and put his blade to his throat. "I knew you would feel it in your . . . fetid blood," continued the frog. "An orphan longing for the simplicity of life in the forest. It couldn't be more perfect really. It wasn't even a question of *if* you would one day come to see it for yourself . . . just a matter of when. Everybody loves a coupon," he said as he shuffled to the side to try and coax a better angle from which to shoot. "On the upside, I had a bevy of new faces to cook for in the years we waited for you. In a way, it was almost like the Barley Days of old. Almost. Now let him go."

"Why? So you can shoot me?" asked Eamon, being ever careful to keep his head hidden behind the rabbit's.

"Quite," said Flackwell, stretching his sling as far as it would allow. "I like my life here, believe it or not. It's quaint and quiet and the closest I will ever come to home again. And I have a feeling you did not come all the way back here just to let Runny and I retire to the woods in peace, did you?"

"I . . . I don't know," stammered Eamon.

"I'm afraid that's not good enough for me. Wouldn't you agree, dear rabbit?" Runny balked at offering an answer as he wondered what it would feel like to have a blade of such fine obsidian open his throat. It would surely mean the end, but the promise of such a release gave him pause, and though he knew it would be nothing less than he deserved, he still found himself too stubborn and too frightened to willingly walk into the spirit's clutch.

"Now, now . . . we . . . surely, we can discuss this, the three of us?" the rabbit bargained. "We're all reasonable creatures, yes? What do you say, Eamon?"

"Why have you come back here!?" barked the frog.

Eamon pressed his knife into Runny's throat as Flackwell raised his sling to eye level. "I needed to understand," he said. "I needed to understand *why.*"

"And do you? Do you understand, now that you've met our families!? Do you see *now!?*" The frog stepped closer as the edge of Eamon's knife began to draw blood from the fur around the rabbit's neck. "Don't you be careless with that knife! You take my rabbit from me and I will take your life, I promise you."

Runny's eyes began to swell with anxiety as he felt the temperature rising on both sides of him. "Now hold on," he eked. "He . . . he came to understand . . . and now he does. So . . . so . . . why don't we all just take a deep breath and retire to the bar and perhaps we can discuss things like rational creatures? There has been enough blood shed this Barley Day, and I should think I needn't see any more," continued Runny, playing the politician as ever. "Our pasts may be filled with horrors, but if we can just find a little common ground . . . perhaps . . . perhaps our futures might be free of them. Perhaps our present too."

His words did not hang empty in the chamber, and even in the timbre of Eamon's breath against the back of his neck, Runny was sure that he felt some understanding. It was slick speech, but it was honest, and as Flackwell lowered his sling and Eamon released his grip on the rabbit, a sigh of relief escaped his muzzle only to be eclipsed by a fleshy whoosh and a gasp of surprise from the frog.

Runny's eyes went wide like saucers when he saw the arrow burst through Flackwell's heart. The life began to drain from his being in an instant, and as he collapsed to his knees and clutched at his chest, Finn's savage form took shape in the doorway behind the ghost of the frog's silhouette. "Charity!?" he bellowed. "Charity for this . . . runt!?

After *all* we've been through!?" There was one last bolt in the fox's hand, but Eamon didn't even have the time to fret about its fate before Runny scurried in between them and gathered the dying frog in his arms.

"No. No, no, no," he moaned as the blood of his favorite creature stained his ragged fur with each desperate reach. "What have you done!?" he barked as Finn stepped across the threshold. "You louse! You . . . you were my brother!"

"No, Rabbit. My brothers are here on the wall, as are yours. But you seem to have forgotten that through the years. You seem to have forgotten the debt we are owed. But I've forgotten nothing."

"Don't . . . don't go," cried the rabbit as he took Flackwell's hand in his paw. "Please don't go. *Please.*" But no matter how hard he squeezed and how earnestly he pleaded, the frog's senses quickly sputtered, and in a matter of breathless moments . . . his frame went limp in Runny's arms. "Flackwell?" he mewed as he watched the life fly from his gaze. "Frog?" he asked again, but his frog was well and truly gone.

"There will be no charity from me," said Finn.

Runny watched his tears mellow into the blood of his fallen frog and sensed a rage welling in his bones that he hadn't felt since the first night he stepped foot in that fateful chamber. He laid Flackwell's body on the floor and gathered himself to his feet, and as he began his march toward the fox he barked, "All of your vendettas. All of your vitriol and all of your loss . . . and for what? For *what!?*" One more soul for the spirit to take!? One more hole in my heart!? One less beautiful thing left to brighten this . . . this horrid forest!? For *what*, Fox!?" He was but a step away from Finn now, his teeth bared and his brow vee'd with bitterness. "Answer me, you vile—"

Runny's wind was cut to nothing as Finn shoved the last of his arrows through his gut. And as he felt the rabbit's bewildered gasp ripple his whiskers, he leaned in and whispered, "I'm sorry, old friend, but I believe this is where we part ways. I wish you peace in the fields beyond."

The rabbit's mouth hung agape as he understood himself to be mortally wounded. He badly wanted to speak so many things, but there was so little strength left to say them, and as he collapsed to his knees and felt the warmth of his own blood climbing the rungs of his throat, Finn pulled the arrow clean through his back, set it in the string of his bow, and swung it toward Eamon only to find Flackwell's sling ready and leveled at his head.

"Clever . . . little . . . runt," he mused as he struggled to focus his one healthy eye on his target.

"You would kill your friends . . . just like that?" Eamon challenged.

"To be perfectly honest, I've never really thought about it until just now, but . . . yes. Do you really think you can take me down with that sling before I loose my draw?"

"Do you really think you can hit me in the heart with one good eye from there?" returned Eamon as they began to slowly circle each other.

"You have something of mine and I would very much like to have it back," said the fox as he nodded to the knife which was now tucked away in Eamon's belt.

"Then maybe you shouldn't have left it buried in my friend."

"Probably right. How is he, by the way?" Eamon said nothing, but the fox needed no words to suss the truth of it, for it was all written on the turn of his enemy's brow and pursing of his lips. "You don't know, do you? Oh, Eamon, did you go and abandon your friend? Isn't it funny how we learn to cope? The things we're taught without knowing it." Eamon's eyes flared with anger at the reminder of his history, but still he steeled his patience. "You know, I rather liked your father. He seemed a fine enough fellow. Quite uninterested in the privilege that his family might bring. Made him something of a maverick among his clan. Well, among *your* clan. Honestly, I felt we could've been great friends if things had turned out differently. Shame about that last name of his though."

"His last name was Buckley. And so is mine."

"You can choose your name, but you can't choose your blood," responded Finn. The slack of Eamon's sling grew taut as he mulled loosing his only bearing with each of the fox's words, but he knew that a miss would surely mean his own death. "Do you know why he came here, Eamon? He came here because I offered him a chance to be free of the thing he feared most. His heritage. And all he had to do was kill me. Did you know that? All the others, they came in droves to claim their birthrights, but your father . . . your father just wanted to be free of it. Wanted *you* to be free of it. Tell me, did you hate him for it?"

Finn's ploy was as transparent as it was expected, and still Eamon couldn't help but give his mind over to the distraction of his past. Still he couldn't help but taste the sting of the fox's insight. Still he couldn't help but silently answer his question over and over until it became all he could hear above the whirlwind that was spinning up between his ears. But Finn was an old fox . . . and no creature is without a history.

"And what about you?" Eamon fired back. "How much of your life have you lived for Edward? Even after he died . . . he still owned you in a way. Told you what to do. How to think. How to feel. What to live for . . . what to fight for . . . what to *die* for. How many sleepless nights did you spend frothing at the mouth over the way he painted you like a coward for the world to see?"

"I am no coward."

"Shame anybody who knows that is dead, don't you think?" returned Eamon as he drew a weapon the fox didn't know he was carrying . . .

> But when he finally saw the beast, five times his size to say the least
> His legs they went to pudding and before the brute he kneeled

"Don't you speak those words to me!" Finn tightened his grip on his bow and pulled his draw tight as they sidestepped each other's line, but his focus was slow to come and he simply couldn't paint a clear picture with just one eye.

He was lost without his knife and without his sight . . . without his prowess and without a plan, and Eamon, sensing his uneasiness, continued to prod him. "Are you really any better than he was? Forcing those hounds to do your legwork while you sit on some hill with your bow? Seems to me that Edward had the right of it."

"Very well," said Finn. "How about I give you the same courtesy I gave your father? Nose to nose and teeth to teeth, the sky above and ground beneath. Seems only fitting for the last of the buffalo. Just you and me. No more games. No more bows. No more slings. And you can even keep my knife until I take it back. I suppose when it's all over we'll *both* be free of this one way or the other. What do you say? Would you like to be free?"

NINETEEN

The trek across the grounds was filled with trepidation, and every step seemed to jar another bit of uncertainty loose from Eamon's shell-shocked sense of self. It had been a night of revelations both endearing and abhorrent, but still he seemed to find some peace in the truth of it all, even though countless pillars of his history had come crumbling to the earth at the quake of the words of others. Both the bow and the sling had been left back in the trophy room, and while Eamon still had his knife and Finn had nothing but his wits, that still wasn't edge enough for him to feel anything in the way of comfort.

"Do you know how I came to have that knife?" said Finn as they worked their way up the side of a grassy hill. Eamon had been wary of some unscrupulous move from the fox throughout the breadth of their journey, but to his surprise, he seemed to be holding true to the honor of his request. "The people of our land once saw my father take an elk at a hundred yards in a stiff wind with one pull of his bow, and from that moment on, they thought him a warrior spirit. They took to leaving him offerings to bring them good fortune before a hunt, and one day, a young brave showed up at his hut asking for courage on his quest to avenge the slaughter of his family . . . and he brought him the blade you're carrying as tribute. I suppose it will only feel right to have it back when I'm done avenging mine."

Eamon had an inkling of where they were headed given the direction and the familiarity of the terrain, but it wasn't until they reached the crest of the rise and the moonlight unveiled the hedge maze cutting a clean square through the middle of the valley that he was certain. "And you think your father would've wanted this for you?" Eamon asked as they made their way toward the labyrinth.

"I think he would have understood. I was the eldest of seven sons, all of them with wives . . . children . . . no different than me. All of them trophies now. All of them trinkets," said Finn as they stopped a dozen yards short of the hedge wall and gazed up at the army of old, dead vines that were still holding it all together. "And *your* father? Don't you think he'd be cross that he gave his life just to have his son end up dead in the very same place?"

"He would've told me to run," Eamon remarked as he scouted the exterior of the maze which bore two entrances, one in front of where they were each standing.

"Smart man. Of course, he wasn't the first smart man to die here. And I'm certain he won't be the last," said the fox as he turned to meet Eamon's gaze. "Life's a funny thing, isn't it? You spend it waiting for that one blinding moment of clarity . . . that one magic thread that sews it all together. And then one day, you wake up an older thing than you ever thought you'd be, and you realize you've wasted your days looking for something that was never really there at all. There are no solutions in this life, Eamon. There are only moments in the sun . . . and moments in the shade . . . and the trick of it all is to understand where you're standing before it's too late to call it home. I wish you peace in the fields beyond, because you will not find it here."

Without another word, Finn darted inside, and though the instinct to flee shook Eamon through and through, he knew it to be a worthless gesture, for there was no way home and no quieting the fox's appetite for what he thought just. And so, with his future and his past colliding in the front of a tireless and quickly gathering storm, Eamon took one last look at the sparkling night sky . . . and stepped through the archway.

He wormed his way toward the center of the maze with his knife at the ready. Eamon was prepared for a fight, though he knew it would be far from fair as there was surely a reason a thing as sly as Finn had suggested they take their quarrel to these grounds. These were tight quarters with little room to maneuver and the night was dark as pitch, particularly under the cover of the vines and thistle, and while one of Finn's eyes was useless, Eamon knew the other could still see night as day. He knew his nose could still track a scent through the garden walls and he knew his ears could still hear the rustle of his gait clear from the other side of the field . . . but above all that, he knew this was all old hat for the fox, and that alone was enough to set his knees wobbling. It was a losing proposition even with a sharp knife at his aid, but Eamon was just as canny, and as he saw a dip in the ground that still held some of the night's rain, he reached out to feel the tangle of vines around him and was buoyed to find they had been whipped dry by the winds.

Finn's steps were swift and silent, and while his suggestion to take their quarrel to the maze had seemed nothing more than a smart stroke of mental warfare, it was the leavings of skirmishes past that he was truly keen on. Destined to face his own blade in a theater so confined, the fox was bullish on extending his reach and quickly sought the spot where Bishop had fallen to a heave of Caroline's pike. Finding the weapon still sitting where it had been pulled from the guts of his hound, Finn plucked it from the ground and gave himself a moment to get acquainted with its balance, turning it through the air and finding its center mass with his paw. It was a far cry from the finely crafted finesse of his knife, but he knew it would give him ambit enough to turn the tide of a scuffle within the walls. Spear in hand, the fox climbed the nearest hedge and slipped through the canopy of vines to find himself a perch, but as he broke through into the air above, he was surprised to see the violent flash of a flare tumbling through the night air . . . and could only watch as it landed behind him and set the brush ablaze.

Eamon soaked his overshirt in the puddle at his feet, and after slipping his windbreaker back over his head, he wrapped the newly damp cloth about his face to shield him from what was to come. He pulled a second flare from his back pocket and struck it to life, and as he ran it along the base of the hedges, he was comforted by the sight of the flames climbing the vines and spreading to the canopy, knowing that his scent would be lost in the smoke and his movements shrouded by the crackling of the fires. He cut further into the maze, expecting to find some fury of fur and flesh around each corner but uncovering only shadows sipping their last breath as the inferno grew fierce enough to eclipse his pace . . . the raw, orangey energy racing past his flanks on its way to where he knew the bamboo dome awaited.

"You are cleverer than your father!" shouted Finn from some distance across the labyrinth. Eamon begged his ears to pin the fox's location, but the raging camouflage of his own design made that a near-impossible task. "He asked to meet me in the cage you know! Nose to nose and teeth to teeth, as you would say! My question to you is, would you be as bold!?"

It was bait clear as day, but still the promise of a certain end to it all hung sweet and lively in the thick, black smoke that had infested the air. Eamon found it odd that Finn was willing to sidestep the value of his wiles in lieu of rugged combat, and knowing he would never make such an offer without an advantage at hand, he thought it best to stay shrouded and silent and continue his march through the once-perfect thicket. He couldn't help but recall the deer-stalking days of his youth and fell into something of a rhythm as he wound his way through the twists and turns of the tailor-made jungle with his senses tuned and weapon readied for a kill. But the moment he heard the cough of somebody overcome with smoke from the other side of the wall, the swing of his step was swallowed by the earnest pounding of his pulse, and he knew he was but a moment away from crossing a threshold from which he might never return.

Eamon breathed as deeply as his mask would allow as he waited for the right moment, and when a gust of wind kicked up a surge of flame above him, he made the turn around the wall in hopes of catching Finn off-guard. He swung himself into the burning corridor and readied his arm to strike, but instead of the fox's grinning maw staring back at him, he saw only the hobbled visage of King outlined in flame. The hound was at death's door by the look of him—his complexion white as china and his ragged frame hanging off his pike like some nobleman's banner, and when King took his hand from his ribs and exposed the grisly wound that Eamon had blessed him with, it was easy to understand why. What wasn't quite as clear, however, was why his posture spoke nothing of war with a weapon at his side.

King hobbled closer and Eamon raised his blade, but the hound only called him off with a wave of his hand and put his finger to his lips, and when he saw Eamon's eyes well with uncertainty, he rolled up the sleeves of his tattered shirt to reveal that he had carved something in the very flesh of his forearms. *My escape is your escape*, it said in still-dripping print on his right wing. And on his left, etched in similarly grisly detail, was a second message wrought in blood—*and I am already dead*.

"Come now, Eamon!" shouted Finn as he danced across the canopy of vines, moving just swiftly enough to stay ahead of the tide of flames that was nipping at his heels and begging to singe his fur. "You want to be free of this, then let me set you free! This is not a young man's game, runt! The time for hiding has long passed!" The fox squinted into the flames, but it was nigh impossible to make out any detail with only one eye to aid him and the fires playing havoc with his vision. He scurried along the hedge tops as far as the blaze would allow, but seeing neither hide nor hair of his target and feeling the sting of the orange storm closing in, Finn slipped back through the canopy and began to creep along the ground. The fire was an overwhelming distraction and it took every bit of the creature's self-discipline to keep himself on task, but when he saw the white of Eamon's windbreaker flash across the end of the corridor, he uncorked his rage and let his instincts take the helm once again.

"There you are," he murmured as he readied his pike about his hip and quickened his pace through the burning tangle. He knew himself to be quicker than the lad, but the need to keep his fur away from the blazing walls slowed him enough that with each corner he rounded, he found himself catching no more than a glimpse of his quarry as he disappeared behind the next bend. "I thought you were done running?!" yelled Finn, shielding his face from a gust of flame as the wind began to whip the fire into a more unpredictable frenzy. The heat was starting to take its toll as the fox felt his skin begin to sear and his sense of direction being carried away with the smoke, but when he carved his way around the next corner and saw it empty into a lengthy straightaway, he pounced on his chance to get clear of it all and hurried ahead.

It wasn't until he found himself in the dark again that Finn noticed he was on course for the center of the maze. He willed his eye to focus on the bamboo cage that he knew to be there, and after a few healthy strides, his trepidation gave way to a warm and familiar savagery as he found the silhouette of a buffalo standing just inside. Finn slowed to a strut as he moved toward the entrance, his gaze bouncing back and forth between the pair of eyes staring back at him and his treasured knife, which was so close that he could almost feel it in his hand again. "You know, for a buffalo you would've made a fine fox in another life. Clever as they come. But you should've listened to your father," he advised as he stepped through the cage door and twirled his pike to make one last accounting of its balance. "You should've run, Eamon."

Finn wasted no time in throwing a flurry of jabs with his spear, but as his thrusts were dodged, he was careful to remain patient, knowing that all he needed to finish this was one careless move to fall his way.

They circled each other and the fox was keen to mirror every step . . . a shift to the right, a shift back to the left . . . all the while keeping the fight at his weapon's length to avoid feeling the sting of his own blade for the first time. "I'm no coward," he said as he calmly parried a few hapless swipes of the knife. "But that doesn't mean I'm much for picking fights that I can't win." Finn could feel the anxiety building in the atmosphere of the cage, and as he saw the hand that was holding his dagger begin to tremble, he knew a little push was all he needed to find his opening . . .

> Brave and bold, the buffalo, he thundered o'er the earth below
> And thought himself the fiercest beast that ever graced a field
> But bravery is as bravery takes, and kings aren't told of their mistakes
> And so, he thought himself the very lord of sword and shield

Those words. Those words that brought them both to this place would've set fire to the labyrinth if it hadn't already been ablaze. They were something beloved that had been taken. They were something pure and perfect that had been sullied and sharpened into the very pike the fox was holding, and when he saw his enemy's chest heave and his eyes flare with anger, he knew the battle had already been won. Finn sidestepped the desperate lunge that followed with ease, brushing the knife aside with the tip of his spear and pivoting to smash his quarry's nose to bits with the back end. He was well staggered from the fox's blow, and when he turned to find a moment to regain his wits, Phineas sunk his pike deep into the back of his knee. The clever creature closed his eyes to savor the anguished cry of his enemy, but as the first pointed yelp tickled his ear, something in the timbre of his voice wrinkled his brow . . . and when he pulled his weapon free, he noticed that his foe's feet were bare and laced with heavy callouses and his nails riddled with disease.

"No," he muttered under his breath, suddenly drowning from the weight of his own hubris. "*No!*" Finn spun back toward the entrance, but it was already too late, for the only thing he saw was Eamon pulling the door closed, and the only thing he heard was the clink of the heavy iron lock being secured around it. His heart began to race with a recklessness for which he had no index. He looked down at the man who had just felt the sting of his spear only to see him unwrap the cloth that covered his face, and for the first time that he could remember, he saw a smile creep across King's lips. The crippled hound removed the windbreaker that Eamon had given him, and as he began to feel the heat from the closing blaze lick at his naked back, he took Finn's knife to his bare chest and carved something into his skin. H-O-N-O-R-A . . . F-A-M-I-L-I-A-M.

He waited long enough for the fox to read it several times over. Long enough for Finn to want nothing more than to sink his spear clean through his heart, and when he was sure that the only solace the twisted thing would have left was to take his life from him a second time, King ran the knife across his own throat . . . and lay down to find the fields beyond.

Finn flew to the edge of the cage, nose to nose and teeth to teeth with Eamon who said nothing as the blaze behind him rode the wind from the hedges to the brittle vines that covered every surface of the bamboo prison. Eamon watched as the fox's eye filled with flashes of yellow and bursts of orange and as the snarl on his face slowly melted into a telling and tight-lipped resignation. And though he held King's pike in his hand and could rightly have slipped it inside Finn's gut as the creature had done to Mark, he was content to let the fire take him. He didn't utter so much as a word as the flames crept onto the sleeves of the fox's jacket and flooded his fur, and while there were countless things that Finn wanted to say and a storm of sanguine screams welling in his throat, he too said nothing. He too stayed silent and solemn in the hope that the inferno would burn away the ingrace of his defeat before it could turn his bones to ash. He too saw it all coming and opened his arms to welcome it. To be free of it.

Eamon thundered through the blazing labyrinth, but with every corner and every dead end, he only found himself feeling more lost. He darted down corridor after corridor, but with every desperate sprint and every panicked breath, he only felt his wind grow weaker in the fast-thinning air. He found himself caught between the need to breathe and the terror of his lungs choking on the thickening soot and ash, charging blindly through the tangle with the hope that each step would spill him out onto unburnt ground, but each step proved to be in vain. His throat began to close and his chest began to burn like he had swallowed the gods' own embers, and as the wind saw fit to kick a surge of flame at his face and the canopy of vines began to crumble in a fiery hail, he could only drop to his knees and crawl toward the next bend in the path. But

Eamon's sight was just as sickly as his breath, and when he reached the end of the passage, he was gutted to find that there was nowhere to go at all.

A heinous cough shook him through and through, and as his seizing became more desperate with each fit, the thought that each croup might be his last began to crystallize in Eamon's mind. He knew there was no time to turn back and become lost again in the labyrinth, and he was sure the burned-out brush was in no shape to let him climb above the fray as he had seen the fox do, and so there was little choice but to push through the heart of the fire in order to escape it. Eamon pulled his shirt over his nose and used his pike to fashion something of an opening in the blazing thicket, and after struggling to squeeze himself through the overgrown hedge, he stumbled out the other side bloody and blackened and hacked up a plug of muddy ash. He begged the air around him for just one clean breath, but the fire had left nothing behind, and he knew that if he couldn't find the strength to soldier forward, he may as well find a soft patch of ground upon which to die.

Eamon burst through the next wall without anything at all left in his lungs, his skin tracked with cuts from the thistles and covered with ever-blackening burns, but still he didn't stop. He willed his way through a second and a third fueled by adrenaline alone, but by the time he found himself mired in the tangle of the fourth, he could no longer stem his need and inhaled a mouthful of fetid fire. It coursed through every inch of his being and burned his insides from toe to tail, and though it was the most singular pain Eamon had ever felt, it brought him no air ... and he had no choice but to take another breath. *Breathe. Please.* He gasped and he wheezed and he retched, but there was still no wind to sip in the clutches of the blazing hedge. There were no stars to guide his way and there were no ancient remedies to cool his burns, and not knowing if he was a moment or a marathon from freedom, he felt himself falling as it all went black.

TWENTY

It was the sensation of vomit running down his chin that finally snapped Eamon back to consciousness, and once he was done hurling the black ash from his system and gratefully sucking the life from the unsullied air, he lay back down and watched the smoke from the still-raging blaze spiral toward the heavens. He had fallen mere feet from the edge of the maze, but it felt like miles to him. He could've reached out and touched the thing if he wanted to, but it felt like a proper ocean of wild, green grass, and as his senses returned and he began to recall the trial he had just weathered, Eamon was overcome with the most present feeling of victory. It was ripe and it was revelatory, and it was almost salve enough to heal his wounds and wipe the blood from his half-cooked skin, but even above all of that, it was his and his alone.

For the first time in his life, Eamon felt free. He felt free of the weight of his past and free of the struggles of his present. He felt free of the doubts that forever seemed to cloud his future and free of the terror that always came with every bit of grace that happened to fall his way, and though he knew these feelings to be false and surely quick to fade, he allowed himself to revel in them anyway.

But it was a pure and unrecognizable peace, and so he was unsurprised when more pragmatic concerns started to bleed into the sanctity of his blinders and the fog of conquest began to clear. Eamon's thoughts soon turned to Mark and Caroline and how they might be faring in their own battles. He wondered if he would be able to convalesce alongside them both once he got back to the mainland or if he would find only Caroline waiting for him in the halls of some hospital she had no business in. It was then that Eamon tasted the familiar flavor of bile that always accompanied his more unshakable regrets, and just as he felt himself being recentered around its bitterness and things seemed to be ebbing toward some measure of normalcy in the most predictable way . . . the haggard war cry of a broken bear split the air like the fiercest of the fox's arrows.

It was a sorry thing to hear. Bing's once ferocious bellow was now just a prayer from his shattered throat as he labored down the hill, pitifully dragging one paw in front of the other with his hammer trailing behind him like some anchor lashed to his wrist. His cuirass was gone and the full spectrum of his scars was laid bare for Eamon to see, though they were hard to parse in light of the fresher injuries that covered most every inch of his fur with blood that had turned thick and grisly during his trek back from the coast. The brute's posture was sad and slumped and his free arm hung from his frame like a sleeve for which he had no use, and as Eamon stood and plucked his pike from the earth, the builder beast stopped and loosed a heartbreaking roar that peppered every breath of his foe's being with crimson and vitriol. There was room to run, but Eamon's heart could no longer bear the shame of the thought, and his head wouldn't brook the torture of the unknown that would surely follow, so with the labyrinth's fire to his back and Addington's own goliath before his eyes, he readied himself for one last fight.

The first swing of the bear's hammer was cold and clumsy, and being that it was only thrown with one arm, Eamon had but to step back from its path to dodge it. The heavy head of the weapon landed on the ground with a thump before Bing gathered the strength to take another pass, the bludgeon this time blowing Eamon's hair back as it breezed past his face. But Eamon stayed ready with his spear about his hip, and when the beast tried to bring his sledge down upon him a third time, he deftly shuffled to the side, watching Bing stumble after the weight of his own weapon and jabbing him in his flank with his pike, drawing both blood and a painful moan from the broken creature.

"*Hey!*" shouted Eamon as he waited for the brute's gaze to meet his own. "You don't have to do this anymore! They're all dead," he continued. "This can be over if you want it to be." He was sure that Bing understood, but when the bear opened his jaws and bellowed war in his face, he was sure that the creature had given him an answer. "I saw your cave," Eamon offered as he backpedaled away from the bear's wobbly advance. "I saw your family. I understand why you fight. But this island is *yours* now. I'm never coming back here and neither is anyone else. Don't you want some peace? Don't you want some—"

Bing flailed his hammer and missed his mark by mere inches, but as his bludgeon landed heavy on the earth, he took his paw from the handle and battered Eamon's head with the back of his hand, sending the young man flying to the ground in a daze. Eamon's wits were slow to return as he writhed on the field, and by the time his vision had righted itself, the brute was all but on top of him, his giant silhouette blocking the light from the blaze that framed his form. Eamon turned and tried to scramble, but Bing had already made his move, and as the bear's claws dug into his ankle, he grabbed at the grass only to feel himself being pulled backward along the ground.

The pain was searing and Eamon could only scream as he felt the beast's talons cut deep enough to scratch his bones. But he still had the wherewithal to grab his pike, and the moment he felt Bing release him to deal a more deadly strike, he turned and thrust his weapon to the sky just in time for the great bear to impale his paw. The creature reared and loosed a frustrated roar, taking the pike in his jaws and snapping it in half before pulling it free of his flesh. Eamon hobbled to his feet and stood unarmed in front of the brute, but as he looked at the scars covering his massive frame and the sorrow in his endless brown eyes, the beast only looked back at him and thumped his own heart with his fist. It was a simple gesture, but it spoke volumes. And as if Bing was now sure that the last of the buffalo understood, he threw the broken spear to the ground in front of Eamon's feet and thumped his heart again.

And Eamon did understand, there in the light of the blazing labyrinth. He picked up his broken weapon and turned it over in his hands and felt the warmth of the bear's blood on his skin. He understood that while the others had learned his own tongue during their days on the island, as that was all they ever heard . . . Bing had only learned violence, as that was all he ever saw. He understood that he had lived his life between his desire for vengeance and his desire to be free of that very thing, and as the most unbreakable beast the spirit ever saw fit to plant, there was simply nobody who could deliver him what he so desperately wanted. He understood his desire to fight, but more importantly, he understood his desire to fall—to be sheathed and stowed away like a sword that had outlived its edge. To be spent and know it was for something proper, just like in Addington's book.

Eamon's heart wept for the giant who had grown to know nothing but war yet yearned for nothing but death. His humanity bled pity for the brute so indestructible that no matter how savagely he fought for his

own end, he knew it would never come. Surely, there was no other reason a thing so capable would have given himself up to be riddled with so
many bullets so many times. Eamon thought back to when he first saw
him in the dark of the Addington's theater, drowning himself in spiced
wine, and he now understood that while Bing was watching to see his
home as it once was, he was also watching to see himself slumped against
the great tree at the end of it all . . . finally free of his history and his woes.
He now understood that Bing surely had seen Gene walking up from the
dock with his pistol at the ready, and that he had raised his hammer not
to take another life, but rather in hopes of taking his own.

"I'm sorry," Eamon said as he raised his gaze to meet Bing's. But his
words weren't so much an apology as they were an acknowledgement,
and now that Eamon understood the bear's mortal conflict, he knew
what was surely to follow. Bing charged him like the brute he once was,
and though Eamon's veins were coursing with a newfound empathy for
the thing that was flying his way, that didn't change what he knew had to
be done. He waited for the bear to pull back his arm to strike, and when
he did, Eamon ducked underneath his hulking frame. Bing stumbled
forward as his paw found nothing at the end of his swipe, landing on one
knee and finding that he needed more than a moment to summon the
strength to lift his heavy chassis from the ground again. His great chest
heaved and his lead-riddled lungs struggled to find the wind to feed his
doggedness, but Bing knew nothing else, and it was only when he looked
to the earth to push himself back to his feet that he saw another shadow
swallow his own.

Eamon threw his exhausted frame atop the bear's mighty back and
locked himself there by wrapping the handle of his broken pike around
his throat. The big brute flailed as Eamon squeezed, throwing his body
this way and that, but as hard as he tried to throw the louse from his
back, Eamon only gritted his teeth and tightened his grip. Bing soon began to wheeze and Eamon could feel his chest pumping as he fought for
air, and even as the builder beast reached behind him and dug his claws
into Eamon's shoulder, he refused to let go . . . and the moment he felt
the crunch of the bear's windpipe, he knew all he had to do was hold on.

The creature's moans were somber and sorrowful as he fell to his
knees. Eamon closed his eyes as if that would quiet them, for there was
no sense of victory as he felt the bear's chest stop heaving, and there

was no revelatory release as he watched his limbs go limp. It wasn't a moment later that Eamon felt the muscles about the creature's neck relax and saw his head hang down like a thing defeated, and as he gave one last squeeze to be sure it was done, Bing fell onto his back, still as a bear in winter.

Eamon's body was pinned beneath the beast's great frame, and as his legs started to turn numb, he thought it fitting that Bing had found a way to put up a fight even in death. It was truly bittersweet, his end. It was laced with everything from sadness to triumph, and as Eamon lay there under the unseemly weight of the brute he had just felled, he couldn't help but think of the words that Finn had shared just before he disappeared into the hedges . . . and he hoped now that Bing had passed on to the fields beyond, that maybe he would feel the sun shine on his fur once again. Eamon tried to shift the bear's weight, but his arms could barely budge his carcass, and as he laid his head back on the earth to give himself a moment to think . . . he heard a voice from the way of the fire . . .

The bison king, for kin and son, was certain that his war was won
And turned to taunt the crowd so they might see his righteous kill
His sword still in the builder's chest, he cried his cry and thumped his breast
But Bing, the bear, was mighty both of body and of will

Finn's fur was smoldering as he made his way toward Eamon with the still-roaring blaze at his back, his precious knife feeling right and ready in his hand. He was a ghastly visage of himself—naked and burned from head to toe and walking with a dire limp, his eyes flaring with hatred and his lips quivering with bloodlust about his fangs. Eamon hurried to try and free himself, but there was simply no time to wrench himself clear of the bear's embrace, and as he grabbed for the piece of his pike that was resting nearby, Finn simply placed a foot atop his wrist and said . . .

One final beastly breath he took, and as his mighty bear paws shook
He bared his teeth and slid the bison's blade from twixt his bones
He stood and growled and gripped the steel, and stunned, the buffalo he wheeled
And just one thrust was all it took to take him from his throne

"Oh, Eamon, were you expecting a happy ending?" asked the fox with a sneer. But Eamon wasn't about to give him the satisfaction of his repartee, even if it meant meeting his end a few moments sooner.

"Well, I suppose it's happy for one of us." Eamon closed his eyes as he felt the tip of Finn's blade pierce his shirt and dig into his chest, bracing himself to welcome the pain of a slow and grisly death in the hope that his silence might somehow be repaid in mercy, but there was to be no mercy from the fox. Eamon felt the weight of Finn's paw press the knife further into his flesh and knew the thing was almost done, but as he looked to the sky to see the same endless blanket of stars that had warmed him during his youth and thought it a fine enough thing under which to die, the report of a rifle echoed through the valley . . . and the next thing that Eamon heard was the rustle of a lifeless body crumbling at his side.

Runny stood on the crest of the hill a broken thing like the bear in the field below. He let his rifle fall to his feet and clutched at the grievous wound in his gut, and when he took his paw away and saw that it was covered in still-running blood, the droop in his jowls and the fall of his brow said all there was to say about the things old rabbits feel at the end of their days. He left without a word for Eamon, as for the first time in his life, he simply didn't know what to say. There was no slick speech that would make any of this better, no toast that would undo what had been done, and no poetry, however lovely, that could ever color either of their histories in a hue other than gray. And so, with his lips sealed forevermore, Runny left for his quiet place in the woods.

He carried his broken body through the forest and past the lake, and as the sun began to peek over the hills to the east, Runny laid himself down in the rye field and unwrapped his ear so that it might feel the island winds and sip the unfetid air. He closed his eyes and his thoughts drifted to better days in the Hollow where he and his frog could run from bog to bog without a care, their minds brimming with the endless possibilities of things that might be beyond the hedge. There were times when those things were surely wild and wonderful and called to them like sirens, and there were times when they were harrowing and horrid enough to keep them but a few hops from their front door. Even now, Runny couldn't help but ponder how different things would have been if he had stayed . . . how unrecognizable his existence would be if he had never heard the name Addington and had never felt the grace of man. It was an important question, but it was patently exhausting, and neither he nor the wild rye had the mettle for it anymore.

The rabbit's head fell to the side and his cheek came to rest on the spirit's green earth, and as the edges of his reality began to bleed white, he could swear that he smelled one of Flackwell's fig-and-onion tarts clear as day. It was sweet and subtle, simple and sublime, and though it was a thousand miles and a hundred years away . . . it smelled just like home. The Hollow was always there for them, winterset to winterrise, and in a way, it was still there now—vibrant and unfiltered by the words of those who never knew its truth. And as the wind left Runny's graces and his ears bent limp to the earth, he was happy that the rye would take its tithing without the weight of where he had been or what he had seen. For he was an old rabbit . . . and the late summer days were long . . . and there was little to do now but rest.

Part Five

The Fields Beyond

The buffalo, they hung their heads, their king upon the barley dead
While Bing, not but a hair apart, was taking his last breaths
They moaned their moans and cried their woes, and as the sacred story goes
They shuddered for his life just as they shuddered for his death

But honor is as honor shows, and fitting of the buffalos
They turned and took the trail that stretched beyond the fields and west
They left their king and took their kin, and quieted the beasts within
And gave back every bit of cress and barley that was left

And when the dust had fled the air, and words were said for Bing the bear
The creatures in the Hollow looked about their land and wept
Held each other tight, they did, and every cub and every kid
Dreamt of leek-and-onion pie and spoonbread as they slept

When morning came and sunshine broke, and all the lovely creatures woke
The promise of a Barley Day was once again at hand
The frogs, they cooked and cooked and cooked, the owls played the chirping rooks
The foxes let the children chase till they could barely stand

The bears, they built the table strong, the rabbits led a sing-along
And soon the scent of sweet potato tartlets filled the air
The elders sipped on barley wine, and now that they were feeling fine
They noticed there were four among their kind who weren't there

Runny hid among the rye, and tossed and turned and questioned why
He had been so brash and cold to venture past the edge
And Flackwell Frog had much to cook, but heartache brewed a somber look
As he saw Runny's spirit sink for hopping through the hedge

And so he watched him from the hill, and so did Finn the fox, who still
Had yet to say I'm sorry for his blunt and bloody deed
But still he felt a twinge of guilt, for at the table Bing had built
There was room for four more that the table didn't see

Heavy were their hearts that day, and as they heard the children play
They stopped into the kitchen camp to gather up a plate
And filled it full of doughy rolls and tarts and pies and pudding bowls
And there, beneath the tree of trees, they sat with Bing and ate

TWENTY-ONE

Eamon buried Olivia beneath the branches of a great redwood made of bones. He felt the cave was a fitting place in which to let her rest, as she had seemed so taken by it during their time together beneath the stars. And when he laid himself down after the digging was done and set his eyes on the ceiling, he noticed for the first time that they were *all* there, in a way—the great bear, the hunter, the rabbit, and the cook. They were as indelible in bone as they were in prose, and though they were just as beautiful set in granite as they were on the pages of Addington's text, Eamon couldn't help but resign himself to the thought that even the night sky wouldn't quite be the same after everything he'd been through. Even the spirit's great canopy would ring differently now that the stars were weighty and hewn on the heels of other creatures' pain.

He didn't think it right to leave Flackwell in a spot where Edward could see him, so he loaded him onto a wheelbarrow that he found in a gardener's shed and followed Runny's bloody trail until he came upon the rye field where the rabbit had fallen. It only felt correct to leave them together as they had gotten along like fountains and filigree since he first saw their names in typeface, and they seemed nothing to the contrary once they had bloomed into living color. Eamon sloughed Flackwell from his shoulder and laid him along the ground, and as fortune would have it, he fell hand in hand with Runny as his bones came to rest among the rye. It seemed so Spirit-sent and proper that Eamon didn't have the heart to bury either of them, for he knew them both better than he should, and he was sure that they would have preferred it that way. He was sure that they had been there many times before, hand in hand under the same stars and warmed by the knowledge that none of it would ever change.

But once Eamon sat himself down among the rye and took a moment to breathe, he couldn't see either of them anymore. He couldn't see the manor or the cave and he couldn't see the river or the coast. He couldn't see a single statue or even a wisp of smoke from the still-smoldering labyrinth and he couldn't see the lighthouse either. He could only see the blue of the sky and the seed heads as they swayed about his nose, and though he knew the trials of life to be but a short journey away, they seemed somehow less vicious now that he had found his field again. They seemed as gray as his past had become, and while he was aware of the work that he would surely have to do to see it all in color again, he was happy to have a say in those hues for the first time.

Bing was as immovable in death as he was in life, and so there was little Eamon could do on his behalf. And though he wasn't sure that Finn deserved his time or his consideration, he gave them to him anyway . . . not because he felt it was anything he was owed, but because in a strange way he understood him. He thought about carrying him back into the maze and letting the dwindling flames take what was left, but he couldn't brook the thought of the ash and soot choking him again. He considered carrying the fox to the top of the hill and laying him upon the empty plinth that he now understood had been meant for him, but the idea of building himself a trophy seemed too callous and unwelcome after everything he'd been through, though he was sure Finn would've appreciated the poetic pettiness of it all. In the end, Eamon felt it best to leave him where he fell, singed from head to toe and with his heart torn open for the world to see. And while he didn't feel the fox was deserving of anything bordering on charity even in death, he placed his knife in his paw nonetheless . . . and hoped his father wouldn't think him dishonorable in the fields beyond.

Eamon tried to use the facilities at the manor to clean his wounds and patch himself up, but as he stood before the great mirror in Addington's chambers, he barely even recognized himself with his broken nose skewed to one side and his skin covered in an endless collage of cuts and scrapes and burns and punctures. He felt the strangest nothing as he toured the house that would have been his. He felt nothing for the hair dye stacked in the corners of the master bedroom, nothing for the ghost of the music still wafting through the ballroom, and nothing for any of the maps or portraits or armor that littered the great hall. Nothing for the family of porcelain foxes dashed about the tea chamber, nothing for the two cages still waiting for their tenants in the basement, and nothing for the study in which he knew Edward had written the book that had brought him here. It was all so diluted, now that he had seen the truth of it all. It was all so gray like the rest.

It only seemed reasonable to set fire to the place as it had set fire to him in so many ways, and as he sat on the dock and watched the flames climb its walls until they licked at the great spire, he pulled from his pocket Addington's note that he first began to read when he awoke in Runny's care and picked up where he had left off . . .

. . . I was born a king and I shall die a king, as I see nowhere above where I reign for me to climb, and no pit below where I stand into which I could conceivably fall. In this way, it is the pauper that I truly envy, for I would give my fortune to be forced to turn thief to eat or grifter to buy new threads, but as I need do neither of those things, it seems I have nothing to keep me whole but my interests, and no choice but to indulge them, however unsavory I might find these things in the final moments of my passing. I care not for that brand of foresight, and I shall not let it dampen the timbre of my existence, vibrant and comely as it is.

I was born a king and I shall die a king, and I shan't shy away from it . . . I have given the world a beautiful thing, and so it only seems proper that I should be able to take from it a trinket or two that would keep me feeling lively and separate from the rest. Why should a castle have walls if not for them to be adorned? Why should a king have grounds if not to gather his friends and hunt upon them? I am as put upon as any man, you see, and I am not immune to problems and wants and needs . . . the only difference between me and them is that I have the means to indulge these things . . . and the status to be free of the consequences. Why have a king at all if he is to act like a pauper? Truly, that's what the paupers are for.

The boats came in droves to see what had caused the great column of smoke on Addington Isle, and when they brought their crafts to idle near the shoreline, they found Eamon aboard *The Standard* as if he had simply arrived before the rest. It was easy enough to find a fellow captain with a spare can of fuel aboard his rig, and once everybody was well preoccupied with the fire that was surely swallowing Addington Manor whole, Eamon simply headed back across the sea to West Rock.

In the days that followed, he read nothing in the news about anything other than a simple fire at a long-abandoned house, so he was confident that the manor's secrets and horrors had been buried along with its most famous tenants. He had gathered the bodies that had been left in the ballroom and set them in the trophy chamber with the hopes that once the flames had cooled and the walls had been turned to rubble, there would be enough bones in the atrium from the beasts alone that it would be nigh impossible to tell that any of them were human. Eamon felt for the families and friends of those that never made it off the isle, and though he promised himself that he would find them all and tell them the reality of what happened eventually, he felt that in their grief, even their wildest assumptions would be more palatable than the truth of the thing, so for the time being he thought it wise just to let them grieve.

Mark survived his injuries, though just barely, and both Eamon and Caroline felt his gnarled scar on their own bellies for the rest of their years. The three of them would always be close, but it was strange to have something so defining in common that they were never keen to discuss. They had always been so good at keeping each other whole, but now there was a pit in the middle of each of them that the others simply didn't know how to fill, and so they had no choice but to leave them empty.

One year to the day after their trip across the sea to Addington Isle, Eamon went home to his father's ramshackle cabin in the woods for the last time. There was nothing left but a husk now. The walls were crumbling and the structure itself was riddled with vermin and overgrown with weeds, and though Eamon picked through the detritus to try and find some keepsake that he might be able to take back to Boise, there was none of that left either. There was only the memory of where the shadows of those things once fell and the specter of the promise that they would always be there. But Eamon understood now that change doesn't come in the cool of the shade, and nothing grows without the breath of the sun. And as night fell on the bones of the hovel where he spent his childhood, the owls began to play their tune . . . and Eamon stayed just long enough to tell them his story in the hopes that they, given all they had seen, might understand.

And once the frog had left his grace and Finn had fled to some far place
The rabbit sat alone with Bing and cried a mighty cry
He cried for those who'd left this earth and those who knew not of their worth
And even for the beasts too big to hide among the rye

He hadn't peace nor appetite and couldn't bear a single bite
Of all the lovely things that were now cold upon his plate
He couldn't eat the onion pie and couldn't put his paw on why
He felt so low and hollow as the other creatures ate

Surely it was more than Bing, some bigger and more pressing thing
The feeling that he'd missed the point of all this blood and pain
The thought that he alone was there to make things right for Bing the bear
The thought that he had missed some righteous truth that had been plain

So Runny paced and paced and paced until he realized it was grace
That stood to bandage up their wounds and keep the Hollow whole
For sure as daybreak there would be another beastly horde or three
That one day or another would come through to take their toll

And so the rabbit toed the edge of all that lay beyond the hedge
And took another look behind him at his broken friend
He saw his matted fur and sighed and bottled up the urge to cry
And promised him that he would make it matter in the end

Runny ran until his paws were red and worn unseemly raw
Until he came upon the leavings of the bisons' tracks
And then he ran and ran some more until the dust had made him sure
That he had caught the tail end of the rough-and-ready pack

I beg you, stop, the rabbit said, I beg you turn around instead
I beg you, come and join our feast and take your barley due
Come and eat our berry pies and sit beneath our starry skies
And have your fill of onion tarts and cress-and-oyster stew

There is no need to travel west, if food you seek, we have the best
And there are fields a plenty just a short jump past the hedge
Why don't you go and settle there, for there is plenty food to share
And you could help us next time there are beasts about the edge

The bison, they were feeling down with no one left to wear their crown
And talked amongst themselves until their hunger ached their bones
They thought the offer fair and just and had no love for wanderlust
And so they followed Runny to the fields they would call home

On that day the Hollow grew at least a hundred heads or two
And all were welcome 'round the greatest feast they ever saw
They ate and ate and danced and sung and tales were told and games were won
And none could hate the other with a smile upon their maw

And there, the buffalo they stayed, and homage to the bear they paid
They buried him beside their king and laid his hammer low
They found their place among the grass and soon a hundred seasons passed
A hundred feasts, a hundred years, a hundred winters' snow

A hundred Barley Days and more, and all without the threat of war
Now that the bison stood their guard around the Hollow's edge
And all because that fateful day one rabbit couldn't bear to stay
At home where he belonged inside the safety of the hedge

The End

Printed in the USA
CPSIA information can be obtained
at www.ICGtesting.com
LVHW052003160923
758386LV00025B/240/J